Brighde Reborn

THE AMULET SERIES 1

Brighde Reborn

LESLIE SOMMERS & JANICE SOMMERS

4 Horsemen
Publications, Inc.

Dedication

Leslie: To my father, the inspiration behind it all.

Janice: To Ernie, for your love and support.

Acknowledgments

Thank you to Lauren – without your help, we wouldn't have been able to see this dream become a reality. To Samantha – your original artwork of the cover is beautiful, and we will treasure it always. To John and Meghan – if either of you didn't spend the year it took to save this book, we would never have been able to continue this series. To Amanda, Maggie, Rich, and all the betas who took a chance on this series – without your unwavering excitement and support, we wouldn't have made it this far. Lastly, to our readers, who are our biggest supporters – thank you, thank you, thank you! If you didn't ask us constantly when the next book would be out or what happens next, we wouldn't have been able to make it this far. Thank you.

Table of Contents

DROLOGUE

Most fairy tales began with the words "once upon a time." Romance novels were almost always another retelling of some Shakespearean play or of a tale passed among circles in local adult book clubs. My story wasn't like any of those. I didn't live in a far-off place inhabited by fairies, dragons, or vampires. The only ghosts haunting me were the shadows of long-forgotten memories of a carefree childhood. I grew up in a small town in Jersey, and while that may have seemed like a mystical land to some people, the only wild animals around were the testosterone-driven high school boys. The only thing those fairy tales had in common with me was that my life was changed by a Prince Charming, too. Well, I thought he was Prince Charming.

If someone had told me a year ago I'd be sitting in the library of a ruined castle, handwriting my life's tale, I would've had them committed. Yet here I was, pen in hand, my messy script covering a wrinkled, yellowed journal as golden sunbeams streamed through the leaves outside my window.

My mother thought it would be therapeutic for me to write what happened. Help me heal or something. At eighteen years old, I'd experienced more death and misery than most people twice my age. How did anyone just bounce back from that? Where did I even begin?

Let me start with the Prince Charming—well, he's just a boy, really. We were in love. Are in love. I can never remember how to describe someone after they're gone. What if they aren't in your life anymore? Do you still talk about them like they're sitting next to you? Or do you speak of them in the same hushed tones grown-ups use when referring to your dead relatives?

Anyway, I should get back to the Prince. More like Enemy of the State, if you ask my family. My friends, on the other hand, couldn't help but giggle and gush over our relationship. And me? I don't know anymore. I can still remember the day everything changed...

Chapter 1

I'd like to say it was a dark and stormy night when Trip Findlay entered our little sleepy town of Corbin City, NJ. That he rolled in on dark thunderclouds using lightning bolts as reins. But that's not even close to being true. It was the last week of August before I would be returning to the illustrious Ocean City High School. The sun singed every piece of skin not slathered with sunblock. The strong ocean breeze carried the tantalizing smells of the boardwalk venders and the salty sea to our noses. I was lying on the beach with my group of friends: Brianna was tanning on her giant beach blanket, Annabelle was sketching something in her notebook, and Cole was finishing up *The Bluest Eye* for his summer reading. I, on the other hand, did what I could to prevent melanoma, my red hair and freckled skin always a magnet for the sun. I was covered with sunblock, wearing a high-neck royal blue one-piece, and hiding underneath the rainbow beach umbrella.

"This book is good, but I'd really rather be out there," Cole said, gazing at the ocean. Using the book to shield his eyes, he flopped back onto the towel.

"I think it's a refreshing change for summer reading. I love reading books by diverse authors instead of the standard canonical literature."

Cole looked up at me. "Canonical?"

"Yes. If I have to read another book written by a pasty guy about how a woman feels, I may have to drown myself."

He frowned. "Dramatic, much?"

"No. Those books leave us women with false hope that a guy will pop up, sweep us off our feet, and carry us off into the sunset. Even Disney wrote it into films. It's fun to read sometimes, but it's not my first choice."

"I think that's my cue to go swim. Want to come, Annabelle?" Bri asked as she hopped up.

"Take me," Cole groaned.

"No, you have to finish. You know they give a test on the first day of school!" Annabelle said as she and Bri ran toward the water.

Clad in slinky bikinis and board shorts, other students from OCHS swam in the rough waves and played volleyball. Cailean and his older brother, Alec, surfed with their group of friends, including my crush, Alec's friend, Kevin, who made up the top tier of royalty at Ocean City High School. Alec McKay was the former reigning king during his senior year, even though the family had just transferred to OCHS last summer. All accounts suggested Cay was the heir to the throne now that Alec was headed to college.

"You're staring again, Bridget," Cole said, as he pushed up his sunglasses.

"Staring at what?" Trying to cover my tracks, I diverted my eyes to Bri and Annabelle.

"Yeah, like you don't know…" I blushed furiously. It was no secret to my friends that I had a huge crush on Kevin, even though he was a year older than me and was going to be a freshman with Alec at the University of Pennsylvania. There was no way he would want to spend his last summer before college tied to a senior at his alma mater, never mind the fact that he never glanced in my direction.

"Shut up," I replied weakly. A couple in front of us rolled onto their backs simultaneously. Their tanning schedule reminded me of the hot dogs on a rolling oven at Jimmy's Hot Dogs on the boardwalk. The thought made my stomach stir, and I remembered I had skipped breakfast earlier in a rush to start the day.

"I'm going to grab something to eat. Do you want to come?" I stood and grabbed my white flip-flops. I could feel the grit of the sand under my feet.

Cole just shook his head. Ducking from underneath the umbrella, I left my sunglasses behind and made my way between the beach bums on their towels and around the sandcastles being built by children of all ages. I squinted and climbed the stairs to the boardwalk. I weaved through the throng of people clad only in bikinis, shorts, or skirts. Lots of skin was showing, some of which I didn't want to see. Finally, the white and red sign of my favorite hot dog joint loomed above me, and my stomach gave an approving growl.

"Hi, Sam!" I greeted the vender.

"Hey, Bridget!" he replied. "How are the waves today?"

Grabbing a plate and a bun, he got ready to make my personal favorite, Sam's Special: an all-beef frank with chili, cheese, onions, and fries. It was full of flavor and absolutely delicious. Sam told me once I was the only person on the beach who ordered this delicious meal regularly.

"Pretty good. Great surfing waves, for sure."

Sam piled on the chopped onions, sank the hot dog into the pocket of the bun, and started in on the layer of chili and cheese. I salivated.

"Excuse me, can I have a bottle of water, please?" a male voice drifted in from behind me. Turning around, I nearly ran into the voice's owner. Tall-ish and lanky, he had dirty-blond hair, lightly tanned skin, and the greenest eyes I had ever seen. Flashing him a shy smile, I moved out of his way. I prayed if he saw the red blush spreading, he would assume it was sunburn.

"That will be one seventy-five," Sam said. The boy patted his pockets.

"Sorry! I only have one fifty." He held his hands out, his palms facing up, and shrugged his shoulders.

"I have a quarter you can borrow. Have! I mean, you can keep it. I don't need it back," I babbled. *Who is this girl?* I was in no way ever this tongue-tied around a guy. I had been on the debate team last year, I had performed in school plays, and I had worked at the local bookstore for the summer. Stuttering in front of a stranger, no matter how likable he might have been, was not something I was used to. He smiled in relief at me.

"Thank you."

I nodded silently in response, placing my payment along with his quarter on the counter. Sam handed me my food, which was positively dripping with cheddar cheese and chili. Just the way I love it. He handed the water bottle over to the guy. I grabbed a few napkins, toasted Sam to say thanks, and turned to walk away.

"Hey, thanks again. I'm sure I'd melt out here if I didn't get a drink." The stranger followed me as I walked back to the stairs.

"You're welcome," I smiled. If I kept looking at him, I would never eat my meal.

"Are you from around here?" he asked. It seemed I had picked up a new friend.

"Yeah. I'm from the next town over." My mouth was only allowing short, choppy sentences to escape... probably my subconscious's attempt to avoid another embarrassing stutter.

"I just moved here," he went on. "My name is—"

"Trip!" I heard someone yell out. We both turned in the direction of the voice. A guy with brown hair and a muscular build came jogging over to us. I had to admit, I was disappointed we'd been interrupted. From the look of frustration flashing across Trip's face, I guessed he felt the same way.

"Hey, wait up!" the new guy said, catching up to us. "What're you up to?"

"Just grabbing some water with my savior, here. She gave me the quarter I was missing." Trip pointed at me. His friend barely glanced at me as I used a fry to wipe some chili that had spilled onto the plate.

"Good stuff. Want to surf?"

Trip shook his head. "Just walking up and down the boardwalk." He flashed me a look again, and I almost choked on my fry.

His friend finally tore his eyes away from Trip and looked me up and down. Feeling judged, I blushed and immediately wished I hadn't just stuffed obscene amounts of food in my face. Oh no... I hoped I didn't have anything in my teeth. I swiped my tongue over my teeth to check for any remnants.

"Well, I should be going," I said, feeling sufficiently awkward in front of this beautiful stranger and his friend. "You're welcome for the quarter." I took two steps toward the stairs. I wondered if anyone had informed Trip that when his wingman sticks around, it kills the mood.

"Wait," Trip said, touching my arm. "I never got your name."

"Bridget."

"Will I see you around?"

"Um, maybe," I shrugged. "I need to be going. My friends are waiting for me." I hurried as much as I could without running. I was sinking in the sand all the way back to my friends. I hoped Trip hadn't seen how ungraceful I was, but once I got back to our group of towels, Trip and his friend were sitting no less than one hundred yards from me. Cue slight embarrassment. Facing the ocean, I noticed Cay glaring at Trip.

"Mom! Dad! I'm home!" I closed the front door behind me, dropped my bag on the floor, and hung my keys on the ring.

"Hi, honey. Dad is still at the firm working on a case. How was the beach?" Mom, wiping her hands on a towel, came in from the kitchen. A sweet fragrance followed her into the hall.

"Hot. What is that smell?" I sniffed again, breathing in the heavenly scent.

"Oh, we have new neighbors two doors down. I figured I'd make them a welcome basket filled with the local favorites." The kitchen counters were covered with various cooling racks filled with cream puffs, chocolate-covered pretzels, and my favorite, chocolate cupcakes with strawberry buttercream on top. Mom was an excellent baker, which was fitting since she owned The Sweetest Shop. It was Ocean City's famous—and only—bakery in town. Her secret for delicious goodies? She grew most of her produce, like figs and strawberries, in our huge backyard facing the Tuckahoe River. The shop was popular not only with kids for the wonderfully tasty treats but also with parents. She was known for slipping vegetables into her recipes all the time.

"Can I have a cupcake?" I'd already tasted the dark chocolate as my salivary glands kicked into overdrive.

"No, but if you want, you can walk it over there with me. Maybe they'll share, if you're lucky." She filled plastic bags with the cookies and twist tied them shut. I scratched the back of my head, feeling little grains of sand against my scalp.

"Deal. Let me shower first."

After shampooing my hair twice and combing out the sand in a hot shower, I got dressed in white shorts, a forest-green tank top, and sandals. Leaving my hair to air-dry, I found my mom waiting in the living room. The basket was sitting by the front door, where my beach bag had been disassembled.

"Sorry. I forgot to unpack the beach stuff first," I apologized.

"No problem. But you're making dinner tonight." Had to love Mom's unusual form of punishments. I was rarely grounded in the normal way, like by being banned from watching TV or from going to parties. No, Mom and Dad felt doing certain chores would be beneficial to my future as an adult—plus, they get out of doing chores they didn't want to do. Making dinner wasn't a bad deal in comparison to the punishment of dealing with the backed up toilet last year. It had been a geyser of urine and feces spewing on the floor, walls, and sink. Even after opening the windows and letting the cold, winter air in, the bathroom still smelled like sewage for two days. "The recipe is on the counter, and we have all the ingredients. I double-checked for you."

I nodded. "Shall we?" I looped my arm through the basket handle and stepped out the front door.

"So, someone is finally moving into the Cartright house?" I asked Mom as we traipsed up the street, passing the old seaside cottage next door. The sun had relinquished its death grip on the earth and allowed a soft breeze to caress my face.

"Yes. After Mr. Cartright passed away, his son sold the property."

"I wonder who moved in. I bet they're famous, like a daytime soap actor or something." We looked both ways before crossing the street.

"Why would you even think that?"

I shrugged. "Why not? This neighborhood is boring. We could use the cast of *General Hospital* to make life interesting."

We arrived at the two-story Victorian house, painted a light, wintery blue. The front yard was picturesque; neat grass with purple irises in the garden lined the pathway leading to the house from the sidewalk. Three cars sat in the double driveway: a red jeep, a blue Honda Civic, and a black Escalade. I pictured a blonde girl, dripping in name-brand jewelry and clothes, receiving the last car like on reality TV. I scrunched my nose.

I followed Mom up the porch steps to the front door where she motioned for me to ring the bell. We heard footsteps thundering, and the door opened. Behind it was a young girl around eleven or twelve. With jean shorts and a striped t-shirt, she was cute with her dark-brown hair pulled into a high ponytail. In her left hand was a tattered copy of Shakespeare's *Othello*. I raised my eyebrows at her reading choice; it was quite an impressive play for such a young age.

"Hi!" Her voice was higher than I'd expected.

"Hi. My name is Samantha, and this is my daughter, Bridget." I waved. "We're your neighbors in that yellow house across the street. We wanted to welcome you to the neighborhood. Are your parents home?" The girl paused for a moment, as if deciding whether to tell us the truth or not.

"Let me go get them. Hold on." She closed the door on us as she turned around and yelled, "MOM!" In all fairness, this little girl didn't know if we were kidnappers or Girl Scouts, so her door slamming was a smart precaution.

I heard lighter footsteps walking to the door, and it opened again.

"Yes?" A tall, pale, blonde woman with a soft foreign accent stood before us. She was dressed similarly to her daughter, in jean shorts and a t-shirt.

"Hi, I'm Samantha MacNamara, and this is my daughter, Bridget. We live across the street, and we just wanted to welcome you to our humble little neighborhood."

"Oh! That's so nice of you. Please." She stepped back to allow us in.

As I stepped in behind my mother, I took in the house's interior for the first time. It wasn't anything breathtaking, but it had clearly been redone after the original Victorian decoration, giving it a certain modern charm. Everything was white: white tile in the kitchen in front of me, creamy white walls, white carpeting on the stairs, and plush white couches that matched in the living room on my right. The wood floor hallway leading to the kitchen had family pictures dotting its walls. A family portrait hung in the center of the hallway. Wait a minute... the dirty-blond boy standing behind the girl who'd opened the door looked familiar. It was the same guy who needed a quarter today! My heart fluttered; warmth grew in my chest, and I remembered our short conversation. I internally kicked myself, but there was no way I could have known I'd be this attracted to him. Or that he'd be my new neighbor.

"I'm Kellyn Findlay, and this is my youngest, Elizabeth."

Drying his hands on a towel, a large man emerged from the kitchen.

"Hello, I'm Nick," he said as he reached to shake my mother's hand. "Sorry, my hand is wet; just finished washing the dishes." He had the same accent Kellyn had, but his voice was much deeper.

"Not a problem." My mom smiled warmly.

"Nick, this is Samantha and her daughter, Bridget, from down the street. They stopped by to welcome us to the neighborhood."

"We brought homemade goodies," I said, lifting up the heavy basket. "Mom is an excellent baker."

"How wonderful! Thank you so much. Here, let me take them from you." Kellyn grasped the handle of the basket and removed it from my arm. Blood pooled in the crook of my elbow. "Can I make you some coffee?"

"Thank you, but we have to get going. Tonight is Bridget's night to cook." Mom wrapped an arm around me and squeezed. "By the way, Sunday is the last night of freedom for the kids before school. We have a barbeque every year for the neighborhood to celebrate. We'd love for you to come."

"Sounds like fun. We'll be there," confirmed Nick.

"Great! We're the yellow house across the street, two doors down. Come by any time after one. See you Sunday!" We exchanged goodbyes and walked out the front door.

"Where do you think they're from?" Mom asked as we walked down the steps.

"No clue, but I really like their accent. Do you think it's British?"

"Maybe. We can ask them at the barbeque." As we reached the sidewalk, a silver Audi pulled into their driveway. The passenger door opened, and out stepped incredibly tan and strong legs, followed by a muscular upper body and a familiar face. It was Trip's friend.

"Hi again," he said as he walked past us up the sidewalk.

"Hey." Mom stayed quiet and shot me a questioning look as we left their yard.

"You know him?"

I shrugged. "Know is a very broad word. I saw him today at the beach."

"He's cute."

Not as cute as his friend.

But that didn't stop me from turning back to see if Trip's friend was looking at us, too.

Dinner was quick and easy that night: macaroni and cheese, tossed salad, and summer squash. Cleaning was a breeze, and by eight o'clock, I didn't know what to do with myself on my last Thursday night before senior year. I was restless, even after the long day on the beach.

"Mom, I'm going for a walk. I'll be back soon." I collected my keys and my cell and headed outside. The sun was sinking behind the opaque river. Needing a direction to aim for, I headed toward the mini park up the street. I thought about calling Cole or Annabelle but didn't feel up for company.

"Hey, Bridget!"

I jumped. There was no doubt in my mind the voice belonged to Trip. Not wanting to be interrupted, I kept walking.

"Hey! Wait up!" I kept walking. "Bridget!" I froze as his shoes slapped against the pavement toward me.

"Hey! Didn't you hear me?" he asked, finally catching up.

I shrugged.

"Cat got your tongue?" He smirked, deliciously adorable. I could lose myself in those dimples for hours.

"No, I was just waiting for your friend to pop up."

Trip's smirk spread into a smile. "Nope, not here. Just you and me."

He had to be doing that on purpose. Maybe if I kept my mouth shut, I wouldn't stick my foot in it.

"So, thank you for the gift basket. Those cupcakes sure were good." He patted his stomach.

Again, he was drawing attention to his abs. Was he trying to make me faint? Thunder clapped in the distance. *Weird, it wasn't supposed to rain tonight.*

"Aren't you going to say anything?" He raised his eyebrows.

"What do you want me to say?" Since nothing was coming to my mind . . .

"Anything you want. Whatever comes to your mind first."

Play it cool, Bridget. I rolled my eyes. *I am cool.*

"Do you realize you never formally told me your name? For all I know, you could be Pennywise."

He laughed and stuck out his right hand. "Hi, I'm Trip. What's your name?"

"Bridget," I said, taking his hand.

"It's nice to officially meet you." Trip smiled politely at me. His toothpaste commercial smile was so contagious; I couldn't help but smile back.

"I was going for a walk to the park. Do you want to come?" I asked as I tucked my hair behind my ears. "I could tell you all the cool places to hang out and then the places that are actually fun."

"Sure." He gestured for me to go ahead of him. We walked past three houses—one in desperate need of mowing—before either of us spoke.

"So, who's your friend?" I asked.

"Who? Today? That's Tomas."

"Is he new, too? I haven't seen him before."

"Yeah, I guess. His family is back home, so he is living with us for … uh … the time being."

He jammed his hands into his pockets. I took it as a sign not to ask about Tomas anymore.

"How long have you lived here?" he asked, clearly changing topics.

"All my life. In fact," we stopped, "this is the park where my father used to take me fishing when I was a kid. This is the best place to fish besides on the preservation."

"What preservation?"

I smiled. "The Tuckahoe-Corbin City Fish and Wildlife Management Area."

"That's a mouthful!"

"It really is, but it's a beautiful hike."

The small park had a large, white gazebo and a few scattered picnic benches broken up by large bushes. Next to the park was a winding wooden path to a dock over the river.

"It's impressive." Trip sat on a gazebo bench and leaned against the railing. I joined him.

"It's just a normal, small-town park. Nothing really fancy."

"I didn't have that as a kid," he said, looking at his feet. I looked up at him, but Trip seemed to be avoiding my gaze.

"No fishing?"

"No fishing with Dad, no playing catch with him." Trip looked a little forlorn watching whatever played in his mind. "We used to move a lot because of his consulting job, so it was hard for us to stay at one school for a long time. Hard to make friends, you know?"

"But you have Tomas, now."

"I do. He's my best friend."

I stayed quiet. Trip's feet dragged on the floor, leaving imaginary crevices with the top of his shoes. Something stirred inside me, and I felt like giving him a hug.

"How come your family moved here?"

"Uh," he cleared his throat, "Dad got a permanent consulting job here at a real estate firm trying to expand their business to the smaller local towns. My parents decided to move us all instead of having Dad travel back and forth on the weekends."

"Oh. Where did you move from?" He didn't answer right away.

"I only ask," I tried to explain, "because your mom and dad have an accent, but I can't place it. And you don't."

"Deidra and I were born in Scotland, like my parents, but Roden and Elizabeth were born in America. That's why they don't have the accent. Moving around a lot, Dee and I picked up a bunch of different dialects, so no accents for us."

"That's really cool! I haven't been to Scotland. Or the UK, for that matter. I've only been to Canada once, but I mostly stay in Jersey."

"Cool. We moved from Scotland to the States when Dee was three."

"Hey, instead of staying here, why don't we go to the boardwalk? I could really use some cotton candy. I'll drive." I stood and shook my foot to release a rock in my sandal. "Race you back?" Trip perked up a bit.

"I don't know the street too well. What if I trip?"

"You'll be fine!" I yelled as I took off running toward my house. "Thanks for the head start!"

"I can't remember the last time I had cotton candy," Trip said in between licking his fingers. The blue, sugary confection melted on the paper cone from the remaining warmth of the night.

The sun had set a while ago, but the air was still heavy with humidity. I pulled a piece of my fluffy treat off and let the sugar dissolve on my tongue. I had to admit, hanging with Trip wasn't so bad. He seemed to be game for most anything I threw at him. We had already walked halfway up the boardwalk, played mini golf at Congo Falls Adventure (I lost), ridden the Ferris wheel at Gillian's Wonderland Pier, and hit up a racing game at the Hollywood Arcade (I won that time). As the night wound down and it came close to my curfew, the shops pulled down their gates as we headed back up to the boardwalk entrance by the high school.

"The last time I ate cotton candy must have been before New York stopped serving soda with a lifeguard," Trip added.

"Really? Cotton candy is a staple of my summer diet, along with Sam's Specials, ice cream, watermelon, and barbeque. And lobster. And pretzels. Oh, and pasta salad! Man, I can't wait for Sunday." My mouth watered at the thought of hamburgers, chicken, grilled vegetables, and all the sides accompanying them. I loved summer.

"I admire a girl who can out eat me," commented Trip. "Seriously." He checked me out to prove a point, but all I did was blush into my remaining cotton candy. Trip was slowly moving his way into my main crush spot. Goodbye, Kevin.

"Uh-oh," Trip muttered.

"What?" I frantically looked down, trying to get a view of my butt. I would seriously drown myself if I'd sat in chocolate or got my period in my white shorts. That would end any chance I had with Trip. But he wasn't looking at my butt. He stared straight ahead with an intense gaze I'd only seen on one other person: Pete Cutter. He was an unknown sophomore last year when he had found a way to unlock porn on the school library's computers. He'd been staring so fiercely at the screen before the gym teacher caught him that his eyes nearly popped out of his head. Now he was the go-to guy for anyone who needed a hacker.

I followed Trip's gaze to a group of people I recognized: Cay and his friends.

"What's the problem? If we don't talk to them, they won't even bother us," I said, a little worried about Trip's sudden change in attitude. He didn't seem to hear me.

"Shocking to find you here," sneered Cay as he walked up to us. I rolled my eyes. He usually didn't torment other students, but every now and then, his class clown attitude crossed a line.

"That's the best you could come up with?" Trip shook his head sadly. "That's weak, man. How about I let you slide on that one, and when you think of a real burner, you can tweet it to me."

I smiled. It was somewhat enjoyable to see Cay taken down a peg.

"I'd rather slide into your sister's DMs."

Cory Birch and Logan Carter—Ocean City royalty—oohed and aahed over Cay's response while the girls and I exchanged glances. Clearly, I wasn't popular on the same level, but the girls and I had a mutual respect for each other. Even though Hilary Thompson and Noelle Patrelli were the "bad girls" of Ocean City, I didn't bother them, and they didn't bother me. In fact, Noelle and I were best friends in fifth grade before cliques were in and elementary school friendships were all but forgotten. Hilary and I'd had our middle school fights over dumb things, but now that we were older, we were over it.

I felt bad for Trip. He was new in town and already had to deal with stupid bullies.

"Lay off of him, Cay," said Alec. Alec was no slouch, but these days, the high schoolers in South Jersey looked like linebackers for the Eagles. "It's not worth it." Cay looked at him in surprise.

"Are you serious?" Alec silenced him with a flash of a menacing look. Cay quieted, but you could see the hate for Trip seething in his eyes. Trip's face remained composed, but his hands clenched in fists at his sides.

"Let's go," Cay grumbled. The group walked through Trip and me, Cory and Cay knocking Trip's shoulder as they passed. Kevin was the last one through, but he didn't touch anyone.

"Hey, Bridget," he said as he passed. I floated out of my body. I didn't even think he knew my name! I know a dopey smile came over my face because when I came back down to earth, Trip was glaring at me. I wiped the happiness away and shot him a sympathetic look back. He just walked away and down the steps, allowing the shadowy darkness of the alley to swallow him whole.

Chapter 2

Friday and Saturday came and went in frantic chaos. For those two days, I was tasked with cleaning my bathroom and bedroom (like anyone was going to see them) and then rinsing the pollen from the deck chairs. Dad mowed the backyard, picked up fallen sticks from the last thunderstorm, and set up the citronella candles around the porch. Mom was checking and double-checking whether or not she had prepared enough food for the entire neighborhood.

"Bridge, did I tell you if Amelia Tanner and her two sons were coming?" Mom yelled from the kitchen. I stuck my head up from the bathtub I scrubbed. Heaven forbid we closed the shower curtain and moved on with our lives. Oh no, it needed to be shiny and Mr. Clean-clean, just in case the Queen of England stopped by and happened to need a shower while she was here!

I blew a piece of hair that had fallen from my sloppy bun away from my face.

"Yes, you told me, and no, they are not. They went to Philly to visit her parents for the weekend!" I shouted. I sprayed more cleaning agents on the stubborn soap scum and attacked it again.

"What about the new neighbors? The Findlays?"

I paused. It'd been almost two full days since I'd seen or heard from Trip after dropping him off. After his tense encounter with Cay, he'd been avoiding me. Who had I been kidding? He didn't owe me anything. Maybe he was doing stuff with his family. It's not like he *had* to spend time with me. We weren't dating. In fact, I wouldn't even call us friends. I shook my head.

"Bridget?" Mom called.

"Oh yeah. Yes, they're coming!" I looked at the obstinate stain and gave up. If Mr. Clean and Mr. Bubbles weren't going to kill it, then there was nothing left to do but relinquish that piece of grout to the soap scum.

"Congratulations," I said to the stain. Standing, I got dizzy from all the chemicals and poor ventilation. I removed my rubber gloves and flopped onto the couch in the living room. Midnight-blue, fluffy ... it was one durable piece of furniture. I had spent my formidable years napping, eating, and having sick days on that couch. I snuggled in more and closed my eyes. A few minutes later, Dad's heavy footsteps were muffled as he came into the living room.

"Hey, kid," he said as he sat next to me. I sank into the couch a little more.

"Hi, Dad." My eyes remained closed. Maybe if I didn't open them, he'd get the hint.

"Mom just mentioned if you were done cleaning the bathroom, she would like you to help her with something in the kitchen. Or you could run to the store for me and pick up a few last-minute things."

"Mm-hmm."

"Bridget!" Mom called again from the kitchen. "Could you help me with something? I was curious if you'd clean the oven for me!"

"Run!" Dad whispered. My eyes popped open.

"Can't! Running to the store for Dad!" I jumped up and rushed out the door.

"If I was an apricot, where in this section would I be?" I muttered and perused the produce section.

"By the peaches, next aisle over," a guy said. I whipped around, a little surprised someone else had heard me. That someone was Cay.

"Oh, um, thanks," I sputtered. I couldn't recall Cay ever talking to me before, let alone nicely. I flashed him a tight smile and walked over to the next aisle. I found the fruit, picked out a few firm ones, and turned smack into Cay. "Are you following me?"

He smiled. "Why would you think that?" He reached around me and picked a few peaches from the pile. Still grinning and never taking his eyes off me, Cay dropped them into his plastic bag. Up close, his dark green eyes were enticing. I saw some of his brother's handsome features in his face. I shook my head and remembered Cay was usually a jerk and a bully. Good looks were nothing compared to a good personality.

"What are you doing here?" I blurted out. He beamed even brighter.

"Hunting reindeer." I raised my eyebrows. Clearly, he was here to do grocery shopping. Score one for Cay.

I nodded briefly and pushed my cart past him, leaving the produce section.

"How come we never hang out?" he asked as he pulled his cart alongside mine.

Frowning, I opened my mouth but closed it quickly. I couldn't think of what to say.

"Well, we should. Hang out. What are you doing tomorrow?"

I was too taken aback to come up with a lie. "My family is holding a neighborhood barbeque."

"Great! I'll see you there." He winked at me and walked off. Had I missed something? Cailean McKay wanted to come over to my house and hang out with me?

I wished the sudden excited butterflies in my stomach would settle down.

That night, I tossed and turned in bed, unable to untangle the ball of nerves lodged in my chest.

"No, Lugh!" I ran after him, slipping on the wet pine needles in the forest. The sweet smell of damp grass and dirt saturated the air I sucked in heaving breaths. My wet dress tangled at my feet, tripping me. Pulling myself up off the ground, I stumbled through low-hanging branches in search of my brother. There! I saw a flash of his burned yellow tunic and white hair through the trees. Pushing myself harder, I practically

flew over fallen trunks and rocks. "Lugh, wait!" He stopped for a minute, suspended in time. Catching up to him, I touched his arm, and the frozen body in front me became my sibling again.

"I can't wait!" he growled. "I need to find her!" I panted next him, doubled over in pain. Lugh took another step up the mountain but couldn't go too far since I still held his clothes.

"I'll help. She can't be too far ahead."

"No! This is my doing! She is the only one who knows. I have to find her." He wrenched his arm out of my grasp and walked away. A sense of panic flooded my body, followed by an overwhelming feeling of urgency.

"Your doing? How? And how can she help us find it?" I called, hoping to slow him down. Lugh turned to face me, his green eyes full of intensity.

"We find her, we find the Amulet." His voice was so filled with doom. It felt like a rock settling in my stomach. Thunder cracked above us, reflecting Lugh's intense anger.

As the dream faded from my memory, Lugh's eyes were the last thing I remembered.

"The weather will be hot and sunny today thanks to yet another side effect of global warming..." the weatherman's voice blared from my radio. Groaning, I rolled and shut it off. Still feeling groggy and over-tired, I flopped back onto my pillows. The unusual dream left a weird impression on my brain. The forest felt like home as if I spent my summers traipsing over every hill and through every shiny brook. My family camped at the Hiltons, not in tents in the rain. Something else pricked the back of my mind. I'd never heard the name Lugh before, yet his face seemed so incredibly familiar.

Stretching, I let the dream fade from my mind as memories of the day before danced into my brain. I wondered if Trip would show today. We hadn't seen each other or talked since we ran into Cay and his friends on the boardwalk.

"Ugh," I groaned through sleepiness. My afternoon adventure with Cay yesterday came rushing back, and I instinctively tensed at the idea of his showing up at the barbeque. At least my friends would be there and none of his would, so I'd be in good company. Pushing my covers off my legs and nearly falling out of bed, I stumbled into the bathroom, yawning loudly as I went.

"Oh, good. You're up," Mom chirped. "After you shower, come help me set up. It's already ten thirty, and I still need to chop vegetables."

I shot her a thumbs-up and closed the bathroom door behind me. Did I really need to shower that badly? I peeked at the mirror above the sink. My not-so-well-rested reflection stared back at me. Cloudy, blue eyes with dark smudges beneath them scanned my face for blemishes or anything out of the normal. Glancing at my hair, I saw what my mother was referring to. The usual wavy, red hair on my head had been replaced by a tangled mess. I brushed my teeth, showered, and hurried to dress. As much as I wanted to make my last day of summer last forever, I didn't want to keep Mom waiting while she was in "party mode." Five summers ago, Dad made the mistake of going golfing in the morning before a big party, even though he knew what Mom is like when setting up. Let's just say he didn't golf as much anymore, and his clubs had a slight bend, even after having them fixed.

"I'm so glad I'm skipping breakfast today," I mentioned to Mom as I entered the kitchen. She handed me a chopping board as I placed my phone on the table.

"Why is that?" Mom asked while pointing to a cucumber and a red pepper.

"Because I want to make sure I can eat everything in sight. I'm talking seconds and potential thirds." I picked a knife from the chopping block and sat at the table. "What did you make for dessert this year?"

The barbeque is themed every year. In the past, it had never been common to dress up, but for the past two years, our neighbors had decided to anyway. Last year was Carnevale, but this year, Mom went low-key: luau. Pink flower leis and tiki huts were everywhere. Thankfully, we wouldn't be wearing hula skirts or flower bras, but I couldn't promise the same for everyone else. The thought of a very old Mr. Sanders dressing in the skirt and bra sent shivers crawling down my back.

"Macadamia Coconut Cake, brownies, and fresh fruit. Nothing too big. When you're done chopping those, I have more you can slice." My phone vibrated, indicating I had a message.

[Trip: Hey, it's Trip.]

[Trip: Can we meet? I want to talk. Fishing park at 1?]

My heart did the Snoopy Happy Dance at the name: Trip. I looked at the clock. I didn't have much time to get ready. Wiping my hands on a towel, I answered back:

[Bridget: Sure. See you then.]

"Um, Mom, how much more do I have to do? I have to run a quick errand before the barbeque."

"You can be done after you finish slicing the pineapple."

I'd never chopped fruit faster in my life. After washing my hands, I changed into frayed jean shorts and a loose-fitting tank top with the Beatles on the front. Who said I had to look like a hot mess when I saw Trip? After dabbing some concealer under my eyes and slipping on my favorite pair of sneakers, I hurried from the house, hoping I wouldn't be late.

I practically ran down the block to the park but was afraid if I didn't beat Trip there, he'd see me running to meet him. Not wanting to come off too eager, I slowed, stopping to tie my shoe and buy myself a little time. Lightning crackled above me and I jumped. Was it normal for lightning to strike in the middle of the day with no warning? Turning the corner, I saw the gazebo where Trip and I had hung out a few days ago. He sat there, his back to me.

Quickly braiding my hair down the side, I walked slowly, afraid to make noise.

"Hey," I said softly as I approached him. He looked back and shot me a quick smile.

"Hey. Wasn't sure if you'd come."

"I said I would. I'd like to think I'm a woman of my word." Playing with the tail of my braid, I made an attempt to appear casual. "So, what's going on?"

He cleared his throat. "I wanted to apologize."

That wasn't what I had been expecting. "For what? Did you key my car?"

"What? No." Confusion painted Trip's face.

"Did you kidnap my cat?"

"Do you have a cat?" he asked, bewildered.

"No, but that's not the point. If I had a cat, would you steal him?"

"Um, no."

"Then you didn't offend me in any way, like keying my car or stealing my cat would. I think we'll be okay."

Trip laughed. "Fine, but I'd like to apologize anyway. If you don't mind."

"Apologize away," I replied, sweeping my hands out in front of me.

"I wanted to say I'm sorry for acting like a jerk for the past few days. I let Cay get to me, and I took it out on you."

"Took it out on me? Did you actually key my car?" I loved my little out-of-date, hand-me-down, red 1979 Pontiac Firebird with a T-top. It had been my dad's midlife crisis car before it was Mom's "need a company car" car. She bought the minivan for deliveries last year, and the Firebird was handed down to me. It was my "I finally have a car" car. It had seen better days, but I loved that thing.

"No! Stop that. I stopped talking to you because..." He chucked a stone into the river, skipping it only twice. I raised my eyebrow, secretly impressed, and waited for him to continue. They say if you stayed silent in a conversation when you wanted the other person to talk, the other person would do whatever they could to fill that silence. I was interested to see if I could get it to work. "Well, I was embarrassed about what happened on the boardwalk with me and Cay. Whatever, it shouldn't have happened, and I'm sorry."

His face was a little flushed, but I wondered if there was more to this story.

"I don't understand something. You just moved here to our small, one-gas station town, right?"

"Yeah." I heard the apprehension in his voice.

"So why would Cay want to fight with you? How did you manage to get on his bad side already?" Panic flashed across his face and was gone the next instant. He shrugged.

"I don't know. Isn't he the school bully? Isn't it his job to pick on the new guy?" Trip looked down again.

"But the way he talked made it seem like he knew you before he saw you on the boardwalk." Trip's face paled and twisted as if he was silently praying I wouldn't push further. A moment later, he was neutral.

"I don't know! Maybe he saw me on the beach earlier that day after I met you on the boardwalk, and he got jealous." Trip couldn't keep the smugness from his tone. I wasn't sure what to do with his mood change, but I let it go.

"Okay, okay. Apology accepted." I smiled to send the message home, but I couldn't understand why Trip was so intent on avoiding my questions. His face flashed relief just as my stomach growled, humiliating me. "I skipped breakfast," I offered weakly. "And I have to get back to help set up for the barbeque. Walk me home?"

Trip brightened at the invite. "Sure."

As we walked back to my house, it began to drizzle. I hoped it didn't stay like this all day. It wasn't fun to wear a sticky and sopping-wet lei around your neck.

"Are you coming to the barbeque?"

"I didn't know I was invited." He put his hand in his pocket, pulled out a pack of gum, and offered me a piece. After I turned him down, he took one for himself and put it away.

"Well, my mom invited your whole family, so I just guessed they would have told you," I explained.

"I'm usually the last to know anything."

"Let me formally invite you then." I put on a British accent. "Mr. Trip Findlay, I cordially invite you to the MacNamaras' Annual End-of-Summer Barbeque. Costumes are encouraged but not expected."

"Costumes?" he asked, skeptical. I shrugged and dropped the accent.

"It's themed. This year is luau."

"So, grass skirts?"

"No," I replied, chuckling. "No grass skirts or coconut bras."

"Will you be dressing up?"

"Not really. I may wear a lei and call it a day."

"Bummer."

Surprised, I looked at him and caught his eye. He grinned. A surge of lust coursed through my body, sending my cells into a tizzy.

Lightning split the sky as thunder grumbled above us, but neither of us paid any attention. I wanted to kiss him. I licked my lips and turned away, feeling my cheeks warm at the strong urge. To add to my suave boy-trapping skills, I was so caught up with potentially kissing him that I tripped. On a rock.

I would have seen it if I had kept facing forward like normal people did while walking. Instead, I fell on my knees, causing my skin to scrape and bleed. If there was any form of a higher power out there, the ground would have opened up and gulped me down without stopping to chew.

"Ow!" *Don't cry. Don't cry!* I had never been good with physical pain. I rolled over and clutched my knee to stop the bleeding.

"Are you okay?" Trip crouched next to me to check out my ridiculous injury. "Let me see." He pried my fingers off and looked at the mess that had formerly been my knee. "You'll be okay. It's just a flesh wound." I kept my eyes big to avoid tears, but the tenderness of his touch and the Monty Python reference made a single drop escape. I cursed that tear.

"You don't have to cry," Trip said softly. He brought his thumb up to my cheek and wiped it away. In the movies, it would have been the moment the new guy—Trip Findlay, in all of his gorgeous glory—would lean over and kiss me. But, of course, that didn't happen.

"Are you alright?" a voice called from behind me. Mrs. Perkins, looking like a banana in her yellow Bermuda shorts and matching yellow t-shirt, was bringing in groceries from her car and had witnessed my downfall.

Taking a deep breath and Trip's now outstretched hand, I stood. "I'm fine, Mrs. Perkins. It's just a scratch." I took a step to prove my point.

She clucked her tongue. "You should watch where you're walking. But I'm glad you're alright. I'll see you at the barbeque later if this rain stops trying to flood us out!" I waved goodbye, silently cursed both my bad luck and Mrs. Perkins's eagle eye, and continued walking home with Trip. It took me a second to realize his fingers still held mine. I bit my lip to hide the smile spreading across my face.

"Ahem." Trip cleared his throat and awkwardly wiped his hands on his shorts, leaving mine cold and empty. "Let's go get you a Band-Aid."

I nodded. Thankfully, by the time we reached my house, my knee had mostly stopped bleeding, so it didn't look as bad as it felt. The rain clouds cleared up, and the sun was drying everything out again.

"Did it stop raining?" Mom asked as we entered. Then, spying my knee, she continued asking, "What happened?"

"I fell."

"It's not as bad as it looks. I promise," Trip piped up. Mom nodded, wearing a frown.

"Oh, Mom, this is Trip Findlay. Remember, we met his family last week?"

"Right, of course. It's nice to meet you." Mom had already pulled down the first aid kit from the kitchen cabinet, so she handed it to me. "Go clean yourself up. Dad already started the grill, and people should be showing up soon. Is your family still coming, Trip?"

"I believe so."

"Wonderful." She smiled and went out the back door.

"Need help?" Trip asked, hopeful.

"Afraid of being left alone for two seconds?" I teased.

"Something like that," he replied with a smirk. I waved my free hand toward the bathroom. I grabbed a washcloth, ran it under the faucet, and sat on the edge of the tub. Trip took the washcloth from me wordlessly and wiped away the dirt and pebbles still embedded in my skin.

"Done this before, huh?" I joked.

"When we were growing up, Mom and Dad had a lot of important business to take care of, so they were around but not always there. Our nanny showed me how to clean a cut. With four kids, she needed all the help she could get!" He smiled at the memory as he washed off the dried blood. I opened the Band-Aid, and he dabbed a little ointment on my skin. Once I placed the bandage over it, I was all patched up.

"Thank you for your help." I chewed on my lower lip, feeling shy all of a sudden.

"Rescuing damsels in distress is merely a hobby of mine," he joked. His gaze landed on mine, and yet again, lust spread through my veins. I leaned in, furiously praying he would, too. He licked his lips, his eyes trailing down my face to rest on my bottom lip. He closed the chasm between us, and I smelled the peppermint on his breath. I should have accepted his gum offer. As we inched closer to each other, I closed my eyes. There was no time for regrets. My body tingled as he placed his hand on my cheek. My breath shortened in anticipation as his lips pressed against mine, softly at first. It was really sweet, but I wanted more. My teenage body demanded it. I deepened the kiss, parting his lips with my tongue. He returned the favor, nibbling on my lower lip.

BANG!

We shot apart like a bomb exploded between us. The front screen door slammed shut.

"Hey, Bridget?" I heard Annabelle's voice coming from the living room. *Oh god*! I had nearly forgotten about the barbeque! I looked at Trip. His pupils were dilated, swallowing the green of his eyes. I put my hand to my cheek, and heat radiated from it. He took my hand, pulling me up for the second time that day, as we shared a telling smile and made a silent promise to continue this moment in the near future. He held it until we hit the living room barrier, where he released me into the waiting arms of Annabelle.

"Hey girly!" she said as we parted from the hug. "What happened?" I looked at my newly bandaged scrape and shrugged.

"I fell and skinned my knee." Trip stood awkwardly next to me. "Oh! Sorry, Trip, this is Annabelle," I pointed to my friend as she pushed her glasses up. "And this is Trip. He just moved in two doors down."

"Nice to meet you," Annabelle said.

"Were you painting again, Annabelle?" I asked and she nodded. The poor girl's shorts had streaks of white and blue paint across the thighs.

"I was painting a picture of the Red Square in Russia in varying shades of blues for my dad's office."

"He'll love that! Before I forget, have you heard from Bri or Cole?"

Annabelle nodded again. "Bri sent me a text saying she'd be here in twenty minutes." The doorbell rang, and I leaped to answer it.

"Hey, Cole!" I was happy to see my other friend arrive. I swept him into a hug, dragging him inside.

"Uh, hi!" He stopped the door from crashing behind him.

"This is Trip. He's new. Trip, this is Cole. He's not new." I shook my head. I was the worst at introductions.

"Hey, man," Trip said, nodding in Cole's direction. Cole repeated the gesture.

"Okay, I'm sure my dad is almost finished with the first round of burgers, and I'm hungry. Anyone care to join me?" I didn't wait for an answer as I bolted for my back door. Everyone trailed behind me as Cole talked about sports with Trip. I hadn't known Trip liked sports. Then again, there was a lot about Trip I didn't know.

I walked outside, and my nose was accosted by the beautiful smells mingling in the air. I caught the gas grill pumping out smoky burgers and hot dogs, along with the sweet scent of pineapple. The normal backyard tents transformed into grass tiki huts with pink, yellow, and green tablecloths covering picnic tables underneath. Streamers of rainbow pineapples connected all the tables together and a fake tiki hut bar complete with bartender sat by the side of the house. Mom even got a giant, roasting pig. She had clearly outdone herself this year. Our back gate opened, and in walked a few of our neighbors. Mom, wearing a Hawaiian-print maxi dress, went over and hung silk flower leis around their necks. They exchanged greetings as I floated down the steps toward the coolers full of drinks.

"How many hot dogs do you want, Bridget?" Dad asked as I passed by.

"One to start, but I'm going for the coconut shrimp first. I'll be back."

"Aye, aye, Captain." I loved that my dad was a cornball sometimes.

"So, why did Cay McKay just text me asking what 'Bridget's addy' was?" Cole asked, grabbing a soda.

"Did you tell him?" I checked to see if Trip overheard, but he was distracted by a conversation with Annabelle. Thank goodness.

"I asked why he needed it, but he hasn't said anything back yet. Want me to tell him?"

"Whatever. I have to talk to Trip." I marched over to the guy I was just kissing. He was laughing at something with my best friend.

Mom intercepted me. "Hey, Bridget? Can you do me a favor and grab the paper bowls for the fruit salad? I left them inside on the counter."

Rats. Detouring, I made my jaunt into the kitchen quick as possible, but I wasn't quick enough. Trip and Annabelle were looking friendlier as time passed, and I wanted to talk to him before Cay arrived—if he showed up at all. Not to mention, I was a tiny bit jealous. We'd *just* kissed!

The sun disappeared behind some fluffy, silver clouds as I dropped the bowls by the salad and rushed over to my friends.

"You two look pretty chummy," I interrupted them, maybe more harshly than I had intended. They both looked taken aback.

"Well, Trip asked me about my painting and was thinking of hiring me to paint him and his siblings for their parents' upcoming anniversary," Annabelle explained.

I suddenly felt very foolish.

"Do you mind if I talk to him for a minute?" I asked her. She looked a bit puzzled but still said, "Sure. I'll go get something to eat." Annabelle left us, and Trip just stared at me in confusion.

"I know we just kissed and all, but there's no need to be jealous. We aren't exclusive yet," Trip joked as I dragged him inside.

"Jealous? I don't care who you talk to!" I scoffed. Pausing for a moment, I put my hands up to stop myself and took a deep breath. "That's not the point. I just came to warn you Cay is probably showing up." I stormed out of the kitchen and into my now-cloudy backyard.

"Hey!" called Trip. He grasped my elbow and spun me around. "What the hell was that about?"

"Which part?" I pulled my arm away.

"All of it. I was kidding about the jealous part, and why would Cay show up here?"

I took a deep breath and let it out slowly. "I ran into Cay yesterday at the store, and he invited himself over."

"Did you want him to come?"

"It doesn't matter because he's apparently showing up anyway." I looked away from him, and my nerves pulsed at my skin, feeling like they were about to break free. Clearly, Annabelle wasn't into him. I just didn't handle stress well, and the potential confrontation between Trip and Cay was driving me insane.

"Hey," Trip whispered. He tucked a finger under my chin and lifted my face up toward his. "There's no need to worry about me and him. I'll behave like a good little boy should."

"It's not you I'm worried about." I stepped back from him. "I'm going to eat. Do you want something?"

"No, thanks," he replied, watching me as I stepped into the yard. Grabbing a hot dog from the tray on the table and taking a big bite gave me time to reflect. There was absolutely no reason for me to feel jealous. I knew Annabelle had a crush on George, another guy at school. She'd been hung up on him since eighth grade, and this year she was hoping to make her move since he was finally single. Even forgetting the Annabelle issue for a minute, Trip didn't seem like a sleazeball who would kiss a girl, then hit on her friend right in front of her ten minutes later. Then again, he could be a heartbreaker who'd had his own heart broken and was now hell-bent on returning the favor to every girl panting after him. I looked over at Trip laughing with Tomas. Apparently, in the midst of my internal diatribe, his family had shown up.

"Hi, we haven't met yet, but I'm Deidra, Trip's sister." I nearly choked on my hot dog at the shock of her popping up and interrupting my staring, but I gave her a small smile.

"It's nice to meet you! Thanks for coming." She had a rainbow lei around her neck to match her yellow, racerback tank and jean shorts. Her long, blonde hair hung loosely around her pale shoulders, and she wore a frayed, threaded bracelet that had clearly once been a light blue on her wrist. It was currently dirty brown.

"I hope you don't mind us coming early."

"Us?" I scanned the yard, but I only saw the four Findlay kids. No parents.

"My dad had to run a quick errand before he came over, and my mom was complaining of a headache earlier. She's lying down," she said, answering my unspoken thought.

"Oh, I hope she feels better." I smiled again and got one in return.

"Thanks. So, what's fun around here?" Deidra picked up a wet can of iced tea from the cooler and wiped it off before popping it open.

"Um, since school starts tomorrow, nothing," I joked. "But normally, it's what everyone else in the world does on weekends. Movies, mall, boardwalk, beach, hanging out with our friends, plotting world domination. Normal stuff." Her eyes widened at the last suggestion I'd made. "I'm kidding about taking over the world," I added.

"Right, of course. Trip's always saying I don't have a sense of humor. I do, but I sometimes miss sarcasm."

"No worries. Have you met anyone else yet?" She shook her head. "Come on, I'll introduce you." We walked over by Annabelle and Cole, joined by Brianna.

"Hey! I didn't see you get here. Why didn't you say hi?" I leaned in for a hug from Bri.

"Just got here. I'm sorry I'm late."

"No problem," I said and shrugged. "Food's hot and ready whenever you are." I jerked my thumb toward the grill and the expansive buffet.

"Thanks. Hi, I'm Bri," she said to Deidra, who waved back.

"Hi, nice to meet you," Deidra said after I introduced everyone. "Do you all go to Ocean City?" I didn't want to leave Deidra hanging, but I was too preoccupied with the newest arrivals to my barbeque to pay attention to the gossip of OCHS. Cay, Logan, Hilary, and Cory had just passed through the back gate and were now standing in my backyard. My eyes darted to Trip to see if he'd seen them, but his back was to the entrance. Good. I shot over to Cay.

"Hi, guys! Um, grab a drink. Can I talk to you?" I hurriedly asked Cay. He flashed me a grin and pushed his reddish-brown hair from his face in one, smooth motion.

"Sure. I'll be over in a second. I want to say hi to Trip first."

"No!" I placed my hands on his chest and pushed him back. "No, no, you and I need to chat before you say hi to anyone else here." I waved the others on in. "Don't worry, he'll be fine." Cory and Hilary waved hello to me and headed toward the buffet, but Logan needed confirmation from Cay before making any movements. Cay nodded once and Logan disappeared.

"So, what's up? Had a good summer?" He rocked back on his heels in a cocky fashion.

"Did you only invite yourself—and your friends—to mess with Trip? Because I'm not having that at my party." Stress built up in my chest again.

"Chill out, Bridge." It needled me that he'd used a familiar nickname. We weren't friendly enough for pet names; we were hardly friendly enough for first names at all. "I'm here to enjoy the last day of summer with some good food and good people. No games or tricks. Scout's honor," he said, holding up his hand in a mock salute.

"Were you even a Boy Scout?" I pushed his hand down.

"No, but I had a brownie once," he retorted, grinning.

"Ugh. One, that joke is so outdated and overused. Be original, for goodness' sake. And two, Brownies are usually in elementary school; you sound like a pedophile." He raised his eyebrows at me. "Forget it. Just leave." I pointed to the gate, and Cay frowned.

"For real, I'll behave. No shenanigans from me."

"Or your friends?"

He rolled his eyes. "We will all be on our very best behavior." I stared at him, trying to determine if he was playing me, but all I saw was sincerity. I frowned.

"Fine, but I'm serious. If you start something, I'm personally picking you up and throwing you out."

"That I'd love to see," he said, laughing as he sauntered past me. I shook my head. This would be a nightmare.

"You okay?" Mom came over to put a bowl of leis on a table. She saw my face and hers swiftly changed from party to concern. "What's wrong? Just take a deep breath and try to calm down."

My neck muscles tensed, and my jaw clenched. Rolling my shoulders, taking that deep breath, and forcing my jaw to relax helped, but I couldn't shake the foreboding feeling nestled in my chest. Suddenly, the gentle breeze turned my backyard into a wind tunnel. Paper plates, leis, napkins, and anything else that hadn't been nailed down swirled around our guests. A guest was pushed back toward the bar. She grabbed the pole holding the awning to anchor herself. Mrs. Perkins was hit in the leg with someone's baseball hat while her husband's fruit salad blew into his lap. The wind startled me out of my anger, but it settled back into its familiar current in a flash.

For a moment, no one said much of anything. All of the guests were probably unsure of what to think.

"Can't ever count on those weathermen to get a forecast right!" Dad joked. People laughed out of politeness, and just like that, the atmosphere was back to the prior, casual mentality. Mom sighed and looked at me apologetically. I stared back, confused, but there was no other response from her. We bent over to pick up the fallen leis while Deidra and Cole pitched in to pick up the plates. Most guests helped with scooping up blown items, but Mom's coconut cake had turned over on the grass. She saw it and sighed sadly. I walked over and gave her a hug.

"I'm sorry," I whispered to her. "I know how hard you worked on this party."

Mom just patted my shoulder and said, "No use crying over spilled coconut cake."

I crouched to help her clean up the mess.

"That was insanely weird," I heard Hilary say to Cay. I looked over just in time to catch his piercing stare.

"Yeah, really weird," he responded.

It was the night before my last first day of school. It's a pretty big moment for parents, but I couldn't care less. I had spent the rest of my Sunday helping to clean up after the barbeque. Most people had gone home shortly after the wind extravaganza, including Hilary and Cory. Surprises had been in abundance today: the fall, the kiss, the weird weather, and the lack of fighting between Trip and Cay. After the midday cleanup, Trip had hovered around me, ignoring his siblings and making sure I was okay. Normally it would have bothered me, but with Cay and Logan shooting odd glances my way all afternoon, I'd been happy for a little positive attention.

"Honey?" Mom knocked on the door as she poked her head in. "You busy?"

"Not really," I said, opening my closet door. "Just figuring out what I want to wear for school tomorrow."

"Are you excited?" she asked, sitting on my bed.

Shrugging, I answered, "I guess. I mean, I've had first days before."

"Yeah, but this is your last first day. My baby is all grown up." She sniffed.

"Mom, really, it's not a big deal." I sat next to her and wrapped my arm around her. "I'll have other first days. Like my first day of college." She smiled sadly.

"Thanks, sweetheart, but it's not the same." She patted me on the thigh. "Do you know what I'll miss the most?" I shook my head. "Getting you dressed in your cute sailor outfit with matching shoes and watching you walk into your first day of school."

"That was kindergarten! You make it sound like I wore that every first day!" I crinkled my nose at the memory. "Do you want to help me pick out what I'm going to wear?"

She brightened. "If you wouldn't mind."

I smiled. Most people hated their moms picking out their clothes, but my mom's style rivaled Victoria Beckham's. "Not at all! This is an important first day of school, so any advice would be appreciated." I rose and stood in front of my open closet. "I was thinking a dress, but I don't know my schedule well yet. I don't want to be running around with the potential to pull a Marilyn Monroe."

"What about jeans?" I moved to another section of my closet.

"Too hot. The weather is supposed to be nearly eighty-eight degrees." I took in my wardrobe selection. My school shopping trip had never materialized. As Mom had once pointed out, I was old enough to buy my own clothes. My job at the boardwalk bookstore wasn't enough for a new closet, hence the slim pickings.

"Shorts?" Mom suggested. I lit up and ran to my dresser.

"Yes! My high-waisted burnt orange shorts, and if Dad will let me, I'll borrow one of his light-blue button-downs to put over it. You know, the ones that are too small for him but that he thinks still fit." I rolled my eyes as Mom went into her room to get Dad's shirt. She came back and handed it to me. I put it on and asked, "What do you think?" Mom studied my outfit, which was now laying on my bed.

"Not bad. I think you'll need a belt." She went over to the hook nailed inside my closet door. "Here, try this." She handed me a skinny, brown belt with a square clasp. I laced the belt through the shorts to see how it would look, and Mom scrunched her face.

"What? You don't like it?" I was rather fond of her choice.

"No, that's not it. Hold on." Mom hurried from my room and down the hall, opened a drawer or two, and practically skipped back in. You'd think she was putting her own first-day outfit together. In her left hand was the pendant I'd always admired, since I was a little girl. Clasped to the skinny, silver chain was a semicircle with two curved, detailed lines tracing the pendant and colors inside. Underneath the clasp was a smoky, purple triangle, reminiscent of the summer evening sky just as the sun settled down for the night. The space next to the triangle was forest-green, much like the pine needles from my dream this morning. On the other side was another band of inky black. Finally, the center of the charm was a cabochon stone with white ribbons swirling in the vibrant, blood orange background.

I took it from Mom's outstretched hand, speechless.

"I know I always said you'd get that on your eighteenth birthday, but I think you're adult enough to wear it now. And it will give an added spark to your outfit for tomorrow." I jumped and pulled her in a tight hug.

"Thank you, thank you, thank you!" I squealed into her ear. "This means so much to me! I promise I won't lose it or ruin it like your favorite pair of dangly earrings you lent me when I was fifteen."

Patting me on the back, she pulled away. "I know, sweetheart. Did I ever tell you how it became part of the family?"

Shaking my head, I sat back on the bed where Mom joined me. "Story goes, this necklace was given to your great-great-great-great—times fifty more greats—grandmother Una by her lover, a poor fish merchant named Andrew. However, her father had engaged her to Lachlan, the eldest son of the best fisherman in the town of Elgol. He was a hardworking young man but spent his time drinking in the local pub, much to your grandmother's dismay. The night before Una's eighteenth birthday, Andrew snuck away from his home to meet her at Prince Charlie's Cave, where they planned to run away and wed on the mainland. Lachlan discovered them and had her lover banished from the isle. The day before

Andrew left, he gave Una half a pendant—the one in your hand—to remind her of him and the love they shared. He kept the other half for himself. Una never saw him again but always held out hoping one day she would see her love again. Eventually, Una married another man and had children."

"That's so tragic! Please tell me she didn't marry the drunken fisherman?"

"No, he fell off a boat and drowned during one of his trips out to sea. She married an outsider, someone from the lowlands."

"Still, this is a kind of depressing story."

"No, it's hopeful! It's said that whoever finds true love just like Una's will find the other half of the necklace on their mate." I gazed at the shiny pendant in my hand, hoping it would bring me good luck in the romance department. Mom must have read my mind wrong because she immediately said, "Thinking about a special boy? Perhaps Trip?"

"What? Mom!" I blushed and shot off the bed as if it had bitten me. "Please, it's weird talking to you about this."

"He's very cute," she teased. I placed the necklace in my jewelry box. It felt too important to wear on an insignificant day like the start of senior year.

"Mom, no. If something is happening there, I might let you know. Maybe." The bedsprings squeaked in relief.

"Fair enough. But please, be careful. I don't want you to end up like Grandma." She kissed the top of my head and smoothed my unruly hair. "Good night. Sleep well."

"Good night." I followed her to the door and closed it behind her. Turning off the light and climbing into bed, I smiled at the memory of Trip's lips pressed against mine. My stomach did a little dance to confirm I was falling fast for the new kid in Corbin City. I snuggled down deep into my fluffy comforter and watched images of Trip and me sneaking off into a cave to confess our true love for one another through my mind. Annoyingly, Cay kept popping up, accusing Trip of something I couldn't quite put my finger on. I pushed him out of my head, but in a matter of moments, he slid back in, yelling for Trip to be honest. It went on until my exhausted mind finally fell asleep.

Chapter 3

"Excuse me, do you know where the main office is?" a nervous freshman holding a book in her hand asked Annabelle. The first day of school was always the best. You had to sort out which tables to sit at during lunch—not the one closest to the gar-bage cans or the bathroom—or where to hide if you couldn't handle the swarms of cliques rushing at you through the halls. You had to dodge the squealing sophomores who were so excited they survived their first year of hell only to return to torture the incoming freshmen the same way. On top of all the social hierarchy you had to suss out while wading through this dark and murky jungle, you had to sur-vive the administration to boot. Mrs. Sharpe was the queen of this jungle, with Mr. Roberts as second in command, complete with his hyena laugh. They were stationed in the main office, sequestered away from the food fights, ditched hall passes, and out-rage of first-day homework assignments. It was a rare sight indeed when our illustrious principal and her infamous counterpart left their adjoining offices due to the appearances of a few famous alumni we boasted. The only two idiots guaranteed to visit the Queen Lioness more than twice a week were Cay and Logan. They were the only monkeys who'd have entered the den and lived to tell the tale.

"Enter the main doors behind you, turn left, and it's the second door on the left," Bri told her.

"Thank you!"

"Good luck!" she called out as the freshman scurried off, clutching the student handbook to her chest.

"Didn't you just give her directions to the girls' bathroom?" Annabelle asked.

Bri shrugged. "She looked like she was going to throw up."

Ocean City High School was a two-floor, red brick building with a sweeping staircase in the front hall. Classrooms were spread around the school on both levels. Lockers were assigned according to rank: freshmen in the back toward the vocation classes, sophomores were on the left side of the school by the TV studio, juniors were by the library, and seniors were by the auditorium and gym. Our cafeteria was in the middle of the school on the first floor, with various food kiosks available in the mornings and at lunchtime on the second floor. The administration was on the left of the main entrance, making it difficult to sneak in late or leave early without someone catching you. To me, it was the same school I'd spent most of my teenage years, continuing my servitude to academic authority, but to newcomers it was largely overwhelming.

My friends and I were sitting in the Senior Square, located in a half-enclosed courtyard facing the ocean and the football field. Last year's seniors wanted to leave a legacy, so they raised money to clean the mess left behind after a few years of negligence. During the summer, the school hired landscapers to restore the Square to its former beauty. It's a known fact the other grades can visit, but only seniors retain permanent residence. The legend says in the '80s, a brave freshman thought he could hang with the seniors. The class clown, Bill Masters, caught the unsuspecting freshman sitting on the bench in the courtyard. Bill ran to the biology lab on the second floor, where freshly dissected frogs were laid on the table. He grabbed a container of their discarded innards and ran to the window. Then he dumped the frog innards on the sitting freshman below. No one knew the freshman's name or what had happened to him, but since then, underclassmen did their best to avoid claiming what wasn't rightfully theirs.

Cole was first to arrive, so he commandeered one of the few stone tables under a Japanese maple.

"Okay, time to compare schedules," Brianna announced. We all reached into our various schoolbags, purses, and pockets to retrieve the piece of paper dictating our lives for the next ten months.

"I have gym first period with Sanders," I said.

"Me too!" Bri replied.

"I have gym but with Dalhaus." Cole slumped on the bench with his head in his hands.

"What's wrong?" asked Annabelle. "She's not that bad."

"She hates me. She thinks anyone who can't run a mile under twelve minutes is pathetic." He ran his fingers through his dark, wavy hair. Cole was the science nerd in our group. Annabelle patted him on the shoulder.

"Don't worry about it. You're a senior. Get a passing grade, and you'll be fine." Cole looked miserable.

Bri chimed in. "Yeah, you don't want to be on the Olympic track team anyway. Your acceptance into Cooper Union doesn't require you to pole vault. You just have to be able to count and graph stuff."

"Okay, who has Statistics and Probability with Furan?" I interjected.

"Not me," said Cole. "I have him for seventh period Calc."

"Bummer. I have him during third." The bell signaling homeroom rang around us. "I guess we'll have to continue this another time, kiddies." I slid off the table. Bri and I headed left toward the gym while the rest of the group scattered to their various first-period classes.

I was happy and hungry by the time lunch rolled around. My morning classes were tolerable, but I was really looking forward to my afternoon electives: Literature and Select Choir. We had a senior thesis in Literature to write by the end of the year, and secretly, I had been looking forward to it. My planned topic was "The Relationship Between Love and the Shakespearean Tragedies." Last year, while everyone had been celebrating the end of school at Gillian's, I was stuck at home with a sudden bout of the flu. Pure misery. Not only did I have a virus, but also the power went out for two days in a freak lightning storm that only hit our neighborhood. My poor parents had been stuck bailing out the basement after the river flooded. Once I was on my way to recovery, I read Shakespeare instead of watching Netflix on my phone to pass the darkened days. Romantic comedies left women with a false hope that a man would come, sweep us off our feet, and solve all our problems while mysteries tended to be based on serial killers or mobsters. Comedies were made to get us to crack a smile. I knew *Titus Andronicus* wasn't one of the more common plays read at my age, but if I'd be reading *Romeo and Juliet* in class this year, I wanted something off the beaten path. Blood, love, revenge. It was so much more interesting than some of his other plays.

Cole dropped his books on the table. "My day is awesome so far! I love Mechanical Drawing."

"What's so great about it?" Brianna asked as she came over. She placed her stuff down and pulled her shoulder-length strawberry blonde hair into a ponytail.

"Nothing special right now, but I'm really excited about what we'll be doing for the rest of the semester." He turned to me. "Want to go grab lunch?"

I opened my mouth to say yes when I saw Trip walk into the cafeteria behind the other new kid, John Michaels. I hadn't seen him or his sister all morning, and I wanted to... I don't know. I just wanted to see him. My peripheral vision blurred as I focused on Trip alone. He scanned the room to look for a good spot until I caught his attention and waved him over.

Cole followed my gaze. "Never mind," he muttered, walking to the lunch line. Trip walked over to me; Tomas trailed not too far behind. I was a little disappointed. Even though my friends were here, I still wanted Trip all to myself.

"Hey," he said. "Is there room for two more?"

"How about three?" another voice cut in. We all turned and saw Deidra standing behind him, her backpack slung on one shoulder.

"Uh, yeah, we can fit in more. If we don't mind sitting on each other's laps," I answered. Trip flashed me a smirk and raised his eyebrows, clearly implying he would love that arrangement. I blushed and tilted my face down. I hoped no one else noticed.

Brianna frowned. "Where is Annabelle going to sit?"

"We'll save her a seat," I promised.

"Great!" Deidra placed her bag on the vacant chair. She opened her backpack and pulled out a brown bag.

"Did Mom make you lunch for your first day of school again?" Trip asked.

"No. I made my own." You know keeping vegan is hard. I don't want Mom to have to deal with that."

"I didn't know you were vegan," I commented as Deidra unpacked two plastic containers, a fork, a spoon, and a bag of sliced red and green apples.

"Since I was fourteen. At our old school," Trip tensed but she ignored it, continuing, "they used to show this horrific video about the abuse the animals endure before being led to slaughterhouses. Did you know cows are stunned with an electrical current before being shot in the head with a bolt gun? After that, I couldn't stomach eating meat." She sniffed delicately and looked at Cole's tray, which had just been set on the table next to her. It was chock-full of dead animals: a hamburger with bacon, a chicken Caesar salad with bacon bits and cheese, and choco-late chip cookies for dessert. As Bri's eyes widened, my stomach rolled a little at the sight of all that heavy food mixed with the new information Deidra had so cheerily bestowed upon us. Even Tomas looked a little green.

"What's wrong with cookies?" Cole asked.

"Made with eggs. Animal by-product," she said, taking a bite of an apple slice.

"That's all for today on 'Deidra's Gross Out,'" Trip said in a mock-announcer's voice. "I'm going to get in line. Anyone want anything?"

Bri looked like she was going to throw up and then pass out, but she managed to shake her head. Cole dug into his hamburger, happily ignorant of the first part of Deidra's disturbing trivia.

"I'll come with you," I volunteered, veering my eyes away from the food on the table. "I'm not hungry for a hot dog anymore."

"Do you want to hear what they put in your hot dog?" Deidra asked slyly.

"No!" yelled Tomas and Bri simultaneously. Trip took my hand, and we walked over to stand in the lunch line. I almost tripped, barely focusing on anything else except for his hand in mine.

"I had fun yesterday," Trip said as we joined the line.

"I'm glad to hear it. The barbeque wasn't too bad. Thank you for not getting into it with Cay."

"You're welcome, but I wasn't talking about the barbeque." Oh, right. The bathroom. The skinned knee. The kiss. Ah, there went the blushing again. "Would you want to try that again?"

"The skinned knee?" I looked at my bandage, hoping to play coy. "Not particularly." He rolled his eyes and smiled.

"Do you want to come over today after school? I can give you the grand tour of the house."

"Oh, um ... yeah. That sounds like fun." I smiled back. He rubbed his thumb over the back of my hand. We hadn't even been on a date, and we were already kissing and holding hands. Was I doing this whole relationship thing backward?

"Good," he responded as we stepped forward. So far, my first day back was going pretty well.

"Welcome to AP Literature and English Composition," Miss Montgomery said as we all clamored into our seats. I was anxious for her to finish the intro and talk us through the syllabus for the year. I had to rush home and change for my date. My nerves got the best of me.

Was this a date? What exactly defined a date? I hadn't had much dating experience since third grade when Scott Heming asked me to join him in a classroom and tried to kiss me. Even the high school dances I'd gone to were with my friends or with Cole as my date.

"Bridget? Bridget?" I heard Miss Montgomery call. Her tone implied it wasn't the first or second time she'd called my name.

"Here?" I said meekly, flushing.

Someone behind me snickered.

"Thank you. Nancy McDonald?" We heard the door behind us open.

"Thank you for fitting us into your busy schedule, Mr. ..." Miss Montgomery spoke sternly. The class turned around to see Cay meandering into the room, taking the last available seat two desks behind me.

"McKay, and it's my pleasure," he replied sweetly.

"I hope this won't become a habit." He smiled again as she moved onto another student in roll call. Amazing. It looked like this could be the one teacher Cay couldn't sweet-talk.

"Psst! Psst! Bridget," he whispered behind me. I ignored him, not wanting to draw attention to myself one more time. There was a tap on my shoulder as Dan Zachariah handed me a folded piece of paper. I took it and slid the note under my own notebook, never taking my eyes off the whiteboard.

"Take a moment to read the syllabus before I go over it." Our teacher handed the first person in every row a small stack of papers to pass back. When I passed mine behind me, I was thanked by yet another note from Cay. Dan tapped me on the shoulder and I turned around.

"Just text him," he whispered, exasperated.

"Sorry!" I mouthed.

Again, I slid the note under my book, not bothering to read it. I picked up my copy of the syllabus and skimmed it. F. Scott Fitzgerald, Homer, Chaucer … no Shakespeare. I scrunched my nose in disappointment. My shoulder was tapped again.

"Last time I'm doing this," Dan said. "Either get his number or switch seats with me."

"I'm not sending the notes. Talk to him," I jabbed my thumb in Cay's direction.

Shooting Cay an annoyed look, I turned back around. In an attempt to recover some goodwill with Dan, I uncovered the notes. After grabbing the first, I unfolded it to see Cay's sloppy handwriting on the page.

> What are you doing today after school?
> Want to hang out?

I caught Miss Montgomery resting her gaze on me, so I quickly hid the notes, pretending to read the syllabus instead. When she looked away, I snuck out the second note and opened it quietly.

> Seriously, I heard you were hanging with Trip. Come hang out with me instead.

I frowned. Cay had never paid any attention to me before. All of a sudden, not only was I on his radar, but also I was his target? I folded the notes back up and slipped them into my folder to toss later. I felt Cay's eyes on me, so I shook my head, indicating that he leave me alone. He sighed and sat back in his seat.

"Did you have a question, Mr. McKay?" Miss Montgomery asked, hearing his sigh.

"No, Miss Montgomery. Thank you for asking." She pursed her lips but finished the reading. I checked the clock on the wall. Another thirty minutes of this, and then I would be free. Again, I got a tap on my shoulder and a note dropped on my desk. This would be a long year with Cailean McKay. I wondered if it was too late to transfer out.

"Hey, why are you avoiding me?" Cay asked as he cut off two other students to follow me.

One flipped him off as the other called out, "Hey!" Cay ignored both.

"I'm not avoiding you." I weaved through the throng of people coming at me. Cay was hot on my heels.

"Then what's the hurry?" he asked, jumping in front of me. I stopped short and glared, impatient with his apparent inability to comprehend my subtle hint to go the hell away.

"As you already guessed, or had previous knowledge of, I have plans with Trip. If I don't want to get caught in the school traffic, I have to leave now." I moved around him and continued walking to my locker.

"Why don't you like me?" Cay asked, his curiosity piqued.

"Why the sudden interest in hanging out with me?" I challenged. Turning a corner, I reached my destination. I spun the lock combination and opened it, dumping my unneeded books into my locker for the next day.

"I've always wanted to hang out with you," he admitted. I lifted an eyebrow. "Really!" he went on. "I was just too shy to ask you last year."

"So you liked me last year?"

"Not *liked you* liked you, but I always thought you were cool, and I wanted to get to know you better." This new side of Cay was weirding me out. I was skeptical this wasn't a play to piss off Trip.

"You swear on your life you aren't trying to play me in any way? You just want to get to know me and hang out?" I stared at him, studying his reaction. He held up his hands in surrender.

"I swear on my mother's grave."

I frowned. "Your mother isn't dead."

He smiled and winked at me as he walked away. Frustrated and confused, I slammed my locker shut and nearly collided with Annabelle.

"Oh! Sorry!" I apologized.

"It's okay. So how was your first day?" she asked, juggling an armful of books. She shifted the pile into her left arm.

"Not too bad. I like most of my classes. World History was fun. Stats will definitely be my hardest class, as usual. One day, I'll learn to add correctly. Yours?" I slung my bag over my shoulder as we both headed toward the exit.

"I enjoyed my media class and government. They sound interesting enough to hold my attention for the full year."

"That's all you can hope for," I said, laughing.

"What are you doing after school? Want to go grab coffee on the boardwalk before my painting class?" We followed our fellow students out into the bright sunshine. I looked up, letting it warm my face for a minute before my ridiculously sensitive skin burst into flames from the UV rays. Oh, it was fun being fair-skinned.

"Rain check? I'm meeting Trip at his house." She grinned and slipped her right arm through mine.

"He's so cute, isn't he? Good for you, scoring the new guy."

"John Michaels is new too," I pointed out.

"Fine. You got the *hottest* new guy in school."

"Touché! What about you? Have you finally garnered enough courage to ask out George King yet?"

She smiled. "Not yet, but it's on my bucket list for this year."

"Bucket list?" We headed out the double doors toward the parking lot.

"Consider it a school year resolutions list. A list of things I want to accomplish before we graduate."

"Sounds like a good idea. What else is on the list?"

We made it to my car. "Finally ride the Ferris wheel and face my fear of heights."

"Good challenge."

"Ask George out, which you know, and get a perfect score on the SATs."

"Wow! That is impressive. If you want help on any of that, let me know. I'll be down to ride the Ferris wheel with you!"

"Great! I'll let you know." She smiled. "I'll see you tomorrow," she said as she headed off.

"See you tomorrow." I unlocked my car door and got in, rolling down the windows. Even though I tried to park in the shade, Mother Nature had different plans and hadn't allowed the tree's branches to extend enough to cover my car for the day. Annabelle waved and walked away in the direction of her art class. I drove off, trying to take a few back roads to make it to the bridge before the rush, but—inevitably so—I got stuck in traffic. I blasted my radio and rocked out to the '80s rock station as I inched forward. At this rate, I would never make it back to Corbin City on time for my potential date with Trip.

By the time I got out of Ocean City and drove home, my shirt was stuck to my back, and my shorts felt a little less soft. I had never been so happy for central air. Depositing my book bag on my desk chair, I headed into the bathroom, stripped off my clothes, and rinsed off in the shower. The cool water refreshed my skin as I relaxed under the stream. Getting out of the shower, I wrapped myself in a sunny, yellow towel and walked back through to my room to plan what I was going to wear. If this wasn't a date, I didn't want to overdress. However, if it was a date, I didn't want to underdress, either. Why was this so complicated? Digging out a light blue t-shirt and a short, black skirt with white hearts on it, I dropped the towel and got dressed. A few accessories later, I threw my wet, fiery hair up into a tight bun on top of my head and slipped on flats; I was ready to go. Checking myself out in the mirror, I looked good. Too good. Too formal for such a casual afternoon. I ripped everything off and started back at square one. I went with jean shorts, a short-sleeved white button-down, and my silver sandals. I left my hair up but changed some of the accessories before leaving the house.

My nerves twitched with anticipation by the time I reached Trip's house. The silver Audi was the only car parked in the driveway. I was happy to see Trip without school, family, or friends to interrupt us. I raised my hand to knock on the door, but it swung open with Trip standing there, a grin painted on his face.

"Hi, sorry," he apologized.

"Were you waiting for me?" I asked.

His face flushed a light pink. "Maybe."

He stepped back to welcome me in. Trip's house held a familiar smell: freshly baked chocolate chip cookies.

"Is anyone here?" I looked around but didn't see anyone.

"Like a chaperone? Not exactly…"

"Good." I reached up and kissed him. I couldn't wait anymore. Trip's hand slipped over my cheek as he deepened our embrace. I sank into him a bit, not wanting this blissful moment to end. My body pulsated with heat as every inch of me craved more. He pulled away first, a little flushed.

"Wow," he said, breathless. "Best hello ever."

I grinned and followed him down the white hallway into their similarly pristine kitchen.

"Are you hungry or thirsty? I could get you water, soda, lemonade…" Tomas sat at the table with a sandwich and a glass of iced tea in front of him.

"Nothing for me, thanks. Oh, hi, Tomas. I didn't expect to see you," I said as Trip grabbed a bottle of water from the fridge for himself. It was weird for Trip to invite me over knowing Tomas was going to be here. Maybe it wasn't a date after all. I deflated as the excitement was leeched from my body.

"He's not supposed to be here," Trip answered for him. A look was exchanged between the two boys. Trip wanted Tomas to leave us alone, but Tomas wasn't going anywhere.

"He's right. I was supposed to go with Kellyn," Tomas explained, "to pick up Roden and Elizabeth, but I asked if it was okay to stay." I had the feeling Trip was overruled by that decision. His jaw was clenched, giving his cheeks a definitively sharper look. I had to resist tackling and kissing him again.

"Cool." I knew I wasn't hiding my confusion very well. Why would Tomas go with Trip's mom to pick up her kids? I didn't remember ever going with Cole or Bri to pick up their younger siblings.

"I promised you a grand tour of the house, if you're still interested," Trip interjected, hijacking the conversation.

"Sure. See you later," I said to Tomas. He had taken a big bite of his sandwich, so he just waved.

"Where should we start? This is the kitchen, clearly," Trip said as we walked out of the room. "The dining room is to your right, through that door over there, and the family room is just off the kitchen to your left."

I peeked at the dining room through the doorway. There was nothing incredibly special about it. The room was midsized with a Swedish-style table: circular with a glass top and dark wood legs along with chairs to match. A China cabinet pressed against the wall directly across from where I stood. A few nondescript pictures hung on the wall around the table, leaving the room a little cold and unwelcoming for my taste. Our own dining room at home was rich in color; bathed in red and yellow hues, it always reminded me of holiday meals with our extended family. I looked back toward the family room, which had a homier feel. Photographs of the kids wearing Halloween costumes, winning trophies, and enjoying family vacations sat on the fireplace mantle, along with Mr. and Mrs. Findlay's wedding picture. The couch was pushed up under the windows and wasn't white like in the other room I'd seen on my first house visit. Instead, it was a dark green. The coffee table had various magazines, fanned out like in a doctor's office. A large flat-screen TV was tucked into a corner, and there was an armchair by the kitchen entrance.

"Come on, I'll show you upstairs."

"Do I have to take my shoes off?" I asked, concerned about the white carpet.

He chuckled. "We can let it slide this time."

Trip took my hand and led me down the hallway, ignoring Tomas as we passed him. Peering into the white living room again, I saw it connected to the blasé dining room. I followed Trip and bumped into him as he stopped two steps onto the wood floor.

"Sorry!" we said in unison. I smiled at him and he smiled back. The annoyance marring his lovely face before was replaced by a sudden calmness. He leaned over to kiss me, and my body spun with heated excitement as crashing waves of pure attraction rolled through me. We stood, learning the shape of each other's mouths. He pulled back, lightly kissing my forehead. Afraid of saying something epically stupid, I didn't want to talk first. The front screen door slamming shut had scared us both into silence the first time we'd kissed, so I hadn't had to worry up until now. But alone, sans Tomas, there was a lot of room in my mouth for my foot.

"I enjoy kissing you," he said, smiling.

I shyly smiled back. "Me too." Still holding my hand, Trip gently tugged me along.

"Deidra's room is behind you." The door was closed, as were most of the others on the floor. Leading me backward down the hall, Trip pointed out the other rooms.

"This one is Roden's, this one is Elizabeth's, and my parents are at the end of the hall. The bathroom is right here," he nodded his head to the left. "And this," he swung the door in question open, "is my room."

It was fairly large room for an old house. Trip had double the closet space I had (and I had a deep closet), a somewhat aged wood dresser, a double window, a desk with a MacBook Pro, a lamp, a notebook, and various writing utensils. His clothes weren't thrown all over the place, as I'd been half expecting (based on my experience in Cole's room over the years). Instead, he had a small pile of presumably clean clothes on the bottom bunk. Yes, Trip had a bunk bed in his room. Granted, it didn't look like he was living in a cabin at sleepaway camp, but it lost him some points.

"Bunk beds? Really?" I asked in disbelief.

"Tomas shares a room with me."

"Okay, I guess that makes sense. I didn't know he shared a room with you." That answered some questions, but I still didn't understand the need for bunk beds. Personally, I was afraid if I slept on the bottom bunk, I would be crushed to death by a freak accident of the top bunk sleeper rolling around, causing the bed to fall. I'd never sleep on the top because I couldn't have that guilt on my mind. I tended to sleep on the floor with my Hello Kitty sleeping bag when a bed wasn't available.

"Yeah, well, it's a long and hard story to explain, but Tomas's parents and my parents were best friends growing up. After his parents died, my parents welcomed him into our home. At the time, our house was a bit smaller, and Elizabeth wasn't born yet. There was an extra room the size of a shoebox, so it was decided he'd share the room with me."

Okay, points regained. I couldn't help but like a guy who was always willing to help out a friend.

"Which one is your bed?" I asked. Trip smirked, pointing to the bottom one.

"I used to sleepwalk when I was a kid, so I slept on the bottom to prevent me from falling out of bed."

I nodded. "So, what do you want to do?"

He snaked his hand around my waist and drew me close.

"You," he whispered, laying his lips against mine. I rested my hands on his chest and gently pushed him away. I didn't want him to think I was ready. He tried to hide his disappointment but didn't do the best job.

"Watch a movie? Do you like horror?"

"Depends. What kind of horror? Ghosts, zombies, gory, killers, twisted doctors seeking revenge, Hitchcockian...?"

"Ah, I see the lady knows her scary movies."

"I know a little. I dabble in the macabre, but I much prefer psychological thrillers. Or fantasy."

"Fantasy, yeah?"

"Why not? It's got to be more interesting than this life."

"How so?" he asked, rather amused.

"I just like the idea of dragons, fairies, magic, that kind of stuff. I don't know. It sounds so... my life here in Jersey is boring. I'm not complaining, but I want more of an adventure in my life. Something to keep me on my toes and remind me life can be more than just repetitive schedules and destiny ending in a nine-to-five with coworkers who are dull, a boss with bad breath, and plain clothes that scream 'I peaked in high school!' Fantasies offer us a gateway to another world within our own but step outside the realm of normal. They're an escape from this monotonous reality." I huffed, out of breath from my speech and feeling silly. I didn't plan on pouring all my inner thoughts about my love of fantasy as a genre in one rant.

"Wow. That's... you must have put a lot of thought into that," Trip said, eyebrows raised. I nodded, deflated. "Well, don't tell anyone, but I happened to agree with that for the most part. Adventure and fantasy give us a reason to dream. My parents don't agree. They think it's just another excuse to distract me from studying."

He rolled his eyes. "Did you decide if you wanted a horror flick?" He pulled open the bottom desk drawer, revealing a stack of horror movies.

"I don't know. You pick, but nothing too gross. After your sister's show-and-tell today, I'm still a little nauseous."

"Yeah, sorry about that. Dee's got a bit of a 'holier than thou' stance when it comes to eating animals. Thriller, but no gore it is." He dug through the stack before selecting one.

"How about *Horsemen*? It's about a serial killer who bases his kills on the Four Horsemen of the Apocalypse. Not too gory."

"I'm game. Where are we going to watch it?" Trip slid the movie into his Mac's optical drive. "On my bed, if that's okay." Flashes of my limbs sticking out from underneath the top bunk crushing me crossed my mind.

"Um, won't it be too cramped under there?"

"I never thought about it, but I guess. We can watch it downstairs if you want."

"If you don't mind." I felt ridiculous letting a stupid fear like a bed falling on me get in my way of snuggling up to Trip, but with my luck, it would actually happen. I couldn't risk that chance. We traipsed down the stairs, surprising Tomas chilling in the armchair with his laptop open.

"We were going to watch a movie, if you want to join us," I offered. I didn't want to be rude with him sitting right there, and it gave a reason for our sudden appearance. He glanced at Trip for approval.

"Yeah, join us." Trip's voice was friendly; he wasn't upset anymore about Tomas hanging out.

"Thanks." Tomas closed the laptop and placed it on the floor. "What are we watching?"

"*Horsemen*." Trip put the movie into the DVD player and turned on the TV.

"Good movie," approved Tomas. As the movie started, I took off my shoes and sat on the couch, sinking in to get comfortable. Trip took a few throw pillows and placed them over the windows.

"I like watching horror movies in the dark. I like the feeling of being creeped out," he explained. I noticed the blazing sun currently hid behind some dark fluffy clouds.

"We are having the weirdest weather," I commented. "Wasn't it a million degrees not even two hours ago? I swear this isn't normal Jersey weather."

"It was really hot out today," agreed Tomas. Trip remained silent on my choice of conversation topic and sat next to me instead.

For the next hour and a half, I watched a grieving police detective solve twisted killings based on biblical prophecies. Halfway through the opening credits, Trip put his arm around my shoulders, and

I snuggled close. Tomas may have faced the movie the entire time, but I had a feeling he paid closer attention to us.

After the movie had ended, I was thoroughly grossed out. It hadn't been too gory, like Trip had promised, but the people hanging on hooks were icky.

Tomas's phone rang, and it was Mrs. Findlay; she and the kids would be home in a half hour. She sent Tomas on a pizza run, finally leaving me completely alone with Trip in the house. I put my shoes back on and gathered my purse as Trip returned the movie to its case and sat on the arm of the couch to wait for me. The air was thick with a concoction of hormones and awkwardness. I was hungry, but I didn't want to leave Trip's presence just yet. He didn't rush me out, so I assumed he felt the same way. I walked over to the wall of pictures, taking in all the smiling faces. I felt Trip breathing quietly behind me. He smelled of faded cologne and a unique scent all his own.

"I like the picture of you as the Cowardly Lion," I said, pointing to a picture hanging right above me. "You're so cute and look one-hundred-percent courageous looking."

"Thanks. My parents dressed us all up as the *Wizard of Oz* characters that year. Deidra was Dorothy, Roden was the Tin Man, Elizabeth was Toto, Dad was the Scarecrow, Mom was the Wicked Witch, and Tomas was a flying monkey. We got a lot of candy that year, too. People gave us more because they loved our costumes."

"Aw, that's so sweet! How old are your brother and sister? I don't even know what grade Deidra is in!"

"Dee is fifteen turning twenty-five, so she's a sophomore." I chuckled. "Her birthday is coming up in November. Roden is fourteen and Elizabeth is twelve."

"Wait, I didn't meet Roden at lunch with you today."

"He wanted to try changing some classes around. Apparently, he was put in remedial math and basic science or something. Not too sure about the science class."

"Ah. So, he can count high?"

"Roden's a math whiz. He can count higher than anyone I know." Trip beamed, proud of his little brother.

I smiled and continued looking at the other pictures. One in particular kept drawing my attention. It was an old drawing, seemingly out of place in comparison to the modern ones surrounding it. The paper had yellowed from age, and even from behind the glass, I smelled the mustiness inside. It showed a young woman standing alone, her red hair blowing in the wind to her right. She was holding her hands up as if reaching out to grab something. Besides the gentle smile hanging from her face, she wore a gray, floor-length fur cloak. Peeping through was a sliver of white, perhaps a tunic underneath. The cloak looked heavy and incredibly warm. Behind her were hills covered in snow as ice and wind drew in frosty gusts.

"Who drew this?" I asked.

"That's been in the family so long. I have no idea where it came from," he said lightly.

"It's lovely. And so moving. I wonder what she's reaching for," I pondered. We both heard the front door open.

"Hello?" Tomas walked in, and the scent of pizza wafted to my nose. Hunger pains poked at me, reminding me to leave and get home to my own family.

"I should go," I said. "I still haven't seen my family today, and I need to eat dinner." My stomach roared at that moment, confirming what I'd said. Trip smiled.

"I'll see you tomorrow for lunch?"

I smiled and nodded, then gave him a small kiss on his cheek and walked away. I passed Tomas and the pizza on my way out.

"See you tomorrow," I said.

Chapter
4

The next morning was a little rushed for me. I couldn't sleep the night before, rolling over every few minutes. Weird dreams involving the drawing from Trip's house kept me awake until my alarm went off. In it, I had been haunted by the shadows of a ghost creature, a reflection of Cay. He swore to me that he was my protector and that giving him some Amulet would keep me safe. The woman in the drawing came to life, declaring Cay a liar, and persuaded me to give her the Amulet. Her face morphed into Deidra's, then Annabelle's, before settling on what I thought my Great-Great (and so on) Grandma Una looked like. It was disturbing, having my ancestor's wrinkled features placed on a youthful and taut body, to say the least. I kept yelling I didn't have the Amulet, but no one listened. I was caught between trusting the ever-evolving distant relative or the boy who had never given me any reason to believe him.

"You look so tired," Annabelle said, approaching me at my locker. My hair was down and damp; I'd just been able to wash it and not the rest of my body in my scramble get to school on time. But I couldn't promise my clothes matched or were even clean, for that matter.

"I didn't sleep well," I yawned. Closing my locker, Annabelle and I headed toward our classes. "Scary dreams kept me awake at all hours." I yawned again.

"Let's get you coffee," she said, directing me to the breakfast kiosk. Surprisingly, there was no line.

"Two coffees, please," she ordered.

"Light and sweet," I added, stifling another yawn. I would need all the sugar and caffeine I could get to stay awake today. Annabelle paid the barista and handed me my coffee.

"Thanks," I said. "I really could use this today."

"No problem, sweetie," she chirped back. "See you later." Annabelle was usually chipper—rarely ever showing any other emotions and always on top of taking care of someone else. If my friends had labels, Annabelle would totally be the "Mom" of our group.

I waved and headed off toward my first class. Taking a sip from that sweet concoction helped keep me awake enough until I got to second period. By the time I got to lunch, I was barely dragging my zombie corpse to the cafeteria.

"Don't bother me for the first twenty-five minutes," I said, resting my head on my arms.

"She didn't sleep last night," Annabelle explained to Deidra, Bri, and Cole.

"Rough night?" Bri asked, spearing the mushroom in her tossed salad. I lazily wondered if Deidra's outburst yesterday had changed at least one mind.

"Nightmares," I mumbled.

"About what?" Bri questioned.

I sat up, feeling like I would never fit in my nap. I needed a double espresso stat.

"Just silly fantasy stuff. I fell asleep watching *Lord of the Rings*. People chasing me, going on about some Amulet." I shuddered slightly at the way my grandmother's face looked on that body. Deidra sat up straighter.

"That sounds interesting. Tell us more?" she asked, looking down at her lunch and playing with the quinoa in her container.

"I don't know what else there is to say. In one dream, a boy is telling me he's my protector, and I should give him the Amulet. In the next, a young but old woman is telling me to give her the Amulet. I kept repeating I didn't have it." I was so exhausted; the physical act of moving my lips was draining.

Someone walked by our table and opened a sugary energy drink. The sudden pop of the can and the sweet smell made my senses perk up. I searched the room to see who brought in the heavenly substance. It was impossible to tell when the entire school has lunch at the same time.

"What did the woman look like?" Deidra pressed.

"Human. Two hazel eyes, a nose, and a mouth. I think she also had hands, feet, and a torso," I snidely responded.

"Whoa," Bri whispered to herself. Deidra looked taken aback.

"I'm sorry. I really am. I didn't mean for it to be that harsh. I'm just exhausted, and I really, really need a nap. Or a silo of coffee," I apologized.

"I think silos usually store grain, not liquid," Cole pointed out. "I think you mean a water tower."

I shot him a death glare. "I don't care what it's stored in. I just want one."

"Eat something," Bri suggested, but I shook my head.

"Too tired to eat."

"You need to. Here." She slid over her untouched croissant. "Food will help. And I'll get you some coffee."

"Ooh, coffee?" Trip asked as he came up to the table with Tomas close behind. "I could use some, too." I reached into my book bag and pulled out a twenty.

"Here," I handed Trip the money. "Medium coffee, light and sweet, and a turkey and Swiss sandwich. Plus whatever else you want." Deidra raised an eyebrow at me as Bri pulled back the croissant.

"Give it a rest, Dee," Trip said, exasperated. He walked away, leaving Deidra pouting into her quinoa.

"Hey, Bridget, can I talk to you for a second?" Cay inquired, popping up out of nowhere.

"If you must." I pushed my chair back, standing. My friends shot me looks ranging from confused to excited to angry. I didn't have the energy to care or pay attention, so I trotted off after Cay.

"What's up?" I asked.

"I was wondering if you wanted to hang out today." Cay took out his phone, typed something, and then put it back in his pocket.

"Honestly, no. I'm exhausted and, frankly, you're freaking me out." I crossed my arms over my chest.

"What? How?" He sounded genuine. His phone vibrated. Again, he took it out, typed a message, and put it away. I was getting annoyed.

"Sorry," he apologized. "It's Alec. Now, how am I freaking you out?"

"Cay, we've been over this. Why the sudden change of heart? Is it only because Trip is interested in me? And why do you hate him so much?"

"Whoa, okay, let's get something straight. I have no interest in you like that. Like I said, I just wanted to get to know you better. As a friend." Thank goodness I was too tired to feel the full sting of that rejection.

"And I see why you think this is because of Trip, but it's not. I just don't like that guy. And I don't think you should, either."

I raised my brow at him. His pocket vibrated again, but he ignored it this time.

"Are you going to elaborate on that?" He didn't reply; he only bit his lip like he was trying to keep any more tidbits from spilling out.

I clucked my tongue. "I knew it. You're full of crap. Congratulations. You still didn't change my mind." Trip returned to our table with two coffees and two sandwiches. My whole body yearned for the food and drink. I adored him so much for fulfilling my order.

"Fine, MacNamara, but I think you'll feel differently soon," he said, his confidence leaving a bitter taste in my mouth.

Trip turned his face toward me after Bri pointed in my direction. He glared at Cay, and I shook my head. No fighting today; I couldn't handle it. Cay frowned, followed my gaze to Trip, and smirked.

"I'll see you in class, Bridget."

"Hey, Cay!" I heard Logan calling for him, waving him over to their table, where the rest of his group was sitting. I walked back to my friends, taking a big swig of coffee before taking a huge bite of my sandwich. I actually sighed in contentment.

"What was that about?" Trip asked, annoyed.

"Nothing," I said, swallowing.

"I thought you weren't friends with him." I took another bite, as I gave Trip the *who the hell are you to talk to me like that* look. I didn't dignify his accusation with actual words. He was being a jerk, but I wasn't in the mood for a fight. Sitting down in my chair, I let the food and coffee work its magic. I felt a little more awake than before, but that could have been a reaction from Trip's jealous anger.

"So you're not going to tell me?" he asked in stunned disbelief.

I took another sip of coffee as I weighed my options. I *really* didn't want this to be an issue between us.

"Trip, it's not a big deal. Stop overreacting."

"Overreacting?" He sputtered. He paused and took a very deep breath, as if gearing for battle. "Bridget, I don't want to see you with Cay anymore."

I barked out a sarcastic laugh. "You can't honestly think that'll happen."

My friends stilled as I stood. Trip didn't flinch; his body remained tense with anger.

"Let me be clear," I began slowly. "You cannot tell me who I'm allowed to speak to. I choose my own friends." Annabelle and Bri suddenly found something extremely interesting in their lunches. Cole didn't move, and Deidra's eyes were as big and wide as an Olympic swimming pool. I gathered my food and belongings and walked out, leaving Trip speechless.

My afternoon classes went by faster than my morning ones, probably because of the coffee I had been mainlining all day. I collapsed into my desk in English, thankful my day was close to ending and I was closer to napping.

"Hello, class. Please come in and take your seats. I want to get started on the novel you will begin reading tonight: F. Scott Fitzgerald's *Tender is the Night*. I hope you've all read the handout I gave yesterday because, at the end of the novel, you will be writing a five-page paper critiquing the role reversal of Dick Diver and his wife, Nicole." Miss Montgomery continued her lecture about good ol' Dick and Nic while I scrambled to read last night's homework without making it obvious. When Miss Montgomery turned her back to us, a wadded ball of paper landed on my desk with a dull thud. I unfurled it; it was from Cay. I seriously needed to transfer out.

Have you changed your mind yet?

I hadn't, but I wasn't telling him that. I should have known ignoring him would actually encourage him to try harder. Another note:

Talk to me after class. I have an interesting proposition for you.

Okay, that one got my attention. Damn my curiosity. I wondered if it was cheaper and less painful to remove it biologically than to spend an afternoon with Cailean McKay. I nodded, figuring he would see my answer, and did my best to pay attention for the rest of class.

"Go ahead. I'm listening," I said, walking past Cay after class. He had to skip a little to catch up.

"I think you should hang out with me."

"We've been over this, many times today. Why?"

"Why not? What do you have to lose?"

"Remember you're the one pushing for this, not me." I opened my locker, dumping my hated math book at the bottom.

"Is there anything I can do to change your mind?" I thought about it, milling the idea around in my head. I was still pretty irritated with Trip after our fight, and part of me wanted to get back at him for being such a jerk.

"How about this? I'll owe you a favor, anything you ask," said Cay.

"What kind of favor?"

"Whatever you want."

Ooh, this could be good. I could have Cay as my minion for a week, doing all my homework. No, I couldn't promise he would get me a good grade.

"Okay, but when I come up with the favor, you have to say yes, no matter what," I countered.

"Deal." We shook hands.

"How about Thursday? We can walk along the boardwalk," I suggested.

"I was thinking, maybe you could come over?" Cay offered.

"I don't know where you live."

"No worries. Just meet me at my locker after school, and we can walk together."

"Sure." He took my number, and we parted ways.

I left school feeling worse than when I had gone in. Trip didn't come find me for the rest of the day. Cay was being somewhat less annoying but still didn't get the hint to leave me alone. Worst of all, my second cup of coffee wasn't helping as much as I had hoped it would. I was beyond thrilled when I dropped my keys on the table and fell face-first into my couch. Kicking my shoes off, I rolled over and switched on the TV as the local news channel came on.

"And now over to our weather woman, Anne Donnelly. Anne, crazy weather we've had lately, huh?" said the news anchor. I wasn't a news fan; there was always so much death and destruction. It was getting depressing. But for some reason, the weather segment caught my interest.

"Thank you, Conner," said Anne. "Following our recent reports on the unusual weather we've been having, many of you have written in to ask how to protect yourselves against the sudden change. What exactly is going on? Well, folks, it's nothing but global warming taking effect. Don't worry, after our five-day forecast, Conner and Katie will tell you how to protect yourself against a weather mishap and what you can do to stop the effects of global warming. But first, the forecast for the next five—"

I changed the channel. I didn't want to fall asleep to images of polar bears stuck on melting ice caps.

Leaving a cooking show on, I tucked myself under a blanket and napped my afternoon away.

"Hey, Bridge. Bridget?" I woke to Dad gently shaking me.

"Yeah?"

"Time to get up. Dinner's almost here. We ordered Chinese tonight because I have to run back to the office, and Mom just came home a little bit ago." I rubbed my eyes, stretching.

"Okay. What time is it?"

"Nearly six thirty." I yawned and sat up.

Dad chuckled. "Come on, kid. The food should be here soon." He tapped my thigh and went into the kitchen to set the table. Looking out the front windows, I saw that the sun streaked the sky, leaving streams of pink, purple, and red to bleed into an orange backdrop. Feeling a little refreshed but still tired, I picked up my bags from where I had dropped them off. My phone kept vibrating, signaling I had missed messages.

[Annabelle: Hey girly! How are you? Feeling better? Call me later Xoxo.]

[Bri: Whoa! I can't believe Trip did that! You go girl! You ok? Text me back.]

[Deidra (who I was guessing got my number off her brother's phone. I'd never given it to her): Hey! It's Deidra. I'm so sorry! My brother can be such a jerk! Good for you for telling him off. I hope you're doing okay. See you tomorrow!]

[Cay: Can we meet tomorrow instead of Thursday? I forgot about a track meeting that day.]

I sighed, still too tired to deal with everyone. I was disappointed Trip hadn't texted me to apologize. I hoped he would do it in person, and if he didn't, it would still be my longest relationship ever. I texted Cay back:

[Bridget: Sure. See you after school.]

I turned my phone on silent. I didn't want to obsess over that missing text from Trip.

Chapter 5

The next day, I waited patiently for Cay by his locker after school, per his request. Today had been much better so far. I'd slept, I'd been able to squeeze in my math and English homework at lunch, and classes were finally getting into actual learning. Trip had yet to be seen since my fight with him yesterday, but I saw Tomas in the halls, so I assumed he was at least showing up to class.

"Hey, sorry about keeping you waiting. You ready?" Cay jogged up to me.

"Yup." The sun was still blazing hot, so I was wearing shorts, a pink peasant blouse, and white flip-flops to avoid any material sticking to my sweaty skin. Slinging my bag over my shoulder, I walked beside Cay out into the sunshine. We walked about two blocks before Cay said anything.

"How was school today?"

"School-like. You?" he replied, bored.

"Same." Another block passed without a word between us. I shifted my bag to my other shoulder and then back again, flipping the magnetic clasp up and down. Cay anxiously played with the strap at the bottom of his book bag and kept looking around like he had never seen the neighborhood before.

"So, how does Alec like UPenn?" I was desperate to fill the silence blooming between us.

"He likes it a lot. He says his classes are cool, and dorming is awesome." Cay smiled and followed suit.

"I'm glad to hear he's happy."

"We cross here," he said abruptly. Cay crossed the street and headed down another.

"How far away do you live?"

"One more block and we'll be there." When we reached his house, it was nothing at all like I'd expected. It was more like a beach condo than the mini-mansion I'd imagined. The bottom level had a two-car garage located next to the front door. We went inside and climbed the staircase to the first level, which held a kitchen and breakfast nook overlooking the beach, a dining room with a fire-place and dark wood floor, and a large family room with a giant TV, a built in bar, and filled (of course) bookcases as well as obligatory family pictures and knickknacks. Cay took his shoes off and dropped his stuff. A German Shepherd came trotting up to Cay from his spot on the floor.

"Hey, boy! Good boy," Cay murmured. He looked at me.

"Uh, sorry, but you have to take off your shoes. House rules," he apologized. "I hope it's okay I have a dog." I nodded as I removed my shoes, placing my bags next to his.

"What's his name?"

"Neit. It's the name of the Scottish God of War."

"Will he bite me?" I asked, hesitant to approach the dog. Cay smiled.

"Not unless I tell him to. Which, don't worry, I won't."

"Thought didn't even cross my mind," I replied as I bent to let the dog smell me. His fur was coarse to the touch but fluffy as a freshly washed fleece. Neit sniffed me and then licked my arm a few times for good measure. Or he'd just been taste-testing me. I couldn't be sure.

"Do you want a snack or something?" Cay opened the fridge and took out a chocolate pudding cup. I stood and wiped my arm on my shorts. I had to admit, it was kind of sweet seeing Big Bad Cay cuddling with his dog and snacking on pudding. I wondered if his mom stocked their freezer with Ellio's pizzas, like my mom had when I was in third grade.

"Sure. I'll have one, too," I nodded to the treat in his hand. He turned a light shade of red.

"I like pudding still," he said sheepishly. I shrugged as he handed me my own with a spoon.

"Who doesn't?" I dug in gleefully. Mmm, pudding, it had been too long. After downing the pudding and throwing out my empty cup of water Cay had placed in front of me, we traipsed upstairs to his room.

"Neit, stay," Cay commanded. Neit curled up on his previous spot in the sunbeam streaming through a window. I was more at ease going upstairs with Cay. We passed the bathroom, Alec's untouched room, a room with the door closed, their parent's room, and finally reached Cay's room. His was the complete opposite of Trip's in just about every way. For one, instead of a bunk bed, Cay slept on a queen-size mattress hardly taking up any space in the room. Besides a desk with a laptop, a nightstand, a flat-screen mounted on the wall across from the bed, and a dresser, there was hardly any furniture.

The double closet off to the left of the room was closed. The most impressive feature of Cay's room was the balcony. Two French doors were to the right of his bed, leading outside to a view of the rolling waves. A small patio table and two chairs were accompanied by a flourishing tomato plant. I would have never guessed Cay liked gardening. He and Mom had something in common.

"What do you want to do?" Cay interrupted my inspection.

"I don't know. I'm kind of game for most any-thing." I noticed his collection of signed baseballs on a shelf over his bed. Any baseball fanatic would have killed to have—or touch—any one of these baseballs for a single moment.

"How about pool? We have a table in the next room."

"Yeah, sounds great." I smiled. I knew I shouldn't be taken with material things, but I couldn't help it this one time. Sometimes I forgot how opulent Ocean City houses could be. Back down the hallway, the game room was just as impressive as the rest of the house. The pool table was clearly the center of attention with the way the rest of the room was setup. Upon entering the space, there was a minibar to my left, complete with a college-sized clear glass fridge filled with water and soda, a tap for various types of beer, and an array of peanuts, chips, and pretzels. Barstools adorned the outside of the bar, and a small, flat-screen TV was tucked into a ceiling corner above. Old-school movie and concert posters lined the walls. In the opposite corner were two arcade games, A-Team pinball and PAC-MAN.

"Rack them up," Cay said, tossing the triangle to me.

"So where is everyone else?" I gathered balls to the end of the table and racked them.

"My parents are at work."

"No, I mean your friends. I thought you would've invited them over." Satisfied with my perfect triangle, I slowly removed the piece of wood.

"If I invited them, I wouldn't be able to get to know you better." I nodded in agreement.

"Touché. What do you want to know?"

"Everything. Start from the day you were born, and end with today."

I laughed. "Seriously?"

"Since I owe you a favor, and I have a feeling this will be a big one, then I want an all-expenses paid trip into your psyche." I was a little surprised. Who knew "stupid Cay" was just an act?

"I honestly don't think my childhood is that interesting for those who didn't live it with me." He indicated for me to go first. I lined up the cue ball and took my shot, scattering the balls all over the table but nowhere near a pocket.

"Try me." He lined up the cue with a solid ball and sank it but missed the second shot.

"I'm really glad we aren't playing for money," I joked.

He smiled. "You say that now, but it could be to lull me into a fake sense of safety before you bleed me dry."

"You overestimate my abilities."

Cay didn't respond to that.

"Anyway, I was born into my family. Two parents, no siblings. Went to school in Upper Township—"

"So, you lived here all your life?" he cut in. I lined up a striped ball with the middle pocket but missed, and it bounced off the wall.

"Maybe you are right about my overestimation."

"Hey!" I said in protest. He gestured for me to answer his question.

I narrowed my eyes at him in mock annoyance. "Born and raised."

He nodded. "Go on."

"Let's see, I had my share of best friends and fights growing up. Scrapes, cuts, injuries of that sort. I used to play soccer when I was in third and fourth grade, but by the time I was in fifth grade, I didn't love it as much, so I quit the team."

"Anything weird happen while you were growing up?"

I paused. "We had a baby duck come live in my yard for a week. It's really the only weird thing I remember happening." That wasn't completely true, but I wasn't going to tell him about the time my cousin Owen and I had done a rain dance to help Mom water her plants. I'm sure rain had already been in the forecast, but before we'd even finished our dance, it started pouring. Everything in the yard was soaked. As soon as we'd scrambled to get to dry land, I'd wished it wasn't raining, and the downpour had stopped. Just like that. Sure, it'd just been a random shower, but as of late, I'd wondered if it was early signs of whatever was going on with the weather.

"Cute, but not what I was looking for. Your shot."

I lined up my shot again and was able to sink my first and second balls into the corner pocket but missed on my third. Eh, victory was fleeting.

"I don't know what to tell you. Why don't you tell me something weird that happened to you when you were growing up?" Cay remained quiet for a minute while he played.

"If I tell you something, can you promise not to tell anyone?"

"Oh my god, did you murder someone?" I was only kidding, but I hoped he didn't answer yes.

"What? No. For real, breathe not a word to anyone." This new Cay was getting a little too serious for my liking.

"Okay, I promise."

"You know how everyone thinks the scar on my upper lip is from a rough tackle from a touch football game from when I was a kid?"

I nodded.

"It's actually from me walking into a tree with my eyes closed when I was five years old."

"That doesn't seem like such a bad secret. Why keep that to yourself?"

"Alec convinced me the hole in the tree was magical and would take me to another world, but I had to walk into it with my eyes closed or it wouldn't work."

"Wow!" I chuckled. "You poor thing."

"I know, right? My brother got grounded for, like, a week. I was so upset I fell for it; I made up the football story."

"Well, no worries here. Your secret is safe with me."

He smirked as he leaned over for his turn.

I leaned my stick against the table. "Why are you only nice to me?"

"What do you mean?" He missed the pocket.

"I mean, you pick on most everyone else, give teachers attitude. I know you've got this badass rep to uphold, but what makes me so special?"

He shrugged. "You just are."

Well, that cleared it all up. I sighed.

"Okay, then. Why did you move to Ocean City?" I played again, sinking another ball.

"My dad's job transferred us here. At least that's what we tell people." I missed my shot. Cay took up his position at the table.

"So, what's the real reason?" I pressed.

He hid the truth behind his smirk. Fine, if he wasn't going to tell me, I wouldn't pry. "Oh! I left my phone downstairs. I'll be right back."

I thundered down the stairs, stopping mid-step when I saw the dog. I'd forgotten about Neit. He poked his head up but didn't move. He just looked at me.

"Good doggie," I whispered, and he laid his head back down.

Grabbing my phone, I took my time going back upstairs. The dining room was spacious and airy; creamy curtains fluttered from an open window's breeze. A clear vase, cradling a bouquet of white orchids, sat in the middle of the wood table. Wandering through the open archway and into the living room, I looked at some of the miniature statues on the bookshelves. Busts of deities I didn't recognize and prized football paraphernalia sat among various cookbooks and assorted family pictures. One picture was of Alec winning a martial arts competition, smiling proudly as he gripped his trophy. Another was of Cay crossing a finish line, the red tape stretching before it broke across his chest, his face frowning and drenched in sweat. The last framed picture in the row made me freeze in my tracks. It was a young girl, facing left, with red hair blowing in a gust of summer wind. Her arms were held up as if reaching for her other half. A summer sky was drawn behind her, green grass growing under her bare feet. A tunic adorned her body while a crown of flowers sat upon her head. I'd seen this picture before. Or, I'd seen the half she's reaching for. At Trip's house. I couldn't believe it was merely a coincidence that both of their houses contained one half of the same picture.

"Hey, there you are," Cay said, walking downstairs. "I thought you got lost."

I whipped around, startled. "Nope, not lost."

"Ah, you're checking out our family pictures," he pointed out, coming up beside me.

"Yeah. This drawing next to the one of your parents is really cool. Did you draw that?"

"Not me. It's been around for generations, so long I wouldn't even know who drew it," he answered immediately. When Trip told me that same lie, I was so quick to believe it, but when those words tumbled out of Cay's mouth, I colored him a liar. There was something more to Trip and Cay's hatred for one another, and I think this drawing was the key to uncovering that truth.

"Funny," I began, "Trip told me the same thing when I saw the other half of this picture at his house."

"Yeah? That's weird. I've never known this picture to be a half of a bigger one." The lie was smooth like melted chocolate.

"So, I have a question for you, if you don't mind continuing the 'get to know me' game?" I challenged.

"No, go for it."

"You moved here last year, right?"

"Correct."

"From where?"

"Everywhere. My family moved around a lot. After Dad's most recent transfer, we decided to settle here."

"Why? I mean, it's nice here, but it's nothing fancy." Determination pressed against the back of my brain.

"The school system." Okay, he got me there. Most, if not all, parents wanted to reside permanently in a town with good education credentials. But that still didn't explain...

"Why do you hate Trip?" I knew I was onto something, but I was missing the last piece.

Cay stopped. His suave demeanor and deflection of all my other questions were just an act. Like being a jackass. He was playing the world, and I finally caught him in a moment of honesty.

"I don't hate him," he said a minute too late. He turned away from me and bent down to pet Neit at his side. Clearly, his calm mask was slipping away. Red creeped up his cheeks.

"Liar. Before you even met Trip, that night on the boardwalk, you tried to pick a fight with him. And you two can barely be in the same room together. In fact, Trip is acting like I'm Helen of Troy to his King Menelaus because I went home with you today, Prince Paris." A bead of sweat formed on my forehead from the building righteousness in my body. "If you don't hate him, this question wouldn't be an issue. And you wouldn't have begged me since before the start of school to spend time with you!"

"I don't hate him," he repeated, staring at me sharply.

"Liar," I scoffed and crossed my arms. "Admit it!"

"Fine! You win! I hate him. Happy now?"

"Why?" I pressed.

"I can't tell you." He sounded conflicted as he turned to walk up the stairs, but I ran and cut him off at the pass.

"Oh no! You can't give in and then not give me details! Why do you hate the new kid?" Some of the rumors floating around school said Cay had a bit of a temper. Let's see how true that was.

He leaned in, his face close to mine.

"You need to leave now," his voice low and rocky. The dog growled softly, sensing tension in the air. The sunny day carrying us from school to here was gone. It might have been the adrenaline pumping through my veins, but I wasn't afraid. Or leaving without answers.

"No. I want to know what's going on between you two. There's too much evidence to prove all of this—" I waved my hand in a circle to emphasize my point, "—is more than just a funny coincidence." Turbulent winds whipped around and through the windows, sending papers scattering to the floor.

We were locked in a standstill. Cay didn't move an inch; there was no other human noise besides his breathing. I kept a steady gaze on him, with my arms still outstretched and blocking his escape upstairs. Cay was clearly firm about holding his ground, but I was more stubborn, refusing to give in. Our eyes latched, his intense hazel eyes boring a hole through my blue ones. Finally, the intensity relented and his body slumped, tired from the internal fight he was keeping from me.

"I can't keep this a secret anymore." He shook his head. "I can't tell you everything, but I will tell you what I can." I knew better than to protest at this moment. I was a mix of excitement and apprehensiveness about what I was about to hear. He gestured to the couch.

"Please sit," he said, and I did.

"Yes, Trip and I hate each other," Cay began. "I have known him before I was born because our parents are enemies, and their parents were enemies from long before any of them were born. Our families have been sworn foes since the days of the Tuatha Dé Danann, the race of gods and goddesses before Christianity invaded Scotland."

"You sound like a textbook," I cut in.

Cay frowned, losing all humor in his body. "You wanted to know why he and I hate each other."

I held up my hands. "You're right. I'm sorry. Please continue."

"During that time, there was the mother of the Tuatha Dé Danann, Danu, a water goddess. She had several children, two in particular. Twins, Brighde and Beira. Each daughter was blessed with the gift of controlling the seasons with the help of their mother and a talisman. When they were about to become women, if you catch my drift, the girls fought over who would control the seasons year-round. Danu, sick of the fighting, split the talisman in half and assigned each girl a certain season. From Bealltainn—"

"Bealltainn?" I interjected.

"The first day of summer," Cay continued after directly acknowledging my question, "to Samhainn, the first day of winter, Brighde was the ruler. From Samhainn to Bealltainn, Beira took control. The compromise worked well for a while, but once Danu fell ill and died, the rift picked back up. Being selfish, neither goddess would give her half of the talisman to the other. The halves were never reunited, leaving the weather unbalanced and out of control."

"I don't understand. How does this rift between the sisters affect you and Trip?" I asked.

"After Danu's burial, the halves went missing. No one is sure how, but it's certain the twins spent the rest of their lives searching for them. While they looked, they each married and had children, who in turn, had children, and so on and so on. The descendants of each line have kept up with the feud and have continued to look for the charmed pieces. My family, the McKays, have the blood of Brighde coursing through us, while the Findlays, Trip's family, are tainted with Beira's blood."

I wanted to laugh. The thought of those high school boys carrying on a silly battle from hundreds of years ago was beyond funny to me. Cay was straight-faced and his voice expressionless. I couldn't do anything but believe him. I looked out the window to give myself time to figure out what to say. Darkness was replaced with sunlight so blinding; it was as if someone had turned on a florescent light in pitch-blackness. A thought hiding in the back of my mind brought a question to my tongue, but like lightning, it faded away in a blaze.

"You're dead serious? About it all? If I went to Trip right now and asked him if this was true, he would say yes?" I questioned.

"Yes." That word hung in the air between us until the garage door opening was the only sound in the room. Heavy footsteps trudged up the stairs.

"Oh hi! I didn't expect anyone home," the new arrival said.

"Hi, Dad. This is Bridget, from school. Bridget, this is my father," Cay introduced us as if our conversation had never taken place.

"It's a pleasure to meet you, Mr. McKay," I said, waving.

"Same to you. I'm going upstairs to change. Be down shortly." He trotted up, removing his tie along the way.

"I should get home. I still have to walk back to my car," I said, standing.

"I'll drive you," offered Cay.

"No, it's okay. I have a lot to think about on the way home." I put my shoes on, picked up my bags, and headed downstairs. "Tell your dad I said goodbye."

"I will. Bridget, I know this goes without saying, but . . ."

"I know. Not a word will be breathed to anyone about this," I assured him.

"Not even Trip."

"Seriously? I just got this giant avalanche of information about you two, and I can't even talk to him about it?"

"It's incredibly important he doesn't know you know."

I held up my hands. "Fine. I won't bring it up."

"Thank you. See you tomorrow."

"Goodbye, Cay."

My ride home gave me the silence I needed to digest everything. I was exhilarated by this new secret information, but this new burden felt heavy. I wondered what would happen if no one did anything to procure these talisman pieces. We'd survived what sounded like forever without the goddesses and their special charm to control the seasons. Why bother keeping with tradition now? And did their parents really want their own children to grow up knowing all this hate and family separation? On top of all of this, Cay had mentioned there was more to the story. What else could there be? My mind couldn't answer all the questions it had, and I was forbidden from speaking to the few people I knew who could.

CHAPTER 6

"Hey, Bri! Wait up!" I chased after my friend, my shoes slick with dew from the morning grass.

"Hey!" We hugged. "What's going on?" The warning bell had already rung for first period, so we made haste to our gym class.

"Nothing. You do anything fun last night?" She smiled lightly at me and nudged my shoulder.

"I bet nothing I did was as fun as what you did," she hinted.

"What are you talking about?" I played dumb, more for the entertainment of the conversation than anything else.

"Please! I know you went over to Cay's! Hilary tagged Cay in her Instagram story about how he was missing their afternoon hangout. Coupled with your fight with Trip about Cay, I put two and two together. Now, tell me about it! What did you do?" Bri's sun-kissed skin flushed with excitement.

I couldn't say I was surprised Bri knew about my hangout with Cay. She usually had the lowdown on the inner workings of the school's social network. I was just hoping the news didn't reach Trip before I did.

"We hung out at his house, played pool, and talked. Nothing earth-shattering." That I could talk about, at least.

"That's it? Did you kiss him?" she squealed as we entered the school.

"No! Gross. I assure you, we don't have feelings like that for each other."

"Uh-huh, sure. What about Trip?"

"What about him?"

"Do you still like him?" Bri asked.

I thought about our fight the other day. Now I understood why he and Cay had been fighting like cats in heat. Let's face it, I had pretty much forgiven him, but I still deserved that apology. No matter how believable (or unbelievable) Cay's story had been, and despite my promise to keep this a secret, I still needed to know how Trip felt about me.

"Hello? Earth to Bridget?" Bri waved her hand in front of my face.

"Oh, sorry." I blinked a few times.

"I'm going to interpret that trip you just took was to a far-off planet, named Trip, where the two of you spend your days kissing, holding hands, and looking lovingly into each other's eyes." She sighed.

I made a face. "I swear I just imagined rainbows and unicorns on that planet, and I've got to say, that's not what Planet Trip would look like."

"No? Then tell me." We clambered in after our fellow female classmates into the locker room to change for gym.

"It would be dark and scary with the threat of a ghost coming to haunt your lost soul at every turn. Where murderers reign supreme, killing and eating the unicorns, for they're a delicacy, drenched in rainbow's tears." I smiled sinisterly.

"Something is very, very wrong with you. Why do you have to ruin my hopes and dreams like that?"

I laughed. "I needed another hobby for my college apps."

After sweating and feeling gross from sprinting around the track in the sweltering heat, I made it to computer science with a minute to spare. Thank the good heavens we had air conditioning at this school.

"Hey," Trip said, appearing by my computer.

I jumped at the sound of his voice. "Uh, hi. You're not in this class,"

"I know. My history class is across the hall. Can we talk?"

I looked around the room as the class spilled in. "Now?"

"No, after school." He rocked back on his heels. I softened a little, touched he was so nervous. I wanted to hold his hand and tell him I wasn't upset. I now understood why he wanted me to avoid Cay so badly. Too bad Cay had sworn me to secrecy. Now being alone with Trip threatened the promise I made to Cay.

"I can't today."

"Oh, what about lunch?" Trip asked hopefully. I shook my head. As much as we needed to have a conversation, I really needed a day to process everything Cay had told me the night before.

"I have some homework to catch up on."

"It's, like, the fourth day of school." The bell rang, signaling class to begin.

"I'm sorry," I said as the teacher walked in. Trip looked at me, disappointed, and left the room.

"Hey, Cay! Can I ask you something?" I asked as he and I left English. I hadn't had a chance to talk to him before class since he was late. I wanted him to confess everything last night was a lie. If he wouldn't, I didn't know when I'd be able to be alone with Trip again.

"Sure, you just did," he replied.

"It's about what you told me."

His face fell. "Then no."

"Come on, you're the only one I'm allowed to talk to about this," I pointed out.

"Bridget, I told you because you basically berated me into telling you." I followed him to his locker, where he opened it and dropped off his backpack. "I shouldn't have told you."

"Well, you did. What would happen if you and," I dropped my voice down, "*him*, drop the hunt? Give it up, let bygones be bygones, and move on?"

"Clearly, the fact you're incapable of following the simple directions of not talking about it means I can't trust you." He closed his locker and turned to walk away. He wasn't getting rid of me that easily.

"How am I to take you seriously?"

He stopped to face me. "Why would you think I was lying?" His eyes narrowed. He didn't give me a chance to answer.

"If you don't believe me, fine. I don't care, but if you really want answers, don't ask me. Ask him." Cay walked to the front door.

"You asked me not to ask Trip."

"Well, I changed my mind. Shoo fly, go away."

I crossed my arms, cocking out my hip. "Seriously?"

"No! No one can know about this," he whispered forcefully. Cay's gaze flitted around the school in a paranoid fashion and finally landed on me. "Just let it go. Forget I told you." He walked off toward Cory and Logan, never once looking back at me. Wow, Cay was really selling this story. He should take this act down the road to the community theater.

I drove home, frustrated and unsatisfied. It was so annoying that Cay shared this huge secret in his life and, when confronted, wouldn't even tell me the full truth. I had half a mind to call Trip and ask him point-blank what the hell was going on. I let out a loud growl. The guy next to me at the stoplight looked over and rolled his car forward. That's it. I picked up my phone and sent out a mass text:

[Bridget: Girls' Night. My house at seven. Bring snacks and movies!]

Within minutes, Bri, and Annabelle confirmed. Deidra texted she had other plans with a winking smiley face. I couldn't wait for the details about that! I felt a little better now I had something else to focus on than the boys and their family feud.

"Oh my god! I love her hair!" Annabelle said, staring at a model in my *Cosmo*. Brianna, Annabelle, and I were hanging out in my black and white room, listening to music and gossiping about clothes, movies, and movie stars.

"What is she wearing, though? I am not a fan of the neon," Bri commented, pointing to the movie star on the page.

"The earrings are nice," I said, popping a piece of popcorn in my mouth. Annabelle flipped the page.

"Ooh, I can't wait to read what else is going to be on the runway during Fashion Week."

"Something we can't afford, even when the knockoffs come out. What else?" I asked. Opening a bag of Cheetos, I sat next to Bri, completing our little circle.

"I like this top," Annabelle pointed to a shirt with an abstract wolf on it. I caught sight of her arm, spotted with plaster of Paris. Her clothes were always stained with oil paints, charcoal, clay, and whatever else she'd used that day.

"I do too, but I like my animal prints less abstract and more realistic."

"Moving on," Bri announced. "Bridget, tell me. How are things with Trip going?" All eyes slid toward me.

"Um, good? I don't know," I said shyly.

"Did he ever apologize for his freak-out?" she asked, taking a sip from her water bottle.

"I haven't given him a chance, honestly."

"Why not?" Annabelle demanded.

"I don't know what to say!" I sat up, tucking my legs underneath me.

"What do you have to say? He begs for your forgiveness, and then you reward him with kisses." I laughed at Annabelle.

"You need to lay off the romance novels," said Bri, shaking her head.

"It's just ... I really like him. Like, a lot."

"So, what's the hang up?" Annabelle asked, chewing on taffy.

"I don't know." I was tired of all the crap Cay fed me, frustrated I couldn't tell Trip, and mad at myself for avoiding him after our fight.

"What about you and Cay?" Bri asked.

"What about him?"

"Anything going on with you two? I heard you had a hot hangout session the other day."

"No hot hangout sessions. Just a normal hangout session."

"What did you two do?" Annabelle asked.

"We played pool, talked, ate pudding."

"Lame." Bri leaned back, disappointed. "Are you holding back? Maybe you two, you know, kissed, but you don't want it to get out because you're afraid it'll make its way to a cute boy who lives down the street?" I blushed.

"I wouldn't tell a soul," she added, looking at Annabelle.

"Hey!" Annabelle proclaimed. "I resent that."

"I have no romantic feelings for Cay!" I exclaimed. "We're just friends."

"Well, be careful. Hilary Thompson has it out for you. It's no secret she drools over Cay every chance she gets," Bri said knowingly. I loved how she knew all the gossip about the school's royalty.

"Can you blame her? I mean, really, Bridge, how did you resist those adorable dimples, that cute scar, and those totally kissable lips?" Annabelle sighed.

"Easy. I don't feel like that about him. We're friends. Remember Trip?"

"Yeah, where did that come from? I mean, you weren't friends before, so out of nowhere now you're hanging out?" pointed out Bri. "What gives?"

"No idea," I said. "He just randomly invited himself to my barbeque and then stalked me until I hung out with him."

"I think he likes you," Annabelle sang.

"Doesn't matter," Bri said. "She's totally with Trip. She's all, 'Cailean who?'"

I smiled. If only they knew the truth.

"Whatever. None of it matters because Trip still needs to apologize," I said.

"Give him the chance to, and he will," countered Annabelle. I fell silent. She had a point, after all. I guess I'd have to take Cay's advice and forget everything he'd told me.

"What about you, Annabelle? Did you ask out George yet?"

She blushed and said, "Not yet, but I'll do it before the holidays."

"The ones that are like three months away?" Bri asked, raising an eyebrow.

"Yes," Annabelle replied firmly.

"Who wants more soda?" I asked, focusing the attention on something else. It seemed neither Annabelle nor I wanted to be grilled anymore on our potential love lives.

Finally, after countless hours of talking, eating, painting each other's nails, and movie watching, the three of us passed out. The girls left just before lunchtime on Saturday, and I went to lie in my backyard under an umbrella with a glass of lemonade and a book. It was a pleasantly warm day, much like one in early spring. Typically, around this time, the sun kept a tight hold on the earth, making people sweat as much as possible before the cool, crisp kiss of fall came around. Global warming in effect, I supposed. Or... maybe everything could be blamed on the missing talisman. Why was I letting myself believe this? Cay was just being manipulative, but what if he was right? I wished I could talk to someone about this. The more I thought about it, the more I'd drive myself insane. I closed my book and sighed. If I couldn't talk to Cay, I'd have to talk to the other person he claimed knew about this family feud.

Trip.

I got up from the chaise lounge just as Mom came outside.

"There you are," she said. "I was going to run to the mall for some new shoes. Do you want to join me?" What better way was there to avoid confrontation and get your mind off things?

"Count me in!" I said.

"Were you able to get any sleep last night?" Mom asked as she turned into the parking lot. "I heard you girls until one, but then I fell asleep."

"Oh yeah, we weren't up much later." With all this stuff about Cay and Trip running through my mind, it was hard focusing on a simple conversation with Mom.

"The bakery has been so busy lately; I think I need to hire another baker to keep up with customer demands." I stayed silent.

"And with your father working on this new case, it's been very quiet in the house," she added.

"Mm-hmm."

"Okay, what's going on? Why are you so distracted?"

I sighed. "A classmate of mine told me a really outlandish story the other day, and I'm having a hard time ignoring it," I answered.

"What's the story?" We walked into the shoe store, and my mind went blank. The smell of leather, rubber, and a dash of other people's feet washed over me. I immediately felt better with the promise of a new pair to walk out in.

"Oh, he told me about goddesses and a lost weather charm, and his family has to rush to find it before another family does. Blah, blah, blah," I picked up a pair of wedge sandals. I like the shape, but not the color. I moved on.

"Who was the boy?"

"Cay McKay."

"Why did he tell you that?" Stopping to try on a pair of black Puma sneakers, she sounded surprised about where my information was coming from.

"Because I noticed a drawing in his house that looked familiar," I said casually. It all sounded silly in my ears. Deciding to keep the shoes, Mom picked up the box and kept browsing.

"What kind of picture was it that made him tell you a story like that?"

I stalled, looking at a pair of sneakers as a cover. "Just a drawing of a red-haired girl."

I absentmindedly picked a pair of flip-flops. "But I also saw a picture like that at Trip's house."

"Same exact picture?"

"No. The one at Trip's was a picture of a girl in a fur coat. The other one is a picture of a girl in a summer tunic. Both had red hair, and they looked identical."

"Interesting."

I frowned at her reply.

"Just interesting?" I gave up on sandals and sneakers, heading toward the heels. It was about time I shopped frivolously.

"How are things with Trip?" she asked, avoiding my question.

"Okay. We're not really speaking at the moment. We fought."

"About?"

"He was upset I went to hang out with Cay."

"Jealous?" She handed me a pair of short, brown suede boots. Cute. I tried them on, but they made my feet look stumpy.

"Trip has nothing to be jealous of when it comes to Cailean McKay."

"Does he know that?" Mom asked, raising her eyebrows at me.

"I guess not."

"Well, for the record, I like Trip more than Cay McKay."

"Why?"

She hesitated a little too long. "There's probably some silly thing going on between the two of them that has nothing to do with you. And that Trip is cuter." She laughed with a wink.

"That's cryptic."

She smiled, slung her arm around me, and kissed the top of my head. Mom's affectionate distraction didn't take me away from noticing her comments about Cay's story. Why was it interesting they both had the same picture, and why had she avoided my question?

Chapter 7

We turned into my driveway after a long after-noon of shopping. Lunch had been tasty, but the three new pairs of jeans, two shirts, and a dress to match my black leather boots sitting in my closet all year really brought my spirits up and calmed the whirlpool of information in my mind. Carrying our purchases, I climbed out of my car and headed up the walkway. Sitting on my porch, with a small bou-quet of wildflowers in his hand, was Trip. He wore a blue shirt and jeans with brown flip-flops to match his belt. His sandy hair was a bit tousled, giving him that sloppy yet put together look, and he shifted uncomfortably from one foot to the other and smiled at me hesitantly. I gave him a full smile back.

"Hi, Trip," Mom said, coming up behind me. She noticed the flowers in his hands. "I'll take these for you." Mom took the bags from me and headed inside.

"Hi," I said.

"Hi," he said, walking down the steps. "I picked these for you."

I took the flowers and sniffed them. "You went to a meadow and picked these for me?"

He grinned. "I picked them out at a nursery."

I chuckled. "That makes more sense." I sat on the bottom step, motioning for Trip to do the same.

"I don't know how to say this really, so I'm just going to come out with it," Trip started as he sat. "I was a jackass. You're absolutely right. I have no claim on you whatsoever, and I'm really sorry. You should be able to hang out with whoever you want, scumbag or not." He pressed his hand to his chest dramatically. "But if you, my friend, are in danger or are going to hang out with scum, isn't it my responsibility as your friend to protect you from such hazards?" He gestured toward Ocean City, where Cay lived. I swear I heard "Battle Hymn of the Republic" playing in the background.

I chuckled. "Smooth. You should be a political writer when you grow up."

"'Ask not what your country can do for you, but what you can do for your country.'"

"Well then, Mr. President, what do you propose I do for the good of my country?"

"Forgive me?" He dropped the act, striking me with a very sincere look. "Joking aside, I really am sorry. That guy just gets to me. Don't ask me why."

"What if I already know the answer?" I teased.

"I don't believe you," he replied lightheartedly.

"Despite my better judgment, I forgive you," I said, breathing in my first bouquet of flowers from a guy.

"Wow, that was easy," he joked. I shoved him, and he pulled away, laughing.

"Want to take a walk?" I suggested. He stood and offered me his hand. I took it, and he immediately laced his fingers with mine. I was light-headed and giddy, but outwardly, I blushed.

"I like that you blush easily," he said.

"Yeah? I hate it! It gives me away."

"I think it's sweet. And you look cute when you do that."

I blushed furiously. We were halfway up the block, heading toward our park—that's what I called it now—and all I thought of was how firmly he held my hand, like he never wanted to let go. My heart swelled; Mom had been right. In the race to be my number one crush, Trip had flown past all the other guys. Kevin was so far behind he was off the list. I wasn't falling for Trip anymore; I had already fallen for him. Hard.

We reached the park and took our normal spots in the gazebo. Even though it was early evening, the sun was shining brighter than ever. The river hung lazily between the muddy shores. The air smelled of freshly cut grass and fishy river water. A family was fishing on the other side of the bank. I smiled and wove my fingers through Trip's as I leaned against him. He rested his head gently on top of mine as we gazed at the scene before us.

"What made you decide to talk to me again?" he asked, breaking the serenity of the silence.

"You sitting on my porch with flowers helped. A lot," I joked. "But honestly, I needed space and some time with my girls."

"And you're good now? We're good?" he asked, somewhat tentatively.

I sat up and kissed him softly, then leaned in and intensified it. He shifted his body to mirror mine and put his hands on my waist. My breath quickened, and my heart sped up. A quick flash of lightning tore through the sky, but we didn't move. We sat like that, kissing in the shadow of the gazebo, as the sun finally decided it was time to go to bed.

"I really like you," he said as we pulled apart. Trip leaned his forehead against mine.

"I really like you, too," I softly said, smiling. I kissed him again, flushing a little.

"We're together, you know." I looked down at his arm to avoid looking at him straight on.

"Yeah?"

"Yeah." I traced the little freckles on his forearm, drawing a senseless pattern.

"Good, because I feel the same way." He lifted my chin with his finger and peered into my eyes. The green of his eyes was bright and clear, as if he glowed from within. I was mesmerized by the intensity, getting drawn further and further in. The blood quickened in my veins as my heart ran a marathon in my chest. I could barely catch my breath. Another flash of lightning appeared, and that time we both jumped.

"We should get back," he said. "I don't want to lose you when I just got you back." He walked me to my front door and kissed me good night. I wrapped my hand around his neck, pulling him in. I didn't want to let go. The kiss ended, and Trip reluctantly headed home for the night.

I tore through her clothes, dragging out her tunics, throwing stuff all over. If she wasn't going to admit she took it, then I would find it.

"What are you doing in here?" my twin demanded, standing in the doorway.

"Just give it up," I answered, determined. "I know you have the Amulet. I want my half back."

She picked up a dress that had landed by her feet. "Brighde, how many times will I have to tell you? I don't have it!"

I turned my back on her and pulled another tunic from the chest. "I know it's in here somewhere!" The top slammed shut, nearly crushing my fingers. I whipped back around toward Beira. "You almost broke my hand!"

My older sister shrugged. "Stop being so dramatic. Your hand is fine." She tossed the dress on her bed. "And I only have my half."

"Liar!" I called. "Who else would have it?"

"I wouldn't know. Maybe someone else in our bloodline?"

I stared at her, dumbfounded. "Are you accusing Lugh?" I answered, eyebrow raised.

She shrugged again. "It makes sense. He is the God of Mastery, after all."

"But... he's the Sun God..." The sentence died on my lips. It made sense. Lugh, our God of Sun, Good Harvest, and Mastery, would need the power of weather to ensure his harvest was bountiful for the humans we protected.

I shook my head. My brother wasn't the conniving one in the family. "It's not him," I told Beira.

I saw her dark blue eyes flash as a gust of snow blew around us. "Is there anyone else you could accuse?" she suggested, knowingly.

For the second week of school, I was constantly plagued by some variation of the Amulet dreams. Lugh kept trying to persuade me as Brighde to work with Beira, yet anytime I stepped near her to make amends, she would scowl and insist she didn't have it. Infuriated, I'd throw her tunics all over the floor or try to zap her with a lightning bolt, but she deflected with an ice shield every time. Waking every day frustrated wasn't how I wanted to spend my mornings. I stopped looking forward to sleep, knowing my feelings in my dream would spill into my waking feelings. I spent our first week of dating in a zombie-like state, relying heavily on coffee and mini naps at lunch to get me through the day. Trip couldn't have been sweeter, allowing me to use him as a pillow or running to refill my coffee. I couldn't even enjoy the onslaught of happiness my girlfriends showered me with over my newfound romance, including Deidra, who'd made a home for herself in our little circle. Cole seemed to have missed the announcement; he kept sneaking longing glances at Deidra. Cay, on the other hand, was like a new best friend, always asking how things were with Trip and me, letting me copy his notes when I zoned out, and actually taking notes for me to copy. I knew he and I still had some unfinished business, but I was happily accepting the help. I just hoped when we did hash it all out, I would be functioning at one-hundred percent. I needed all my energy to go toe-to-toe with him.

When I made it home on Friday, I passed out, sleeping until the middle of Saturday morning. I padded out into the kitchen, wiping sleep from my eyes. Waking to the smell of homemade waffles drenched in syrup and butter was glorious. Dad was standing at the waffle maker, pouring more batter.

"Morning, kiddo," he greeted me. His cotton, drawstring sleep pants bunched around his t-shirt, and his graying hair stuck up everywhere.

I yawned. "Morning. Where's Mom?" I opened the fridge and pulled out the orange juice.

"She had to work this morning. Her Saturday baker, Belinda, called in sick."

"Ah, okay. The waffles smell good." I poured the juice and took a sip. "What're your plans today?"

"Um, homework, followed by homework, and homework if I get that all done."

"So, you're doing nothing all day?" He placed two waffles on my plate, and I doused them in syrup.

"Pretty much." Being a lawyer, Dad was a big stickler for doing homework and keeping up with responsibilities, but he also loved relaxing when he wasn't in court.

"Well, if you get tired of doing homework, want to shoot some hoops with your old man?" He sat straddling the seat across from me.

"Old man? Come on, Dad," I scoffed. "Yeah, I guess. If I get it all done."

"They weighing you down with homework?"

"I'm a senior now, Dad. More responsibilities as you get older... You know the drill." I finished my waffles and drank my juice before putting my dishes in the sink. "I need to get a head start if we're going to fit a game in." I left a sticky kiss on his head and went to take a shower.

Later that day, I closed my notebook with a large thud and sat back in my desk chair. It felt good getting all my weekend homework done by five o'clock.

I left to go find Dad. He was sitting on the couch watching ESPN.

"Hey, Dad," I collapsed next to him. "I'm sorry my homework took all day."

"Don't worry about it. Did you finish?"

"Yup, all of it."

"Nice. Pizza for dinner?"

"Oh, yeah. Wait, where's Mom? Tell me she didn't work all day!"

"No, she called and said she was going to see how Belinda was feeling. Just you and me for dinner." The doorbell rang. "Plus, our mystery guest."

When I opened the door, Cole stood in front of me.

"Hey! Come on in," I said, happy to see my friend.

"Hey, thanks, but is it okay if we go for a walk?" He looked a little nervous.

"Uh, sure." I slipped on my flip-flops discarded from yesterday and walked out.

"I'll order the pizza!" Dad called as I closed the door.

"That means I have twenty-five minutes before I have to get back," I said as we crossed the yard.

"Then I'll make this quick. Do you have a date for the Homecoming dance?"

"Oh, I don't... know." It was true, I hadn't even considered going with Trip, regardless of our new status. The idea had never struck me.

"I know you're dating Trip, but I was curious if you would go with me, if he doesn't ask you?" Cole was sweating, despite the cool weather we were suddenly experiencing. Wishing I'd grabbed a sweatshirt, I wrapped my arms around myself to save some heat.

"So you want to be my... backup date?"

"You don't have to call it that," he responded.

"I'm sorry, but that's what it sounds like to me!" I sighed. "Cole, why do you want to go with me when you know I have a boyfriend?"

He shrugged, avoiding my look. "I just got used to going with you."

"Cole, seriously. There's no other reason?" I stopped and faced him directly.

"I'm worried the person I want to ask will turn me down."

"Who do you want to ask?"

He sighed and fidgeted a little. "I was thinking of asking Deidra."

I smiled and gave him a hug. "Cole, that's awesome! You should ask her!"

"You know I don't do well with rejection."

"No one does; how do you know she'll reject you?"

He didn't respond.

"Ask her. If she says no, you can come with Trip and me. No third wheeling. I promise."

He smiled. "Deal."

Sunday came and went, followed—thankfully—by an uneventful week of school. It was the end of September, and the Homecoming football game and dance were upon us. The school was plastered with bright posters of girls vying to be the next queen. Cheerleaders were selling giant lollipops and bags of movie theater candy to raise money for the parade float. The varsity football team had been working overtime with extra practice in the hope of defeating our nemesis, Mainland Regional High School. The pep rally was scheduled at the end of the week with the game following that night, and honestly, I was sick of it all already. I had to deal with the inquiring questions like "What is he like?" and "Is he a good kisser?" from random classmates about Trip. On top of that, I had to deal with Cay's newfound interest in my relationship with Trip, the incessant school spirit being jammed down my gullet, and Cole's whining about asking Deidra to the dance. By Wednesday, I was in an incredibly snippy mood no one was able to lift.

"Hey." Trip came up behind me after lunch let out. "What's going on?" His voice was concerned as his hand nestled into mine, and all I wanted to do was bite it.

"Nothing, I'm just in a bad mood."

"All week?" he asked, doubtfully.

"Yes." I sighed. This wasn't his fault. "I'm sorry. I'm just overwhelmed and stressed by everything. If one more person asks me about you, I swear I'm going to scream. Or claw their eyes out. I haven't decided yet." Trip was smart enough not to outright laugh at me, but he did crack a smile.

"Who's asking you about me?"

"Everyone! It's like you've charmed people or something. Underclassmen girls are following me to the bathroom to ask me if you're a good kisser! Even Cay has taken a very creepy interest in you. Are you famous on Tiktok or something?"

"No?"

"And to top it off, the dance is this weekend, and I don't have a da—" I stopped myself.

"A what?"

"Nothing, never mind. Oh, there's my classroom. See you later!" I went to leave, but Trip held my hand tightly.

"Is that why you're upset? Because I didn't ask you to the dance?" Feeling silly and deflated, I leaned against a grouping of lockers.

"It's not just that. It's everything. But mostly, it's that."

"We moved a lot when I was a kid, so I didn't really have the chance to go to dances or have many girl... girlfriends. I didn't even know you wanted to go!"

"It's okay. I shouldn't have assumed you'd want to go just because we're dating."

"Well, would you like to go with me?" he asked with a touch of timidity.

I broke into a smile. "Yes, I would. But we don't have to if you don't want to go!" I added.

"Ha! And risk disappointing you? Plus, I don't know if my celebrity status can handle such a blow. Not taking the prettiest girl in school to the Homecoming dance? I wouldn't survive the fall." He grinned cheekily at me. "Yes, we're going." He kissed me on the cheek—I wasn't a huge fan of PDA. "Go to class, I'll send Dee to come find you after school tomorrow."

"Why?"

"Because every celebrity's girlfriend has a personal shopper!" He winked at me and sauntered off.

"So, with your red hair, I think an emerald-colored dress is best for you," Deidra said, holding a strapless dress to me. Thursday afternoon, Deidra and I stood in the dress section of the department store. Rows and rows of silky, shiny fabrics surrounded us, smelling like the food court and the candle store next to it. My mood lifted slightly.

"Here." She shoved a bunch of dresses into my arms. "Go try these on."

She turned me and pushed me toward the dressing room. It's not that I didn't want to pick out a new dress—I enjoyed shopping, after all—but I was too preoccupied to really worry about one. I'd been planning on just wearing an old dress from my closet that hadn't seen the light of day yet. But when Deidra showed up on my doorstep, ready for battle, I couldn't really turn her down. I looked at myself in the mirror. My blue eyes were dark today, murky and mysterious. My hair was tossed back into a messy ponytail, my skin dull after a day at school. I made a face. I really needed to snap out of this funk I was in. Not only was I dragging myself down, but also I was probably making Deidra miserable.

"Did you try a dress on yet?" she called from the other side of the door.

"One minute and you can zip me in!" I answered, stripping fast. Being naked in a dressing room made me uncomfortable. Even though the door was locked, I felt like anyone could walk in at any moment. I stepped into the first dress, royal purple chiffon with cap sleeves and a tie in the middle. I opened the door.

"This doesn't really flatter me," I said as Deidra closed the zipper.

"Hmm... nope! It flattens your boobs."

She unzipped me and closed the door behind her before I could say, "Hey! I'm not flat chested!" Hanging that dress up, I checked out the next one. *Not happening.* I wasn't even going to put it on. I skimmed through the rest. The pale dress wasn't my color; the orange was gross and looked like a stain; the short boatneck dress was too boxy; the next dress was the wrong size; and the red one was too long. Oh wait! Hiding behind my giant stack was a cerulean blue dress with a sweetheart neckline. It was floor-length with a gold embellishment nestled underneath the bust. I had no idea if the shopping gods had left this for me or if Deidra slipped it in when I wasn't looking, but it stood out like a ray of hope among the sloppy cast-offs. Deidra knocked again.

"Seriously, you're taking forever, and we still have to shop for shoes!"

"Hold on, I'm putting on the last dress!" I zipped the side and held my breath as I looked in the mirror. I glowed. Outlining my seventeen-year-old curves, the dress hung beautifully on my thin frame. Its color highlighted my hair, giving me a halo of ruby sunshine around my face.

"Okay, I'm going to burrow underneath this door if you don't come out!" she threatened.

I unlocked the door and let her in, still admiring the dress.

"Oh my goodness, Bridget. Trip is going to fall all over you in this dress," Deidra gasped.

"I have to admit, you picked out the best one," I said, spinning around. The dress floated out beautifully.

"I didn't pick this out."

"No? Either way, I love it." I pictured Trip and me dancing in the middle of the gym, pressed against each other, my dress swirling at our feet, as he leaned in to kiss me. I gazed dreamily into the mirror.

"Okay, let's buy this and go get shoes before you decide to make out with yourself." Can always count on my friends to snap me back to reality.

"Are you going to the dance?" I asked as I hung the dress up on the hanger.

"I was planning on it," she replied. I got dressed and opened the door.

"Going with anyone special?" I hinted. I hoped Cole asked her and stopped lamenting over it.

"No, no one asked me, and I didn't know who to ask."

"I bet someone in our friend's group would love the honor of having you on his arm." I hung up the discarded dresses on the rack and headed toward the register.

"Like who?"

I looked at her. "No one specifically came to mind? Not the dark-haired sweetie who has been sneaking glances at you since the beginning of the school year?"

She furrowed her brow. "Cole?"

"Yeah. Why don't you go with him?"

"I hadn't thought about it. Doesn't he have a date?"

"I have firsthand knowledge he does not and would love to go with you." I smiled knowingly as I handed the dress over to the clerk.

"Really?" She looked at the rack of dresses in an attempt to hide her smile.

I shrugged. "If you don't believe me, ask him yourself." As I paid, I saw Deidra take out her phone to send a text.

Two shoe stores and one department store later, I was going home with an entire Homecoming outfit. My bad mood was officially over, and I was ecstatic to call my friends to tell them about this dress.

"You know, my brother is completely smitten with you," Deidra said as I turned out of the parking lot.

"Well, that's good because I like him a lot, too." I watched as the other cars passed us before making another left-hand turn.

"He's never been this hung up on a girl before," she hinted.

"Deidra, what are you trying to tell me?"

"Just don't hurt him."

"Is this the 'be careful because I'll hide the body where no one can find it' speech?" I asked. She smiled coyly at me.

"Maybe, but I'm serious. There's something different about you that he really likes. I'm asking you as a friend and as his sister not to mess with him."

"I promise I won't intentionally hurt your brother."

"Intentionally?" she asked, eyebrows raised.

"Take or leave it," I firmly answered.

"Okay." We turned down our block, passing my house on the way to hers.

"Thanks again for dragging my moody ass out. I really appreciate it," I said.

"Anytime," she smiled. "Elizabeth won't let me take her shopping yet, so I'm just going to do this with you for a while."

"Sounds good. See you tomorrow," I said as I dropped her off.

The school bell rang, signaling the end of our last period. Normally, kids of all ages would be rushing to their lockers and then to busses or cars to escape these boring, brick walls. But today was the last day of the week which meant pep rally. Instead of racing to get the best seats on the bus, we were dismissed by grade, racing to get the best spots on the bleachers. As a senior, I was able to leave class first, along with a few of my classmates.

"You excited about the dance tomorrow?" Cay asked as we trotted off to the gym.

"Yeah, for the most part. How about you?"

"I guess. I'm really just going for Hilary."

"Oh?"

"Yeah, she asked me."

"You don't sound too excited," I pointed out.

"She's my friend, that's all. I... sort of like someone else."

My face fell. "Oh lord, please don't say it's me!"

"What? No! I told you already. It's not you. For the love of—stop saying that!" We walked through the gym doors and headed toward the senior bleachers.

"Okay, just checking. Don't want to go through that again. So, who is she?" He smiled and shook his head. "You'll never know." I watched him walk away and then chuckled to myself as I joined my friends.

"I love pep rallies," Annabelle said.

"Since when?" Bri asked.

"Always. I love getting out of class early," she said, grinning. I sat next to Bri, trying to catch Cole's eye. I was dying to know if Deidra had asked him to the dance.

"Personally, I like the cheerleaders," Tomas added, sitting next to Annabelle as Trip sat next to me. I heard the word "pig" floating around us, most likely originating from Bri.

"You do realize that you're surrounded by girls?" I asked. "Not including Cole and Trip, of course."

"Hey, I don't want to be a part of this!" Cole announced, holding his hands up in surrender. Trip remained quiet.

"I need backup!" Tomas argued.

"Sorry, dude, I'm out."

Trip shook his head. "Bro Code, man."

"I thought Bro Code applied to not dating your friend's ex?" Bri piped up.

"The Bro Code is so much more than that," Cole cut in.

"Like what?" Annabelle asked, wiping a smudge off her glasses.

"Can't reveal the Bro Code to a h—"

"You better not make that word rhyme," she warned.

"Girl," Cole amended.

"Speaking of girls," I said. The marching band came in playing the school song while the cheerleaders performed a borderline sexual dance. I sat back in the bleachers, at peace for the first time in a while.

Chapter 8

"Mom, I'm going to be late!" I said as she made Trip and me pose for a million pictures. I delicately patted the curls bobbypinned much too tightly to my scalp. The hairdresser really dug those suckers in. I smoothed the skirt of my dress, mostly because I liked the feeling of silk on my skin. Trip wore a casual suit with a white button-down shirt and no tie. He kept the top buttons opened, which gave him a lazy, James Bond kind of air. My boyfriend and I were placed strategically in front of the bay window outside my house. Our audience consisted of my parents, his parents, and Elizabeth. Tomas and his date, Andrea, were busy taking selfies by one of the trees toward the side of my house as Deidra and Cole kept sharing little smiles with each other.

"Stop wriggling!" Trip laughed in my ear.

"I can't help it! I'm so excited for Cole and Deidra. They look so happy."

Trip just gave me a kiss on the cheek and said, "just for a second, so we can get the picture and leave." I looked over at Roden and his date, a sophomore named Jenny who I hadn't known until that night. They were getting their own pictures taken by Kellyn, Trip, and Roden's mom, who left our photo shoot for theirs. You'd think this was the last time we would ever go to a dance. There was still prom, after all.

"Just one more, I promise," Mom said. She pressed the button, and the blinding flash went off.

"Okay, bye now!" I said, gripping Trip's hand.

"Wait!" Kellyn said, coming over to us. I stopped. She'd been patient with my mom's amateur photography, and I couldn't very well deny her. "I wanted to take one picture of all my children together." I moved away from Trip and went to stand next to the other non-Findlay dates. The sun was starting its dip into the ends of the earth earlier now, leaving girls donning wraps and their boyfriends' suit jackets. I rubbed my hands up and down my arms as I tried to dispel a chill that was settling into my bones. My strappy gold heels sank slightly into the cooled nighttime grass.

"You look really pretty," Jenny said sweetly to me. I smiled.

"Thank you. I really love your hair! My hair would never cooperate like that." Her black hair was swept into an intricate design of braids pulling it all off her heart-shaped face. She beamed in return.

"Mom, we have to go, or we'll be late," Deidra announced. With that, the parents and children said goodbye, and we all piled into our respective cars.

I was excited when we pulled into the parking lot. Everyone in town was in great spirits after winning the game against the Mainland Regional High School Mustangs by a staggering twenty-one points. Trip flashed me a big grin, taking my hand as we walked into the school gym. The Homecoming committee really went all out this year. The walls were adorned with stars of red, black, and silver, our school colors. The ceiling was covered in silver balloons to represent stars. Tables outlined the dance floor, each with black and red tablecloths on top.

"This looks great!" Tomas yelled over the music pumping through the speakers. I nodded in agreement and scanned the room for my friends. I didn't see them, so I snagged a table away from the noise and put my stuff down. Andrea and Deidra followed suit.

"Would you like to dance?" Trip asked me, offering his hand. We glided out onto the dance floor and nearly bumped into Cay and Hilary.

"Sorry!" I yelled to them. He smiled, and she glared at me. Trip spun us away from them. I had to admit, that boy could really dance. I was having so much fun I barely noticed my friends' arrival. Annabelle, sans art materials, wore a slinky, black dress accentuating her dark skin. Her date, George, wore a suit and tie. I grinned at Annabelle and flashed her a thumbs-up when George wasn't looking. She grinned back and blushed as she ducked her head. I didn't see Bri right away, but sure enough, she walked in wearing a red dress, short and flirty, with black heels and jewelry. She was leading Marco Santos in by the hand. He looked incredibly handsome in his gray suit and tie. Bri saw me on the floor and waved.

"I'll be right back," I said, excusing myself from Trip.

"I'll get us something to drink," he said. "Water?"

"Please!" I made a beeline for Bri.

"You look amazing!" I squealed as I gave her a hug.

"Me? You look stunning! I love your dress!" Something behind me caught her eye.

"How did I not know that Cole and Deidra came together?" She asked as her mouth dropped open.

I gave her a knowing smile and laughed. "When Dee and I went shopping, I may have left a breadcrumb or two to lead her to ask him to the dance."

"Is matchmaking considered an extracurricular or a hobby? And how much are you charging for your services?"

I laughed again. "Marco looks good. I don't think you need my help!"

Bri grinned widely and looked back at her date. "He really is dreamy. I'm going to dance with him. I'll catch up with you later!"

I nodded and went to find Trip. He waited for me at the table, two bottles of water sitting in front of him. Roden sat without Jenny.

"Hey, I was wondering what happened to you," he said as I downed half a bottle.

"I had to talk to Bri about something." I looked around and didn't see Jenny. "Where's your date?" I asked Roden. He was crestfallen as he pointed to the dance floor.

"Logan Carter asked her to dance." I turned to watch the two of them practically grinding. Classy.

In my personal opinion, Roden was better off without her, but what did I know about his love life?

"One dance should be okay," I said.

"One dance would be okay. Except it's been three dances in a row now." I gaped at him for a minute.

"I'm sorry. Want to dance with me?"

"No, thanks. I'm just going to sit here for now."

"Roden, if you want to dance with her, go get her back," Trip said.

"I haven't decided yet." A slow song came on.

"Oh! I love this song! Want to dance?" I asked Trip. He led me to the dance floor, and we swayed with other couples to the romantic lyrics. Tomas and Andrea were slow dancing to my left, her dress swaying with her body. Tomas's expression was blissful as he pulled Andrea a little closer to him. He took me by surprise. I hadn't thought of him beyond being Trip's friend, but looking at him now, I couldn't help but wonder who he was underneath that label. I promised myself I would make it a point to get to know him.

"You're beautiful. You truly look like a princess tonight," Trip said, drawing my attention back to him. I was thankful it was dark enough to hide my blush.

"Thank you. You look really handsome yourself." I fingered the collar on his shirt and stared at his exposed skin.

"No, I really mean it. Bridget, I know we've only known each other for a little while, but I care about you so much."

In the dim lighting of the gym, I could make out the sharp features of his face, and I heard the sincerity in his voice. His eyes were focused on me, and I felt my heart burst with such elation and tenderness. It was nearly unbearable. Trip lightly pressed his forehead against mine.

I kissed him in the middle of the floor, ignoring rules—and even the few cheers we got. I was happy and warm all over. The cheers got louder, and I pulled away from Trip, embarrassed. It was only then I realized the cheering wasn't for us but for the commotion going on behind Trip.

"What is that about?" I asked him. He shook his head. People were crowding around two guys and a girl ... Jenny. That meant the two guys had to be Roden and Logan.

"She's my date, so yeah, I'm asking her to dance with me!" Roden yelled at Logan.

"Well, we weren't done dancing. So you get to wait." Logan's baritone was loud enough to hear over the music clearly.

"Where's your date? Did your cousin turn you down ... again?" Roden threw at him. Logan took a step closer to him, clenching and unclenching his fists. Apparently, the date issue was a sore subject.

"I don't need a date when I have yours!"

I poked Trip. "Go help your brother." I had barely finished the sentence before Trip took three huge strides to step in with Tomas hot on his heels.

"Hey, hey, what's the issue?" he asked his little brother.

"Not your fight, man," Logan said, pushing Trip out of the way. Trip knocked Logan's arm away from him.

"Don't touch me." All the softness marking his features before was replaced with protectiveness and anger. Trip's body was loose and clearly ready for a fight. I hoped it wouldn't come to that.

"Go away." Logan turned his back on Trip and focused all his anger back on Roden, who looked like a combination of pissed and nervous. Jenny, still standing on the side, looked a little smug. She, a sophomore, had two guys—both seniors—fighting over her. Her friends must have been so jealous. I rolled my eyes.

"Break it up! Break it up!" One of the new freshman teachers I didn't know came over to end the fight before it really began. Apparently, Roden had recognized him because he'd backed up before he hit anyone. The teacher stepped in between all three guys. "Break it up or leave."

The crowd dispersed, disappointed there had been no punches thrown. Tomas, Logan, and Trip stepped back into their neutral corners. Jenny just stood there, not knowing who to go with, her date or her dance partner.

"The dance is almost over anyway. Why don't we just go home?" I suggested quietly to Trip as I stepped behind him. He turned to face me.

"Yeah, that's a good idea. I'll get Roden," he said, looking around. I left him to go get my own stuff, pushing my way through the tight mass of sweaty bodies. The music had dropped off a bit, giving our tired ears a break, but now it was loud again, the bass pounding thunderously. I said my goodbyes to my friends and left to wait outside the gym for Trip. A group of students standing outside the building caught my attention. Logan, Cay, Tomas, and Roden were facing off yet again. I looked for Trip but didn't find him, so I went outside to see if I could help. Or at least be a credible witness.

"You did it on purpose!" Roden yelled. It was clear his calm anger before had been a teaser for the main show.

"Hey, I can't help it if a pretty girl like Jenny wants to dance with a man and not a boy," Logan retorted.

"It's true. She was all over him," Cay chimed in, nudging his friend in the ribs. Ugh, Cay was so slimy. I rushed down the steps to confront him.

"You have to get him to stop," I said, tugging on his arm.

Cay turned, looking happy to see me.

"I won't."

"What? Why not?"

"You'll see." He moved next to me and faced the fight.

"Well, if you won't do anything, I will." I took a step forward without a solid plan in mind when an arm wrapped around my waist and pulled me back.

"Trust me," Cay said in my ear. I shoved away from him, disgusted by everything in this moment, but I didn't move closer.

"You're lying!" Roden yelled.

"So what? You can't do anything about it," Logan sneered. Roden shoved Logan, sending him back a few steps. Before Logan retaliated, Cay stepped in and punched Roden in the jaw, knocking him flat on the grass. Roden sat up, dazed. If this had been a *Looney Tunes* cartoon, there would've been blue birds flying around his head. Tomas then stepped up to Cay, picking him up by his shirt. Cay was no slouch, but Tomas had a good six inches and an additional forty pounds on the bully.

"Don't!" Roden yelled. He staggered, anger marking every move. "Let me do it."

Tomas dropped Cay in a bundle on the grass and turned to his friend.

"Roden, calm down," Tomas said, his voice darkly serious. There was a freezing chill in the air. My arms and legs were covered in goosebumps, and I could see my breath in swirls around me.

"No! I'm tired of being bullied all the time by these two idiots," Roden growled, wiping blood from the cut on his lip. Cay had been bothering Roden? I thought he only had a problem with Trip. I was furiously shivering at this point, the air thick with the promise of snow. The grass around Roden's feet was crisp with ice, and it spread to Logan as well as Cay, who was already on his feet. Suddenly, a door behind us burst open and out ran Trip and Deidra.

"Roden!" Deidra yelled. "Roden, please calm down!" Trip reached him first and nearly tackled him.

"Take a deep breath. Relax," he said in a muted voice. The temperature rose, and I felt warm blood pump to my fingers and toes. The ice on the grass melted and evaporated, as if nothing had happened. There wasn't a puddle in sight. My eyes widened as I watched the ... magic take place. What the hell was going on?

"Bridget," Cay called, looking over at me. "Remember what I told you?"

"Cay, don't," threatened Trip.

"Remember what I told you about who controls the weather?"

"Cay!" Deidra said impatiently. "Stop!" He didn't acknowledge them.

"There's more than what I told you. Ask him." He nodded in Trip's direction. "He owes you the truth."

Trip let go of his brother and swung at Cay, missing within inches.

"Trip, we should go," Tomas suggested. Logan pulled Cay by the shoulder, out of the way of any further attacks.

"Promise me!" Cay insisted. "Promise!" I nodded, more out of confusion than the need to keep a promise to Cay. He seemed satisfied with my response and allowed his ridiculously tall friend to drag him away.

The ride home was quiet. Jenny got a ride from one of her girlfriends, so it was Trip, Roden, Deidra, Cole, and me in the car. We dropped off Cole first. Deidra walked him to the door and gave him a kiss on the cheek. I watched Cole's face as she walked away. He smiled as he watched her climb into the car. We continued our commute in silence. Anger and frustration from both boys were practically palpable as Dee grasped her hands until her knuckles turned white. I was still reeling from Cay's announcement. What did he want Trip to tell me? And what Roden had done with the grass and the air? Did he have ... powers?

I looked in the side mirror back at Roden. He was still on the smallish side, not hitting his big growth spurt yet. His blond hair was mussed from the fight, and a bright blue-purple bruise was flowering under his skin. Overall, he looked frazzled. But his hazel eyes were what caught my heart. They were filled with defeat and disappointment. I didn't know if he was upset about the fight with Logan or losing Jenny, but whatever the reason, he was beating himself up over it. I wanted to comfort him, but I saw he didn't want to be coddled. He was barely tolerating Deidra rubbing his back like a baby who needed soothing. He was just insanely upset about what happened tonight. Roden and the other Findlay kids didn't have powers. I couldn't believe I'd let Cay into my head again. It was clear something was going on, and I wasn't sure who or what to believe. Trip pulled into my driveway and got out, leaving the car idle.

"I'll be right back," he said to his siblings. They nodded but didn't say a word. I slid out of the passenger seat, only waving goodbye at Deidra and Roden. We walked slowly to my front door, not speaking.

"Well, I guess this is good night," I broke the never-ending silence.

Trip just nodded.

"I had fun," I added. "You know, up until the end." Trip barely looked at me. I could see he wasn't just a seventeen-year-old boy in that moment. He was a young man with a family's burden on his shoulders. Bending over to kiss me, Trip let his lips linger on mine. After all the excitement, a little romance was desperately needed.

He cleared his throat as he pulled away. "I'll call you later."

"What about what Cay said?" I asked. I didn't want to bring it up given the situation, but I couldn't allow it to dissipate from my mind.

"Please, don't ask me about that," he whispered, taking my hand. "I really can't tell you."

"So, Cay's not wrong? The story about your families is true?"

Trip closed his eyes. "Please. Just let it go. I can't—"

"I know. You can't tell me."

He looked like he was going to cry. I reached up and wrapped my arms around him. "I'm sorry about everything tonight. I won't ask you about it."

He pulled me close, pressing me into his hard chest. "If I could, I would," he mumbled into my hair. I pulled away again and kissed him harder this time, as if I could transfer comfort and the feeling of safety through our lips.

We broke apart. "I have to go, but I'll call you later. Probably not tomorrow."

"Good night, Prince Charming."

"Prince Charming?"

"You called me a princess before. Every princess needs a Prince Charming."

"Right. Good night, my fair maiden." He bowed deeply.

"Good night," I said, opening my door. He was gone before I even had a chance to take off my glass slippers.

Chapter 9

I woke up late on Sunday with my hair in a knotty version of my updo. I sat up, looking at my discarded dress and haphazardly thrown about shoes. I'd been so exhausted from everything the night before; I hadn't even cared if my clothes ended up wrinkled or dirty. I checked my phone for messages, but there wasn't anything from Trip. Bri texted me in our group chat with Annabelle, asking about the fight. Cay texted me, too, around ten in the morning.

[Cay: Did you ask him yet?]

I didn't answer, still upset about his part in last night's catastrophe. How could Cay be so callous toward Roden? I knew the family fighting was just tradition at this point, but when it reached a physical level it became barbaric and so ... stupid! I got out of bed and went to the bathroom to brush my teeth and wash my face. The more I thought about Cay's involvement last night, the angrier and harder I scrubbed. By the time I finished, my face was nearly as red as my hair. Oops. I took a deep cleansing breath and tried to think of something positive, like how Cole and Deidra looked like they were starting a new relationship or how much fun my friends and I had dancing. But my favorite part of the whole evening was Trip. I grinned at myself in the mirror. Just thinking about dancing with him and holding him made the butterflies from last night pop up in my stomach again. When he'd dropped me off, it'd been incredibly nice to kiss him. Even after all the drama. I heard my phone chirp from down the hall. I hurried back, hoping it was Trip. Nope, Cay again.

[Cay: Hey! Let me know when you ask him.]

I turned my phone off and threw it on my bed in frustration. As easy as it was to ignore Cay today, it would be that much harder tomorrow. I tilted my head back and groaned.

After digging all the bobby pins from my head and taking a long, hot shower, I was a bit more refreshed. I turned my phone back on only to see another text from Cay.

[Cay: What did he say?]

[Bridget: I didn't ask him.] I lied.

[Bridget: He was a little distracted by how you punched his brother.]

Three little bubbles popped up as Cay texted back.

[Cay: I had to.]

[Bridget: Punch him?]

I pulled the towel from my hair and squeezed out the excess water as my phone chirped again.

[Cay: No. I didn't plan that.]

[Bridget: What was the plan then?]

The bubbles came back but disappeared. I waited a moment but got no reply.

[Bridget: Fine, keep your secrets.]

I turned the sound off on my phone as I headed to the kitchen for breakfast.

Monday morning rolled around, greeting me with a chill in the air and frost on our lawn. It was only the first day of October, and I wanted to snuggle into my fur-lined boots and heavy sweaters. I already missed summer. Gathering my books and slipping on my quilted bomber jacket, I hurried to school, hoping to catch Trip before class.

I didn't see Trip that morning, unfortunately, but I saw my friend.

"Hey, Bri!" I called, rushing to meet her. "Want to grab some coffee before class?"

"Hey! Sure," she replied. We hurried down the hallway, hoping to beat the swarm in front of the coffee kiosk.

"How was the rest of your weekend?" I asked.

"Good. After the dance, Marco took me home." She beamed at me. "He gave me a good night kiss."

"Oh my goodness! Does this mean you two are a thing now, or was it just one, blissful night?"

"I hope the former and not the latter, but who knows? He texted me yesterday about how we should go out again."

"When's the date?" We stood in line at the kiosk, not fast enough to beat the morning rush.

"Next Friday night. I think we're going to the movies."

I squealed and did a little dance. "Maybe soon we can double date!"

"That would awesome!"

"How was the rest of your weekend?" she asked, changing the topic. I debated telling her everything about the fight, all the behind-the-scenes details, but then I remembered how Roden looked on the drive home, and I just couldn't.

"It was okay. Sunday was a slow day for me. I caught up on all my homework."

"Okay, seriously?" she looked at me skeptically.

"What?"

"There's a huge fight involving two of the hottest guys in school. One has a sudden interest in you, and the other is the little brother of your boyfriend. You aren't going to give me *anything* about it?"

"You didn't ask!"

"I was giving you the opportunity to volunteer the information. As a best friend, I didn't think I had to beg!"

"Beg about what?" Annabelle asked, sliding in line next to us. There were a few complaints from underclassmen behind us, but we ignored their whining. Being a senior had a few extra perks.

"Details about the famous fight," Bri answered. We moved up.

"There's nothing to tell," I said. "May I have a large coffee, light and sweet?" The barista nodded and poured my drink.

"Please! The whole dance was about that fight after you left," Annabelle said. "You are the only witness who wasn't involved."

"Dee wasn't involved," I pointed out, handing money to the cashier. I took my cup and moved out of the way.

"Orange juice, please," Bri ordered. "Roden is Deidra's brother. She was involved in one way or another." She paid and took her drink.

"Fine. What are you dying to know?" I asked dramatically.

"Everything," Bri demanded. She gulped down her orange juice. "I didn't see what happened. What was the fight even about?"

"Oh, I know! Logan was making out with Roden's date, right on the dance floor!" Annabelle sounded scandalized.

"I heard Roden bribed his date to dance with Logan so he could start the fight," Bri gossiped.

"Why would he do that?" I questioned.

Bri shrugged. "To up his reputation."

"That doesn't even make sense," I pointed out. "That's insane."

Annabelle was the last to receive her drink. She paid the barista, and we headed toward the senior wing, seeing as it was too cold to hang out in the Square.

"Well, if you know so much, why don't you tell us?" Bri sniffed.

"Nice try. All I know is Roden was upset Jenny had danced with Logan. That's all."

"Jenny? The sophomore with the dark hair who'd won the science award last year?" asked Annabelle. I nodded. "Well, that makes sense. She's also got a huge crush on Logan. Poor Roden."

"She does? I didn't know that." I took a sip of coffee. My goodness, I loved this delicious concoction.

"Oh yeah. She tweeted about it all weekend, how she got to dance with her favorite senior. It was really annoying," Bri responded.

"That's funny. I heard Logan didn't even know her name when he asked her to dance. Someone posted that the whole thing was a set up by Cay," Annabelle disclosed. "I wouldn't put it past him. He's got this weird grudge against any of the Findlay kids. I bet he bribed Logan to provoke Roden so he would get kicked out of the dance."

"Can we really give Cay that much credit? I mean, come on, he's cute and a total ass, but he's about as smart as a stop sign," Bri said, brushing a strand of recently-dyed pink hair out of her face. I thought about that. When I'd hung out with Cay that one time, I never got the impression he was the dumb bully we all knew. Clearly, he was smarter than we all give him credit for. But why was he playing the village idiot?

"Either way, I feel really bad for Roden. He's so sweet and cute. Like a small puppy," Annabelle commented. We stared at her.

"That's a weird thing to call him," I told her. The bell rang, alerting us for first period. "See you at lunch."

I left my friends, their information rolling around in my head. If Cay had set Roden up, what was his endgame? I didn't believe it was just to mess with him, and lately, he'd been kind of nice to Trip, so I couldn't believe that idea. Had strategically planning the fight merely been a ploy to get me to believe his story, knowing I would somehow get drawn in? I still had my doubts about the goddess weather stuff, but coupling that story with Roden's weird icing incident ... maybe Cay's story did have some credibility to it. Except I didn't know the whole story. I guess I'd have to talk to someone about this. I really didn't want it to be Cay if I could avoid it.

"Hey, so did you ask him?" Cay asked as soon as the final bell rang.

"No. We didn't have time to hang out this weekend," I answered, swinging my bag over my shoulder.

"What about when you saw him today? Like at lunch?" He pressed. I took a deep breath. Lunch had been jam-packed with talk about the football game and gossip about dresses at the dance. Much to my relief, no one had brought up the fight. Because of all the social news that needed to be discussed, I hadn't been able to excuse myself to speak with Trip. On top of that, I didn't think it was a conversation that should be held in school. I couldn't risk someone hearing us.

"Nope. We haven't really been alone." We left the classroom and turned down the hall.

"Come on. You expect me to believe you didn't think about Saturday night at all?"

"Rumor has it you bribed Logan to dance with Jenny to get to Roden. Is that true?"

He wavered for a moment, probably debating what to tell me. "Yes, but not for the reasons you think."

I scoffed. "Just when I believe you're not the jerk everyone tells me you are..."

He threw his hands out in front of him and begged. "Bridge, I swear!"

"Why would you do something like that? And spare me the family warfare story again. It's getting old and, quite honestly, rather predictable."

Cay ushered me into a corner, allowing the other students to file past us. "What do you remember from the story?"

"There were goddesses, they controlled the weather with a talisman, it went missing, and now you and Trip hate each other."

"Right, but you're missing the main point. The goddesses had the power to control the weather with the Amulet."

"Okay."

"They had children who had children..." he prompted me.

"I'm not following you down this hole, White Rabbit. Get to your point." I crossed my arms.

"Okay, think about this: Beira and Brighde had powers they got from their mother, so when they had children, those children had powers." He waited for me to fill in the blanks.

"Right. So, every child born into Beira's or Brighde's family line has powers?" I asked, skeptical.

"You don't believe me? How about believing your own eyes?" I moved to leave, but Cay stepped in front of me. "You saw what happened last night; you *felt* it."

"The below-freezing temperatures? The ice? You're telling me that freaky, frozen grass incident was Roden?"

Cay's lips parted into a smile slowly spreading across his face. He tapped his nose twice, pointed at me, and disappeared into the last remaining group of students who hadn't left yet, leaving me hanging in a corner by myself.

I couldn't wait anymore. I needed to talk to someone else.

Chapter 10

The urgency to talk to Trip was so overwhelming; I thought it would crush me. Forcing myself to wait until the majority of the kids left, I got into my car and took off. I couldn't sit in after-school traffic trying to make it to his house. Sitting in my car at a light, I revved the engine a few times, more to release some tension than to rush the person in front of me. She didn't see it like that and flipped me off just as the light turned green. I didn't take offense; that's the Jersey thing to do. Giving the middle finger was practically "hello" in this state. I needed a plan of action for when I saw Trip. I knew I'd promised I wouldn't say anything to him, but Cay wasn't going to leave me alone. He was forcing my hand. I headed home first to get my thoughts in order.

I let out a breath I didn't realize I'd been holding. My phone buzzed from inside my purse, and I jumped. At the stop sign, I looked at the screen. It was a text message from Dad. I'd check that later. Driving slower than a snail, I turned onto my street.

When I pulled into my driveway, I peeked down the street at Trip's house. The silver Audi was parked in its usual spot, next to the black Escalade. I closed my car door and went inside for a snack. The refrigerator hummed in the background, the ticking of the clock on the wall getting louder and louder. I bit into my apple, savoring the sweet juices as I chewed. Forget it, I couldn't take this anymore. Walking out onto my front yard, I figured I would probably go mental before I got any real answers. I'd promised Trip I wouldn't say a word, but I had to know if Cay was right. Before I could protest, my feet were marching me down the street.

I paced in front of his house nearly a million times debating if I could keep Cay's promise. What did I owe him? Technically nothing, but he had shared what he claimed was a big family secret with me without truly knowing me. Sure, we'd had random classes together in the past year, but I wasn't braiding a BFF lanyard bracelet for him anytime soon.

I walked up to his front door and knocked. My palms were sweaty and, soon, so was my neck, dampening the back of my shirt. It was like the sun had kicked into high gear all of a sudden after a very cool weekend. If all this was real, I hoped either the McKays or the Findlays found these talismans or amulets or charm pieces soon enough. I didn't know if I could take these sudden climate changes much longer. One day, it was blazing hot; the next moment, lightning struck, and it was chilly. I didn't know how to dress for the weather anymore.

The door opened, and Deidra stood in front of me.

"Hey!" she said. "Long time no see." She backed up and welcomed me inside.

"Is Trip home?" I asked, stepping out of the raging inferno.

"No; he, Tomas, and Roden went skateboarding."

"Oh, okay. I just wanted to ask him a question. Can you let him know I stopped by?"

"Sure. Is it something maybe I could help with?"

An idea struck me like I'd been knocked upside the head with hail. I didn't have to talk to Trip directly. Maybe I could get something out of Deidra with a little chat.

"Actually, I think you could help me," I said, grinning. "How well do you know Cay?" I asked. We moved inside to her living room, where we sat on the couch. Deidra was sitting. I was, again, pacing. Apparently, lying and extracting information make me a bit twitchy. Her mom was in the backyard with Elizabeth, preparing her garden for winter, and her dad was at work, leaving Deidra and me alone.

"Not really at all. I only met him when we moved here." Oh, she was good. So casual in her reply as she crossed her legs and sat back. Clearly, I'd underestimated her.

"That's not what I heard," I answered.

"What? What did you hear?" Her tone was casual, but I heard underlying tension. She had been interrogated before.

"Nothing of importance but a small rumor or two."

"About what?"

"How you two actually know each other."

She frowned and leaned forward, uncrossing her legs. "Care to elaborate on that?"

I sighed, sitting next to her.

"I know you know Cay more than you're letting on." Her jaw tensed and her hands closed in tight fists on her lap. She kept her mouth shut to let me talk. "What I'm about to tell you is incredibly insane, I know, but I need answers, and I don't know who else to ask. I came to ask Trip because of what I promised Cay at Homecoming."

"What are you talking about?" Her voice was tight.

I looked at the family pictures on the wall; the drawing of the red-headed girl dressed in fur was placed in front.

"I saw the other half of that drawing at Cay's house," I said, pointing to it. "When I confronted him about it, he broke down and told me about the goddesses, the feud, the talisman, the weather going crazy, all of it."

Deidra wiped her face of any emotion, which was creepier than actually showing feeling. I had no inkling of what she was thinking.

"And I came to ask Trip some questions because now Cay won't stop bothering me about it. He also hinted Roden has ... powers."

I felt really stupid. I mean, what if Cay had told me all that to mess with my head? And I had just rambled to Deidra, who would probably have me committed and tell her brother not to date me. I waited for her to talk; I thought she'd stopped breathing.

"Dee?" I asked. Barely blinking, she stared at the picture. Oh my god, she was catatonic! "Deidra!"

"I'm going to kill him." That wasn't the answer I was looking for, but ... yeah, I'll go with that for now.

"You weren't supposed to know." Her voice came out weird and slightly robotic.

"Me specifically? Or like, me as a representative of the rest of the world?" I asked.

"What exactly did he tell you?" She looked directly at me.

"What I said. The goddesses fought over an Amulet, it went missing, they blamed each other, and now your families have to look for it."

"Nothing else?"

"Well, there was a small misunderstanding that you could fly, but other than that, nothing else." Deidra was already pale, but I swear, she turned translucent.

"I'm joking! Flying wasn't involved, I promise!" Wow, it was not the time to joke. Deidra, never saying one word, jumped off the couch like I'd bitten her. What was it about this family feud that had everyone acting so strangely whenever it was brought up?

"Wait, can you actually fly?" I asked. She looked at me, her eyes wide as the ocean.

"Not fly." She slipped from her crazy state for a second to become viciously angry. "I'm going to kill him. That seems like the best course of action here." She paced while it was my turn to sit, confused, on the couch.

"Okay, what the hell is going on here?"

"He shouldn't have told you."

"Well, he did, and I'm tired of being left out in the cold and of only getting scraps of whatever Cay deems worthy to tell me. Why is it a big deal if I know? I'm not telling anyone! And technically, I kept my promise to your brother. I didn't ask him. I asked you," I argued. I wasn't a good liar, but clearly, I could bend the truth like nobody's business.

"Trip needs to know about this," was all she said. Deidra grabbed her cell phone and dialed a number.

I was becoming more and more frustrated with being ignored. If I had known I would be treated like a hostile witness, I wouldn't have come over.

"Wait, you can't tell him!"

But it was too late; he'd already answered.

"Hey, it's Dee," she said, pacing back and forth. "Yes, I know you have caller ID."

She paused a second.

"Really? Whatever. I have Bridget here, who has some very interesting information you should hear." She started pacing again.

"She knows. I didn't say anything!" Her eyebrows raised with the octave of her voice.

"Right, okay. See you then." She hung up.

"What the hell is going on?" I asked. I was exhausted by the game of spy vs. spy we were playing. I wanted answers, especially since her convoluted conversation with Trip had ended with a very specific, "She knows."

"Trip will be here soon. He'll tell you."

I stood. "No, I want answers now." She remained quiet. "At least tell me why it's the end of the world if I know about this?" Deidra looked unsure if she should answer.

"Nothing?" I asked, surprised.

"It's not technically the end of the world if you know."

"Meaning what?"

"Meaning," she took a breath. "You knowing is not the best news for us, exactly."

I gestured for her to continue. She looked me dead in the eye.

"Because *you* change everything."

CHAPTER
11

"What does that mean?" Thunder cracked outside of the Findlay house. Getting used to the crazy weather patterns, I ignored it.

"Just wait until Trip comes home. He'll fill you in." Deidra walked into the front hall and put on rain boots.

"What're you going to do?" I asked, worried to be left alone right now. Being told I'm a game changer was a little unnerving. Even though Deidra was acting like a lobotomy patient, I still felt a little safer with her here.

"Going to get Cay with Tomas." With that, she grabbed a set of keys and left.

I paced around the Findlay house, unsure of what I should be doing. I was too restless to sit, given what had just happened with Deidra, and too anxious to do anything else, considering what Trip might be telling me. What did I have to do with Trip and Cay's family feud? Thinking about it, I was a little excited about what that meant. I stopped pacing. That probably meant I'd have the fate of the cosmos on my shoulders or something. Just then, the sliding glass door to the backyard opened, and in stepped Elizabeth and Kellyn.

"Oh, hi, Bridget!" Kellyn said. "I didn't know you were here."

"Hi! Deidra said Trip would be home shortly. And she went out ... to run an errand," I covered. I wasn't sure if I was supposed to let Kellyn know what I knew. I think it was bad enough I knew anything. "She just left!"

"Oh, that's okay. Can I get you anything to drink or eat?" She washed the dirt off her hands in the kitchen sink.

"No, thank you. Hey, Elizabeth, are you reading anything new?" I asked, trying not to appear nervous.

"Not for fun. We're reading *Jurassic Park* in English now."

"Wow! That seems old for your age group. Not that it's a bad thing. I don't believe in censorship. Do you like it?"

She shrugged. "It's okay. It's not my favorite."

"I didn't really love it either," I said, and she brightened.

"Hey, do you want to see some of my other books? When we first moved in, Dad built a bookcase into my wall. Like, the whole wall is a bookcase. Want to see it?"

"Yes! That sounds awesome!"

"Wash up!" Kellyn called as we headed upstairs. "Dinner will be soon!"

"Okay!" Elizabeth replied.

As we reached the top of the stairs, the front door opened, and I heard the guys come in. I froze, unsure if I should ditch Elizabeth.

"Come on," she ushered me.

"Hey Mom," Trip said as he walked into the kitchen. "Is Bridget here?"

I followed Elizabeth into her room. I wanted to stay in partial ignorance for a few more minutes. Her bedroom was like every other tween's out there. Posters of musicians and pictures of her friends decorated her pale, green walls. Tucked into the corner across from the door was her bed, under a hanging canopy. Wooden blocks hanging above the headboard spelled out "Elizabeth Rose" and the closet door was open, revealing the mess inside. A desk sat opposite to the foot of her bed, and her dresser was cluttered with young girls' jewelry. But my favorite feature in her room was the wall of books built into the whole wall. Painted childhood characters from beloved books were scattered around the backdrop of the bookcase, which was brimming with books. I walked to get a closer look at what she had. Beverly Cleary, Walter Dean Myers, Neil Gaiman, Lois Lowry, and Gennifer Choldenko were some of the authors punctuating the shelves.

"Wow, this is awesome!" I said. "Hey, where's the Shakespeare play you were reading?"

"Which one?" she asked, sitting on her bed.

"The day I came over with my mom you were reading a Shakespearean play. I think it was *Othello*?"

"Oh yeah! I stole that from Deidra's room. It's hers."

I smiled. That's something I would have done if I'd had an older sibling.

"Yeah, I liked it more than *Antony and Cleopatra*." *Color me impressed*. This was one of the brightest twelve-year-olds I'd ever met.

"There you are," Trip said. I jumped.

"You found me." I looked back at Elizabeth. "I have to go, but we'll do this again soon. I would love to talk books with you!" She smiled and nodded.

"Thanks for keeping her entertained for me, Liz." With that, Trip took my hand and led me into his empty bedroom.

"I think we need to talk," he started.

"You don't say?" I crossed my arms over my chest.

"Please, before you say anything, listen."

I nodded, against my better judgment. It was probably the smarter plan to let him talk first. I may finally get some of the answers I had been waiting for. Trip motioned for me to sit on the bed, but I chose the desk chair.

"Go on," I said.

He sighed. "I wanted to tell you, but I wasn't allowed."

"By who?"

Trip smiled apologetically. "I can't say." He ran his fingers through his hair, leaving it tousled, like he was fresh from the barber. "I honestly don't know where to begin."

"I've always liked the beginning."

"Okay, well, a long time ago, around the time of the Ancient Greeks, there were two goddesses: Beira and Brighde—"

"I know. And there's a charm missing, and that's why your families have been fighting for generations. Cay told me."

"What else did he tell you?"

"To ask about Roden and the dance."

"I can't tell you about that! We already discussed this." He looked at me pleadingly; his hands were clasped together as he begged.

"Why not?"

"Because, I can't." He crumpled a little, deflated.

"That's a fantastic answer."

Trip just stared at me.

"You can tell me! You can tell me anything! I don't understand what the big deal is about me knowing anything about your stupid family war!" I shouted, leaping up. "If I'm something special like Deidra says I am, shouldn't I be able to know everything about this?"

"Deidra?" He jumped up. "I thought Cay told you everything." I stood.

"He told me the background history. She filled in some blanks. What does it all mean? Am I supposed to change the course of history? Or stop the polar ice caps from melting? I don't understand!" The rain fell in sheets outside, pelting the window. Thunder boomed over our heads, shaking the house with every crash. I couldn't help but cry. It was a stupid family trait, crying when things went wrong. I was overwhelmed with everything, pissed at Trip for avoiding my questions, and becoming increasingly frustrated.

"Where is Dee now?" Trip asked, his tone still sharp.

"Still getting Cay?" I mumbled. I took a shuddering breath, trying to stop the outpouring of emotions. He walked over and wrapped me in his arms.

"I promise I'll explain everything you want to know, no holds barred, once Dee returns. Shhh, calm down," he soothed, stroking my hair. "It's going to be okay." I let myself melt into his arms and cry for a minute. It felt good to let go of this tension I'd been holding on to.

The tears slowly dried, but not before leaving a huge wet spot on Trip's shirt. I heard thunder grumbling in the distance; the heavy downpour on the roof morphed into a calming patter instead of an angry storm.

"Are you okay now?" he asked.

I nodded, rubbing the edges of the spot. "Sorry about your shirt."

He half smiled. "It'll live."

"Trip?" Kellyn called from downstairs. "Are you up there?"

"Yeah, Mom?" he bellowed back.

"Your ... friend is here."

"Wow, I can hear the disgust from here," I whispered.

"Be right down!" Trip yelled. I wiped my eyes and followed him. By the time we reached the kitchen where Tomas, Roden, Deidra, Cay, and Kellyn sat, the rain had stopped completely.

"Thanks for the shower, Bridge," Cay said, as he dripped all over the floor.

"Shut up!" Trip snapped. "This is your mess I have to clean." Something told me he wasn't talking about a towel. Cay just shot him a cocky smile and sat at the table.

"Trip, a word, please," Kellyn demanded. The two of them went into the dining room. The house was quiet enough that I could catch snippets of their whispered conversation.

"I don't like him being here," Kellyn said.

"I know. I don't like it either, but he told Bridget." Their voices dropped for a minute until I heard Trip again.

"Okay, okay! I'll try," he said, stepping back into the kitchen. Kellyn followed, her beautiful face marred by frown lines.

"I'll be upstairs," she said curtly, then left. Trip flicked his head toward Roden and Deidra, who moved away from Cay and toward me. Tomas stayed where he was, like he was guarding Cay from us ... or us from Cay.

"I see you finally started asking questions," Cay said. "About time."

"I thought I told you to shut up," Trip retorted. Cay raised his hands in mock surrender.

"Does anyone mind if we get the Q and A part of the evening over with?" I said, sitting across from Cay. He sent a genuine smile to me, and I sent a tight one back.

"What is going on with you two?" I looked at Cay, but Trip answered.

"I don't know how to answer that."

"Figure it out," I said as my eyes slid over to him.

"Come on, Trip, doesn't she deserve to know why everyone is suddenly so interested in her?" Cay kept his tone light.

Trip crossed his arms and took a deep breath. "Fine. Bridget, the reason why Cay has taken a new interest in you is that he found out you're his very distant ... cousin." He finally looked at me, and I heard the thickness in voice.

"Seriously? That's it?" I analyzed Cay, trying to find any familial resemblance. Maybe our cheeks were a little round? Other than that, my red hair and blues eyes didn't match his reddish-brown hair and hazel eyes.

"Yup, we're family. That's why I'm not interested in you like that," Cay confirmed.

"So that's all? Cay and I are related? Is that how I change everything?"

"Do you understand what this means?" Cay said.

"No, not really. This is all feeling like a monumental waste of all our time." I stood, very tired. "If we're done here, I'm going home."

"It means you're a descendant from Brighde." Deidra stared at me. I looked at the three Findlay children, realization smacking me in the head.

"What? What exactly does this mean?" No one, not even Cay, looked me in the eyes. Now he'd decided to stop talking?

"Are we suddenly enemies? Because I can't hate you guys! You're my friends!" I waved my finger at them. "I'm not getting in the middle of two feuding families."

"Bridget, that might not be an option," Dee said softly.

"What?" I turned to Trip, hoping he'd refute her statement. "Is this true?"

He just looked sad.

"When is your birthday?" he asked.

"June twenty-first. It's the first day of summer," I answered with a sinking feeling in my stomach. "Why?"

"Did Cay tell you the whole story about the goddesses?"

"I didn't think he left anything out." I glanced at Cay who still felt the need to remain silent.

"Descendants on either side who are born on the first day of summer," Trip gestured to me, "or on the first day of winter," he pointed to himself, "are very special."

I crossed my arms and waited. I was over asking questions and getting almost nothing in return.

Trip sighed. The room was silent.

"You promised," I prompted him.

"We are the Cuardaitheoirs." It sounded like he had just choked on his tongue.

I blinked. "Come again?"

"Seekers," Cay answered. "It's your job to find the Amulet of Danu and her daughters."

I fell back in the chair.

"I know this is a lot to take in," Trip said tenderly, sitting next to me.

"A lot doesn't even come close." I didn't know how to process this information. "So, now what? I look for the talisman? Where do I look? In cookie jars or couch cushions?"

"Amulet and no, nothing like that," Trip said with a smile. "Normally, Cuardaitheoirs are trained from birth to search. We tend to travel around the world."

Another lightning bolt went off in my head. "You didn't move a bunch because of your father's job?"

The Findlay kids looked a little uncomfortable but shook their heads. I felt incredibly stupid and gullible, so ready to believe whatever I'd been told. I should've read between the lines or something.

"There's more," Cay volunteered.

"Cay..." Trip threatened.

"You promised," he taunted.

As if my mind could handle anything else, a memory swam its way through the sea of information.

"Does it have something to do with what happened at Homecoming?" I asked cautiously.

"Sort of," Roden chimed in. "I don't have powers like you or Trip."

"Hold up! *I* have *powers*?" I gaped at everyone but mostly Cay because, apparently, we were family. He should have kept me in the loop. This whole thing was becoming more and more absurd. My mind was on the verge of exploding. "What didn't anyone tell me?"

"We were ordered not to," Deidra answered.

"By who?"

"You've always had powers. You just didn't know it," Trip cut in, sending Deidra a look.

"This has to be a sick joke. I don't have powers." I stood and paced like a caged animal.

"Nope, you have them. Just like the rest of us," Cay commented, sitting back in the chair.

"What kind of powers? Can I freeze stuff like Roden?"

Cay shook his head. "You're a summer descendant. Our powers aren't winterized like theirs."

"Ours? What's your power?"

"Healing," he responded.

"Healing? Like Wolverine?"

Shockingly, Cay didn't roll his eyes. "Any living thing. The true weather goddess, Brighde, can heal anything."

"Healing is considered a season now?"

This time, Cay rolled his eyes. "Not directly, but in the spring and summer, plants and animals are growing, being renewed, being born, and that translates to healing."

"Show me," I challenged.

Cay deferred to Trip, and he nodded. Tomas walked over to the knife block and pulled out a small knife. He moved back to the table and, without pausing, sliced his palm open. I flinched and closed my eyes for second, smelling the tang in the air. Blood welled in the cut and spilled over onto the table. Cay took Tomas's hand in his own, closed his eyes, and focused. The blood slowly dried, and the halved skin sewed itself back together, leaving nothing but fresh, unharmed skin. I felt my eyes popping out of their sockets.

Okay, maybe I believed them a little. "Can I do that?" I asked, my voice coming out strangled. Blood didn't bother me, but seeing that display caused bile to rise.

"No, sweetheart, you can't," Trip said. I was too involved to even appreciate the endearing term.

I took a calming breath. "What can I do?" I assumed I hadn't fallen asleep to *Alice in Wonderland* and dreamed all this.

"Bigger and better," Cay said.

"Bigger and better than that?" I pointed to Tomas's healed hand.

"You can control the weather," Trip said plainly.

I stood there, thunderstruck. Maybe I didn't hear him right.

"So... global warming is my fault?" I asked, confused. A few scattered laughs from my friends littered the air.

"No. That's why it's important we find the Amulet," Cay said, invigorated. "And not them. It's our family who is supposed to settle the weather."

Amulet... That word stirred something in my memory, but I couldn't reach it. Had I read that somewhere?

"Beira was older than Brighde by mere minutes, so technically, it's our family's right to control the weather," Deidra said. Cay's eyes flashed with anger.

"Wait," I said holding my hands up, "I'm still a little lost."

"With what?" Roden asked.

"Everything! Why do I have weather powers and you don't?" I asked Cay.

"Because I wasn't born on the first day of summer. My birthday is in July."

"Who else has powers?"

"Most everyone in the families," Trip answered.

"I feel like I'm missing vital information. What kind of powers are there? And what do I do with mine?" Wind blew in huge gusts outside, whistling like a train.

"That's my doing?" I asked. Five heads nodded at me. Unbelievable. I sat and dropped my head on the table. All this information in one shot was making me dizzy. I heard the chair next to me scrape against the floor.

"I know it's a lot to take in," Trip repeated, rubbing my back. "But eventually it will make sense and become normal to you."

"I still don't understand," I mumbled. "How do I use my powers? And what am I supposed to do with them?"

"You don't have your full powers yet," Deidra said. "You get them on your eighteenth birthday."

"What happens then?"

"Brighde's full powers are bestowed upon you."

"Among other things, which I'll tell you when we are alone." Cay glanced in the direction of the Findlays. Deidra rolled her eyes while Trip's jaw tightened.

I didn't even know what to ask anymore. My mind whirled with information, and I was having a hard time getting a grip on it all.

"This is the pinnacle year. It's been over five hundred years since the Amulet pieces have gone missing. The weather is more turbulent than it has even been before," Trip added, a little aggressively. There's that word again. Why can't I remember where I had just heard Amulet?

"It's beyond important that we find them," said Deidra, desperately.

"What happens if we don't?" Again, my question was answered with silence.

"We don't know for sure. But it can't be good," Cay nearly whispered. His tone scared me more than anything else. I stayed quiet, absorbing more news. I looked at those around me and noticed Tomas hadn't moved or spoken since this whole thing had started.

"What's your power?" I asked Tomas.

Without moving or looking at me, he answered, "I have none."

"What's your story then?" I asked.

"I told you. He was adopted by my parents after his died," Trip interrupted. He shot a look at everyone. No one countered him.

"Really? After everything tonight, you're still keeping secrets from me?" I asked.

"I swear it's not my choice," he said apologetically. "If I could tell you, I would."

I was suddenly very tired. The adrenaline in my system had slowed to the pace of a drowsy snail, leaving me sleepy.

"Well, then whose choice was it?" I yawned. Again, an exchange of glances took place. No one said a word. "Still keeping secrets. Forget it." I stood. "I'm going home."

I headed toward the front door with Cay and Trip hot on my heels.

"No!" I said, turning to face them. "You stay. I just ... need some time." Trip looked pained but remained silent.

"Ask your mom," Cay said as he went back into the kitchen. I waited for Trip to explain. He was too busy shaking his head and glaring at Cay's disappearing silhouette.

"What?"

Trip sighed and faced me. "Your mom didn't want anyone to tell you. Ask her about it." Then he left me as I turned on my heel and sprinted toward my house.

Chapter
12

My mom had known about this all this time and had never told me? Rushing up my front steps, I threw open the door.

"Mom!" I yelled. "Mom! Where are you?" The house was filled with the smell of beef stew simmering. I walked into the kitchen, expecting to see her at the stove. Nope, not there. I checked her room, but she wasn't there either.

"Mom!" I called again. I heard the sink in the bathroom turn on. She came out of the bathroom.

"What's wrong?" she said.

"How could you keep something like this from me?" I shouted.

"Voice down, please. And what did I keep from you?" She walked past me into the kitchen. She was annoyingly mellow as I followed her.

"Everything! Let's start with the fact that you've been keeping my family history a secret from me?"

"What are you talking about? Here, taste this," Mom said, holding out a spoon brimming with delicious stew. For once, her food didn't distract me.

"I know about my powers." She put the spoon in the pot.

"Let's sit."

"I don't want to sit. I want answers."

"Please?"

I sat across from her at the kitchen table, my hands resting on the tabletop. Mom looked resigned, as if she's been dreading this moment all my life.

"I knew this day was coming. Please, keep in mind I've only kept it from you for your own protection."

"Why didn't you tell me?"

"I'm sorry, sweetheart." She covered my hands with hers. "With your powers, things like thunderstorms and cement melting heat were bound to happen. Dad and I wanted you to have a happy childhood without worrying about it."

"Dad knows?"

"Yes." I pulled my hands from hers and sat back in my chair.

"Does he—?"

"No. Your powers are only from my side of the family." Mom looked stressed, but I was tired of being kept in the dark.

"Of course, you have powers. Does everyone have powers?" I paused. "Why didn't you tell me before I was seventeen? Like maybe when I hit high school?"

"I wanted to protect you. To keep you safe." She got up and began heating water. Mom usually drank tea when she needed to calm her nerves.

"From what?"

"Beira's clan."

"What are you talking about?" I asked, alarmed. College apps, midterms, college applications, boyfriend, friends, finals, prom, graduation, and now I had to fight unknown assailants?

"Those Amulet pieces are very important to the people of Scotland. They took pride their goddesses controlled the weather, and it seems after all these years, well, the weather around the world is out of control."

"What does that have to do with me?" Mom poured two cups of tea, placing one in front of me as she sat back down.

"Honey, you are the direct descendant of Brighde with her strongest powers. The stories I heard growing up told of Brighde's child being the one who wields the full power of the Amulet. Every generation in the NicBodach line, my family, a child is born on the first day of summer. Normally that child is trained from a young age to be the Cuardaitheoir: a Seeker who hunts for the Amulet and defends our family from the Winter Clan," Mom explained.

"Wait, defend?" I was incredibly unprepared for this life being shoved into my hands. The warmth of the cup soothed me a little as I took a sip.

She nodded. "I know this is a lot to take in, but Daddy and I wanted to delay your future a little bit longer. We hoped we would have had more time to train you for this."

"Like martial arts?"

Mom smiled at me. "Yes, but more about how to control your powers. When you were born, Daddy and I wanted you to have as normal a life as possible."

"So you mentioned," I replied.

"Can you understand why we did this? Knowing what you know now, do you see why we hid your potential destiny from you?"

My destiny. I hoped Mom didn't expect me to answer her question because I felt as if my life was out of my control. Powers, goddess ancestry, and now a giant scavenger hunt with fellow Seekers coming after me?

This Amulet was going to be the bane of my existence. I just felt it.

"So... is this what I have to do?"

Mom swallowed her mouthful of tea. "No! You don't have to do anything you don't want to."

I raised an eyebrow. "But—"

She took my hand in hers. "No buts. Just remember that."

"Mom, I don't get it. Wouldn't it have been better to help me control my powers instead of leaving me vulnerable all this time?"

"I thought about it, but I was hoping when my family moved from Scotland and settled here, we would've escaped this. It worked for my childhood, and I was hoping it would work for you."

I paused. "You have powers? Are you a Seeker, too?"

She didn't answer right away, but she gave me a small smile. "I'm not a Cuardaitheoir."

"So, what are your powers?"

"Brighde was known for many powers, including the power of fertility." She wrapped her hands around her cup.

I blanched. "Are you telling me I'm not an only child?"

She burst into laughter.

"No! No. Her powers manifest in different ways. I grow my own produce, and because of my power, it tastes better than anyone else's. Let's just say I have the best green thumb there is."

I nodded, weighing this information in my mind. There were so many more questions I couldn't hold back anymore, but only one kept bubbling to the surface. "Mom, why did I hear about all this from Cay and Trip?"

She sighed. "I know you don't agree with me keeping this from you, but I had to keep you safe. I spoke with the boys' mothers, and they agreed to not say anything. This, of course, was before social media and the terrible fact I placed my trust in someone from Beira's side of the family." Did I detect a hint of bitterness in her voice?

"What are the next steps?" I asked.

"What do you mean?"

"Do I change schools or start training?"

Mom took a long sip of tea before she replied.

"You stay in school. I'll speak with Dad about starting your training. He needs be included in the loop."

I felt a little better before a horrible thought crossed my mind. Did this mean Trip and I were over?

CHAPTER
13

I woke up late the next morning, with a note taped to my mirror from Mom.

Turned off your alarm. Thought you could use the day off, sweetheart. I'll be home early tonight. See you then.

Love you,
Mom.

Yawning, I sat up, a little lost from having a surprise day off from school. Out the window, I saw the sun was shining, but it wasn't hot. The crisp, autumn air rustled the leaves still hanging on the trees. This was all on me? I stared out the window. How could this be my fault? October weather was cool, edged with the last of the summer warmth. If I was in charge of summer, how could the crazy, fall weather have been blamed on me? I shook my head. Why had I even considered this whole story to be real? I must have been gullible. Cay hadn't blinked in my direction at all last year, and now I was to believe he's my magical distant cousin from a goddess I'd never heard of? And my boyfriend had powers—along with the rest of his family—and we're fighting over a dollar store trinket that controls the weather for the entire world? To top it all off, my mother had confirmed their claims! I rubbed my forehead. Mom had been right: I did need a day off.

I got up and went to the bathroom. While I brushed my teeth, I peeked out the window again. I didn't think it would hurt anyone if I tested my so-called powers. What was the harm of me playing Harry Potter in my yard? If all three of them were telling me the truth, I should probably learn the rules before it was too late.

Pulling on gray sweatpants, a long-sleeved shirt, and sneakers, I walked into my backyard, thankful most of the neighbors were more than likely at school or work. Okay, let's see. Where did I start? I waved my hands for thirty seconds before feeling like an idiot. Nothing stirred. I stretched my body, mostly because I didn't know what else to do.

"Abracadabra!" Not one leaf lifted off the ground. What would a witch do? I didn't remember any witches using a spell to call up their powers.

A cool breeze danced around me, sending a chill down my neck. I wished it was summer again. I closed my eyes and concentrated, wishing for warmer weather. For a minute, I swear I felt heat. But nothing happened. The breeze floated past again, mocking me. I stretched my muscles a bit and cracked my knuckles. Closing my eyes again, I concentrated harder... nothing! I think I'd actually made it colder. I sighed, feeling ridiculous. Honestly, if Mom hadn't vouched for them, I might have still believed this was all a big joke.

One more try, and I was going inside. It was getting too cold to be out without more clothing on. What else could I do? Maybe I had to think of summer things, like the warm sand on the beach underneath my sun-kissed skin or the ocean washing up the shore, cooling me from the scorching sun. I felt the light summer wind blowing around me. My wet hair tickled my shoulders, and my eyes popped open. The wind... I'd done it! I'd made the weather a little warmer. I spun laughing, reveling in the summer wind I'd conjured. Suddenly, the temperature dropped, and it was fall again. I was too excited to care. Trying again, I pulled forward the memory of Sam's hot dog and the smell of the crispy fries nestled on top of the spicy chili. I tasted the bite from the onions on my tongue as I scooped up the chili with a piece of the bun. The last time I'd had this, I was walking back to the beach, swimming through the humidity to find my towel. I touched my forehead, felt the thin layer of water clinging to my skin, and opened my eyes. Gone was the memory along with any semblance of heat I'd mustered. Not a problem. The third time had to be the charm. Again, I pictured warm nights on the boardwalk, absorbing all the bright lights and sounds being piped into the air. I stilled and waited for something, any minuscule weather event, to happen. All I felt was extremely cold; my breath ached in my lungs. I sighed, disappointed. Well, not too bad for my first time ever. I'd take it for now. Going inside, I looked back toward the river behind my yard. Dumbfounded, I had to believe them now.

After my interlude with the weather, I painted my nails, watched a cheesy movie on TV, and gave myself a facial. As I dried my face, my phone lit up; Annabelle was calling.

"Hello?"

"Hey! Are you feeling okay?"

"Yeah, I just needed a day off. I didn't sleep too well last night," I lied, wiping the water off.

"More nightmares?"

"Something like that. How was school?"

"The usual. I tried to get your homework, but I couldn't make it to all your classes."

"No problem. Thanks for trying, though."

"Anytime. Um, I ran into Cay as I was trying to get your homework for English, but he offered to take it to you instead."

"What time should I expect him?" I asked, dryly.

"Soon. When I saw him, he was running to his car." The doorbell rang.

"I think he's here. Thanks again," I told her. "See you tomorrow." We hung up. Rubbing his hands together, Cay stood on my front steps with a goldenrod scarf tucked into his black jacket.

"Hey," I said, feeling the bite of the cool air.

"Hey, mind if I come in?" I stepped back and returned to my spot on the couch to turn the TV volume down.

"How are you feeling?" he asked.

"I'm fine. After last night, I needed a day off," I replied.

"I'm really sorry about all that." Cay sat on the chair across from me. "I didn't mean for you to find out like that."

"Yes, you did. You purposely told me the story about your—I guess I should say *our*—family and Trip's family, then pushed the issue at the dance. Tell me, did you set up Logan with Jenny so Roden was forced to use his powers?" I raised an eyebrow as he looked directly at me.

"You needed to know. You needed to see it with your own eyes."

"Weren't you told not to tell me?" He looked away.

"Yes, but you have to understand; it's important you know."

"Why?"

"So we have a better chance of finding the pieces!" He jumped, startling me a little. "You don't get it! We have to find that Amulet. The weather around the world has gone insane. We, the descendants of Brighde, have to fix it! You are part of this equation. You possess the goddess's powers!"

"Why is it all on me? I thought there were others."

"Mistakes were made, and now you're the last one in our family."

Gulp.

"What kind of mistakes?" I asked tentatively.

"People died," he replied, his tone serious. "The battles between the families were horrible and bloody. Until you came around, there'd been no Seeker on our side."

I stared at him, slack jawed, as he continued. "We've wasted enough time as it is. You're The Cuardaitheoir of Brighde, and your family needs you."

"Cailean McKay. I'd appreciate it if you'd stop scaring my daughter." Cay's head whipped around to find my mother, standing in the doorway, glaring at him.

"Mrs. MacNamara, we need Bridget's help. Yours, too," he said.

"You need nothing from my daughter. I've spoken with your parents about this. We're in agreement—you stay away from Bridget until this situation is resolved." Mom's icy tone sent chills down my back. Cay looked back at me, his eyes begging for me to jump in.

"Mom—"

"No. No discussion about this. Cay, you need to leave." Indecision flicked across his face, not knowing whether to fight or to go, but Mom held her ground. With a sad parting look, Cay left.

"I know that was harsh," Mom said. Her voice softened, "but it needed to be done. I don't want you getting dragged into this. I've kept you safe so far, and I intend to finish that job." Fear flashed across her face as well. Everyone except me was afraid of the Big Bad coming. I couldn't decide if ignorance was bliss or a nightmare.

Chapter 14

I awoke to a creepy tapping noise coming from my window. It sounded like the sharpened fingernail of a serial killer rapping on glass. I froze, sweat beading on my forehead. I didn't breathe. This was silly. No one had ever been killed by a deranged ax murderer in Corbin City. I pushed back my covers and crept to the edge of my bed. I admit I'd never been happier that my bed had been positioned away from the windows. A shadow moved past the glass, and my heart fell out my chest. I grabbed my alarm clock. The plan was to throw it at the stranger. I started walking away, clock in hand, when I was yanked back. The stupid thing was still plugged in! Abandoning that, I scrambled for the next closest weapon. Hairbrush? No. A book sat on my nightstand. Maybe. Turning, I spotted my hairspray on my dresser. Clutching the beauty product in my hand, I inched my way to the window and pulled back the curtain. A guy's face stared at me. I screamed and clamped my hand over my mouth when I realized it was Trip. He ducked, and I waited to see if I'd woken my parents. Silence definitely was golden. I opened the window, letting cool air in.

"Trip? I'm going to kill you!" I whispered to him.

"I need to talk to you. Can you come outside?"

"Only if you stand still so I can kill you!" I hissed.

"With hairspray?" he asked, with one eyebrow raised. I glanced at my hand and put the hairspray on my desk.

"I could blind you," I said, climbing through my window. Thank goodness my room was on the first level.

"Or make my hair stand still in a really strong wind," Trip teased. I smacked him on the arm.

"Never, ever do that again! Or it'll be the last time you're physically able to tap on a window."

"Okay, *ow!* I'm sorry!" I hit him again for good measure and remembered I was standing outside in my pink, piggy pajama pants and white tank top with my boyfriend.

"What do you want? I'm cold and it's late." I shivered.

"To see how you're doing. You missed school today, and last night was ..." he drifted off, rubbing his hands along my arms.

"Overwhelmingly informative?"

"Sure, let's go with that," Trip reluctantly agreed.

"You couldn't call? E-mail? I know this is old school, but there's this weird system old people have where they write on paper, put it in another folded piece of paper, and stamp it. Rumor has it, the correspondence reaches its intended destination.

"I'm just saying, as romantic as a midnight rendezvous with the boyfriend is, it's also going to zombify me tomorrow at school. So, what's up?"

"First, this." He bent his head and placed his mouth against mine. Leaning into him, I let go of the tension I held onto. I lost myself in the kiss, in his skin against mine. He moaned, and I kissed him harder, pressing my body to his. I ran my hand down his arm, over his stomach. Not wanting to push anything further, I stopped for air. We both blushed bright red.

"That was nice," Trip said, brushing a piece of hair from my face.

"All our kisses feel nice," I said. Trip grinned.

"I feel the same way, too." He furrowed his brow and bit his lip before saying, "I know a lot is going on right now, but—" He looked away from me.

"But what?" He clenched his jaw, and his Adam's apple bobbed.

He shook his head. "Never mind. It's not important."

"So, what did you come over for?"

"I wanted to apologize for unloading on you like that last night. It wasn't how you should have found out, from Cay's big mouth," he mumbled, kicking the hard dirt in front of him.

"It's okay. I guess eventually I would have found out."

"Yeah, but... still."

"Wait a minute, are you jealous you didn't get to tell me?" I nearly laughed as I crossed and leaned back slightly.

"What? No." He averted his eyes and shook his head.

"Oh my goodness, you are! Trip," I took in his hand in mine, "there's nothing to be jealous about. If anything, you dodged a bullet. Cay came today to drop off my homework and convince me to join the search, but Mom chewed him out before he made his case."

"Cay's so stupid."

I shrugged. "True, but apparently, he's my family. Also, I tried my powers today. On purpose!"

"Yeah?"

"Yeah. I was able to make a small but warm wind." I grinned. Trip scooped me up into a tight bear-hug.

"I'm so proud of you! I knew you could do it!" He released me. "How'd you do it?"

I shrugged. "I don't know. I thought of summer warmth and bam! I was caressed by a breeze."

"Okay, now I'm jealous. I want to be the one caressing you." He smiled wickedly.

I playfully pushed him. "I wish I could pinpoint how I did it."

"Don't worry. I'm sure you'll figure it out."

"Yeah. I hope so." I stifled a yawn.

"Sweetheart, you need to sleep." He pulled me close, kissed and hugged me, and sent me back through my window.

"I'll see you tomorrow," I whispered from my room.

"Good night."

I closed my window and snuggled into bed, hoping to play out what else Trip and I could have been doing beyond kissing.

"We've been to Germany, Ireland, Scoti, the Dano-Norwegian Kingdom, even our own home. Nothing was found!" I cried as I collapsed into a chair.

"You can't give up, little sister," Lugh said, perched on my bed. "The Amulet is here somewhere."

"Where? We've traveled the world! Scoured beneath the filth dwelling on our lands and have come back empty-handed," I pouted. "And look outside!" I gestured toward the window where the wind blew furiously, bending the trees backward and breaking waves against the rocks on the shore. "I can't stop this madness without the help of the Amulet."

Lugh sighed. "You need to calm down. You know this tantrum of yours won't help settle the storm."

"Staying calm won't do a thing for me! I can't control this alone." The wind whistled loudly in my ear. I attempted to focus my thoughts on the eye of the storm, the peaceful center, but couldn't sense it.

"See?" I snidely pointed out.

"Enough. There are two of you who have this power," Lugh said. "Perhaps if you and Beira reunited, the weather would settle."

"How can I reunite with someone who stole the one thing to end this muddled mess?" I launched myself from the chair and started combing my hair. My mother had always done it to help me find peace as a small child.

"I'm not saying you two should be the best of friends again," Lugh explained, walking behind me. "But if you two came to ... an understanding. The world would be right again."

My muscles relaxed as the tension melted away. Perhaps Lugh was right. Playing nicely with my sister shouldn't be too difficult, especially for the greater good.

"Maybe," I responded, but Beira's accusation crept into my mind. I shook my head. I refused to believe our older brother had stolen my necklace. Why would he be searching for it with me if he'd had it all along?

"Maybe he's distracting you from the fact that he's the real culprit..." Beira's voice whispered at me from the shadows of my mind. "What better way to throw you off his scent..."

Hoping to dispel the feeling slithering down my back, I shuttered at the suggestion. I slammed my comb on my table.

"I'm not working with Beira. She's evil and a thief. I'll find it by myself, and I'll be the one who controls the weather," I announced to Lugh. Thunder boomed, and lightning flashed across the sky. The wind howled against the castle walls.

"Whatever you say, little sister," Lugh said. "But if you can't fix it, don't say I didn't warn you."

"No!" I shot out of bed, gasping for air. I shivered at the lingering whispers of Lugh's voice. I didn't want to believe he'd be so underhanded as to steal something from his own flesh and blood. But then again, Beira was Brighde's blood as well, so what did that say about her? Rubbing my shoulders, I couldn't shake the impending feeling of deceit and betrayal. According to the alarm clock on my floor, it was only 3:22 a.m. Crap. I'd only been asleep for three and a half hours since seeing Trip. I replayed my dream again, not by choice. My legs were tired from the countless hours searching across the world, and my face was slick with sweat. When I'd had these dreams before, it was like something I'd imagined from bits and pieces of my subconscious. Now, knowing about my family, they felt more like clues. I understood Brighde's desperation to find the necklace; it was something slowly building inside me. I looked around my room, seeing it blanketed in the silver light.

I wanted some connection to my distant relatives; I took out the necklace Mom had given me the night before the first day of school, the one rumored to be a love token for my great-grandmother, Una. The white swirls gleamed in the moonlight, the red blazing in my hand. I rubbed my thumb over the shiny top of the stones. If Andrew had given this to Una, where had he gotten it from? Could it have been more than a simple necklace? The yellow stone seemed to wink at me, confirming the answer to a shared secret. Replacing the necklace back in the box, I got back into bed. If I was right that one half of the Amulet was sitting in my room right now, there were a lot of people who would kill for this information.

Sleep didn't come easy for the rest of the night. I tossed and turned and flinched at every squeak from the house settling or every tap from the trees on my window. By the time six o'clock rolled around, I looked and felt worse than death. In those hours of insomnia, I had decided to keep my dreams and the necklace a secret for now. My suspicions wouldn't help anyone; it only dragged the fighting out even longer, increasing the possibility of danger for everyone, including me.

Chewing on my salad at lunch, I half-paid attention to what my friends talked about. Cole joined our little group, sitting between Deidra and me. I moved my tray to give him room. He smiled at me and took a bite of his pizza.

"I give up!" Trip said, slamming his math book shut. "Trig will never help me in the real world, and I don't care what Mrs. Harding says!" He took a huge bite of his hamburger. Looks like someone else hadn't slept well last night. I rubbed his knee.

"Math isn't the easiest for most people. Just ask for help or get a tutor," I suggested.

"Maybe," he muttered through beef and bun.

"Okay, new topic," said Deidra. "I hear this school has a Halloween dance. What's everyone going as?"

"I thought about being a water nymph," Annabelle answered. "I could wear a blue dress with wings and have shimmery fabric over my skirt." Folklore was always something Annabelle had liked. She studied the history and their myths for as long as I've known her. A lot of her art was inspired by Greek mythology.

"Not bad," I commented. "I like it." She smiled at my approval.

"What about you?" Deidra asked me.

"Oh, I didn't plan anything this year."

"Why not?"

"Honestly, I haven't had the chance. I don't know, maybe I'll go as a nymph with Annabelle." She brightened at the idea.

"Yeah! We could go as two water nymphs, or you could be a flower fairy, and I could be a mud sprite!"

I chuckled at her. "I'll consider it."

"I thought you and Trip would be themed," Bri chimed in.

"We haven't really talked about it," Trip replied. We looked at one another.

"We could go as a devil and an angel?" I offered.

"Lame!" Bri said. "It's your first Halloween together. Be something fun, not redundant."

"Okay, fine. We'll think of something better," I told her.

"Thank you. Also, no Sonny and Cher, no Romeo and Juliet. Everyone has been there and done that."

"Noted." We dumped our food as the bell rang, ending the lunch period and the conversation.

"Hey," Trip said as we headed to class. "Want to hang out after school?"

I sighed. "I'd love that, but I can't. Not only do I have to catch up on a ton of schoolwork, but also I need to rest. After our midnight make-out session, I didn't really sleep."

"I'm sorry about that," he apologized. I intertwined my hand with his and squeezed gently.

"It's okay, I promise. Minus the whole potential-sociopathic-killer thing, it was kind of badass sneaking out of my house to make out with my boyfriend." He grinned at my remark.

"Should we do that again?"

"Yes. In the summer when it's not so damn cold!" He clucked his tongue.

"You know," his voice dropped low, "you could warm yourself up. Being practically made of sun has its advantages."

"I don't know how," I whined. "Not all of us were privy to certain knowledge since they were drooling in diapers."

"How about this weekend we go onto the reservation you told me about and play around a little? I'll help you learn how to control your powers."

"The Tuckahoe-Corbin City Fish and Wildlife Management Area?" I smiled. "Sure. You know, no one ever answered my question about how I'd even summon them."

"I think I know how you did it," he said with a twinkle in his eye.

"Okay, go on."

"Isn't it obvious?"

"No." We reached my classroom and stood outside the door, having another two minutes before class started. Trip gave me a quick kiss. It surprised and excited me as lightning sizzled in the air. I flinched at the spark in front my face, expecting it to burn me. Matthew Smith came down the hall, and I prayed he didn't see. Clearly, it had been more than just static shock.

Ignoring everything around us, Trip kissed me again and lingered for a bit. This time, the heat in the hall rose as the sun streamed brightly through the windows.

"Do you get it now?" Trip asked. I bit my lip and shook my head.

"Your emotions," he said with a wink.

"So if I control my feelings, I can control my powers?"

"Yup." He leaned in for another kiss, but I held him off.

"Go to class before I set a tree on fire," I said with a smile. Trip kissed me before I could protest again. Thankfully, I saw it coming, so I was prepared to stop the butterflies from causing a commotion.

"See you later." My heart jumped a beat, and the bell rang. I was officially late for class.

Thursday and Friday dragged on and on, with homework piling on in preparation for midterms. It left me no time to work on my powers. At this rate, I'd never learn to control anything. The final bell rang on Friday, and I sprinted to my locker.

"Hey, want to hang out tonight?" Cay asked behind me.

"I'm not allowed, remember?" I didn't even look at him.

"So don't tell your mom."

"I can't not tell her." I shoved two books in my bag and closed the locker, hearing it click.

"Then tell her you're hanging out with Annabelle. Please?" He followed me down the hallway and out into the bitter air. Colored leaves lay on the ground, giving the football field the appearance of a patch-work quilt.

"I'm not going to lie to hang out with you," I said, facing him. "You need to realize this is not my fault. You're the one who pushed the issue, not only with me but also with my mother. Now you're the one who has to deal with the consequences."

"I only did that—"

"For your own interest! Don't twist the truth, Cay. At least be honest with yourself."

"Fine. I'm sorry! Is there any way you could get your mom to say yes to seeing me again?"

I sighed. "Give it a few more days, and I'll see what I can do, okay? Until then, I'd back off."

"Deal." Cay saluted me and went to join Logan, Hilary, and Noelle to watch Cory's football practice.

Chapter
❧ 15 ❧

Saturday morning rolled around, and I leaped out my bed. I crammed all my weekend homework, plus makeup work, into Friday night, so I had freedom to work on my powers. I danced around my room while getting ready when my gaze fell on my jewelry box. My necklace, potentially one half of the Amulet, hung in there, threatening my family's safety. Excitement left my body. My phone rang from under my covers. A text from Trip.

[Trip: Eat light today. I'll bring snacks. You don't want to practice on full stomach.]

[Bridget: There goes the continental breakfast I had planned.]

I was too nervous and excited to eat. I finished getting dressed, grabbed a granola bar, and left to meet Trip on the Wildlife Reservation.

"Hey, you," Trip greeted me with a smile. He was dressed in jeans, a shirt, and a thick hoodie. A black canvas bag sat by a tree trunk behind him. "You ready?" The sun hid behind clouds, casting a gray darkness over the earth. A consistent wind, smelling of pine and wet leaves, blew my hair around my face.

"I guess. What should we do first?"

"Stretch."

"Um, okay." I lifted my arm over my head and pulled as Trip laughed.

"No! Not your body, your mind." He sat on the forest floor, closed his eyes, and took a deep breath. "Follow me. Empty your mind."

"How is this going to help me?" I plopped down in the dirt, feeling the dampness through my pants.

"If we don't dig deep into your inner subconscious, you'll never tap into your power."

I took a steadying breath and let it go. *Erase your mind; let nothing in but the sound of your own breathing.*

We sat like that for a few minutes. There were no other noises besides the whistle of the wind and sporadic chittering from the animals in the trees. The road was too far away to hear any cars. We weren't close to the riverbed, but the wet slap of the waves was carried to us each time a gust blew through.

I tried to keep my breath paced, but I was cold and slightly shivering from the wetness of the ground mixed with the cool air around us.

Trip opened his eyes and let out a sigh. "It's not working, is it?" I shook my head. "I see we have to start from the beginning."

"The key to controlling your powers is to know where they stem from," he continued. "I can harness mine because it's tied to my inner thoughts. Heads up, if I'm having scary dreams, prepare for a snowstorm." I nodded.

"With you, if I'm right, your powers come from your emotions. Think about how you've been feeling recently and what's happened."

I thought back to all the weird weather we've had: the turbulent winds at my picnic, the blazing hot days, the frequent thunderstorms. Most of these things happened when I was upset or scared or excited. The night the truth had been revealed to me, I practically drowned the entire town. And whenever I thought of Trip, I blushed and the sun burned hotter than ever.

Frowning, I asked, "Okay. How do I fix this?"

"It's not going to be easy, but you'll get the hang of it. Keep that in mind."

"Patience isn't a virtue of mine."

He smiled. "You'll learn some, or you'll never have full control over your powers. Now, close your eyes and try to clear your mind, letting whatever happens happen."

I tried allowing my mind to go blank. No success. At first, I got distracted, allowing the animals' chirps and chattering into my brain. I tried again, blocking out all noise but the drumming of my heartbeat. Nothing happened. I slumped over and put my head in my hands. Thunder boomed above me, signaling my frustration. Sitting up and resting my hands on my knees, I rolled my shoulders and forced myself to chill out. After several moments of pure concentration, it got easier, and the thunder dissipated. Ribbons of purples and blues swam through the seas of my black mind, permitting me to delve deep into my subconscious. I pushed through the colored streams and found myself floating in a sea of hazy red. It was silent as a stone on this level. I didn't even hear the sound of my breathing. I dove into the redness, swimming down further and further, crossing through greens and oranges, shapes and abstractions. I hit a pink flower that morphed into a brown, muddy cloud. Ignoring the oddities of my mind, I kept moving. Finally, I stopped in a yellow field. There was a sense of calm, the kind kids have before they grow up, knowing nothing but happiness and serenity. I smiled, peaceful. I was drawn up through the levels of my mind, retracing my steps, crossing through the rainbow of my subconsciousness. The blood rushed to my ears, and I was bombarded with the sounds of the forest again. I sat still, catching my breath.

"Are you okay?" Trip whispered. I nodded slowly.

"You can open your eyes." When I looked around me, the sun was out, shining brighter than before with gentle warmth beaming from it. The dark clouds were replaced with white ones, and the breeze was soft and comforting.

"Did I do that?"

Trip nodded and smiled encouragingly. "Yes! That's all your doing."

"I feel so ... at ease with everything. Just calm."

He nodded again, his smile widening. "It's that simple. Now that we're sure your powers lie within your emotions, let's take them for a test drive. Think of something that makes you really happy."

Instantly, my mind flew to the memory of my dad and me fishing in the Tuckahoe River for the first time when I was five years old. The blue dingy rowboat we always used floated in the middle of the water. Dad in a white t-shirt, plaid shorts, and boat shoes, me wearing my rainbow zebra-print one-piece. I was covered in a thick layer of sunscreen, my father's old college baseball cap, and flip-flops. Mom never wanted to fish, so it was up to me to keep Dad company. Our lines were in the water, waiting for something to bite.

"Dad, is this it? There's nothing else we do to catch the fish?"

"Afraid not, baby girl. You just sit and wait."

I didn't want to tell him I was bored; I wanted something just for us, so I kept my mouth shut and leaned back, letting the sunshine warm my skin.

"Bridget, quick! Look!" My line bobbed. "Grab on!" I wrapped my fingers around the plastic pole as Dad covered my little hands with his. We pulled and pulled, slowly reeling in the small, wriggling fish as it tried to swim from the boat.

"Good job! You caught your first fish: a baby trout." I watched the little guy hanging in the air, gasping for breath.

"Daddy, what do we do with him now?" I felt bad for the fish. I didn't want to see him die.

"Well, he's too small to eat, honey, so we'll cut him loose." Dad maneuvered the hook from the moving mouth and tossed the fish back into the river. He darted below into the murky darkness.

"You did good," Dad said, pulling me into a hug. "You're going to be the best fisherman yet."

"We can't eat the fish."

"No, he was too small."

"None of them."

"Bridget, that's the idea of fishing. Catch them and eat them."

"Daddy, would you want me to be eaten?"

He sighed. "No, I would never want anything bad to happen to you." He pinched my cheek softly.

"Their daddies wouldn't want them eaten."

"Okay. We only fish for fun, not for food." Dad reset the pole and pulled me into his lap. I leaned against him, feeling the pressure from a kiss on the top of my head. I turned my face toward the sun, blissfully happy I was hanging out with my dad.

I felt the same, warm sun on my skin in this moment with Trip as I did with Dad all those years ago. When I opened my eyes, the light was blinding, the heat index rising.

I flinched and covered my face.

"Bridget, you can control this. Think of something else!"

"Like what?"

"Sadness!" I remembered the time the teacher's pet, Nancy Dowton, called me a "cheater, cheater, booger eater" in second grade because I had spelled "planetarium" on our spelling test, and she couldn't. It might not have been the saddest moment in my life, but I'd really been hurt by that, and it was the first thing that came to mind. Immediately, the sun cooled, and the gray clouds were back, dropping rain on us.

"Note to self: be prepared for all weather," joked Trip, wringing out the bottom of his sweatshirt.

"Ha, ha! I'm new at this! I'll get better." I wiped my wet hair off my face.

"I know. Want to give it another try?"

"Sure. What emotion should I tap into now?"

"Something to stop the rain. Embarrassment?"

The night of my first kiss popped into my head. Being thirteen at one of my first co-ed parties without parental supervision had been exciting and a little nerve-racking. I went with Hilary Thompson since she was my best friend and could navigate parties better than me. As we walked in, I saw my crush at the time, Justin, standing by the chips and dip. He worked on the school's literary magazine with me, and I loved working on the layout with him. I tried to look causal as I went to pick up a bottle of water.

"Hi," I said.

"Hey," he nodded back. I opened my water, trying to avoid feeling self-conscious. Hilary then came over to grab some chips.

"Hey, Justin," she purred. I frowned slightly. I knew my friend didn't like Justin the way I did, and I also knew what her purr meant.

He gave her a smile. "Hey yourself." Justin turned so his back was to me and grabbed a napkin. "Here. For when your hands get greasy," he offered to Hilary. She smiled her flirty smile—the one where she fluttered her eyelashes—and accepted the napkin.

"That's thoughtful of you, Justin. You're like my knight in shining armor."

I gaped at her, fully knowing how this was going to play out.

"Justin," I said, tapping him on the shoulder. "I'm really excited for the next magazine meeting. I have some ideas for the class superlatives."

He faced me and said, "Cool, can't wait to hear them," before turning again to face Hilary. I blushed and moved from the table. Feeling a little bummed

Justin was ignoring me, I took a long sip of my water, not completely sure of what else to do.

"So, do you want to dance?" Justin asked my friend. She grinned and took his hand, leaving me standing alone next to the food. I tried to not watch as they danced *very* closely together but, from a mix of fascination and disappointment, couldn't look away.

Suddenly, Dan Zachariah suggested we all play spin the bottle. Everyone squished next to one another, grabbing a spot around the table. I noticed Hilary didn't sit next to me, and neither did Justin. When it was Justin's turn, he grinned at the bottle and closed his eyes, like he was praying for it to stop at just the right time. The bottleneck landed on me. I blushed but was secretly thrilled he was going to kiss me. Justin didn't look unhappy it was me, but it was clear he was hoping for someone else. He leaned in, closing the gap between us. I closed my eyes, anticipating his lips touching mine. I smelled his cologne, a little vanilla combined with a hint of spice. It was a pleasant smell until it tickled my nose, and I sneezed all over him before I could catch myself.

"Gross! I'm covered in snot!" My eyes flew open, and my hands covered my nose and mouth. Some guys laughed at me, but most of the kids were grossed out. I heard gagging and a small chorus of "Ew!" as I leaped up and left, holding back tears the entire time.

The rain slowed down, but the clouds didn't disappear. They darkened until the sunny skies were tarnished by the blackness. Fog hung thick around us. I reached out and grabbed Trip's hand, somewhat afraid I'd lose him in this weather.

"Try relief," he suggested. Instantly, a soft wind blew the clouds apart and tore through the dense fog. Trip appeared in front of me, still grasping my hand.

"Not bad, newbie. You're doing good. How do you feel?"

"Tired. It's taking a lot of my energy to control all this." I yawned, as if to prove my point.

"Aw, poor thing. Want to take a break and have some lunch?"

My stomach gurgled. "Yes," I replied, laughing.

"First, I'm doing something about this," he said, waving his hands around. The weather had become a hodgepodge of heat, fog, silver clouds, wind, and dampness. Gazing at me, Trip concentrated. Instantaneously, the air cleared, and the sun came out, but the cold was still there.

"Show off," I shivered.

"Sorry. I only make things colder. Such is my luck."

"Don't worry. I know how we can heat things up." I grinned and shifted myself, so I was snuggling into his coat. He embraced me, hugging me close to his body.

"I like the way you think, MacNamara," Trip whispered in my ear.

"Mm-hmm. Feed me now, get kisses later," I purred back. He chuckled and reached behind him for the bag full of snacks.

We ate and practiced for the rest of the afternoon. I wasn't even close to master level yet, but I had started to understand how to control my emotions and my powers. Trip left me with homework.

"Pick one emotion a day and strengthen the power going with it. Learn to make it bigger and smaller. Play with it."

I couldn't after the day I'd just had, but I looked forward to it more than my regular human homework. I texted my girls, but no one was available to hang out. Exhilarated from my day, I called Cole that night after dinner. I didn't want to spend the night at home.

"Hey! What are you up to tonight?" I asked as soon as he picked up.

"Hi and nothing. Just finishing some calculus." I imagined Cole sitting at his very organized desk, his notebook open, filled with numbers and equations.

"Come out with me," I said.

"To do what?"

"I don't know," I whined a little, feeling restless. "Coffee, movie, ice cream?"

"It's too cold for ice cream," he pointed out. I scrunched my nose. It was the middle of October, after all.

"Fine, hot chocolate." He didn't respond right away.

"Come on! You can finish your work tomorrow!" I pressed him. He sighed.

"Hot chocolate does sound tasty right now."

"With whipped cream," I sang lightly into the phone.

"Sorry, but I can't," he apologized.

"Boo! Okay, I'll see you on Monday?"

"Absolutely."

"Bye." Well, now I wanted hot chocolate. Wandering through the kitchen, I discovered we were out.

"I'll be back!" I called to my parents as I left the house.

I drove to the grocery store and popped inside. Grabbing my hot chocolate, I wandered the aisles a little before getting to the marshmallows. I felt a little creative and wanted to flavor my hot cocoa, something besides peppermint. Turning down the candy aisle, I nearly ran over Deidra... and Cole.

"Hi," I said brightly. Deidra smiled and gave me a hug while Cole looked very uncomfortable.

"Hey! What are you doing here?" she asked me. I held up my basket, showing her my items.

"In the mood for some hot chocolate, but we were out. What about you two?" I looked pointedly at Cole, but he avoided my stare. I didn't understand why he didn't tell me he was hanging with Dee.

"Snack run. Cole and I couldn't decide what movie to go see, so we decided to stream one instead. The family's out, so we're watching it at my house."

"Some free time from the family. I get it," I smiled.

"I spend enough time with everyone as it is," Deidra said, a little tired.

"It's cool. I get it."

"Oh! We forgot ... chips," Cole said quickly. "Be right back!" He darted out of the aisle. Deidra looked confused by his sudden disappearance.

"I didn't know you and Cole hung out outside of school," I said.

She grinned. "Since the dance, Cole and I have been spending a lot of time together. He comes over after school sometimes, or I'll go to his house." She paused. "I really like him."

"That's sweet! I wonder why Trip didn't tell me," I mused out loud.

"Probably because he's still dealing with how you're handling the—" she lowered her voice, "news."

"Oh. Well, I'm already working on my powers, so I would say I'm handling it okay," I smiled.

"That's awesome!" She hugged me again. "I'm so happy you finally know everything."

"Me too!" I hugged her back. "I'm also happy you and Cole are together. He's such a good person. One of my favorite people."

Deidra smiled. "He is."

"Well, I have to get going. Have fun tonight!" I said.

Leaving Deidra in the aisle, I headed over toward the popcorn, wanting to balance the sweet and savory.

"Hey!" Cole said from behind me. I jumped, not expecting him there.

"Is calculus code for 'I have a date with Deidra?'" I asked, playfully pushing him.

"It's not like that."

"Liar." I crossed my arms.

"I did have calc!" he protested.

"Uh-huh. Last night. And tonight is what? Biology? Oh no, wait! Chemistry!" I bent to pick up the popcorn kernels and some cheddar cheese powder.

"That was lame."

"But true. I don't understand why you didn't tell me you had a date tonight," I replied. "I wouldn't have minded."

"I know, but I haven't told anyone, really."

"Why not?"

He shrugged. "You've been busy with Trip, so when would I get the chance?"

He'd gotten me there.

"Fine, you win," I sighed. "But let's not keep anything from each other anymore. Especially big life events." *Well, all but one big life event,* I thought. "I love you two together."

"Sure," he said as he smiled. "I really like her."

I grinned back. "See you later!"

He waved goodbye and left. I waited about six seconds for him to leave before I texted Trip.

[Bridget: Why didn't you tell me Cole and Dee are dating!]

[Trip: I thought you knew.]

I rolled my eyes.

[Bridget: How was I to know when lately all we've done is share family secrets and work on my powers?]

[Trip: Are you saying you want to do more than that?]

I frowned. Was I saying that?

[Bridget: Yes.]

He didn't text back. A few minutes later as I headed to my car with my bag, my phone chirped.

[Trip: Stay tuned.]

Chapter
16

The week flew by so fast; I blinked, and it was already Thursday. By the time I dragged myself to English, I was desperately bored of school.

"Okay, class, now that we've finished our final discussion on Dante's *Inferno*, it's time for the dreaded mid-marking period test," Miss Montgomery told a chorus of groans and whines. "The test will be this Tuesday, so you have the weekend to study. Monday is a review session, so over the weekend I want you to come up with questions that could be on the test."

The shrill bell rang out. "Class dismissed!"

I packed my belongings, not rushing. Today was a lazy day for me. I spent last night practicing my powers and no matter what—even with a full night's sleep or coffee—I had a hard time getting the hang of it. If I didn't need to be in school, I would have stayed home today in pajamas to nap.

When I reached my car, Cay leaned against the driver's side.

"Off my car," I commanded.

"Aw, but it's so comfy here," he responded, moving away from the door.

"Are you here for the English homework?" I unlocked my door.

"Nope. I'll just copy yours."

"No, you won't. Test next week." An icy breeze from the ocean blew past us, and I shivered. I looked to see if Trip or his siblings were nearby, but I didn't see a Findlay anywhere.

"You know, you don't have to shiver," Cay pointed out.

"Because of my awesome powers?" I replied, opening my door and throwing my bag onto the passenger's side.

"Yes. Because you can use your powers to bring up your body temperature."

I didn't reply.

"I can help with that."

"Thanks, but Trip is already helping me."

Cay tensed a bit, but I didn't care. Trip was my boyfriend. "You know, you shouldn't be taking lessons from him."

"Why not?" It was my turn to rest my arm on top of the door.

"Because, he's the enemy. And if he learns your secrets, he can use them against you."

"He's your enemy, not mine," I responded. Cay took this whole rivalry thing way too seriously. "And he's been helping me control my powers."

I scanned the parking lot for any other students and teachers still hanging around. Even though no one knew what we were talking about, I couldn't take chances.

"I can help."

"So you've said."

"I can show you how to warm yourself up."

"That's easy. Run in place."

Cay rolled his eyes at me. "Or use your powers. Come on, let me help you!"

"Why are you so intent on spending time with me?"

"We're family. Family should help family." He shifted his book bag on his shoulder.

"I haven't decided if I'm trying to find the Amulet yet."

"You have to! Bridget, do I have to explain to you again how—"

"No! I get it, but this is my life, and I make my own decisions. Now, I'm going home." I sat, starting to close my door.

"Wait," Cay said, pulling on it. "I'm sorry. I'll give you space, even though it's becoming a pressing issue... Are you having a hard time with your powers?"

I looked at him, narrowing my eyes. "What do you mean?"

"Are you tired a lot more lately after you've used them?"

"How did you know that?" I asked, folding my arms over my chest.

"It happens every fall. You're turning to stone."

I raised an eyebrow. "Come again?"

He rolled his eyes again. That little habit was really getting on my last nerve. "It's symbolic. When Brighde's time of reign was over, she would turn to metaphorical stone as Beira took over the winter. For us—more specifically, you—our powers become a little weak instead."

"Oh." I frowned. "Is that why I can't call up my powers as easily?"

Cay nodded. "More or less, yeah." I stayed quiet while I considered it.

"Let me guess. Lover boy didn't mention that piece of info to you, did he?" He smirked.

"Don't be so smug. I'm sure Trip would have told me at some point."

"What would I have told you?" Trip asked. I jumped from the car to see my boyfriend standing on the passenger side of my car.

"That my powers are a little crazy because it's fall." All the good humor on Cay's face erased, replaced by irritation.

"Were you even going to tell her?" Cay demanded.

"Cay, don't," I warned him. Trip walked around the car and took a place next to me.

"Why would I hide it from her?"

"Because you want to keep her in the dark. Help your own family out trying to find the pieces. We both know she's your biggest competition."

Trip stepped forward, getting close to Cay. I closed my door and moved away from my car. I had this dark feeling that if I didn't, I'd end up bruised.

"I also know I'd never lie to her."

"What about keeping stuff from her?" Cay took a step closer to Trip, getting right up in his face. Trip didn't flinch.

"Never."

"Liar. I told her about her destiny. You couldn't even man up to do that."

"You only told her so she would join your ranks."

"She needed to know."

"Selfish bastard."

Before I blinked, Cay swung his fist. It connected with Trip's jaw with a sick *thwack*, and he stumbled back into my car.

"Stop it!" I screamed. I jumped in front of Cay and shoved him. "What the hell is wrong with you?"

"Get up! Come on! Fight me!" Cay shouted at Trip around me.

I pushed Cay back again. "Leave. Just go. Get out of here!" He didn't move, but hatred burned in his eyes as he glared at Trip.

"Go before I do something to you," I yelled, pointing toward his neighborhood. The light gray sky darkened, and pellets of hail rained down on us.

"Trip, stop," I pleaded, facing him. Ignoring my presence, Cay advanced toward a bleeding Trip. Continuing to bombard the parking lot with hail the size of ping-pong balls, Trip wiped the blood from his split lip and pushed himself off the car. I didn't know what to do. Helpless, I watched Cay get nailed with ice. Neither boy listened to me. Trip curled his fingers into a fist and stomped in Cay's direction. Remembering my training, I tapped into my anger and frustration. The hail stopped as thunder growled above us, and strong winds pushed the boys apart. Trip was pinned to my car as Cay struggled against the tennis court fence. Seeing some phones held up in our direction, I released them immediately. I just hoped no one had been able to catch the beginning of that.

"Enough!" I ordered, quietly. "I'm sick of this fighting. Cay, I'm done with you. Family or not, I will not stand for this violence."

"Get used to it," he warned.

Cay straightened his jacket and walked away, limping slightly. I saw my betrayal marking his every move. Cay had hurt me badly, but it was clear I'd hurt him worse.

"And you," I said to Trip. "You need to get in my car like this was a normal fight. There's a good chance some of this was caught on video."

I took a tissue from my pocket and put it on his lip, wiping some of the dried blood. "Let's get some ice on your face. Where are Deidra and Roden?"

"Dee stayed after for some club, and Tomas took Roden home," he replied, never taking his eyes from the fading silhouette of Cay.

"Good. Let's go." We climbed into my car. I caught some kids still watching us as we left the parking lot.

CHAPTER
❧ 17 ❧

"Ow!" Trip flinched as I placed a pack of frozen peas on his face.

"Stop moving! You won't feel the cold as much because of the towel." I sat in a kitchen chair. "This is your own fault, you know."

"Mine! How? He sucker-punched me!" Trip collapsed into a chair next to me.

"You didn't have to egg him on. Cay was itching to punch you, and you gave him a reason."

"So you're saying I deserve this swollen jaw? Unbelievable."

"No, I didn't say that, but you didn't make the situation any better." I leaned forward.

"This fight between our families is getting more and more dangerous."

"I know."

"You could end it," I urged him. He pulled the peas away from his face and winced. I saw exactly how red and swollen he was.

"Bridget, this is never going to end. Even when one family finds the Amulet, what makes you think the other family won't try to steal it and gain control?"

That thought never occurred to me. What did I expect? That everyone would just accept the outcome and get on with their lives?

Trip continued. "You want me to try to end over three hundred years of fighting? Do you really think that could happen?"

"It could," I said, leaning back in my chair.

"I highly doubt it." He placed the peas on his face again.

"It could," I said, my determination flourishing. "Who's to say that if our generation gives up this stupid feud, it wouldn't end? If we teach the future kids of the families to be at peace, it would be over!" I laid my hand on the table.

"Bridget," Trip said, covering my hand with his, "that's never going to happen." His tone brimmed with sympathy like I was stupid.

"Think of the out-of-control weather we're having. If you don't end this fighting, everyone will suffer and pay for your stubbornness. You're not willing to even consider this idea?"

"I considered it, but it's an idea, nothing else." He patted my hand as a sign of comfort. I pulled it back.

"Stop that."

"What?"

"Don't patronize me. Just go home." Trip sat forward as I stood.

"No! I wasn't trying to—" I took the peas and the towel from him. "I'm trying to make you see it wouldn't work!" He exclaimed. "You're talking about taking on hundreds of years of bitter hatred and in less than a year, fixing all that? Changing stubborn attitudes? It wouldn't work!" He winced.

"And that means we shouldn't try?"

He got up to face me and put his hands up. His jaw was puffy and bright red. Cay had really done a number on him.

"Listen, I get what you're saying, but please be reasonable. Think about it."

"Fine, but I still want you to leave." I folded my arms over my chest.

"Come on, Bridget. I don't want to fight about this anymore." He wrapped his hands around my arms, pulling me toward him for a hug, careful to keep his jaw out of the way.

"Stop." I brushed him off me and walked to the kitchen sink. "Just go."

He left without another word.

CHAPTER 18

"What's going on with Trip?" Bri asked before anyone else had the chance to arrive. Trip and Tomas were sitting with Roden and his friends.

I opened my book bag and pulled out my minuscule lunch. After all the fighting yesterday, my stomach wasn't feeling too well.

"He felt bad about ignoring Roden a bit this past weekend, so he's making up for it," I lied. Normally, I wouldn't hesitate to tell my friends about a regular fight with my boyfriend, but this wasn't even close to normal.

"That's so sweet of him," she gushed. "But are you sure it doesn't have anything to do with his fight with Cay?"

I gulped. "Who told you?"

"Bridget," Bri tilted her head forward and raised her eyebrow, "you really don't understand how technology works?"

My tongue felt like I'd licked sandpaper as my heart beat faster. "What do you mean?"

Bri pulled out her phone and showed me the video. "I can't believe you didn't see this."

The video showed Cay punching Trip and me shoving Cay while yelling at them. It showed the hail appearing.

"What the hell? Is that hail?" The videographer laughed. Thankfully, at the exact moment where I push the guys apart, he brought his phone down to show a cracked car window. Giddiness flooded my system as my heart slowed to its normal pace.

"I don't want to talk about it," I replied as I handed her phone back.

"What?" Bri tilted her head slightly.

I shook my head. "It's not something I'm ready to deal with."

"Deal with what?" Deidra asked as she placed her stuff next to mine.

"Trip and Cay's fight," Bri answered, shooting me a perplexed look. Deidra sighed.

"Yeah, I heard about it," she said, looking at me knowingly. I ignored it.

Bri stared at her expectantly, waiting for details from Dee.

"If you think I'm going to sit here and gossip about my brother, you're out of your mind."

Bri puffed her chest out and looked defeated all in one moment.

"Do you know what you're going as for Halloween yet?" Bri asked Deidra, avoiding a confrontation. I'm glad the question wasn't directed to me. With everything going on lately, I'd completely forgotten the holiday was just two weeks away.

"Not sure. I was thinking the tooth fairy. I have my eighth-grade dress I wore for our school dance. It's pink and girly. I can borrow wings from Elizabeth's costume last year. All I'll need are some fake coins." Deidra opened her lunch and took a bite.

"Sounds great!" Bri said. "I love it! What about you, Bridge?"

"No, nothing. I haven't come up with anything yet," I said.

"Well, if you need help, you can ask me. I'm done with my costume," she said as Cole and Annabelle walked up.

"School is boring today," Annabelle commented. "I'm over it already, and we're barely into the school year." She collapsed heavily into her chair. Cole leaned over and gave Dee a quick kiss. He sat next to her and took out his lunch: a vegetable sandwich, chips, and an apple. Wow. Deidra must have left an impression on our resident carnivore.

"I can totally relate," Deidra said. "I mean, after a while, school is redundant. You've seen one, you've seen them all."

As the conversation at the table became filled with gossip and silliness, I felt increasingly separated from my friends. Here I was, dealing with some huge changes in my life—badass powers, newly revealed family, and fights with my boyfriend—while they discussed costumes and recent breakups among our classmates. None of my best friends had any clue about the biggest secret in my life, and I couldn't tell them a thing. I looked at Trip again, and my heart went out to him. Fighting with him was getting old. His face was still purple and swollen from the punch, but I was sure the fight we'd had hurt more. Deep down, I knew I'd been wrong for yelling at him, but my pride stood in the way of my apology.

"Bridget? Hello?" Cole waved his hand in front of my face.

"Hi, what?" I answered.

"Where did you go just now?"

"Nowhere. I just remembered I have a test to study for, and I'm falling behind. I'm going to the library. I'll see you guys later?" I grabbed my stuff and hurried from the cafeteria without waiting for a response.

One unrecognized bonus of having the entire school eat lunch at the same time was the library always being dead during lunchtime. Our two librarians nodded to me as I walked in, but they left me alone, seeing as I was one of three students in the whole room. I hunkered down by the literary criticism books, one section guaranteed to be empty. Pulling out a random notebook to make it look like I was working, I leaned back against the shelves. Being a senior was exhausting. School got more intense with work. The seniors last year had made classes look and sound like a breeze, but I was under a lot of stress with the workload. Plus, college applications needed to be started to get them in by their January deadlines. On top of that, I had an added bonus: the personal homework of learning to harness my powers. If what Cay said about the stone phase was true, I could theoretically take winter off. Why bother practicing full throttle when it was just going to zap all my energy anyway? Maybe I could use the downtime for catching up on real life, like my schoolwork, friends, and family. The last time Mom and I had gone shopping felt like a lifetime ago, and I couldn't remember the last time Dad and I went fishing. It seems I'd been spending more time with Trip than anyone else.

Trip, my illustrious boyfriend.

He seemed to appear from thin air and shake up my life in ways I couldn't even fathom. It felt like the whole school buzzed with his arrival, from my friends to the new branch of my family tree. Knowing what I know now, Trip's sudden entrance felt more like a calculated arrival than a regular, old job transfer. I sensed more to this idea but couldn't hold onto it.

Sighing, I closed my notebook and slid it back into my bag. Lunch was almost over, and I wasn't one step closer to the answers I reached for. Heading out of the library, I ran into a group of kids walking the halls. They laughed over something someone said, and I envied them for their carefree attitude. The bell rang, and the moment passed. I shook my head. I was too young to feel like this! Every person went through rough patches with their significant others, and I couldn't name one student in this school who never felt crushed by the amount of homework assigned. Plus, who else got to discover they are secretly related to one of the most popular guys in school and have incredible weather-controlling superpowers from their ancestor, a Scottish goddess? No one else I could think of. And just like that, I felt better.

Friday night was the best night of the week for all teenagers. It meant sleeping late the next morning, no school, and total freedom.

All teenagers, except me. Not only was I not enjoying my Friday night the way a normal seventeen-year-old would, but also I did it with increasing frustration. I was trying to finish all my other weekend homework so I could focus my attention on studying for English, but at six o'clock, Mom called me in tears. Belinda, her assistant baker, had gone into early labor and couldn't finish the wedding cake Mom had been making for a customer. In the whole process of rushing Belinda to the hospital, some moronic emergency technician knocked the half-iced cake on the floor and rolled a gurney over it. So at nine o'clock at night, I was dressed in jeans and a flour and fondant-covered t-shirt, helping Mom re-bake and decorate the wedding cakes instead of being out like a normal teenager.

"What time does this have to be ready by again?" I asked as I poured sugar into the mixer for the fillings.

She sighed and rubbed her nose with the back of her hand, smearing batter on the bridge. "It has to be baked and decorated by nine o'clock so Matt and Chris can pick it up and deliver it to Egg Harbor by ten."

"I thought I wouldn't have to pull an all-nighter until at least college." I poured myself a cup of coffee and took a huge bite of a carrot cupcake as the mixer spun.

"Well, I'm training you early. Can you hand me that spatula?" Mom asked. In the two and a half hours since we'd been here, Mom and I had baked the four tiers of cake for the main piece plus a smaller, two-tier cake for the groom. Belinda had only been able to mix the batter of that cake before her water broke. Why did a groom need a cake all for himself anyway? Isn't the regular wedding cake big enough for, like, four hundred guests? The cakes were odd, too. The bride's cake was an orange chiffon filled with lemon buttercream frosting and white fondant with fall leaves made of sugar adorning each tier. The groom's cake, on the other hand, was a chocolate cake with a blood orange filling decorated with lime fondant and mummy caricatures trick-or-treating at a witch's house. Both cakes required more than twelve hours, but Mom and I had no other choice but to pull it off.

"Mom, if you're an amazing gardener, how did you get into the baking business? I mean, why wouldn't you own a nursery?"

"I never told you?"

I shook my head. Turning my mixer off, I stuck a spoon into the frosting and tasted it. The lemon stuff tasted pretty good. I pulled the bowl off the stand and filled the bottom tier of the bridal cake.

"Gardening didn't interest me. Ironic, I know. When I was in high school, we had to take a mandated home economics class. I wasn't very good at sewing, but the cooking part always came easy. When I graduated high school, I thought I'd be a chef. I even majored in culinary arts, but after taking the basic baking class, I was hooked and changed majors." She helped place the next layer of cake on top of the frosting.

"That's really cool. Did you always want to own your own bakery?"

"Not really. I thought I'd work in some high-end hotel or restaurant, but that lifestyle never suited me. Once I met your father, my priorities changed, and I didn't want to work for someone else."

I downed another gulp of coffee. Mom was the best. She added nutmeg to the grounds.

"Mom, how did you know Dad was the love of your life?" I placed my cup on the desk and went back to work.

"He made me laugh. I always told Grandma I'd marry a man who'd be able to make me laugh." I smiled gently. Listening to Mom talk about Dad made me miss my own boyfriend.

We finished filling the bridal cake and started on the groom's as I thought about Trip. Did he make me laugh? Taking a quick peek at the clock, I saw it was quarter past ten. Trip would most definitely be awake—he didn't fall asleep until eleven most nights—so I went to grab my phone.

"Are you ready for fondant? If we get it on fast enough, we can add the decorations and get home earlier," Mom asked. The promise of sleep enticed me more than texting my boyfriend at this moment. I took a long sip from my coffee cup.

"Okay, I'm ready," I said.

"So how are you handling everything?" asked Mom as we gently laid the green fondant on the groom's cake.

"As well as can be expected, I guess. I mean, finding out I have powers is pretty mind-blowing." We smoothed the fondant, and I trimmed the excess while Mom rolled out the bridal fondant.

"Have you tried using them?"

"Oh, yeah! Trip helped me unlock the secret to tapping into them, and I've been practicing nearly every day."

"I'm glad you're getting used to them." She sighed and stopped rolling. "Bridget, come here for a second."

I put my knife down—I think it used to belong to my Swirl n' Scoop Play-Doh set—and walked over to her.

"I'm sorry, honey, for not being the one to tell you." She draped her arm over my shoulders. "I guess I was hoping if I didn't talk about it, it wouldn't happen. That was silly of me, I suppose."

"No, Mom. I get it. That's the only way you knew to protect me. But now, it will be okay. I know about everything, and I'm working on my powers. I'm getting better with them all the time."

She gave me a sticky hug. "Please, be careful. I couldn't even imagine what I would do without you."

I hugged my mom back tightly. "You don't have to worry. I'm not getting involved."

To her credit, she hid her surprise. "Oh, I just assumed you would," she said, trying to sound nonchalant.

"I know, but I thought of all the stuff I have to do, and hunting for this Amulet isn't worth my effort right now. Especially since my powers are weak from the 'turning to stone' thing."

"What are you talking about?"

"Cay told me." She tensed a little. "Whenever I've been practicing my powers, I'm getting tired faster than before. He said it was because summer was over and that's when I shine, so to speak."

Mom sighed. "He's not wrong, but Bridget, you're tired because you're new at this. I told you. You have the strongest powers since Brighde herself. Plus, you're a Seeker. Changing seasons wouldn't affect you the same way it does him."

"Oh. So the more I flex this muscle, the stronger I'll become?"

"That's the idea." I nodded and walked back to my station. I've got a lot to mull over.

"Mom," I said, "what if I don't want to accept this?"

"Accept what?"

"Everything! The powers, the responsibility, joining the scavenger hunt for the Amulet."

She put her rolling pin down. "Well, I guess you don't have to. But maybe you should."

"Why? You spent my whole life keeping me safe. Now I've been let in on the secret, I have to sign on to be a superhero?"

"Who is telling you that you *have* to be a super-hero? If you don't want to be one, don't be. You're old enough to make that decision."

I wrinkled my nose. I suppose I should have been all excited I had awesome powers and a destiny to save the world. But I just wanted Mom to tell me I didn't have do it. I didn't know if I was ready for this. The Halloween dance was a week away. Shouldn't I be focused on that instead of this impending family war?

"Whatever you decide, I'll be okay with it," Mom said, rolling fondant. "Just keep me in the loop?"

"I will, Mom," I said with more confidence than I felt. "I promise."

CHAPTER
19

"Bridget? Are you home?" Dad called as he walked in the front door the next day. I was sitting on my bed, reading. My body was still weary after my marathon baking session with Mom.

"In my room!" I yelled back.

"Hi, honey." He poked his head in. "How're you doing?"

"Tired. How was working out? Show all those young guys how it's done?"

He smiled. "They were jealous because all the women were drooling for this bod." He flexed his arm and pretended to kiss it.

"Gross, I don't need details. You hungry? I want pizza, and I was waiting for you."

"I'm starving, but I called your mom and talked her into a quick date night at that Italian place. Do you want to come?"

I thought about leaving the house, but eating pizza on the couch sounded better. "Not this time. Thanks, though, for the invite."

"Okay, well, if you change your mind you can always come. I'm going to shower." He walked out of my room. Well, that changed my plans. I was hoping to put off studying for one more night, but it looked like it's what I'd be stuck doing. I closed my book and walked to my desk, preparing myself for a night of quizzical math problems and a journey through the nine circles of hell.

"Bridge? Why don't you invite your friends over for dinner and a little company?" Dad called from his room. I made a sharp turn and headed back to my bed. *Thank you, Dad, for my excuse note.*

"Okay!" I furiously texted my friends. Without missing a beat, both Bri and Annabelle were in. I scrolled through my contacts. Should I invite Deidra? Would it be weird when her brother and I weren't speaking? Well, her parents were out of town, and I bet she was sick of seeing her family. I'm sure she could use a night off. I texted her and went to the kitchen to grab a drink while I waited for my friends to arrive.

"Oh, I love this part." Annabelle grinned as we watched a marathon of comedies while scarfing down pizza, ice cream, and candy. Pure sugar overload. I loved every minute of it.

"Me too!" Bri sighed. I grinned at two of my best friends. Feeling a little better after eating and resting for the day, I was happy for a night in to be a normal, seventeen-year-old girl. I grabbed a couple of Skittles and popped them into my mouth.

"Can we pause it? I need to use the bathroom," Annabelle requested. I froze the screen and she dashed into the bathroom.

"So, do you know what you're going to be yet?" Bri asked me.

"For Halloween?" I took a sip of water. "Not yet. I haven't felt inspired this year."

"What do you need inspiration for? Look around; anything can be a costume."

I shook my head. "Yeah, I know, but I want something I can connect to. Plus, the dance is, like, a week away, and I don't have time to go shopping."

"One, the dance is a whole week away and two, we'll shop in your closet. There has to be something you can use for a costume. What did you and Trip talk about?"

"We... didn't. Just never came up in conversation." I stuffed a spoonful of vanilla ice cream in my mouth.

"Why not?"

I let the ice cream melt in my mouth to give me a chance to come up with a lie. I'd already told Bri I couldn't talk about the fight with Trip and Cay, which was the reason Trip and I were fighting.

"I just keep forgetting to ask him to go," I replied. Bri eyed me.

"Is everything okay with you two?"

I nodded, a little pebble of doubt forming in the bottom of my stomach.

"Totally. With college apps coming up, midterms, and everything else, it just slipped my mind."

Bri frowned and a pinch of worry washed over me.

"Okay," she said. "If you need to talk, you can come to me."

I smiled, grateful she'd accepted my answer. "Thank you."

"Now, didn't you save any costumes from when you were a kid?"

"I think so, but they're in a box either in the basement or in the attic. Not sure anything will fit."

"Hmm, okay. Let's see what you have in your room and go from there." Annabelle walked back into the living room.

"Okay, you can press play," she said.

"Change of plans. We're playing dress up to see what kind of costume Bridget can wear for the dance," Bri said as she pointed her finger to my room. "Move out, soldiers!"

Annabelle gave her a mock salute and followed us to my room.

"What do you have?" Bri flung open my closet door and immediately shifted through the hangers. "Dresses, pants, shirts... What about a hippie?"

She pulled out bootcut jeans and a brown vest with fringe that once belonged to Mom. Bri threw them on the bed, dug around in my shirt drawer in my dresser, and pulled out a tie-dyed t-shirt we each got from our guidance counselor at freshman orientation. Our freshman counselor had been a weirdo. She dyed all the shirts herself and handed them out, claiming we were all made of beautiful colors, and we could be whoever we wanted to be. She left school before we broke for winter break.

"What do you say?" Bri had arranged the clothes into a costume.

I mulled it over. "Eh."

"Eh?"

I shrugged. "Not my thing."

"Okay, fine." She put the t-shirt back.

"How about a Grecian princess?" Annabelle asked as she pulled out a dress I'd worn for Homecoming junior year. The strapless gold and eggplant silk chiffon dress was a personal favorite of mine. I remembered feeling glamorous as Cole and I spun on the floor. The gold design swirled around my bust before it dashed across my shoulder and down my back. Annabelle was right. It did look Grecian.

"I could do that," I said.

"You could," Bri responded as she opened my jewelry box. "But what would you wear with it?"

"Earrings? An armband?" I suggested.

"Oh my god, I've got it!" Bri announced. "You can go as a flapper!"

"Well that was random and unforeseen," I said. "What are you talking about? What happened to the princess idea?"

"We're reading *Tender is the Night* in English. Everyone is going to be a princess, Bridge. The thing about costumes is you have to be original."

"Like no one has ever been a flapper before," Annabelle rolled her eyes. "It's been overdone by everyone." I smiled. I liked the Greek princess idea.

"Oh, it's been done but not by our fabulous Bridget here." Bri dumped my jewelry box on the bed. Earrings, rings, bracelets... and necklaces. The one Mom had given me. The one that could be the Amulet and the harbinger of death and lead to an all-out war between my family and Trip's.

"You have a lot of cool costume jewelry," said Bri. "This ring would match the black fringe dress my mom has in her closet. If your mom has opera gloves, I think you could be the most fashionable flapper yet!"

"I don't know," I answered.

"I think you should do it," Annabelle chimed in.

"You, too?" I said, facing her.

Annabelle shrugged. "You could do your hair in those little waves." I saw Bri's excitement catching on, and I had to stop it before it got any more out of hand.

"I really like the princess idea," I pressed. "I already have most of the pieces for the costume."

"But everyone has seen you in that dress," Bri pointed out. "No one I've talked to has thought of a flapper costume. They all want to be Ms. Marvel or Hermione."

"Yeah and think of how Trip will react when he sees you embodying the pinnacle of women's liberation!" Annabelle grabbed the potential Amulet. "This would be the perfect accessory for the costume!"

The Trip comment needled me more than it should have. I still hadn't talked to him since our fight the other day. It felt like a million years since I'd last seen him. I chewed the inside of my cheek, wishing I could abandon this costume hunt and text him.

"You and Trip could be Bonnie and Clyde!" Bri nearly jumped out of her skin with excitement. I was fighting a losing war.

"Those costumes are always cheesy."

"No, they're not! Why don't you want to be a flapper?"

"The Greek princess has a pretty crown to wear." Oh man, what a lame excuse. I barely believed myself.

"So what? Crowns are so last year. Even Disney has done away with them," Bri said flippantly.

"Yeah, I don't think that's true," said Annabelle. Bri waved her off.

"Not the point. The point is you can wear 1920s clothing. Besides the jewelry and dress, flappers wore garters, high heels, lots of makeup, those head-bands with feathers, come on! I'll be one with you," she offered excitedly.

"I don't know," I wavered. Damn it, this was sounding cooler than the princess. My friend clasped her hands and gave me puppy eyes.

"Fine! But you have to do my makeup," I conceded.

"Yay!" Bri threw her arms around me and hugged me close.

"Is it okay if I'm not a fairy with you?" I asked Annabelle. She nodded as she gazed at the purple dress with a dreamy expression on her face.

"Go ahead," I said to her. "You should be Athena with that dress. You'd look great."

Annabelle brightened at the suggestion. "Really? I'd appreciate it. My fairy costume wasn't working out the way I'd planned."

"Okay, now that we have settled this costume debate, can we get back to the movie marathon?"

"Absolutely!" Bri grinned. Allowing Annabelle and Bri to leave the room before me, I glanced back at the necklace, sitting exposed on my bed. Worry sat at the pit of my stomach, and I quickly stuffed the necklace into my sock drawer, vowing to deal with it later.

Chapter

20

I spent most of my Sunday studying for my *Inferno* test and finishing my other homework, all the while having Trip and the Amulet weighing on the back of my mind. I didn't know what to do with either problem. I was afraid of revealing the Amulet to anyone. What would happen if half the Amulet was discovered in my house? I could only guess. Should my loyalty be with the McKays since we were blood, albeit distant, or should I hand the necklace over to the Findlays, since I felt I could trust them? After all, Trip was still my boyfriend. Not to mention, all Mom and Dad's hard work to keep my powers a secret would be for naught if I started to wave this around. But at the same time, if the necklace presently snuggling with my socks *wasn't* one half of the ancient Amulet, there was nothing for me to worry about. So why did I still feel paranoid?

I picked up my phone and scrolled through some of the Homecoming dance pictures other kids had posted on Instagram. Before the fight—and not to my knowledge—Bri was able to snap a couple of shots of Trip and me slow dancing. I gazed at the photo, remembering how hot his hands felt through the slinky material of my dress. So distracted by his fingertips slowly grazing my waist with every turn we made, I let my arms drape around his neck in a desperate attempt to stay on my feet. Our eyes locked; the only focus was on him, me, and that moment. My heart lurched. Fight or no fight, I missed Trip. I cleared the site away and pulled up his number. Biting my lip, I froze. Did I really want to say what I had to say to him on the phone? I sighed. *No.* I needed to speak with him in person. Looking back at the open books on my desk, I decided my schoolwork had to come first right now. I would find him tomorrow and fix us. This silent treatment was a huge distraction.

I fell asleep clutching my phone with the picture of us at the dance as my lock screen.

"You said you loved me!" my boyfriend growled. "You just don't go changing that in mere seconds!" We were in a palace garden, standing in an alcove of hydrangea bushes.

"I do love you! That hasn't changed, but I can't do this anymore! Constantly worrying about Beira—"

"Beira is dead!" Trip yelled.

"But her descendants aren't!" I cried and shook my head. "Everything has become too much, and something had to give." I reached for his hand, but he yanked it away from me.

"So, I have to go?"

"It's either you or the Amulet!" A sharp pain pierced my chest as those words tumbled out of my mouth.

"That has become more important to you!" His face was red with rage, and my hands trembled. Thunder groaned above us as small snow flurries drifted from above us. I raised an eyebrow. It was summer, yet Trip called upon his power. Lightning flashed behind us, and the sky lit up for one, bright moment.

"No! But right now, the Amulet calls for me. If I can feel it, so can Lugh's line and everyone else in my bloodline. I can't risk you losing your life over the necklace. Please understand," I begged.

"I would give my life for you! You are more important than this piece of cheap jewelry!"

Trip pointed to my half of the Amulet around my neck. I clutched it in my left hand.

"You lie!" I cried. He sneered at me and turned away. "If you can't be truthful with me, then be honest with yourself. I have seen your so-called passing glances at my neck, and when you touch my skin, your touch lingers in the same spot, directly under my necklace."

"Ha!" he barked, never looking at me. I shook my head as the sadness welled up in my eyes. He will never understand the depths of my sorrow over this decision. I fretted over it for days, always coming to the same result, but I couldn't chance losing him and the Amulet.

"I fear your love for me has been muted by your growing attachment to the Amulet." Trip whipped around to look at me, his face hardened and his voice silent after hearing my words. I know deep down he knows I'm right. Hopefully, he will forgive me, but right now, the Amulet needs my undivided attention.

"I will always love you, no matter what happens between our families. But for now, our bond must be

severed." With that, I stepped into the bright moonlight and walked on the grassy pathway lined with purple thistles that led to the castle.

Monday morning, I awoke crying. Tears streamed down my face as I tried to accept my supposed ex-boyfriend's obsession with my necklace. The grief of the dream was so overbearing; my waking heart brimmed with sorrow and pain. Fear constantly threatened my dreams lately; this one was no different from the rest. The choice between my love and my destiny wasn't easy. Why couldn't the dream version of Trip get that? I felt desperate. I wanted to go back to sleep and explain to him I could never choose the Amulet over him, but I had to put his safety first which meant leaving him to find the other half of the Amulet to end the war. Unfortunately, I needed to get to school. I only hoped my real-life conversation with Trip would have a happier ending than my dream conversation.

I pulled my coat closer around my neck. It was the rain that left a chill in my bones. No matter the color I put on this morning, it didn't help my attitude. Giving in to my dark side, I dressed like I was in mourning for school. A black boatneck sweater, dark boot-cut jeans, and black boots together clearly stated "Stay away from me at all costs!" Yet some people didn't get the message.

"Join the yearbook committee!" a junior said as he waved a flyer in my face.

"No thanks," I muttered as I moved past him and his group. Wasn't it too early for the yearbook committee? Whatever. I didn't want to be a joiner today.

I quickly scanned the hallway for Trip but didn't see him. I knew his parents were still out of town, so I guess he was busy dealing with the younger kids. I just needed a quick look. I hated to admit it, but I was hopelessly addicted to my boyfriend. Mom would have been so proud.

Wandering down the hall, I noticed Roden chatting with Tomas. Trip wasn't in sight.

Without a second thought, I marched right up to them.

"Hey guys," I said as I approached the Findlay boys. "Is Trip around?"

Tomas looked a little uncomfortable and stayed silent.

"Uh, he was just standing here," Roden answered. "But I don't know where he went." He looked around to prove his point.

"Oh. Well, when you see him next, can you tell him that I'm looking for him?" I asked.

"Sure."

"Thanks." The bell rang for first period. "See you later."

By lunch, my mood wasn't any better. Just like a lingering cold, I couldn't shake my sadness. After I bought my sandwich and went to sit at our table, I searched the cafeteria for Trip but didn't catch sight of him. I wasn't worried. He would show up at some point.

"Okay, I want all the details," I said to Annabelle. I hoped gushing about my best friend's date with her dream boy would make my rain cloud disappear. She looked at up me and smiled.

"The date was really nice," she said, taking a sip of iced tea.

"Aw! I'm glad. Tell me everything. Leave nothing out."

"Well, he picked me up at seven and took me to—"

"Wait!" Bri interrupted as she walked up. "I want to know what happened, but I have to get a drink real quick. Say nothing else!" She dropped off her books and scurried off.

Annabelle looked at me and shrugged her shoulders.

"It's okay," I said as Cole sat next to me.

Bri came back. "Okay, spill," she said.

"So, George picked me up at seven and took me to Jeremiah's."

"Oh," Bri and I said in unison.

"I love that place," swooned Annabelle.

"George who? King?" Cole asked. Annabelle nodded.

"Yeah, he's a dork. I wouldn't date him." Cole leaned forward and stole a chip from Bri's lunch.

"Good thing no one asked you," snipped Bri, swatting at his hand. She faced Annabelle again. "Ignore him. He hasn't liked George since last year when he beat him out of the top spot in science class." The rest of us just stared at Cole.

"What? I know he cheated! He was such a kiss ass to the teacher! There had to be something there!"

"Uh-huh, sure," I said.

Cole stuck his tongue out at me.

"So, after Jeremiah's, what did you do?" Bri interjected.

"He took me to a skating rink, and we sipped hot chocolate afterward by the giant fireplace." Cole scoffed.

"That's so sweet!" I gushed. "I'm glad you had fun." I chomped on my sandwich for a bit, noticing neither Trip nor Deidra sitting with us.

"Now we're past all that, did you kiss him?" Bri leaned over, closing the distance between the girls.

"Brianna!" I gasped. "Leave her alone."

Bri tilted her head and raised an eyebrow. "Like you don't want to know?"

I thought about it and then whipped around to face Annabelle. "Okay, I do. Did you?"

Her face flushed and nodded her head. I smiled at her while Bri squealed in delight. Cole shook his head.

"I can't hear this. I'm going to get lunch and then head to lab." He stood. "See you three later."

"How was it?" questioned Bri as I took a sip of water. "Was it good? Or is he a drooler? Because he looks like he slobbers all over you like a teething baby," Bri scrunched her nose. I nearly spit my water as Annabelle giggled.

"No! It was dry and really nice. Soft, with light pressure." She zoned out, and I assumed she was reliving the kiss in her head. Bri snapped her fingers and brought her back.

"That's all we get?"

"No. After he dropped me off, he said he would call me later for another date!" We all squealed this time.

"This calls for cookies!" Bri announced, standing. The Bri-shaped hole in my vision gave me a clear shot of the table against the wall, a few spots away. Roden sat there with his friends, Tomas ... and

Trip. A sudden pang pinched my heart. Why didn't he say hi? Did Roden tell him I wanted to see him? I heard laughter and noticed Deidra was sitting across from them. No one from their table even peeked in our direction.

Suddenly, my bleak mood returned, and I didn't feel like celebrating anymore.

"I'm going to the library," I said abruptly. "I just remembered I have to read something for English today."

"But what about cookies?" Annabelle asked.

"You can have mine," I offered. The sadness in my dream slowly leaked back into my memory, and it weighed heavy on my heart. I was afraid if I stayed there any longer, the wall I built would crack and the midnight-blue misery would drip all over the table, ruining everyone else's celebratory mood. "I'm really happy for your date. I'll see you later." I grabbed my stuff and bolted before anyone could say another word.

I hurried to the library. If our school wasn't littered with teachers patrolling the halls, I would have sprinted. Rain still dripped from the sky, as if the world cried on my behalf. I burst through the doors of the silent sanctuary in the library, waved to the librarians, and headed to my spot in the criticisms section. Leaning my head against the shelves, I gulped in air, trying not to cry. The tears slipped from my eyes before I could protest. With my mood manipulated by my dream, I had no control over my emotions. The rain came down harder, pelting the windows and echoing around the cavernous room. Thankfully, it was loud enough to cover my quiet sobbing. I didn't think I could deal with the embarrassment of people knowing I cried in the literary criticisms section. If Trip was intentionally avoiding me, what else could I do? Any effort I put into speaking with him would be a frustrating waste of my time. I cried for another minute, letting the tears flow from me. Had my dream last night been more of a premonition? Was my subconscious telling me I needed to end it with Trip? Panic hit me like a wave. Was that what I really wanted? To end our relationship over a stupid fight? If he could just make friends with Cay and his family, maybe there was potential of getting the weather under control. I sniffed and wiped my nose on my sleeve. Glamorous.

"Hey," I heard a soft voice above me. I jumped at the sound. Looking up, I saw the last person I would have ever thought to find me there.

"What do you want?" I sniffed.

"I wanted to talk to you, about the other day," Cay said. "Are you okay?"

"Why do you care?" I really wasn't in the mood for this.

"Seriously? Just because you blacklisted me doesn't mean I still don't worry about you."

"You have nothing to worry about." I pushed myself off the bookcase. "I have to get to class."

"Yeah, in about twenty minutes. Please, just let me apologize."

"I'm not the one you need to apologize to."

He sighed. "I know you don't understand, but I can't apologize to him." I crossed my arms.

"Why not? You punched him!"

"He's my enemy. Why would I be nice to him at all?"

"Because he's my boyfriend! And if you cared about family as much as you claim, you would tell him you were sorry for being such a hotheaded jackass for me!" I pushed past and stormed toward the door.

"Wait a minute! What about him?" Cay scurried to grab his bag and followed me.

"What about him?" I snapped.

"Shh! If you're going to yell, take it outside," Mrs. Barone, the librarian, said in a harsh whisper. I looked back at her with tears staining my face and saw her look change from upset to sympathetic. She curled her mouth into a half smile and tilted her head slightly. The motion caused a piece of her black hair to slip from the clip holding it in place.

"He should apologize too!" retorted Cay, who had clearly ignored the direction from Mrs. Barone. I whipped back around to face him.

"Why? He was only defending himself." I stormed through the door and stood in the hallway.

"Not to me. To you!"

"What are you talking about?"

"Why does he still keep you in the dark about everything? How can you trust him knowing secrets still exist between you two?" Cay kept his voice low, but the intensity was still very present.

"There aren't any secrets between us! Not any-more, thanks to your insistence."

Cay snorted. "Don't kid yourself." He moved closer to me.

"There will always be secrets, ones that have yet to be revealed. Don't you think it's weird he hasn't told you about his family?"

"You sound like a comic book villain. And I know about his family."

"Yeah? All of them? What about Tomas? It has to be annoying that he's always hanging around."

"The same way Logan is usually at your heels?" I nodded to the lurking silhouette of the high school boy just down the hall. Cay smirked.

"Exactly the same way." I frowned, not following the breadcrumbs he left for me.

"That's something for me and him to figure out. Not you," I responded. "I don't care why you feel it's your job to get in the way of him and me. I don't care why you're fighting with Trip, but it needs to end before it consumes you both. I'm giving you the chance to be the bigger man right now. Take it." With that, I huffed down the hall and to my next class.

As I drove home from school, I decided to find Trip and talk to him. When I pulled into my driveway, I saw I'd beaten him home. I dumped my books in my room and went outside to wait for him in a calmer state than I had been an hour ago. It had stopped raining, but there was still a cold dampness in the air. Fifteen minutes passed, and the silver Audi hadn't arrived. I shivered in my coat. Twenty-five minutes gone. Okay, another five minutes and I would be going back inside. My determination to wait had run out about ten minutes ago, leaving me vulnerable to the bone-chilling cold. This was silly. I'd just go over later tonight. I had a test to study for anyway. As I went inside, I knew Dante and Virgil wouldn't be enough of a distraction. I unpacked my notebook and my copy of *Inferno*, laying them open on my desk. Pulling out the study guide we were given, I flipped to the first question: Who is Beatrice to Dante, and why does he travel to Hell to save her?

I wasn't interested in answering the question right away, so I moved down to the next question: "Many scholars agree Dante's *Inferno* is an allegory. Argue why it's not."

Pushing away Dante and sliding my statistics book toward me, I opened up to the fifth chapter. Staring at it, my mind went blank.

I texted Trip after three fruitless attempts to study.

[Bridget: Hey, missed you at lunch today. Can we talk?]

Obsessively, I checked my phone every three minutes for a response. I groaned and threw my phone across my room. It landed on my bed softly.

"Things okay?" Mom asked as she poked her head into my room. I didn't even hear her come home.

"Yeah, I'm just frustrated about something. I'll be fine."

"How was school today?" she asked, coming into my room.

"Boring, like normal." I liked school. With the way things were slowly going insane around me, I liked the stability of it.

"I'm sorry to hear that. If you want to take a break from studying, I could use some help making dinner."

I swung around in my chair and stared at my books again. The words swirled around and cha-chaed off the page. I slammed the book shut. "Sure."

After helping Mom make dinner and eating, I cleaned and washed the dishes to put off my inevitable homework. When I got back into my room, I grabbed my forgotten phone. *Sigh.* Still no messages from Trip. I flopped back onto my pillows. This whole avoidance act was getting really old. The radio silence was driving me insane. My anxiety practically shot out my fingertips as my heart pounded in my chest. Maybe this was his way of breaking up with me. I took a huge breath in and released it slowly, counting to ten. Repeating this process helped slow my racing heart and return my hands to normal again. I glanced at my books one more time. The thought of studying made my brain flatline. I needed a mental break. It was dark outside, but that didn't matter. I got up and went into the yard to practice, waning powers be damned.

With the sun setting earlier, it took a lot for me to get my powers into full swing. I breathed, closed my eyes, and cleared my mind. "Okay, now what?" Trip's voice floated from somewhere in my memory.

"Think about how you've felt," he told me. Right. I'd been feeling broken, mostly, mixed with hurt and a dash of disappointment. Drawing from those emotions, it rained heavy droplets pelting the earth. Letting it pour down on me was comforting. I knew I controlled it, but it felt like the world sympathized with me, and I suddenly didn't feel so lonely.

Thoroughly drenched but with the weight lifted off my shoulders, I ended the rain. I summoned a quick heat wave to dry off. Focusing my mind again,

I thought of a memory from earlier this summer. Right after school had let out on the last day, the ocean waves beckoned my friends and me. We all had our bathing suits, having worn them to school. I stashed my stuff in my car and ran to catch up with them. The sun beat down on my skin and warmed my flesh as we hurried to get a spot on the already-filling beach. The crash of the waves made me ache to dive, and Gillian's roller coasters filled with the high-pitched screams and laughter of children of all ages. We finally found a good spot in the toasty sand and settled down. Along with every other high schooler, I stripped off my clothes and slapped on sunscreen before racing into the water. I basked in the innocence of that moment. The freedom of summer, the blissful ignorance of what was coming, and the happiness of drinking in the sunshine.

I felt my own skin heat up, on the verge of sweating, and my clothes dried on my body. I opened my eyes slowly, expecting a blinding sun to be waiting, but nothing but damp darkness welcomed me. I was so caught up in my own thoughts; I forgot it was October. I patted my body and looked down. My pants and shirt were now dry with a few still-damp patches behind my knees and upper thighs. Everything else around me was still wet from the rain. I smiled. Finally, I could warm myself up! No more freezing in winter. Happiness and pride flooded my body. I needed to tell someone. I ran up the porch steps, my sneakers squeaking on the kitchen floor, and hurried to my room. I grabbed my phone on my bed, went to text Trip, and froze. Right. He was avoiding me. My heart sank as I stared at my empty inbox. I would give him until after my test tomorrow to try to contact me. I put my books away, turned on my TV, and sank into my bed with the intent of drowning myself in sitcoms.

CHAPTER
❧ 21 ❧

School the next morning was frantic. Everyone buzzed with excitement about the latest gossip, which meant they slowed down the traffic to homeroom. No one wanted to rush off just after hearing Cory Birch had broken it off with Noelle Patrelli for another girl. Rumors flew as people speculated who the other woman could be.

"I heard it's Hilary," Annabelle said knowledgeably.

Bri shook her head. "Impossible. Everyone knows she has a thing for Cay."

"Plus, Noelle and Hilary are BFFs. That would kill the friendship if Hilary hooked up with her ex," I added. "Not to mention, Noelle would kill Hilary."

"I heard it was Melissa Palmer," Annabelle said, scandalized.

"That's possible," Bri said, "but I've never seen him look in her direction."

"What about Amanda Wykowski?" I suggested. "They used to date freshman year. Rekindled romance?"

"Maybe, but I thought she was still dating Ryan Trainor," Annabelle said.

I shrugged. "Kyle Perkins? She's part of the pep squad, and sophomore year, Cay had a thing for her."

"All I know is whoever the 'other woman' is, she better hide until the year is over. Noelle is on the warpath. She's out for blood," Bri said.

"How do you know that?" I quizzed her.

"Twitter." Bri looked at her nails casually.

Annabelle looked at her phone as it chirped. "Class is about to start. I'll see you at lunch."

Our little group broke for studying instead of intense gossiping.

On my way to lunch, I caught sight of Trip, laughing and hanging out with Tomas and some other guys in the hall. He seemed so happy without me. There I was, miserable, unable to concentrate, and he was living the good life. Had we broken up and I'd missed it? I just stared at him as students passed by, heading toward the cafeteria. He looked up and caught my eye. His smile fell a little. Confirmation. I closed my eyes for a second and took a deep breath. When I opened them again, he was on his way toward me. I couldn't do this in school. I just couldn't handle it right now. I shook my head, holding back tears, and headed toward girls' bathroom.

Thankfully, it was empty. I closed the door to the handicapped stall and leaned against the wall, the least offensive part of the enclosure. I felt the cool tile through my shirt. It was refreshing against the heat of my body. Deep breaths. A knot formed in the center of my chest, expanding with every second. Tears burned my eyes as I slid down, sitting hard on the floor. *Think of something else.* My fists clenched by my side until white knuckles appeared. *Puppies, baseball, math, bugs, anything else but him.* I turned my face and pressed it against the wall, hoping the chilly touch of the tile would stop the fire spreading in my cheeks. *Calm down. You have the* Inferno *test today. Who is Dante's childhood love? Beatrice. Who guides him through hell? The poet, Virgil.* I started calming, the building tension in my chest subsiding. My breathing slowed, so I wasn't panting anymore. The bathroom door opened, and someone walked into the stall next to me. I walked out, washed my hands, and checked my appearance in the vaguely scratched mirror hanging above the sink. My hair was pulled halfway up, waves cascading down my shoulders. Skin, not too bad, eyes, slightly red, but that will clear up. Overall, I shouldn't look like I was on the verge of tears a few minutes ago. I opened the door and turned right to meet my friends.

"Hey," Trip said, stepping from his perch against the wall. I froze in my tracks.

"Hi," I breathed. *Just be cool.* Oh, who was I kidding? I never hid my feelings.

It would be a miracle if I didn't turn into a blubbering mess right now.

"How've you been?" he asked. My bathroom buddy walked out and headed across the hall into a classroom, never looking once in our direction. Beside us, the hallway was empty and felt endlessly long. I looked down it toward the cafeteria, appearing millions of miles away. I'd been dreading this moment, but it was time to rip off the bandage. "If you're going to end it, just do it already," I said, feeling that knot building again. *Puppies, baseball, bugs...*

"What?"

"I don't want to drag this breakup out. Just get it over with." I swallowed hard.

Trip opened his mouth, but I cut him off. "And just for the record, breaking up with me over a fight just shows how juvenile you are! When things get tough, you work them out!" I pointed my finger in his face. "I can't believe I fell for your good looks and charm." I shook my head. "I'm just as shallow as you." Shrugging my shoulders, I folded my arms over my chest. "It doesn't even matter anymore. Break it off or don't, but make a decision so I can move on with my life." I took a deep breath. "Okay, now you may speak."

Trip burst into laughter.

I frowned. What the hell?

"I'm sorry," he said, calming a bit. I jokingly punched him in the arm. Hard.

"Ow! What the—Bridget, I'm not breaking up with you!" he said.

Confusion clouded my mind. "I don't understand. You've avoided me for days. If you aren't breaking up with me, what the hell is going on?" Trip became serious.

"I'm sorry for the way I've been acting. I was mad at you and needed to cool off."

"Ignoring me for nearly a week and looking positively cheery without me is your way of cooling off?"

He shook his head. "No; with my parents gone until tomorrow, I had to play the responsible brother role for my siblings. If they report back to my mom and dad that I was distracted by a fight with my girlfriend, who knows if they'd leave me in charge again? Plus, I couldn't leave all the responsibility to Dee. She takes care of us enough as it is. It's not fair to her."

I wanted to believe him. Believing him would be so easy, but there was more to his story. Maybe Cay's words were getting to me.

"That's all?" I asked. He flashed a smile that didn't quite reach his eyes.

"That's it. I'm sorry I've been so distant. I really am." He moved to take my hand but stopped himself. "Are we good?"

I bit my lip. "So you didn't sit with me at lunch because you were still upset with me, but you were faking happiness for your siblings?"

"Yeah."

"What did you say when Deidra or Roden asked why you weren't sitting with me, if they didn't know about our fight?"

He sighed. "Dee knows, but Roden doesn't. She helped me cover, okay?"

I felt I'd only scratched the surface of this half-assed apology. Trip eyed me carefully, probably trying to figure out if I bought his story. I rubbed the back of my neck for a moment, taking it all in.

Shaking my head, I asked, "That's it? That's why you've been avoiding me?"

"Yeah. You don't believe me?"

"It's not that," I started. His eyes filled with concern. "I just... I feel like there's more you aren't telling me." I shifted my weight to my left foot and put my hands in my back pockets.

"Like what?" The concern was replaced by a shadow of dread. I gave a tiny shrug.

"I don't know. Why don't you tell me?"

Trip cupped my face in his hands and stared into my eyes. "There's nothing else to tell you. I promise."

I didn't know who he was trying to convince more, me or himself. "Okay. If you say there's nothing more, I believe you."

"Are we good then?" He asked with his eyebrows raised and an inquiring smile on his lips.

"Yeah," I said. The gnawing in my stomach wasn't going away. He held out his hand to me, and I took it. Not long ago, interlocking my fingers with Trip's had given me a squishy, happy feeling that made me blush deep red. Now, the gesture felt foreign to me. Looking up at Trip, he smiled genuinely. I gave him a small smile and looked ahead. I couldn't tell who was lying to whom anymore.

Trip and Deidra sat with the rest of us at lunch. I tried not to act like a zombie, but I was preoccupied with what was going on with Trip. For the life of me, I couldn't figure out what he was hiding, but I knew his apology had been off.

Someone nudged my knee. I looked up from my sandwich and at Trip, who was sitting on my right.

"What's running through your pretty mind?" he whispered.

"I'm just worried about this test I have in English. I studied for it, but I still feel unprepared."

"Well, don't worry. You're the brightest person I know," he said, giving me a kiss on my temple. He jumped right back into the conversation swirling around me without a second thought.

I stared out the window and caught sight of some light snow falling. I glanced at Trip for a moment, wondering what was running through his mind.

Was he the reason for the sudden snowfall? Tomas laughed loudly at the other table, drawing my attention and forcing my thoughts back. I knew Trip was hiding something from me. What if it was about his bunkmate? If I wanted the answers to my questions, I should ask Trip, but how could I trust he'd tell me the truth? He's never lied to me before, but as much as I hated to admit this, Cay had always been the one I could turn to about this stuff. Would he tell me, even after our fight yesterday? He seemed so hell-bent on telling me everyone's deep, dark secrets. Either way, I would have to ask someone. I surveyed my options. Deidra could help, but I knew she'd back up her brother's cover story before breaking his confidence to me. Roden would do the same. I appreciated the family loyalty, but it would get me nowhere. A loud noise followed by roaring laughter came from a table behind me. I turned to see Logan acting like a moron for the amusement of his Neanderthal friends. Cay laughed so hard I thought he'd to pee himself. I might as well ask him.

I dug into my lunch with newfound vigor. If I hurried, I could catch him before he rushed off to class.

"You late for an important date, White Rabbit?" Cole asked as I scarfed down my grapes.

"No. Why do you ask?" I chugged my lemonade and wiped my mouth with a napkin before going back to grapes.

"Because if you don't slow down, you'll choke," Bri said, raising an eyebrow.

"I'm just really hungry. I feel like I haven't eaten since yesterday," I lied. I polished off the rest of my fruit and gathered my garbage. Ten pairs of unblinking eyes stared at me.

"What?" I asked.

"Are you okay?" Annabelle asked.

"Yes." Five doubtful faces looked at me. "I'm fine. Really. I'm running to the library real quick to cram some last-minute studying in," I told them as I picked up my backpack and trash. "See you later!"

I barely made it into the hallway before I felt a hand on my shoulder and turned.

"Are you sure you're okay?" Trip asked, concerned.

"Yup," I said, giving him the wide-eyed look.

"I mean, with us. You aren't running off to get away from me, are you?" He looked slightly pained to say it. I hated wondering if this was just a cover play.

"Nope. Avoiding someone isn't usually my thing," I said, my voice light.

"Right." He furrowed his brow and tilted his head down. "Why don't I believe you? You said we were good."

I sighed. "We are. This test is just weighing on my mind more than I expected." Cay got up from his table with his things. This might be my shot to talk to him. "I want to do well since it's a huge part of my overall grade."

"That's all?"

"Yes."

"You promise?" Ooh, he caught me there. I hated lying, but I hated even more to promise I wasn't lying when I was. The test weighed on my mind, but not as much as the urgency to speak with Cay did. I nodded.

"Why don't you meet me after school today, and I'll treat you to hot chocolate to celebrate the good job you'll do?"

"I don't know. I don't want to jinx it," I said, shifting my weight. Cay walked out of the lunchroom and past us, shooting us both a look. Talking to him may be harder than I thought.

"Please? Believe it or not, I've … missed you these past few days."

"Really? If you missed me, you could have talked to me," I pointed out.

"Come on, don't be like that. I told you I needed some space. What's going on with you?" I looked down the hall again, more to give myself a chance to think than anything else.

"Let me get through this test, okay? And we can talk later?" I shifted my bag from one shoulder to the other and bit my bottom lip.

"Fine. I can't meet you in the parking lot because I have to be there when Liz's bus drops her off. But after that?"

"Sure."

He leaned in for a kiss, and I obliged. It still felt good to kiss him, I'd admit, but I couldn't let go of that gnawing feeling he was hiding something from me.

"See you later," I said and rushed off down the hall.

Chapter
22

I didn't find Cay after lunch, and I almost bombed my test because I was too anxious about talking to him. After school, I closed my locker once I deposited my books, taking my time. Cay had left already, sprinting once the bell rang. I didn't have anywhere to rush to, and it was always nice not to sit in traffic. As I walked toward my car in the parking lot, I heard my name being called out. Turning, a breathless Annabelle ran after me.

"Hey! What's going on?" I asked. She slowed and took in huge, gasping breaths.

"I need ... to work out ... more," she panted. Her cheeks were red, and there was a slight sheen to her forehead. She bent over, resting her hands on her knees.

"Deep breaths, you'll be okay." I patted her on the shoulder. "Is there an emergency making you exercise?" She shook her head no.

"I just wanted to talk about the dance." Annabelle took a deep breath and blew it out. "Wow, note to self:

ask Santa for a gym membership for Christmas," she said. "Anyway, what time do you want us at your house?"

"My house?"

"Yeah, remember? We girls are getting all beautified at your house and meeting the boys here."

"When did I sign off on this?"

"Today? At lunch? I asked if it was cool with you, and you nodded." Oh, crap. I needed to stop spacing out in public.

"Right! Come around after school. That way we can get ready and hand out candy to the little kids that come early."

"Great! I'll text everyone," she said, pulling out her phone.

"Super! So, anything else you wanted to talk to me about that could have been done using a smartphone?"

Annabelle's fingers frantically typed out a message on her iPhone. "Hmm? Oh, yeah. Sorry about that." She finally looked up from her phone.

"Earth-shattering news?" I asked.

She blushed a light pink. "No, I'm just really excited for the dance. George is taking me." Her blush depended.

"You really like him, don't you?"

"Yeah," she replied. "Every morning he texts me, 'Hello, Beautiful.'"

"Aw! That's so cute!"

She grinned. Happy looked good on Annabelle.

"I hate to do this," I said, "but I got to run. Gush to me later?"

"Of course!"

"See you tomorrow," I called as I headed off.

Driving home, Annabelle's excitement tumbled around my head. I was so happy for her. I remembered how excited I'd been when Trip and I had first started dating. Did everything with him have to be so ... hard? My parents loved me, so they did what they could to protect me. Annabelle's mom gave her the freedom to make her own choices, trusting she would make smart decisions. In the sixth grade, when Cole got the flu, his dad had waited all night for Eagles tickets in a snowstorm just to give him something to look forward to. That's what we did for those we loved. Trusted and protected them. This was the relationship I shared with my friends and family, yet I couldn't offer the same courtesy to my boyfriend? I didn't know if I loved Trip. I'd never experienced romantic love before, but I did care for him—a lot—and I didn't want to hurt him. I let out a deep breath. He trusted me and was always supportive; the least I could do was return the same feelings. I felt silly and dramatic for my behavior today. He'd needed space, and I'd panicked, thinking we were breaking up? Shaking my head, I turned left into my neighborhood. I was overthinking again. I'd let Trip tell me what he was hiding in his own time. I drove past my house and pulled on the side street next to Trip's.

I inhaled the woodsy fireplace and embraced the brisk temperature, not bothering to dispel the cold snaking down my neck. The chill in the air burned in my lungs, making me feel rejuvenated and vibrant, different from the liberated spirit of summer. I climbed the front steps, enjoying crunching the leaves under my Converse. I knocked on the wooden door and waited. It opened slowly, as if the person behind it was unsure of their decision.

"Hello?" a voice said.

"Hi!" I smiled brightly. Deidra's face peered out.

"Hey," she replied, her voice cold as the weather. "What's up?"

"Is Trip here?"

"Yeah." She didn't move.

"Well, can I see him?"

"I'll ask." She closed the door in my face. Um, what had just happened? The door opened again, and Trip stepped outside, closing it behind him.

"Hey," he said with a big smile. At least my boyfriend still wanted to see me. Not wasting a minute, I tilted my head up and kissed him. He leaned into me, his lips eager to touch mine. His arms encircled my waist and pulled me closer to his warm body. My shirt slid up slightly, and his fingertips pressed firmly against me, like he never wanted to let go. His tongue flicked against my lower lip ever so gently; I nibbled his lip and closed the remaining space between us. He laced his hand in my hair and grasped. I placed my hands on his chest, feeling the firm muscles beneath and lightly pushed him back.

"What's wrong?" He frowned with concern.

I chuckled. "We're outside? I'm not old enough to put on this kind of public show."

He scanned the neighborhood behind me. "Let's take this inside, shall we?" Trip kissed me again—shorter, but just as urgent—and pushed the door open. I followed him inside where the heat from the house mixed with the crispness from outside, causing a blast of warmth on my face. The earthy fire smell was inside the house too, creating a cozy atmosphere.

"I hoped you'd come by," Trip said as I removed my jacket. "I was still a little worried things weren't okay at lunch, but after that hello, I'm guessing it was just me?" He wiped his hands on his jeans and shoved them into his back pockets.

I smiled tenderly. "Things are fine."

His mouth curved up. "Good. Tomas made a fire for the girls, and I was getting them hot chocolate. Did you want some? I promised you a cup, though it comes from a packet, fair warning."

Sweet milk chocolate wafted from the kitchen, and my mouth salivated a bit. "Yeah, sure, but a little later, if that's okay."

"Yeah, we can make ours then," he replied. "Want to go upstairs?" I nodded. The fire and promise of hot chocolate were incredibly inciting, but they had to wait. We headed into his room, messy from lack of attention. Messy was too weak of a word; it looked recently ransacked by blind thieves. Dresser drawers lay open in various degrees. I didn't know where to stand since the floor was covered with clothes. I couldn't tell if they were clean or dirty. Beds were unmade, sheets dangling off the mattresses. I tried to hide my disgust.

"Sorry," Trip apologized sheepishly. "Tonight is 'clean like crazy before the parents come home' night." He picked up some stray socks and pants, tossing them to the side and clearing a path for me to the desk chair. I wrinkled my nose at the stale smell and sat as he perched on the bed. "What's up?"

"So many things, but first, thank you for the apology. I'm sorry too, for everything. My craziness today, all of my insane family history, spending time with Cay even though you hate him. A lot. I get that now."

"Good," he replied.

"Seriously, I'm sorry for the fight." I put my hands up. "I don't think I'm wrong. There has to be a solution, but I didn't have to flip out like that."

"It's okay."

Chewing on my inner lip was a family habit, one giving me great comfort, and right now, I was chewing like crazy. I wasn't sure how the rest of this speech would go. "I want this—us—to work. I like you, and I like us together. And if we can't be honest and trust each other, one hundred percent, then we need to either fix that or..." I took a breath, "end this."

Trip stilled as cautiousness settled on his face. "Is that what you want?"

I frowned and chewed some more. He raised his eyebrows, waiting for my answer.

"I want to fix this," I finally said. "But I need to know if," I paused, "you still are going through something."

He stared at the floor for a full minute before he faced me. "Please don't tell me we're going back to this again."

"Trip, I need to know I can trust you." He ran his fingers through his hair.

"Bridget," he started with his eyes glistening slightly, "you know you can trust me."

I licked my lips but didn't say anything. I was tired of this fight. I wanted to believe him, so I ignored the little voice in my head and nodded.

"Okay," I said, interlocking my fingers with his. "I'm just saying I know there is something else going on with you, and I'll be here if you want to talk about it. But I won't ask anymore. I trust you'll tell me when you're ready. I'm asking that we stay open and honest about stuff. Please remember I was lied to about a lot in my life; I don't want that with us. I don't want us to have any secrets when it comes to big stuff."

Trip did nothing but study me for a minute. I couldn't read his expression, and I got nervous. He moved forward and kissed me, hard.

"No more secrets," he promised, then kissed me again.

"I really did get lucky with you," he added between kisses.

I moved away and looked him in the eyes. The green of his eyes inflamed with a happiness I haven't seen there for what felt like a long time. He brushed a strand of my hair away from my cheek and kissed me, sweetly this time, as if I was a porcelain doll—so precious I would break at the touch of a feather.

"Ahem," Deidra fake coughed from the doorway. Instead of jumping back, Trip leaned away from the kiss like he knew she was standing there this entire time. I looked down at a pulled thread on my shirt. If her attitude now was the same as it was earlier, I wasn't in the mood to deal with it.

"What's up?" Trip asked casually.

"You promised Liz you'd hang out with us. Are you coming down anytime soon ... or are you too busy?" I shook my head. What was her issue? I looked over at her, but she ignored me. Deidra leaned against the doorjamb and crossed her arms.

"Yeah, I'll be down in a minute."

"Right." She sent a look of disbelief toward him and walked back downstairs.

"Sorry about her," Trip apologized. I gave him a tight smile. "Do I have to apologize to her too?"

He coughed a laugh. "No, she's just ... being over-protective. She knew how upset I was and went on defense. Dee's like ... a protective mama bear, even for her older brother."

"And you're her baby cub? Weird image." I scrunched my nose at the thought. Trip chuckled.

"I'll tell her to back off."

"Great. Talk to her soon, please?"

"Sure." Trip rubbed my arms gently and sighed. I blinked.

"What's wrong?"

He smirked and gave me a long kiss. "I really don't want to go downstairs."

I smiled slowly, ducking my head to hide my blush. He trailed his hands down my arms and continued until they stilled on my upper thigh. I felt his eyes on me, and I looked up at him shyly.

"Trip, I told you, I'm not ready." I covered his hand with my own and moved it lower to my knee.

Trip shook his head, as if his mind was an Etch A Sketch, and he was shaking it clean. "I know. I wasn't trying to pressure you. I was just ... feeling like maybe you felt differently. It's okay you want to wait." He stood and pulled me up. "Come on, let's go downstairs."

My knee where his hand had been instantly became cold. I let the conversation slide, mostly because I needed to think about this more for myself, but I told him, "We have to talk about it at some point, you know."

"I know."

I pulled on his hand. "Wait." Trip paused and faced me. "I'm not upset with you for that. I just don't think now is the best time."

He turned and stared down the landing. "Right. Good point," he said and rubbed the back of his neck. "Honestly, I'm not ready for sex either. But I would like to do more than kiss. If you're okay with that."

It took me a minute, but I caught on. "Oh, oh. I haven't thought about it." I felt so weird about this. I'd never talked so seriously with a boyfriend before. Not that I had much previous experience, but discussing this with my girlfriends and now my boyfriend? Two totally different things. I didn't know what else to say, so I blushed furiously instead. The bright sunlight turned blurry through the window.

"Bridget, if you don't calm down, my family will know something is up," Trip said with amusement in his voice.

"I know! But I can't help it. This whole thing is really embarrassing." The sun was being swallowed whole by the fog. "I've never had this talk with a guy."

"Hey," he caught my eye. "I promise it's okay. No pressure. We can hold off on it all until you're ready." He kissed me, but I felt like I should have thought about this earlier. I'd had the talk with Mom and had taken the sex-ed class. I knew I wasn't ready to have sex, but I didn't know how far I *was* ready to go.

"We'll talk about it," I said firmly. "I promise. Now I want some hot chocolate and some snuggling, if that's still on the table." He smiled and led me downstairs.

"Took you long enough," Deidra muttered under her breath as I went to sit on a pillow by the fireplace.

Elizabeth toasted some marshmallows over the blue flame as Roden and Tomas attempted throwing them into each other's mouths. They looked like panting dogs with their tongues hanging out.

I shot Deidra a cold look. "We needed to talk some stuff over."

"You have a funny way of talking," she snapped back.

"Leave it alone, Dee," Trip rumbled.

"Do you need help with the hot chocolate?" I asked Trip, while looking at his sister. "I think Deidra's offering."

"Yeah, I could use a hand. Come on, Dee." She made a face at me but got up anyway and went into the kitchen.

"Bridget, watch this," Roden said, tossing a marshmallow up into the air and moving like a viper to snap it between his teeth.

"Impressive. How long did you have to practice that?" I leaned over and grabbed one sugary morsel for myself. The sweet treat melted as I savored its flavor. Wonderful. I could eat these forever.

"No practice. I got skills like that," he boasted, grinning, white fluff squishing between his teeth. Trip and Deidra returned, carrying two mugs of steaming chocolate each. He looked a little relieved while she had softened from the stone-cold attitude she'd given me before. Trip gave one to Elizabeth as Deidra gave both mugs to Tomas and Roden.

"I couldn't carry yours, too," Deidra said to me. "Plus, I wasn't sure if you wanted whipped cream or not. Come put how much you want on." She turned on her heel, blonde hair swinging, and walked away. I cocked my head to the side and glanced at

Trip. He gave me an encouraging smile. I trotted after her, unsure how this would turn out. The can of whipped cream waited on the counter for me as Deidra stirred my drink and slid it over.

"I should apologize," she started, pouring an open packet of chocolate into her own mug. I grabbed the whipped cream and sprayed some cream into my cup as she stirred her hot chocolate. "Trip told me what happened, and I was upset with you for being so..."

"Naïve?" I asked dryly.

"No. Lucky."

Color me confused. "I'm sorry?"

She sighed. "I've prepared for some kind of epic battle my entire life. Our parents did everything to ingrain in us that the only option was winning. It's our family's birthright to wield the Amulet and all the power that comes with it."

I put the can down and rested my hands on the counter. I didn't have to agree with her to understand where she came from. Nothing I said in an hour speech would dissuade her from that.

"And then we moved here," she continued, putting her spoon in the sink, "and you came along, the Seeker for the Clan of Brighde. And you knew nothing of it. You got to have that innocent childhood of reading fairy tales and living a life of blissful freedom."

I didn't know what the hell kind of fairy tales she'd been reading, but my life—though not horrible, let's be clear—was no princess story. Though, I keep thinking, it's destined to be.

"I would give anything to be like that, even if just for a minute. When Trip told me what you said, I was jealous I couldn't see past what my parents taught me. You have a point—who's to say we couldn't stop the war? But after thinking about it some more, both sides have come too far just to give up that easily," she finalized.

"That may be true, but I think there's a way for all of us to compromise. Think about Cay. You guys hate him, but you still put up with him!"

"Because of you."

"Why me?"

Deidra pressed her lips together. "Trip likes you, and Cay is your family. So out of respect for you and your power, we're nice to him. Well, except Roden. But even you have to admit Cay pushed the line."

"I do and told him that," I replied, nodding in agreement.

She smiled. "I'm sorry for the way I acted earlier this week and just before. There's a lot of stuff running through my head, and I was taking it out on you."

"Thanks. But it's not all spring days and sunshine over here. Well, I guess it is ... but that's not my point. What I'm trying to say is it's hard being the new kid. Everyone else knows the rules of the game, and I'm expected to pick it up by osmosis. It's not easy to sit out during a game you didn't know you were playing."

Deidra nodded and sighed again. "I'm just glad my parents come home tomorrow. I can't handle being the adult for much longer."

I blinked at her. "I thought Trip was the one left in charge?"

She barked out a laugh. "Please, did you see his room? If I let Trip be the only one running things, we'd order in every day and eat off the floor, so he could avoid doing the dishes." Picking up her cup, Deidra smiled and walked into the living room. My gaze followed her. I got it. Trip might have been my equal magic-wise, but Deidra was the power behind the throne.

As Trip and I took the long way to my car, the sun set, and the air turned from crisp to biting cold; I didn't want to leave, and I was doing everything to drag this goodbye out.

"Hold on a second," I said, pulling on his arm. He stopped as I slipped my hand into his and peered at the falling sun. I snuggled into him, smiling lightly to myself. "What's up?" His eyes followed mine, searching for something.

"Nothing."

"Okay." Trip frowned and went to take a step forward, but I wouldn't let him go.

"Wait, hold on!" I giggled. I moved in front of him and kissed him on the cheek. "I missed you ... so much."

He smiled and gathered me in his arms. "How much?"

"A lot?" I joked.

Trip pressed his soft, warm lips against mine, and we stayed there, swimming in the happiness of reconciliation.

"So, I was thinking," he took a breath, "how about I take you on our first official date this weekend? My parents will be back, so it's the perfect time."

Smiling, I said, "Yeah, I'd like that." Then I kissed him again. The kiss was simple and sweet but edged with the suggestion of something more. I couldn't read into it any further than that. I pulled away.

"What's wrong?" I asked.

Trip slightly smiled. "Nothing's wrong." He moved his left hand to my face, cupping my cheek and kissing me again. I allowed this to happen for another minute before I backed away again.

"I love kissing you, but I feel like more is on your tongue than the taste of hot chocolate and my lip gloss." I slid my hand up to the nape of his neck and ran my fingers through his hair. "You can tell me."

He smiled. "I'm happy."

"Me too." I stepped out of his embrace. "I should get home."

"I wish you could stay longer," he said, drawing little swirls on the back of my hand he still held .

I sighed. "If only, but I genuinely hear my homework calling my name."

He laughed and lightly bopped me on the nose. "Is that your mom's new name?"

I grinned at him. "Why would my mom be calling me to come home? It's not even close to my curfew."

"Maybe your mom thinks I'm a scoundrel trying to take you from her," he said, scooping me up, my legs dangling over his arms.

I tilted my head back and laughed. "Why do you sound like a pirate?"

He laughed again and put me down gently. "I don't know. When I think of the word scoundrel, I think pirate."

"Well, if tonight is any consideration…" I teased.

"Wait, what?" Trip dropped the goofy smile he wore.

"What?" I lost my smile, too.

"Why would you say that?" He took a step away from me.

"I was just joking! You know, because you thought ... we would do more than kissing." I tucked my hair behind my ears and played with the belt on my coat.

"I thought we were on the same page about that."

"We are!" I ached to step toward him, but the stone in my stomach kept me in place.

"Then why joke about that? I was being serious about my feelings for you. You wanted to keep the conversation honest." He shoved his hands into his pockets.

"I know, but we've only been dating for two months, not even two full ones."

"Right. So why is that a bad thing I brought it up?" He shrugged. "I thought we could talk about it, but you said you weren't ready, so I backed off."

I sighed, desperately wishing I hadn't opened my mouth. "You're right. I'm sorry. I tried making a stupid joke that didn't work."

He nodded and didn't say anything.

"What are you thinking?" I asked. Trip looked up at the twilight sky, took a deep breath, and released it.

"I don't think you're ready to have that conversation."

"About what you're thinking?"

The weather reflected my confused state. Fog popped up in patches, rubbing against my jeans like a hungry cat and covering my thighs. The temperature ran the spectrum of warm to sweltering hot and back down again. I was damp from a sudden rain cloud appearing over my head to spit droplets into my hair. It probably looked like the weather was convulsing. To top it off, a flash of lightning split the sky.

"Whoa!" He moved toward me and gave me a hug. "I meant I didn't think you were ready to talk about moving past kissing. I didn't understand why you joked about it when we just had the conversation. You sounded really serious about it." He let me go but kept his hands on my arms. I was able to control the rain and calmed the rainbow of varying heat waves. The fog was stubborn and didn't move, but at least the lightning didn't reappear. My mind slowed a bit, and the awkwardness and embarrassment dissipated. Relief popped up, but colorful ecstasy pushed its way to the front of my mind and held on. A comforting warmth flooded my veins. I couldn't deal with the onslaught of everything. It exhausted me.

"I'm sorry," I said, feeling deflated.

"It's okay." He hugged me again. "I'm ready to have that full conversation when you're ready to talk about it."

I sniffed, trying to hold back tears. I pulled away from him. "I really need to do my homework."

He put his finger under my chin, lifting my face to meet his, and said, "We're good. I promise."

I smiled, gently, and swallowed the lump in the throat. "Okay. I'll see you tomorrow?"

"You can see me whenever you want," he said, giving me a kiss on my cheek. I smiled and left, fighting tears as I walked home and leaving a little trail of fog in my footsteps.

Chapter
❧ 23 ❧

After a tender and revealing night with my boyfriend, school was easier to get through the next day. My morning passed quickly, and the conversation at lunch was dominated by the Halloween dance and everyone's costumes. I finished my meal quickly and spent the rest of the time either keeping my hand on Trip's leg or pressing my leg against his. I still stung from my idiocy last night just before I went home, but I felt closer to Trip more than before our fight. Now he understood where I was coming from.

"We're meeting at Bridget's house around five to get ready. Then, the boys will come meet us, and we'll head to the dance," Bri announced.

"What are you going as?" Trip asked me. I smiled coyly in return.

"You'll find out Friday," I teased as I took a sip of water. He made a silly face at me and went back to his lunch. A second later, he looked at me from the corner of his eye and winked.

"Cole, have you decided on a costume yet?" I questioned. He swallowed a bite of his chocolate chip cookie and nodded.

"I was thinking of going as a superhero."

"Which one?" Trip asked, moving his chair over as Annabelle arrived, putting her snack down.

"That line was insane! I didn't think I was ever going to make it back before the bell," she said, collapsing into the chair. "What are we talking about?"

"Costumes," Bri said.

"I don't know yet. I've got two costumes, one from DC and one from Marvel," Cole answered my question.

"Are you two going in a couple's costume?" Annabelle asked Deidra. She shook her head no.

"I'm not into superhero stuff. I'm more into mythology," she hinted. Gee, I wonder why.

"Me too!" Annabelle exclaimed. "I'm going as Aphrodite."

"Aw, the goddess of love," Deidra sighed. "That's a great idea."

"Well, I'm going as a naughty nurse," Bri declared.

"What happened to Bonnie and Clyde?" I asked.

Bri shrugged. "No Clyde."

"I'm sorry," I said.

The lunchroom fell into a lull as Cay McKay and Kyle Perkins walked in holding hands. Last year, Kyle had been a semipopular cheerleader. She hung out with the cool kids but was in no way considered a mean girl. Cay's silent announcement of his relationship with Kyle sent her status into the high school stratosphere.

All eyes flickered to Cay's table, where Hilary Thompson's eyes barely registered acknowledgment of her crush's new beau. Cay led Kyle to a table, his hand on her back, her dark-brown ponytail swinging low against her shoulder blades. I noticed Bri's slight nod of approval of the skinny jeans, riding boots, and white button-down combo Kyle wore. Cay pulled out a chair and pushed it in as Kyle sat. He took the seat next to her and drew in close, as if he had something incredibly important to discuss with her. Personally, I was impressed. I don't know if I'd handle the questioning eyes on my back with such class. By now, I would probably have had the school filled with fog so bad it would be dangerous to breathe. Woe to the kids with asthma.

Over three hundred kids held a collective breath as we waited for some drama to unfold. Five minutes of dead silence passed, and Cay turned toward the school, shooting us a look that clearly read "back off." Instantly, the chatter jumped up again, as if someone had turned the volume up all the way and pressed play. Cay turned back to his new girlfriend, and for a second, everything was back to normal.

"Whoa, I can't believe they're not sitting with his friends," Annabelle breathed.

"That's like saying she's better than them," Bri added in her own, breathless whisper.

"I think it's not worth talking about," Cole said. "Who cares who he dates?"

Two pairs of eyes whipped toward him in shock and disapproval.

"Um, he's the most popular guy in school," Bri said. "It matters."

"I don't know," I chimed in. "I can't say I genuinely care. He doesn't rule the world." That much I could guarantee. The bell rang at that moment, signaling the end of lunch.

"Well, whatever you believe," Bri said as she stood, "Cay may not control the world, but he totally controls everyone's attention."

"Thank you for gracing us with your presence, Mr. McKay," said Miss Montgomery, as Cay sauntered into English late.

"Anytime, Miss Montgomery."

She gave him a stern look. "I'd like to speak to you after class today."

He saluted her and settled into his desk, not bothering to take out his notebook.

"As I was saying, now that we've finished with Dante, we're going to dive into the second half of our class. Last night, you read the first three books of Homer's *The Odyssey*. I would like you each to take ten minutes to jot down a few ideas of why Poseidon hated Odysseus so much. Go ahead and start."

As the class worked, some of us wrote furiously while others stared into space. I blinked at my blank piece of lined paper. Normally, this page would be filled with ideas brimming over the edge, but lately Trip had been dominating the space in my brain reserved for learning. I tapped my pen on the paper, anxious to get to my date tonight. I looked down. My pen was bleeding, leaving blue smudges on the paper. I looked at my classmates. Ally Cohen chewed on her nails, her eyes darting up at Miss Montgomery every three seconds. Dan Zachariah had already finished. I turned and saw Cay had taken out a piece of paper and written something on it, but I couldn't read what. Man, if Cay could do his work, why couldn't I?

"Okay, class. Time's up." Miss Montgomery put down her pen and stood.

Had that really been ten minutes? I looked down at my empty page, dread growing in my stomach.

A warning bell went off around us, causing me and few others to jump.

"Leave your belongings, and please head outside for the fire drill."

Fire drill, yes! I loved whatever higher power controls the fire drills and got me out of class! I was totally converting.

"Hey, Cay," I said, jogging a little to catch up, avoiding my classmates. He glanced back to see who had called him.

"Hi." Cay's tone was flat, void of any feeling toward me.

"Can we talk?" I pulled my hood from the back of the coat.

"Now?"

"Well, no, not now. Today, after school?"

"Why?" He didn't look at me as we kept walking.

I sighed. "I wanted to discuss something with you."

"About what?"

"Cay—"

He stopped and faced me, rigid in his movements. "If I remember correctly, you were the one who said you didn't want to talk to me, but lately, everywhere I turn, there you are."

"In all fairness, we have class together." He continued walking with me trailing after him.

Cay snorted. "Cute."

We followed the throng of people out into the warm sun. I expected it to be colder outside, but I guess my feelings messed with the weather.

"Come on, Cay. What do you want me to say?" I grabbed his sleeve and stopped him again.

"Nothing. I've heard everything you wanted to say. Loud and clear." He turned from me.

"Cay! I need your help!"

He whipped back around. "You don't say?"

I ignored his snarky tone. "Yes. Please?"

I saw his thoughts bounce between helping me and not. He sighed.

"You should've taken the offer the first time, Bridget ... but I'll think about it." Cay moved away from me and joined some of the guys by the field post. I didn't know what else to do, so I followed the rest of my class to the side of the field as Miss Montgomery took attendence.

When I got home, I didn't glance at my homework. Instead, I stripped off my sweaty outfit and stared at my open dresser drawers. I've done this "what to wear" dance before. Right on cue, my phone chirped, announcing a text message:

[Trip: I hope u had a good day at school! Date for tonight will be different than the normal dinner and a movie. Ready for your first clue?]

[Bridget: Clue?]

The phone chirped again.

[Trip: Don't you worry about what we're going to do,]

[Trip: Dress warm for tonight,]

[Trip: And wait for clue number 2!]

Dress warm? Clearly, I'd be outside. I checked the weather on my phone for the nighttime temperature. Cold. I scrunched my nose. I was not a fan of the cold, but I'd play along this time. I grabbed a pair of skinny jeans, my favorite buttoned shirt, and my black riding boots to finish off the look. I had better not be hiking in the swamp tonight. No way did I want to ruin these shoes. On my way to the bathroom, I noticed my reflection. Damn, I looked good! There was no way Trip would be able to keep his hands off me... Wait, was that my goal? I quickly went into the bathroom and took out my makeup. Hadn't I just told him last night that I wasn't sleeping with him? I applied some mascara and blew out the breath I subconsciously held.

I frowned. "Chill out!" I yelled at the mirror. *You know Trip won't do anything you don't want him to. Tonight will be fine.* My phone beeped on my dresser.

[Trip: Changing it up,]

[Trip: Throwing something new into the mix,]

[Trip: Be ready for your ride at a quarter after six!]

I looked at the clock; it was already a little after four. I felt like I swam in time, but in reality, it would take me a while to fix my hair and finish my makeup.

Between brushing my teeth—*Cosmo* said fresh breath is always important for potential kissing—and swiping on blush, my phone chimed again, this time from Mom.

[Mom: Dad working late and I'm grabbing dinner with some friends. Want to come?]

I texted back:

[Bridget: No thanks! Date night with Trip. Have fun!]

Rushing through the rest of my beauty regimen, I grabbed my purse—packed full of crap I probably wouldn't need—and dumped it. I threw in keys, wallet, phone, lip gloss, gum, and a hair tie in case it got windy. I zipped the bag and sat on the couch, anxiously waiting for my ride.

At quarter past, the doorbell rang. Hopping up, I rushed to the door and threw it open, nearly ripping it off its hinges. Tomas jumped.

"Sorry," I said.

"No problem. I'm your ride tonight. And this," he handed me a slip of folded paper, "is for you."

What fun would this be if we ended before dark? Got to keep playing—

Your next clue will be at the park!

I looked at Tomas.

He shrugged. "I'm just here to drive. The writing is all him."

I chuckled, grabbed my scarf and blue coat, and trotted out the door after Tomas.

"So how did you get stuck with this job?" I asked, sliding into the back seat as Tomas held the door open.

He smiled. "I volunteered." He closed the door and got into the driver's seat. "Now, I'm not at liberty to answer any more questions, so I suggest just enjoying the adventure."

"Not even if I ask about you?" He looked at me in the rearview mirror.

"Those I could answer, but nothing about the date."

"Okay. How do you like Corbin City?"

"It's okay. Not like other places we've lived."

"Where else have you lived?"

"You know, all over." I frowned a little. Weird that he'd avoided the question.

"So, when you aren't playing chauffeur for Trip, what do you do in your spare time?"

Tomas made a left turn and said, "Stuff."

"You aren't very chatty, are you?" I asked.

He laughed a little. "I'm just not great at talking about myself."

"I get that." He didn't say anything else, so I let our conversation die. I settled back in the seat and peered over the Tuckahoe River to watch the last bit of the sunset.

Tomas parked the car and turned to face me.

"I have another clue for you: This is clue number four, and yes there is more, so go to the building that has no door."

I laughed at him. "I'm sorry!" I said between giggles. "I couldn't hold it back anymore. These clues are just so silly!"

He broke into a wide grin. "Yeah, I get it. Now go ahead and find clue four."

I hopped out of the car and scanned the park. The white benches sat on my left side. They looked dull in the fading light. Tied to the dock were boats, floating in the water, waiting for their next ride out. My eyes landed on the gazebo. I walked to the entrance. Lying on a bench was a bouquet of pink and yellow roses, my favorite colors. Smiling, I picked them up and sniffed. The moonlight grazed the tips of the roses, giving the appearance they glowed. A card drifted from the bouquet to the ground. I picked it up.

Congratulations! You found the
fifth clue!

Head back to Tomas.

He'll know what to do.

I followed directions.

"Where next, driver?" Tomas smiled and headed toward Ocean City.

"What do you like to do?" he asked me as he made a right at the end of the street.

"Read, bake, hang out with my friends." I sounded boring.

"You sound like Liz. She reads all the time." I smiled, thinking Trip's little sister and I had that in common. I wondered what she was reading at this moment.

"I've seen her bookcase. It's the kind I would have loved when I was her age. Actually, I would probably like it now!"

Tomas smiled as he headed over the bridge into Ocean City.

"Yeah, it's pretty cool."

I pulled out my phone to see if I had any messages. Nothing but my lock screen picture of my friends and me at our summer barbeque junior year.

"Do you like sharing a room with Trip?" I asked, as I put my phone back into my purse.

"It's okay. We respect each other's privacy, so it feels like we have our own rooms sometimes." Tomas pulled into the first fast-food restaurant off the main road and parked the car.

"There's no formal dinner tonight. I'm to buy you whatever you want and give you clue number six."

My stomach rumbled at the smell of French fries and hamburgers. "Okay, how many clues are there?"

"Like, two more. Don't worry, it's almost over. What's for dinner?"

I gave him my meal choice as he ordered for us both at the drive-through, and in between handfuls of fries and mouthfuls of burger, he rattled off:

"Two clues, six and seven, head back toward home for the last stop: Heaven!"

I shook my head and scarfed down the rest of my meal. Tomas peeled from the lot and drove back to Corbin City.

"Why are we in my driveway?" I asked as we pulled in.

"Last clue should be found here," he answered. "On the steps."

I hopped out quickly, excited to see how this would end. Leaning against my front door were a chocolate candy bar and another piece of paper.

Bring the chocolate, bring the flowers,
this is clue number eight. Hurry now
for our official first date!

"Let's go!" I said, jumping back into the car.

Tomas laughed. "Someone's in a rush."

"Drive now, comment later," I directed. The ride lasted two seconds before he stopped the car, opened my door, and gestured for me to exit.

"This is where Prince Charming comes in. My night is over," Tomas said. "Have fun!"

I thanked him and watched him get back in and drive off. I wondered where he was going. I turned and headed to the front door. Clutching the flowers and candy, I didn't know if I should walk into the house or wait for Trip to get me.

An earthy smell of burning wood drifted past from the backyard. I followed my nose to my boyfriend standing next to a roaring fire and a bag of marshmallows.

"Hey, you," he said, grinning.

"Hi to you, too." I smiled back. He strolled to me, and I immediately fell into his arms.

"Thank you for the flowers," I mumbled into his chest.

He pulled me closer. "More than welcome. Are you cold? Come sit by the fire."

Trip directed me toward two chairs with a blanket resting on top. They were pulled close to the flames.

"I figured if I was going to make it cold tonight, the least I could do was keep you warm." He winked and wiggled his eyebrows. As he moved the blanket away, I sat on the cushion, feeling a draft of cool air.

"No, this is perfect."

Trip took a seat next to me and offered a tray full of treats. "S'mores?"

"Yes, please!" I picked up the fixings and roasted my marshmallow. We sat in silence for a few minutes with nothing but the sound of snapping wood to entertain us.

"You know," Trip started, "I know all this stuff about you, like the fact that your emotions control weather, whether or not I wear a jacket," he said teasingly. "But I don't know your favorite color, or favorite food, or anything basic like that."

"Aren't we a little past basic?" I answered.

He nudged my knee with his. "Maybe, but it'd be nice to know who you are now..." *As opposed to who I'm supposed to become.*

"Fair enough. Ask away."

"Favorite thing to do?"

"Besides eat?" I grinned, thinking for a minute. "I really love to bake. I'm a horrible cook."

"Really?" Trip raised an eyebrow.

"Ironic, I know, but toast and mac and cheese are the extent of my amazing chef skills. I'm a better baker."

"Well, I'd love to try anything you make." He took his roasting marshmallow off the stick and bit into it.

I smiled at him. "What's your favorite dessert?"

"Red velvet cupcakes." He licked the sticky bits off his finger before grabbing another one.

"Easy! I'll make them for you." My marshmallow caught on fire, so I blew it out and squished it into the graham cracker and chocolate. "Birthday gift, perhaps. Or Christmas."

"As long as it's not a twofer."

"A what?"

He sighed and leaned back. "Growing up, since my birthday is so close to Christmas, my gifts were counted for both days. One year, my parents gave me a t-ball set for my birthday, and for Christmas, I got the ball." Trip scoffed and shook his head.

"Seriously?"

"Yeah. I mean, looking back now, it's not that bad. Turns out they forgot to add the ball in the original gift, so they just stuck it under the tree. But when you're a kid, you don't realize that right away."

"Noted. No double-dipping on gifts."

"Thank you." He offered me the tray of goodies, and I snagged another marshmallow to roast.

"Let's see, I already know your favorite color is green... what do you do for fun?" I asked.

"Guy stuff. You know, skateboard with Tomas and Roden. Train, go to the gym, play video games."

"Train?"

"Yeah." He cleared his throat. "To be the Seeker."

"Oh." I remained quiet, letting the only noise be the crackling of the burning wood. Trip has been training to find the Amulet pretty much his whole life. How in the world could I compete with that? I'd only known about this whole mess for maybe a month! I pulled the melted mallow off the stick and pressed it between chocolate and graham crackers to give myself some time to mull things over. I attempted to stuff the whole thing in my mouth.

Instead, the crackers crumbled on me. **Smooth going, MacNamara.**

"You got a little..." Trip chuckled as he wiped some sticky marshmallow off my cheek. I blushed.

"Thanks." I paused. "Trip, what would you be if you weren't,"—*stuck*—"destined to be a Seeker?" I asked, licking melted chocolate off my finger.

He hesitated. Then he said, "I guess I never really thought about it. It was always just assumed I'd follow in the family business." I nodded.

"How about you?" he asked.

I shrugged. Planning my life has always been hard for me. I knew my parents would love it if I mapped out what college I'd attend, what degree I'd get, and what job I'd be stuck in forever, but I was only seventeen. It was hard living up to that kind of pressure. Most of my college applications sat on my desk at home, buried under my stack of *Cosmo and Teen Vogue* magazines and half a bottle of Coke that had been sitting there for two weeks.

"I know my mom would die happy if I followed in her footsteps with the bakery, but I don't think that's me. I mean, does it matter anymore now that I know everything?" I answered.

Trip became very serious. "Of course, it matters. It's important you keep part of yourself grounded. It helps with the search. It helps keep you sane."

I watched as he drifted off to some memory I was locked out of. His eyes muddled as he pressed his lips into a tight line. Shadows waltzed across Trip's face while he stared at the fire in an unbreakable trance.

"Hey," I said, touching his arm. "Are you okay?"

Trip shook his head. "What? Yeah, I'm fine." He smiled, but he still wore a mask of darkness.

"Where did you just go?" I asked softly.

"Nowhere." He grabbed another marshmallow and stuffed it into his mouth. More secrets? I'd thought we were past this.

"Trip, if we want this to work out, we have to be honest with each other," I pointed out gently. "What were you thinking about?"

He sighed. "I'm not ready to talk about it yet, but when I am, you'll be the first to know."

I nodded. "Alright." He still looked a little distant, so I leaned over and kissed him lightly on the cheek. "Thank you for tonight. This is the best date I've ever been on." He smiled again, the happiness finally reaching his eyes.

Trip kept that smile on as he leaned over. Even with the heat of the fire, the sweetness from the s'mores, and the comfort of being with my boyfriend, I felt when Trip kissed me, he was still distracted.

Chapter
❧ 24 ❧

The next night was the Halloween dance, and I stood in front of the mirror, doing the best I could not to smear my liquid eyeliner.

"Can I borrow that when you're done?" Annabelle asked. Her chestnut hair was piled on top of her head with a gold, double-strand headband woven through and loose curls dangling around her face. She had my yellow bathrobe wrapped around her dress to keep it clean while she put on her makeup.

I sighed. "Sure. I'll never steady my hand enough anyway. Hand me that mascara?" I closed the bottle and traded with her. Deidra, surprisingly dressed as a zombie housewife, completed her own look with a fake zombie baby and curlers in her hair. She stood precariously in tall, black heels against my doorframe.

"I'm really excited about tonight," she said to me. She held onto the doorjamb for a second, as if she was going to fall over. I wasn't sure if it was from her shoes or her excitement.

"How come?" I swiped mascara over my lashes.

"I'm looking forward to dancing with Cole," she blushed. I smiled back at her, happy for both of my friends.

"Bridge, do you have any dress tape? I don't want my boobs popping out when I dance," Bri asked as she tugged the top of her dress. The white nurse outfit was a little tight on my friend's curvy body. Her hat sat quaintly on the top of her head, and big blotches of red dye were splattered all over, giving her a macabre look.

"Check my bathroom medicine cabinet. If it's not there, then no."

"Or we use duct tape," Annabelle suggested as she blotted her lips.

"Ha, ha," Bri stuck her tongue out.

"What time is it?" I asked, smudging eye shadow on my lid.

"Almost seven; the boys will be here soon," answered Deidra. Thankfully, I was almost done. I smoothed my hair again, feeling a touch of anxiety over the frizz. With the gallons of hair gel, my tight waves wouldn't move in an earthquake. I straightened my black dress, untangling the strands of fringe at the bottom. Slipping into my black kitten heels and pulling up my garters, I felt sexy in my costume. Good girl image be damned.

Turning around, I asked Deidra, "How do I look?"

"Pretty!" She played with the hem on her baby's dress. "You look really good."

"Thanks. Your zombie baby rocks!" She grinned.

"I would never have expected this creepy costume for you!" Bri said as she reappeared. "Looks so good!"

"Thank you," Dee said, widening her smile.

"Bridge, you need jewelry," Bri said as she adjusted her nurse's cap in the mirror.

"I know, but I wasn't sure what to wear." I opened my jewelry box, and Annabelle peered over me.

"Wear this necklace," she advised, pulling out a long strand of fake pearls. "Flappers are big into layering, so double it up."

"Maybe even triple or quadruple it. That thing's like a jump rope," Bri added. "Also, they wore big, flashy things, so any piece with crazy shapes would work."

Just then, my doorbell rang.

"Bridget, the guys are here!" Mom called.

"Okay!" I yelled back. I turned to my friends. "Am I good?"

"Yes," Annabelle said as Deidra nodded.

"No," Bri answered. "You need something more."

"Like what? A bracelet?"

"No, one more necklace." She dipped into my tangled necklaces, separating one of them.

"Bridget?" Mom said as she popped her head into my room. "The boys are waiting for you."

"I know, Mom. Almost ready. I promise we'll be out."

"I'll go keep them entertained," Deidra volunteered as she followed Mom to the living room.

"Wear this one," Bri said, shoving the necklace in front of my face. My blood cooled in my veins—the potential Amulet dangled before my eyes. I could've sworn that was still in my sock drawer.

"Ooh, yeah!" squealed Annabelle. "It's perfect!"

"I don't know. I don't think it matches," I stammered.

"No, come on! It'll look great!" pressed Bri.

"If you don't, I'll wear it," Annabelle promised, reaching for it.

"No! I'll put it on." I grabbed it from Bri's fingers. "It wouldn't look right with your dress." I slipped the Amulet around my neck.

"Perfect. Let's go," Bri said, marching from my room. I tucked the necklace into the top of my dress, covering the outline with the tripled strand of pearls. With a final look in my mirror, I followed Bri and prayed nothing happened tonight.

The ride to school was quiet. The fake smell of plastic from the store-bought costumes choked me as if it was trying to squeeze the freshness from the air. Bri fidgeted with her dress as we tried not to touch in the back seat to make room for the puffy coats we wore. As we drove up to the gym, the bass boomed in my chest; it was a new rhythm for my heartbeat. I was almost desperate enough to jump out of the moving car.

"Have I told you just how much I like your dress?" Trip flirted as we sat inside. He traced his finger on my knee. I blushed.

"Yes, but a girl could always hear it again," I replied with a smile.

"I really like your dress," he said again, leaning in for a kiss. Moving closer, my necklaces pressed against my chest and were trapped by his blue velour vest. We broke apart, and Trip dug out his vampire teeth from somewhere inside his matching blue jacket.

"Who are you supposed to be again?" I asked.

"Lestat? *Interview with the Vampire*?"

"Oh yeah! Such a good book."

Trip shrugged. "I liked the movie." He adjusted his vest as I glanced around.

We sat in the bleachers, barely acknowledging our fellow classmates. I recognized almost no one, given the amount of face masks this year. Even Cole was hard to identify with his Captain America mask. If he hadn't been at my house before, I wouldn't have even known it was him. He and Deidra were already dancing, swaying closely together.

"Let's dance!" I stood, taking his hand in mine. He nodded and followed me to the dance floor.

Excitement hung in the air amid the flurry of chiffon, polyester, glitter, wings, superheroes, bumblebees, and gods. Kids in store-bought costumes bumped into each other as they gyrated and twisted their bodies to the music. Trip's body curved against mine as we danced to the pounding bass line. I spun to face him, and we locked eyes as we swung our bodies back and forth. The dance committee had gone all-out this year. Hanging above us were black and orange streamers. In the corners of the gym were decently scary vampires, a Grim Reaper, a raging werewolf, and a zombie that jumped and twitched to chomp your brain when you walked past it. Fake fog settled around our feet as kids grabbed handfuls of candy and pretzels from a vinyl cafeteria table. My flapper costume was going over great; I was getting lots of compliments on my dress and, especially, my jewelry.

"Great earrings," Kyle Perkins said as she walked past. She and Cay were dressed as Ariel and Eric. Cay's hair was slicked back, and her seashell bra was sewn onto a tan mesh top. Kyle was taking dainty steps, thanks to her constricting tail skirt.

"Thanks! Great costumes," I replied.

"If she was keeping true to the story," Trip whispered into my ear, "She would've come as sea foam."

I looked up at him, a tad shocked he knew that.

"I read the original story to Liz and Roden when they were younger."

I grinned. He wrapped his hands around my waist as the music switched from fast to slow.

"Ashley! Ashley!" Someone called from behind me. I was jostled forward, stepping on Trip's foot in the process. My body slammed into his, and the long strand of pearls caught on his hand. As he moved to steady himself, the necklace snapped, scattering pearls all over the floor.

"Oh my god! I'm so sorry!" a girl dressed as a cop apologized. She bent over to recover some lost beads. "I totally didn't even see you there! I was looking for my friend and didn't mean to bump into you—"

"Whoa! It's okay. It was an accident," I told her as I knelt. "I'll live. My necklace, though..."

She collected a few beads and handed them to me. "I'm so sorry! I'll buy you another one. Where did you get it? Dollar Express?"

I gave her a dirty look. "No, but lucky for you they were fake anyway." I gave up collecting pearls. They were hard to find in the fog and under people's feet. This scene already drew enough attention as it was.

"Well, at least you still have the other necklace. It's really cool," she said, pointing to my chest. My eyes widened, and I slapped my hand over the Amulet before anyone could see it.

"Are you okay?" Trip asked me. Based on my bug-eyed expression, he thought I was pissed.

"You should watch where you're walking," he said at the cop.

"I really am sorry." She shot me a sympathetic smile and shrugged her shoulders slightly.

"No worries. Go find your friend." I smiled gently at her, but I was distracted, attempting to tuck in the Amulet. She returned my smile and walked off.

"What happened?" Bri rushed over with Cole and Deidra behind her. I turned my back on Trip and faced my friends.

"Nothing, some girl just ran into me, and my necklace broke. It's okay." The string from the pearls tangled in the Amulet's chain. It kept tying to my spaghetti strap, making it hard to slip under my dress.

"Bridget, you're bleeding!" Cole pointed to the hand clasping the Amulet. I looked down and saw a scrape on my knuckle.

"I'll live."

"Come on, let's get you a bandage," Deidra said pulling on my nonbleeding hand. I flinched back, but she was too quick for me. My fingers slipped off the necklace, and instantly her eyes flew to what hung around my neck. Deidra's expression was all the confirmation I needed; she looked like Golem drooling over the One Ring. Time slowed, and I couldn't hear the music over the sound of my own breath. Neither of us moved.

I was five again and caught with my hand in the cookie jar right before dinner. I swear I heard one drop of blood well up in my cut and drip onto the rubber floor.

"Bridget? Dee? Are you two okay?" Trip's voice swam above me, out of reach.

In this moment, no one else mattered.

I should have stayed home.

Someone bumped my arm, jolting me back into the present. Time sped up, and the music blared from the large speakers.

"Hey, what's going on?" Trip put his hands on my shoulders. The Amulet lay on my chest, hanging out in the open. If I wasn't screwed before, then I was now. I ripped my hand from Deidra's grasp and covered the necklace again.

"Everything's fine. I need to wash my hands and get a bandage. I'll be back!" I rushed out the gym before anyone asked any more questions.

Hiding in the same stall that had prevented me from breakup humiliation earlier this week, I panted like hunted prey. What the hell was I going to do? Ugh, why was I so stupid! I should've taken this thing off before I left the house. Oh my god, my mother was going to kill me! She'd trusted me to keep the Amulet, the powers, and my heritage a secret; and I went and flaunted it in front of the entire school, which included my boyfriend and his family—the sworn enemies of my family. The toilet next to me made a strangled noise. I stared at the cool, reflective water.

I could flush it.

I shook my head hard enough to cast off that foolish idea. Dumbest thing I could do. The whole point of my newly revealed destiny is to find this stupid thing! I shook my head. It'd make no sense for me to flush it and then hunt it down again. I rested my head against the blue tile and closed my eyes. I wished I could talk to someone about this. My friends were still in the dark, and I couldn't tell Cay because he'd try to convince me to use it to destroy the Findlays. What was I going to do? I had to get out of here!

I heard the bathroom door creak open, and a pair of heels clicked on the tiles.

I froze.

The owner of black the heels went into the stall next to me. The roll rattled in the dispenser as she blew her nose loudly, flushed the paper, and walked out. I cringed, realizing she'd never washed her hands.

My pulse slowed to a normal pace as my adrenaline dipped back down.

The door swung open again, and I saw another pair of black heels, a pair I recognized.

"Bridget, I know you're in here," Deidra said. Her voice was slippery like black ice, and the hair on my body that wasn't plastered down stood up.

Oh, crap.

Her heels stopped in front of the stall, and she pushed the door open.

"Hi," she smiled.

Oh, double crap.

"Hi." I remained glued to the wall, as if it needed me to hold it up.

"So, I guess you know what you have there," she nodded toward my chest.

"I wasn't sure until tonight."

"What're you going to do with it?"

"I was just deciding when you walked in," I gulped. Heat crept up my neck into my cheeks.

"I'm more than willing to take it off your hands." She was mesmerized yet again, her eyes staring at the half of the Amulet sitting around my neck. She reminded me of a snake in the basket, and my neck-lace was the snake charmer.

"No, thanks, I think I'll keep it. It matches my costume better." I'd never been happier Deidra was heavily lacking telekinesis. She took a step into the stall.

"I don't mind, really. It wouldn't be any trouble." Her zombie makeup and intense stare were really freaking me out. If this was a contest, she'd win for freakiest costume.

"Deidra," I said, my tone even, "back off. I don't want to hurt you."

She raised her eyebrows. "Like you could?"

Fury flashed through me, leaving deep gashes in a wake of smoldering fire. Tension built around us, leaving the air charged with energy. I moved my fingers slightly, the static shock throbbing.

"Hello? Raise your hand if you're the more powerful goddess descendant in the room." I raised my hand. Deidra raised her eyes to meet mine.

"I could take you."

"Ha! Not in those heels."

Her gaze dropped down to her feet, and I took my chance. I darted forward, knocking her from the stall and into the trash can. Deidra tumbled, limbs flopping all over as she tried to grab hold of the sink. I didn't wait to see if she would get up. I ran for the door and grabbed the handle. Deidra came up behind me, yanking my hand off the handle. The static electricity pulsated under my skin. I grabbed her arm and released some if it into her. She jolted back. I grabbed the handle again and bolted out. Kicking off and grabbing my own heels, I sprinted down the hall toward the parking lot.

"Bridget!" Deidra called. I heard her shoes hit the ground as she kicked them off and then the thumping of her feet hitting the ground. Oh god, if she got close enough, she'd kill me for this necklace. Ignoring the blast of cold air sizzling against my skin, I pushed through the main door and crossed the front walkway. I stopped. What the hell was I running for? I was more powerful than her, even with my waning powers. I could destroy her.

I turned as she ran to the door. "I'm right here, Deidra," I called, dropping my shoes. "You want this necklace? You're going to have to fight me."

She burst through, skidded to a stop about three yards away from me, and dropped her shoes in a bush. "Let's do this."

Deidra leaped at me without a pause. I dodged her, but she was able to punch me in the arm as I moved. *Think of something, any feeling, right now!* My internal voice screamed. Instantly, lightning cracked overhead

"Ooh, scary," she taunted. "Did Trip teach you that?" Another flash. I grinned.

"Let me show you what else I've learned." Thunder rumbled above, growing louder as it drew closer. Rain dripped slowly, leaving our clothes soaked.

"If this is all you ever learned, I'd get a new teacher." Deidra lunged at me again, this time knocking me to the pavement. I wrestled her hands away from my neck, struggling all the while. The attack shook my attention, and the rain let up. My adrenaline was at an all-time high. I felt a change in temperature as the air grew hot and humid. Black clouds rolled in, and heavy winds whipped around us.

With her hands otherwise occupied, Deidra leaned in, her mouth getting close to the necklace. My fist flew up, and I punched her in the throat. She coughed and loosened her grip. Taking the chance, I shoved with all my strength and pushed her off me. Still coughing, she got up as buckets of rain poured down on us. I stood, pushing wet hair off my face. Deidra looked at me. Her mouth curled into a snarl as her eyes got big and black; the pupils devoured her irises. I felt hard pinches as big welts appeared on my body. I panicked. No one had told me about this! She wasn't supposed to have this power! But the welts weren't from Deidra; they were from the ice that had fallen from the sky. She'd turned my thunderstorm into an ice storm!

I gritted my teeth and started thinking of the fire the night before. The blue and green flames dancing into the night sky as if in a ritual ceremony. The hazy aura of heat surrounding the fire. I panted and fought the pain of ice slicing into my skin, but the ice slowly turned into water droplets. Unfortunately, Deidra still had a hold on the weather. I could feel her power as it flexed against mine, keeping the water a mix of ice and rain.

"What the hell is going on out here?" a male's voice said. We both snapped our heads toward the door where Trip, Roden, Tomas, Cay, and Logan all stood. We were caught off guard, and the inclement weather let up.

"She has the Amulet," Deidra explained.

The looks ranged from Trip's shock to Tomas and Roden's surprised looks to the relief on Logan's face to Cay's excitement.

"I didn't know!" I only spoke to my boyfriend. "I suspected, but I wasn't sure, and I didn't know until Deidra tried to kill me to get to it!" I faced her again, a flash of anger pulsed through my body. Lightning cracked above us.

"Did you hear me? She has the Amulet!" Deidra hollered.

"Well, I'm glad no one else saw this, but we should be going. Come on, Bridget," Cay said smoothly, waving me foward. I didn't move. Trip took a step toward me but stopped. He breathed heavy and switched his gaze from me to his sister. With his brow furrowed and his fists clenched, he remained frozen between us.

"I didn't know," I said softly. "I didn't know. I didn't ... know." My mind was stuck. "Please, you have to believe me."

"We need to talk," he said to me with an eerily level voice.

"Talk? Talk! We need to get the Amulet!" Deidra screeched.

"Okay," I replied to Trip. "When?"

"Not today, but soon." He still didn't move toward me. The fear in me was unleashed, and I lit the sky. I didn't want to lose my boyfriend, but I couldn't stop the feeling that I just had.

I took a breath and counted to ten. The light in the sky slowed until it was completely gone.

"Okay," I whispered.

"Grab it! Just rip it off her neck!" Deidra was practically bursting a blood vessel. Her makeup was smeared from the rain, and she was shaking. I wasn't sure if it was from the cold or the lure of the Amulet.

"Enough!" Trip growled at her. "I will handle it."

Deidra snapped her mouth shut, but the rest of her was still quivering. Trip looked back at his brothers.

"We're leaving."

Tomas and Roden went to stand by Deidra without question. Trip turned to me again.

"I'll call you." I nodded, unsure of what else to say. He joined his siblings, and the four of them walked to their cars. Cay, Logan, and I remained still, watching them drive away.

"Bridget—" Cay said.

"Don't. Just... don't." The main door opened again and out popped Annabelle and Cole.

"Bridget? What happened? Are you okay?" Annabelle rushed over to me, her dress swirling around her. I looked at my dress. It was torn from the physical fight and sodden from the weather. Bruises bloomed, and I had scrapes on my legs. My shoulder hurt from impact, and exhaustion hit me like a Mack truck. I wanted to go home, crawl under my covers, and never leave my room again.

"Can you take me home?"

"Sure. We can leave right now. Cole, go grab our stuff. Don't forget my jacket." I shivered. My jacket sat in the backseat of Trip's car.

"You poor thing." Annabelle wrapped her bare arms around mine. "Come on, I'll take you home."

We left, and I never once looked back at Cay or Logan.

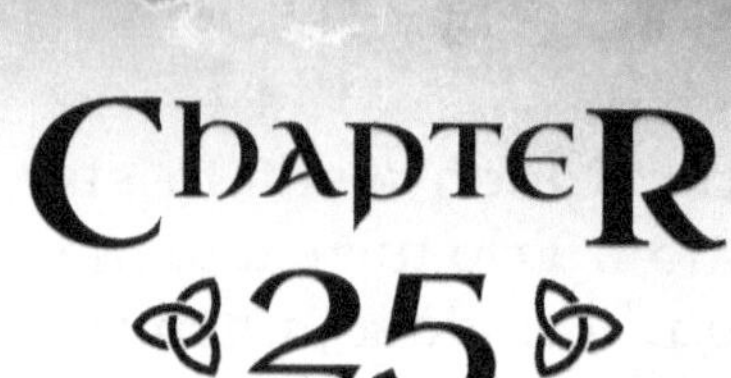

CHAPTER
25

"**B**ridget, are you okay? Oh my—what happened?" Mom jumped off the couch when Annabelle walked me into the house.

"She didn't talk on the way home, Mrs. MacNamara," Annabelle said. "I came out of the dance and found her standing outside like this."

"Thank you for driving her home. I think she could use some rest." Mom put her arm on my shoulder. "Come on, sweetheart."

"If you need anything, please let me know."

"Thank you," I said to Annabelle. She gave me a worried smile and left. Mom waited a heartbeat before turning to me.

"Are you okay?"

I nodded. "Besides some light physical damage, I'll be alright."

She nodded and gave me her own worried smile.

"Let's get you cleaned up, and then we can talk about what happened." Mom gently guided me to the bathroom as I limped slightly from a cut on the ball of my foot. The bright light of the bathroom was jarring after the dim glow of the living room.

"We need the first aid kit. I don't know if we have enough bandages," she said. "You'll have to take a shower, too. To get the mud out of your hair."

"Okay. Can I have some tea?"

Mom smiled. "Sure. I'll make you some cinnamon toast, as well." She hugged me with restraint to avoid more pain.

Looking at my beat-up appearance, I saw the dark circles my mascara left under my eyes. Hot mess over here. I pulled off the dress and rolled down the stockings. The necklace hung against my bare skin. It was the last thing I removed. Holding it in my hands, I couldn't imagine the magnitude of this family heirloom. I got into my first fistfight over this thing. Undoubtedly, it wouldn't be my last. I took a hot shower first, savoring the warmth on my sore body. When I dried off, my skin was rosy. I had a few scattered bruises and scrapes on my upper thigh and torso, but overall, I wasn't as badly hurt as I had initially thought.

"Bridget, your tea is ready," Mom said from outside the door. In my fuzzy Hello Kitty flannel pajamas, I grabbed the Amulet and ambled into the kitchen.

"I put it in the living room. I thought you'd feel more comfortable with it there than on the hard kitchen chairs," Mom offered.

"Thanks." I slowly moved into the next room as I breathed in the minty tea and took a nibble of the toast. Mom poured herself a mug and joined me on the couch.

"So, tell me what happened," she said gently.

I handed her the Amulet. Mom took the necklace in her hand and drank it in; her eyes traced the lines of the black outline. "This is it, isn't it?"

I nodded. "It's half of it. When Deidra saw it, she went psycho and attacked me."

"All this time, the one thing my parents moved around the world to protect me from was hanging in my jewelry box."

"You really had no idea?" I took another bite of the toast.

Mom just shook her head. "You know how families have those stories they pass around at the table during the holidays? I just ... assumed this was one of those stories."

"Irony is a cruel mistress sometimes," I said, breathing in the steam from the tea.

"Tell me everything that happened."

I started from the beginning with the dreams, then about Bri and Annabelle making me wear the necklace, and finally about Deidra and the fight.

"And then Trip left with everyone, and Annabelle came and dropped me off," I finished. "I didn't talk on the way home because I didn't know what to say. I can't tell my friends about any of this, so how am I going to explain my bruises?"

"Don't worry, we'll figure something out." Mom looked down at the necklace again, studying it. "I think we should put the Amulet some place safe."

"Where?"

"I'll keep it. I'll have to discuss it with Dad."

"What? Mom, no," I sat upright.

"Bridget, I can't spend more nights like this, watching you come home hurt."

"Mom, please. It'll be safe with me."

"Bridget—"

"No, Mom! It's my responsibility to find it, right? That's what everyone keeps telling me. I'm the one who protected it tonight! I'm stronger than Deidra and anyone else who comes after me!"

"You don't know that," she said sternly.

"I do!"

"What if Trip comes after you?" she exclaimed.

My breath caught in my throat, and I couldn't speak, let alone breathe. What would I do if my boyfriend came after me? I frantically tried to think of an answer, but I came up empty.

"Could you stop him?" she continued. I still couldn't answer her.

"That's something I see you didn't think about before. Bridget, I'm not saying this because I want to control your life. I want you to have one that's safe. You shouldn't be coming home bruised from school dances. You should be calling me, begging me to extend your curfew so you can go out after." Mom cupped my chin in her hand. "So for now, I will keep the Amulet and discuss with Dad what we will do with it."

I looked into her eyes. "Mom, please, let me keep it. I can protect it."

She shook her head vehemently. "No. There will be no discussion of this. As long you have the Amulet, you aren't safe, and I can't allow that. End of story. Now go and get some rest. You've had an exhausting night." She kissed me on the forehead.

"Good night," I replied, feeling disappointed. The conversation was far from over, but I was too tired to fight her anymore. If I had to, I'd find the Amulet and keep it with me.

When I woke up the next morning, I groaned as I tried to get out of bed. This would be a long day if I couldn't function at a somewhat normal level. I stopped by the bathroom and looked in the mirror again. No major improvements since last night with the exception of a washed face. It took a lot for me to make it back to my bed. I did nothing but a bit of homework and spent most of the day in bed. My body was still recovering from the fight, and I wasn't up for doing anything else but watching a marathon of whatever was on TV. My phone blew up with messages from everyone, except Trip. Apparently, Annabelle had told our friends what happened, and now they wanted a firsthand account. Cole's message was the only one that surprised me.

[Cole: Hey, Dee told me what happened.]

Ice ran through my veins. How much did she tell him? I typed back with shaky fingers.

[Bridget: What did she tell you?]

I watched as the three little bubbles popped up, stopped, then popped up again. My anxiety fluctuated with every blinking dot.

[Cole: She said you attacked her.]

My heart dropped as my anger flared.

[Bridget: Did she tell you she went after me first?]

[Cole: Yes.]

I didn't know what to say back. I held my phone in my hand and stared at the screen. Those bubbles returned.

[Cole: I think we need to take a break from being friends for a while.]

I burst into tears. Cole had been one of my closest friends since Freshman Orientation, and his choosing Deidra over me dug into me in a way I hadn't expected. Laying my face in my hands, I sobbed; the hurt welled up inside me and sat there like stagnant water.

With tears still streaming down my face, I shakily typed out:

[Bridget: Don't believe everything she tells you.]

I told everyone else I was resting—I would see them on Monday—and turned my phone on silent. I didn't know what else to tell them, and I still had to figure out a cover story. Until I talked with Trip and processed the loss of Cole, I couldn't face anyone just yet. Snuggling back into my pillows, I flipped channels until I landed on some cooking show. I let visions of cranberry muffins and stuffed breads lull me to sleep.

I rolled over and out of bed, the smell of warming bread and sweet cakes inviting me to the kitchen.

"Mom? Did you make all of this?" I said, rubbing sleep from my eyes.

"Doesn't she always make the best food?" Deidra answered. Wearing Mom's handprint apron I'd made in kindergarten, Deidra turned around from the counter. She had a dusting of flour on the front.

"The best," I agreed. Looking at the spread in front of me, I grew famished. I moved to the table and picked up a slice of almond cake from where it cooled on a rack. I crammed it into my mouth without taking a bite. Grabbing a handful of butter cookies, I popped one at a time into my mouth, not bothering to savor them. I washed the cookies down with a mini cupcake and cream puff. My appetite had never been so ravenous.

"Feeling starved?" Deidra asked me.

I nodded because I was chewing another three cupcakes.

"Would you like something to drink?" She held a pitcher of lemonade that hadn't been there before. I nodded again. I took the glass she poured and gulped it down. The intense sweetness made my teeth hurt.

"More?" She offered the pitcher again. I held out the glass. Biting into a slice of crusty bread, I chewed slowly to absorb the sugar.

Deidra sighed happily. "I'm so glad you like everything! I baked all day to make everything just the way you like it."

I sipped again and immediately puckered my lips. My salivary glands tingled. I bit a brownie to counteract the sour but nearly spit the bite out. It tasted ... salty. I swallowed to be polite but took a cookie to get rid of that taste, too.

"Thank you," I said, and I prayed my mouth would stop hating me from the barrage of flavors. My breath caught in my chest, and I practically coughed up a lung. I doubled over, leaning against the table. Something swung out from underneath my chin, and I jumped. The Amulet dangled in midair above my clavicle. I stood, confused. I thought Mom took this last night. Deidra handed me another glass, and a sick feeling grew in my stomach.

"Here's a glass of water," she said. Wiping away tears from my eyes, I took the cup and sipped carefully.

"That's a lovely necklace," Deidra pointed out. "May I see it?"

No! No! My mind screamed, but my body was no longer under my control.

"Sure." I rested the cup on the table and brought my hands up to my neck, slipping the chain off. Holding it out toward her, Deidra's eyes gleamed in the overhead lighting. The muscles in her hands were tense; she was restraining herself.

"You know what?" I asked, pulling the necklace back. "It's not really clean. I think I dropped powdered sugar on it. I'll wash it." I turned, but before I stepped, Deidra snapped a hand down on my arm.

"I don't see anything wrong with it," she said. I tried to pull away, but her grip held fast.

"No, really. See there? Sugar." She leaned in closer.

"Let me see," Deidra said, reaching for the Amulet. Her fingers trembled slightly, but I was in no position to stop her. Enclosing the pendant in her palm, she pulled, trying to rip it out of my hand. I pushed her away, but she remained glued and dragged me forward. I stumbled into her as she landed against the counter.

"Let go!" I cried, clawing at her hand.

"Never! It's mine!" She yanked at the chain again, and the clasp broke. She shoved me hard, and I knocked into the edge of the counter. My back stung from impact. I tried calling on my powers, but nothing happened. What the hell was going on? Deidra swung her leg out at my knee, but I jumped onto the counter. I called on my powers again. Nothing.

Deidra barreled at me with a thunderous gait, her arms stretched out. I slid down, readying myself in a defensive stance. As she pulled her clenched fist back and swung, I ducked and turned, pushing her into the counter. The chain clinked against the granite. I lunged for it, knowing my movement was useless.

My hands landed on something cold and soft. Snow. I whipped my head up to find I was no longer in my kitchen, but in a clearing surrounded by pine trees. A blanket of reflective gray covered the sky, only allowing the glow from the sun to escape through its weave. A mini avalanche fell from the branches, landing quietly on the forest floor. Expecting to hear wind or maybe an animal, I was greeted with intense silence. I stood, brushing snow off my pjs.

That did me no good. Wet patches of pants stuck to my skin.

"I thought I said I would contact you," a voice drifted to me. I looked around but didn't see anyone.

"Trip? Is that you?" I called. My words were absorbed by the snow.

"Why didn't you just wait?" the voice asked.

"Wait for what?"

"You let her take it from you!" This time the voice sounded more like Cay.

"I didn't let anyone take anything!" Frustration settled in my chest.

"Then why aren't you wearing the Amulet?" the voice taunted. I touched my neck absentmindedly.

"She ripped it out of my hand! My powers didn't work, and I couldn't stop her!"

"I should've kept it safe." Mom's voice danced above my head. I didn't know where to look, so I tilted my head to the sky.

"It wasn't my fault!" I screamed, and pent-up anger spilled from my mouth. "I didn't do anything, and she attacked me!"

"You must get it back..."

"You can't lose it..."

"If you'd waited for me, I could've helped you..."

The voices overlapped each other, repeating the same phrases. I pressed my hands over my ears, trying to keep them out. Their words burrowed into my ear, penetrating my brain. "Shut up!"

I blinked in the darkness of my room. My nerves twitched as I lay in bed, covers half-thrown on the floor. The voices in my dream still echoed in my head. I shuddered. I felt like I'd disappointed everyone all at once. Pulling the covers to my waist, I took a few breaths to calm myself and gave up on sleep altogether.

Chapter 26

Mom was a peppy cheerleader, party of one. Stumbling around the kitchen, I grabbed a bowl and cereal and then crashed on the couch. I knew I should be doing homework or scrolling through memes, but I'd liked my day yesterday so much. I was going to repeat it.

Two bowls and an hour nap later, I dragged my lazy self off the couch and back into my room. My phone looked like a strobe with the amount of blinking it did. Two missed calls and six texts. The calls were from Mom, and the texts were from my friends responding to yesterday's message.

My phone lit up again with a new message.

[Trip: Hey. Can we talk?]

Trip.
My heart fluttered.

[Bridget: Sure. When?]

I wiped sweaty palms on my pajama pants. My nerves were strung tight. Why? Somehow, I felt like I was in trouble. I'd defended myself against my boyfriend's sister after all.

[Trip: 6. Park.]

I wrote back:

[Bridget: See you then.]

After showering and completing some last-minute homework, I jogged to the top of the street. My body didn't ache as much as yesterday, but there was a sore spot on my shoulder still. Wind blew harshly across my face, danced past me, and skipped over the river as I approached the gazebo. My nerves twitched as I couldn't stop the confusing mix of anxiety, defensiveness, and uncertainty. Fragments of touching moments with Trip flashed in my mind: our first conversation turned first date, the bouquet of flowers from our actual first date, our first kiss... Heat rushed to my cheeks, and I smiled.

Something romantic stirred in the deepest part of my heart.

I saw Trip's silhouette in the fading sunlight. He stood with his back to me, hands resting on the banister, facing the Tuckahoe River. My sneakers crunched on fallen leaves as I approached the gazebo.

"Hey," he said, turning around.

"Hi." I stood outside the fixture, not sure what to do. I desperately wanted to hug and kiss him and snuggle into his arms to keep warm. But something held me back. Right now, I couldn't guarantee he wanted to keep dating me. His sister and I *did* have a knockout fight.

"How are you?" Trip asked.

"Sore, but I'll live." I paused. "How's Deidra?" I couldn't say I actually cared, given what had happened, but Miss Manners—my mother—would've made me ask.

"Same." He half-smiled. "I think her pride hurts more than her body."

"Yeah, well..." It was eerily quiet. The wind stopped blowing, and even the river lapping on the shore muted. Porch lights blinked on all the way up and down the block.

"I don't know what to say," I offered.

"Me either." He blew out a deep breath. "I'm ... not even completely sure how I feel."

I understood that. My mind was a constant whir of emotions, ranging from scared to angry and all that fell between.

"I'm pissed at Dee for attacking you."

A spark of hope ignited in my chest. "Yeah?"

"I ... yelled at her," he took a deep breath and let it out. "I've never done that before. She's usually the calm, put together one, you know?" He shook his head. "But when she admitted to me that she went after you, I just... snapped." Trip shrugged and shoved his hands into his coat pockets. I didn't speak.

"We fought. Mom and Dad overheard and broke us up."

"Are you grounded?" I asked, putting my hands into my pockets. I hadn't moved from my spot. No, he needed to be the one to take the first step.

"No. They didn't know what to do with us. We never fight." He was upset again, but maybe at himself this time for losing his cool with his sister.

"But the thing is?" he continued. "She's not the only one to blame."

"No?" I held my breath.

"No. You aren't innocent in all of this."

"What? What did I do? She's the one who cornered me in the bathroom!"

"Bridget, come on. You had one half of the Amulet around your neck! What did you expect her to do?" He threw his hands in the air.

"Not try to kill me!" Frustration flowed through me. How the hell had it all been my doing?

He snorted. "Right. She wasn't trying to kill you. Stop being so dramatic."

Fury flared under my skin.

"I get that you didn't tell anyone else about the necklace. But you kept it from me. Me! Your boyfriend! I thought we were going to be honest with each other!"

"I didn't know!" I screamed. I drowned in the betrayal rolling off him in thick waves. "I don't know anything about this whole stupid story! The Amulet, the goddesses, my powers, it's all new to me! So how was I supposed to know the necklace was one half of the most magical item on this planet? What would you have done?"

Trip didn't say anything, let alone walk toward me. He stood there, glaring at me. Even from where I was, I saw the storm brewing behind his light-green eyes.

"I'm waiting," I rasped. "You're the one who's known about everything since you were born, so enlighten me. Share your infinite wisdom!"

Icy wind picked up, whistling as it swirled past us. A huge gust blew by and threw the blue recycling bins, tipping them and spilling their contents. Paper from people's recycling fluttered in the air and pressed against the benches, struggling to break free. I held my own, but if it was any stronger, I would've been slammed into a tree. Then it died down.

"I don't know," he mumbled, lowering his gaze.

"I did what I thought I was supposed to do. And I get blamed because you thought I was keeping secrets? That's beyond unfair." I crossed my arms over my chest. Trip leaned against the railing and looked out over the river. Neither of us moved for a long while.

"I'm sorry," he whispered. Trip turned to face me; his expression was a combination of regret and misery. "I'm just so confused about everything."

"Me too." Again, silence.

"So... now what?" I prompted.

"I don't know." Silence stretched on as I waited for him to continue. He sighed again. "I don't know. Everything's still so confusing. I'm going to need a few days to clear my head."

"Okay." Disappointment expanded in my chest. I was afraid he'd say that. "Well, I'll see you tomorrow, then."

"Yeah, see you."

Chapter
❧ 27 ❧

Three weeks passed before we said anything to each other besides our morning greetings and lunchtime chitchat. Things between Trip and I were unsettled at best. Everything I did or said led to a breakup, and my feet hurt from all the eggshells I walked on. It drove me insane. It didn't help that when I walked past Cole, he did everything in his power to avoid making eye contact. He nearly walked into a garbage can one time when he was trying to dodge me. Now, with things strained between Trip and me, Cay felt this was the best opportunity to get chummy with me again.

"Yo, cuz," he said at my locker after English.

"What do you want?" I shut my locker and slung my bag over my shoulder.

"So, have you found it yet?" He followed me down the hall. Since the dance, Cay and I had been in cahoots, trying to find the Amulet piece Mom has and the one still missing. I needed something to distract me from pining for Trip, and school wasn't cutting it anymore.

"No. I texted you last night; I don't know where she put it." Truth be told, with all the crap with Trip, my focus wasn't on the damned jewelry. But I wasn't going to let Cay know that. I still needed someone to clue me in on anything in the feuding history if I was meant to find the other half of the Amulet. Of course, that was assuming I was following my pre-determined destiny.

"Want to meet up today to study the family history again? We may have missed something the other day."

Spending time with Cay was a double-edged sword. On one side, I finally felt I could hold my own in a family history trivia game, but on the other, it was hard to learn when every other sentence began with "the evil Winter Clan." Being caught between your family and your boyfriend was not the feel-good time one might have hoped for.

"I can't tonight. I'm busy."

"Come on, Thursday is Thanksgiving. We have a five-day weekend. Whatever you have to do, do it later."

I brushed my hair off of my face. "Cay, I just can't."

"What about Friday?"

"You don't give up, do you?"

"Not now, no. Not when we're getting close. I just know it."

"How can you tell?"

He dropped his voice. "That story about your grandma, who got the necklace from the lover? Well, I looked into it, and I think there's a clue to telling us where the other piece is."

I blinked. He grinned.
"See you on Friday."

Thanksgiving was one of the best holidays ever. I looked forward to seeing my aunts, uncles, and cousins sit around eating turkey and pie. This year, I floated through the day, barely participating in any of the festivities. My mind swirled with Cay's revelation. How had Andrew's family found the Amulet? Had it been in pieces before then? I constantly checked my phone to see if Cay dropped any more hints, but there was nothing from him. And Trip? He sent me the perfunctory 'Happy Thanksgiving!' that could have been part of a mass text. I couldn't wait for tomorrow.

The next morning, Neit barked as I waited on Cay's doorstep. The sky was an icy blue, streaked with strips of white. A chill hung in the air as I shivered and pulled my scarf up closer to my ears. I sent a small burst of warmth down into my toes, but that withered out fast. Every day, I did at least one thing to work my powers, but I kept failing. It could have been the turning-to-stone thing or my lack of training, but either way, Cay needed to hurry the hell up.

The door opened, and the wrong McKay boy smiled at me.

"Hey, Bridget," Alec said warmly. "Cay's upstairs in the shower. So, you're stuck with me for now." He backed away from the door to let me in.

"No problem! How's UPenn?"

"Pretty great. Much harder than high school, but the freedom is cool. Drink?" He offered as we reached the kitchen.

"No thanks." I kept shifting my weight from one foot to the other and tapping my nails on the counter.

"You okay?" His forehead creased with concern. I smiled shyly and nodded.

"Hey, chill. Cay told me everything." I raised an eyebrow.

"Powers... Pretty freaking cool, right?" Alec smirked.

"Oh yeah! Total shock! I mean, weather control?"

"Pretty badass."

"What can you do?" I asked.

He grinned. "Hand-to-hand combat is my specialty. I never lose."

I looked back toward the pictures on the bookcase. Martial Arts awards, all with Alec's name inscribed, dotted the shelves.

"That all comes from Brighde? I thought all she controlled was weather."

"She controls a lot more than that."

A door closed as Cay walked downstairs, drying his hair with a towel. "Hey," he said. "You ready?"

"Mom and Dad always kept this family history book, but I didn't really look at it until now."

"Why not?"

He shrugged. "Never mattered before. I spent hours looking for anything to clue me in about Una and Andrew." The book flopped open on his bed with a garbled thud; its mouth opened wide and revealed pieces of torn notebook paper tucked inside the pages.

"Any luck?"

"Not until I saw this." Cay flipped to a yellowed page. "See right there?" I turned the book around and read the beginning of the paragraph.

> *When the sun goes down and doesn't rise*
> *And mist adorns the hanging trees,*
> *broken halves wash across open Skye,*
> *and a Seeker travels the summer breeze.*
> *Endless rains and icy winds gather up ahead,*
> *and so begins the quest for the Lovers' charm,*
> *for only their Amulet will calm this dread,*
> *and bring the world away from harm.*

"Yeah, it's the same story I keep hearing. So what?"

"Keep reading," he urged.

> *Love will bring and bind the pieces,*
> *soothe the storms that threaten man.*
> *Who will come to smooth the creases,*
> *and set the world right again?*
> *Racing to uncover what's concealed,*
> *Through forest and valley, mountain and field.*

"I don't get it." I sighed. I hate poetry.

"Right here." He pointed to the line "the Seeker travels the summer breeze." "This has to be talking about you!"

"I thought you were looking for Andrew and Una connections." I looked up at him.

Cay groaned. "Work with me here. I was looking for that, but that line talks about a summer Seeker, Brighde's kin, being the one who finds the Amulet."

"Why is "Skye" spelled funny?"

"Bridget. Focus."

"I'm trying, but I never understand poetry. Why can't anyone just come out and say what they're thinking?" I pouted.

"You two need help?" Alec stuck his head in. "I've studied the prophecy a few times." Cay frowned.

"No, we got this."

"No, we don't. Alec, I don't get it," I whined a little. I really, *really* hated poetry.

"What's going on?" Alec pulled a chair close to the bed and flipped it around, resting his arms on the back. He pushed his hair from his face and stilled, ready to help.

"Nothing! That's the problem!" Cay threw his hands in the air. "Our Seeker here doesn't believe she is destined to find the Amulet!"

"Cay, chill out. Bridget knows we have to find it before Beira's family does." He looked at me. I nodded.

"Now this line here," Alec pointed to the second stanza, "... quest for the Lover's charm ... could be the ticket. The clue we need."

"How?" Cay demanded.

"Bridge, didn't you say before that the Amulet was broken in two by Andrew?" Alec asked.

I nodded.

"So, if love broke the Amulet in half, then love will make it whole again."

Cay and I both blinked at Alec.

"Meaning if Una had one piece..." Alec prompted.

"Then Andrew had the other!" I called out excitedly.

"Right!"

Cay rolled his eyes at me. "Well, we can't go back in time and fix it now."

"And that's why you need to find that piece your mom hid," Alec said to me as he slouched a bit.

"I've been looking but no luck so far."

"Bridget, do you know where my parents are right now?" Cay asked.

I frowned. "No, why would I know that?"

"They aren't Christmas shopping. They're in Scotland. The weather is beyond out of control. And we can't do anything until we find the Amulet. Bridget, our people are suffering from the extreme temperature drops. Every day, it's a new season. It falls on our family to harness it."

"I'm trying, okay! I've been doing what I can to find out where she hid it, but it's not in all the normal spots. I don't even think it's in the house." I sat back, a bit sullen. It wasn't like I didn't want to find the Amulet.

"You need to break it off with Trip," Cay said.

"Says who?"

"You're dating the enemy." He threw his hands up again. "How else do you think it's going to end?"

All the anger washed out of me. Weren't all fairy tales about star-crossed lovers who survived all challenges and obstacles in their way, only to prove love would prevail? Did Trip feel we could survive all the odds? Did I?

"It doesn't matter. I'm not breaking up with him because you tell me to." Cay dramatically groaned into a pillow.

"We're doomed."

Chapter 28

I spent the rest of my holiday weekend hunting for the Amulet while avoiding any cover-blowing questions from both my parents and my friends.

[Annabelle: Hey Bridget. Is everything okay with you and Cole?]

She asked me in our group chat.

[Bridget: Cole and I aren't friends right now.]

Bri responded right away.

[Bri: !!! Is it because of Deidra?]

[Bridget: Yes and no. Long story. Can't really talk about it yet. It still hurts too much to relive it.]

All I received from Annabelle was a heart emoji.

Putting my phone down, I opened a box full of summer clothes Mom kept up here. I dug through them, hoping the necklace popped up.

"Bridget, why are you in the attic?" Mom called up to me.

I peeked over the side. "I thought some of the Christmas stuff was still up here. I didn't want you and Dad to come up and fall through the ceiling and hurt yourself!"

"Well, that's nice, sweetheart, but all the stuff is in the basement now. Be careful coming down."

"I will!" I shimmied from view, waited five minutes, and then climbed down the ladder. I checked in my parents' room, the kitchen, the basement, the attic, the living room, and a briefcase in the closet with all our important documents. No dice. I looked around the garage only to turn up grease and grime, but no necklace. After reading the prophecy, I was genuinely worried. If I didn't find it, what would happen to the people in Scotland? In the world? I'd be guilty for causing millions of deaths worldwide. My phone buzzed in my pocket.

[Cay: Any luck?]

I turned it off. As if tearing the house apart and thinking of the deaths of innocent people weren't stressful enough, Cay texting me every five minutes wasn't helpful, either.

"Hey, kid," Dad said behind me, as I stood in the center of the garage. I figured it couldn't hurt to look again. "Taking up a new interest in mechanics?" He looked at the grease smudges and dirt on my jeans and face.

"Something like that. I got to go shower." I quickly moved past, trying not to wipe the grime on his clean clothes.

"Wait."

I froze. "Yeah?"

"It's not in here," he motioned around us.

"What's not?" Innocent was never a look I could pull off.

"Think about it. Would Mom keep an invaluable item in this grease trap?" I blushed. "Look, I know how important this whole Seeker destiny thing is to you, but Mom and I are trying to keep you safe."

I nodded, crestfallen. I totally thought he was going to tell me where to look.

"Give me a few days, and I'll see if I can work something out with her." He smiled.

"Seriously?" I squinted, not sure I believed him.

Dad winked. "Hey, I can't have the fate of the world resting on my shoulders knowing I could have helped you save it. Now, go shower." He turned his back on me as I stared at him in astonishment. Clearly, I had misjudged Dad.

"Hey, can we talk?" Trip asked me on Monday morning. The chill temperature had taken a plunge, and I wondered how much control Trip really had over the weather now. He held open the front door as a stream of students filed past.

"About what?"

"Us. Things are ... unsettled."

"I know." I shifted the strap of my backpack and looked past him.

"Tonight?"

I nodded. He smiled and kissed me gently. I returned the tenderness of the kiss, but my heart wasn't into it anymore. So many things ran through my mind; I couldn't focus on being happy with Trip when I had the threat of world destruction haunting me.

I couldn't remember what I did in school anymore. The days had been blurring together into a blended mix of tests, papers, friends, lunches, Amulets, stress, and Christmas shopping. Seeing Cole not looking in my direction at all, walking next to Deidra, stung every time we passed each other.

Concerned I was stepping into enemy territory, I met Trip at his house that same night.

"I figured since no one was home, you'd want to come here to chat," he said as he poured two cups of hot chocolate. I wrapped my fingers around the handle of the cup and breathed in the steam. The tension in my chest wove tight, and it hurt to take a breath.

"Even Tomas?"

"Yes. I sent him off on some errand that will take a few hours." We both sat at the kitchen table.

"Okay." I focused on my drink, not wanting to start the conversation.

He placed his down. "Look, I'm sorry for the stuff I said. I know it's not your fault. Dee was wrong for attacking you like she did. The pressure to save the world is crippling sometimes, and I think it's my doing."

"How?"

"With Mom and Dad gone most of the time, it falls on me to teach my brother and sisters about our family's responsibility. I think I pushed the idea on them a little too hard, and Dee just did what she felt was right."

"To kill me?" My stomach flipped over and clenched.

"No! God, that is never an option. Bridget, please understand." He ran his hand through his hair in frustration.

"That your sister is insane? Yeah, I got that." I stared at him, not wanting to let him make excuses for her.

"Hey! She's not more insane than anybody else around here. I'm trying to apologize."

I shook my head and put my cup down. "You shouldn't be apologizing for her. She's the one who slammed me against a wall!"

"I know, but I can't control her. No matter how many times I've told her, she refuses to speak to you. What else do you want me to do?" Trip held his hands up, as if I could hand him the answer.

"Nothing. There's nothing else you can do." I slumped in the chair, a little deflated. "Why do we do this anymore?"

"What?"

"This. The fighting! What does it mean if all we do is fight?"

"It means we care about each other."

"How?"

"Bridget, I don't ever want anything bad to happen to you. And if I have to fight to get you to see that, I will." He covered my fingers with his and squeezed gently. "I'm sorry Dee attacked you. She shouldn't have done it."

"No, she shouldn't have. Trying to take something that isn't hers," I pointed out.

He sighed. "But she has the right to go after the necklace."

I pulled my hand away. "Since when? According to everyone on both sides, the Amulet is exclusive to one family, and we can't share ownership."

He fixated on me with a determined stare.

"It doesn't exclusively belong to you."

"Well, it's not yours, either!"

"Says who?" He got up and dumped his mug into the sink. "Beira is older than Brighde, so by inheritance law, my family owns it."

I snorted. "Inheritance law? Well, according to possession law, my family has it in our possession so it belongs to us." I crossed my legs and sat back.

He shook his head. "God, Bridget, you can be so…"

"So what?" I challenged.

"Nothing." Trip sighed and gazed at the window. I looked out at the big, sliding glass door behind Trip. The wind kicked up, blowing the little bits of leaves around. It blazed bright outside, turning everything white with sunshine.

Little flakes of snow appeared as the sun dimmed. It was as if someone had turned the lights down. More flakes fell every second, covering the world with a fluffy coating. A minute later, the sun was back again as my blood heated once more. The snow melted before it'd had a chance to cool.

"Well, how do you expect me to believe you had no clue about the Amulet? And then you just decide to wear it in a public place? That sounds more like you wanted to show off the fact that you're closer to total weather control than we are!" Trip said.

A light went off in my head. The Findlays didn't have the other half. My family had the advantage now.

"So, what do you want me to do?" I asked, calmer than before.

"I think you know my answer."

"Look, if I didn't care about you at all, I would've ended us the minute I found out about my family." I walked back to the table and took a sip from my now-chilled hot chocolate.

"Are you saying I'm more important to you than your family? Than your destiny?"

I never said that, but did I feel that way? Was my family really worth less than my high school romance? Was Cay right in telling me Trip and I needed to break up? A sinking feeling in my gut told me I knew the answer to these questions, even if I didn't want to say it out loud. But now that Trip knew I had the Amulet, what was left for us? Too many times have I been told we're enemies, and we won't find a compromise to suit both families.

So, I asked the question I couldn't answer.

"Are you... are you still dating me because I have the Amulet?" I stared at him point-blank and steeled myself for the response. I imagined little iron walls growing around my heart, clinking as they inter-locked like puzzle pieces.

His silence spoke volumes.

Chapter

❧ 29 ❧

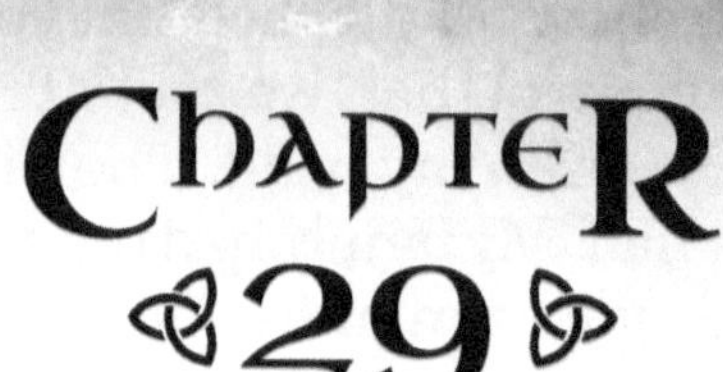

As I walked home in freezing temperatures, Trip's silence echoed in my mind.

He really was only dating me for the Amulet, and I felt numb. My emotional range was stretched thin, and I couldn't tap into those emotions anymore. I didn't have enough feeling to summon a small spark to fight off the cold. Trip's question followed me as I trudged to my house. Was he more important to me than my own family? I still couldn't answer that. I rubbed my temples with my gloved fingers. It seemed like winter showed up overnight, and my fingers were chilly even wrapped in fuzzy fabric.

A soft buzzing came from my pocket.

[Cay: I found something.]

Excitedly, I texted Cay back:

[Bridget: Details?]

I tucked my phone into my sleeve and shivered in my coat. The cold had attached itself to the insides of my bones, and even with my struggling powers, I couldn't get it to release its grip. I jumped at the vibration on my wrist.

[Cay: Tomorrow. Lunch. Library.]

I quickly typed back I would see him then.

Turning the icy doorknob to walk into the house, I was drained from everything. My nerves were wracked from fighting with Trip, and I hate that I felt unsettled about his accusations. Tossing my jacket on my floor with my shoes and socks, I curled up under my blankets and turned on the TV. For now, old reruns of *Law and Order* drowned out the parade of questions dancing in my head.

"Hey," I whispered to Cay as I dropped into a seat. He slid his chair closer to me, shrinking the space between us, and then pulled out a book from his backpack.

"Hey. Last night, Alec and I were working on where Andrew's family is, and we found an old drawing of what he may've looked like." Cay flipped open to a page toward the back of the book where a yellowed sketch of a young man stared at me. He had big, chocolate eyes fringed with long lashes. Andrew could've made a killing with an endorsement deal for Maybelline. His long, brown hair was pulled back with a piece lying across his cheek. I totally saw how Una swooned over him. My eyes traveled down the collar of his faded, white shirt. There hung the other half of the Amulet, clear as a raindrop for anyone to see.

"What does this mean? How does knowing what Andrew looked like help us?" I asked, my eyes still stuck on the drawing.

Cay smiled like the cat that swallowed a canary.

"Turn it over." On the back of the picture, in faint script, were the words: *Andrew, Helvetia, 1687.*

"Helvetia was the old name of Switzerland," Cay clarified.

"I repeat, what does this mean?"

"It means we need to find a way to get you to Zurich."

"Switzerland? I hear it's nice this time of year," a snide voice chimed in above us. We both swung our heads to see Deidra peering down. Cay's hand slid over the picture, just in case she saw something.

"Weird, I don't remember asking for your opinion," I shot back. My body sung with anticipated tension. I'd never thought I was one for fighting, but I was ready to take her on again, powers or not.

"Weird, I remember asking you not to hurt my brother, and yet, that's all you do these days. I can barely remember his smile. Can you?" Her snotty smile made me wish we were in the dead of summer.

"I think there's no smile because every day he has to realize he's stuck with you as a sister," Cay cut in. Deidra flushed and narrowed her eyes.

"What do you want?" I needed to distract Deidra from finding out about Switzerland.

"Trip has been nagging me since Halloween to apologize to you."

"Great, I don't accept. You can go away now." I turned my back on her and closed the book as Cay stood, forcing her to step back.

"I'm not apologizing," she said. "I don't care if I hurt your feelings. You have the Amulet, and it belongs to Beira's kin."

"Here we go again," I muttered and followed Cay's lead, standing. "Get out of my way."

She crossed her arms over her chest. "No. Not until you give me the Amulet."

"Oh well, why didn't you just say so!" I rolled my eyes at her. "You really must be dumb to believe I would hand it over."

Her eyes flickered to my neck and then met mine again. "It wouldn't be the first time you made a mistake."

The sky outside darkened as clouds dark as coal covered the sun. Thunder crackled, and lightning lit up the sky.

"Shall we take this outside?" I smiled sweetly at her.

"Bridget! What're you doing?" Trip demanded as he stormed into the library.

"There is no yelling in the library!" Mr. Capri, one of the school librarians, scolded us from the next aisle. "If you must speak loudly, take it outside." He motioned toward the hallway, then walked into his office and closed the door.

"Bridget, what the hell is wrong with you?" Trip said more quietly.

"Me! Your sister started it! She was eavesdropping on a private conversation."

"They were talking about the Amulet," Deidra sang.

"Actually," Cay said, "to keep everyone honest, the word 'Amulet' was never spoken. Bridget's right. Dee did involve herself where she didn't belong. It's not like you witnessed it. Why are you here, anyway?"

"It's the library. Why else would I be here?" Trip snapped. He pointed out the window. "Clearly Bridget was upset over something. Note the instant thunderstorm."

I didn't flinch. "I'm so done being blamed for stuff I didn't do! Ever since you showed up on the beach, my life has been a nonstop carousel of lies."

"Lies? What lies?"

"Yeah, what lies?" Cay leaned against the table.

"The fact we all have powers, the goddesses, the Amulet." I took a breath and looked at Trip. "Our true destinies."

Trip rolled his eyes and shook his head. "Those weren't lies. I can't help if your mom didn't tell you anything! Remember, I helped you find out the truth!"

"Actually," Cay chimed in again, with his finger in the air, "to keep you honest, I'm the one who made you tell her."

"Yeah, fat lot of good that did her!"

"It did her a lot of good! Not only did she discover that she is one of the most powerful people in the world, but also she found out the truth about you." Cay remained cool.

"What the hell is he talking about?" I demanded from Trip.

Cay sang, "Go ahead and tell her, Trip," the same way a first-grade kid sings on the playground.

A vein in Trip's neck twitched, and I frowned. "I don't know."

"Sure, you do." Cay turned his face toward me. "Ask him why he moved to Corbin City." His arms crossed over his chest.

"Shut up, Cay," Trip's voice darkened as he clenched his fists.

I was really sick of the mind games between them. "What the hell is going on with you two?" I exploded.

Trip didn't answer me, but Cay did.

"Let me clue you in, cousin. We moved here for you. Because of your family status. The Seeker. What makes you think he didn't move here for the same reason?"

The wind rushed out of my lungs like I was punched in the stomach. I was nothing more than a pawn in this vicious family war.

"You moved here for me? To do what, kill me?" I whispered shakily. I put my hand over my stomach and leaned on the table for support.

"More like date you," Cay responded. Trip, avoiding my gaze, shoved his hands in his pockets and licked his lips.

My legs wavered. I felt like a heavyweight boxer going down in a fight.

"Nothing to say for yourself, Findlay?" Cay moved in front of me and crossed his arms.

"Why bother when you're going to say it all?" Trip responded, visibly hurt. Defeat marked his voice.

I felt like throwing up. "There's more?"

"I should let you tell her you're dating her because you needed to know how much she knew about her destiny," my cousin said smugly, "but I'm going to enjoy watching her destroy you."

Trip looked away from me.

"Is that true?" I asked, the quiver in my voice betraying me. My anger boiled up and over as I stood to face Trip. "Were you dating me to find out if I knew about the Amulet? If I knew where to find it?"

"Not... completely," he admitted, finally looking at me. I gaped like he'd slapped me in the face. Trip shot daggers at Cay with his eyes.

"I knew it. I called you out on that, and you blew me off!" I shook my head in disbelief. "I'm such an idiot."

"No, you're not!" Trip took a step toward me; his hands were open, like he wanted to take mine into them. "Bridget, I was only supposed to find out if you knew about any of this. If you didn't, I was to back off. But I couldn't. You're a wonderful girl, and I just..." His eyes pleaded with me to believe him.

"What? You just what?"

"I didn't want to lose you."

I shook my head, and I took a step toward him. "Too late. I can't date anyone I can't trust." Turning my back on him, I headed toward the door.

His hand was heavy on my shoulder as he touched me. "Bridget!"

"Enough!" I sent a huge gust of wind through the room, blowing books off shelves. "I'm done."

Trip's powers overcame mine, and the dark clouds outside were replaced with heavy wet snowfall. In a matter of thirty seconds, two inches of snow blanketed the grounds.

"No! I won't give up until you believe me."

"Good luck with that." I ignored the pain stabbing at my chest as I continued to the hallway.

"I don't know what else to say to get you to trust me."

"There's nothing else you can say!" I brushed past, firmly pressing the book to my chest. Maybe it would muffle the sound of my heart breaking.

"Bridget!" Trip called. I turned to face him. "Are we really over?"

"Are you that dense, Findlay?" Cay came up next to me, flanking my left side. "She said it's over."

"I thought I loved you," I said softly, "but I can't take the lies anymore."

Deidra's eyes grew brighter, and she smiled widely. "Good. Game on. We're going to find the Amulet before you."

Cay scoffed. "Good luck trying. We're already in the lead."

Trip said nothing, just staring at me. His mouth upturned and quivered as his arms hung limply at his side. He swallowed the lump in his throat and straightened his posture. I watched as the fire he held for me morphed into something else.

Surrender.

"Fine," Deidra said. "But don't be surprised if we find it first."

"If," I said. Cay waved his fingers at Deidra. She flipped him off. I glanced at Trip once more, secretly hoping he'd pull off some romantic gesture, but there was nothing. I walked toward the door as the ball rang, and I accidently bumped into the table.

"Are you okay?" Cay asked.

"I think so. Ouch," I winced, rubbing my hip. "What the hell did I trip on?" Underneath my feet was a small spattering of black ice.

"Did you really just try to hurt her?" Cay growled at Trip.

"Don't be so dramatic," Deidra jumped in. "She tripped. Bridget's clumsy. We all know that."

"How pathetic. Letting your little sister defend you," sneered Cay. "Fight your own battles."

"Cay," I cut in, pulling on his sleeve. "Let's leave. I can't stand being around him anymore."

"I'd watch my back if I were you, Findlay," he threatened. "No one hurts my blood and gets to sleep soundly at night." He held open the door, and we left.

Cay pulled me into an alcove and waited until the hallway was clear.

"I'm sorry about Trip," he said softly. "I know I hate him, but you don't." Tears formed behind my eyes and slipped down my cheeks.

"Thank you," I said, leaning my face against his chest. There in the seclusion of the nook, I cried quietly into Cay's shirt. He just hugged me close, like a big brother, comforting me.

Chapter 30

I stayed home from school the next day. Cay must have informed my friends because, miraculously, I was left alone to recover. It involved lots of crying, sulking, wallowing, and sappy movies. I glossed over the breakup with Mom and Dad. Whoever said being dumped hurts must have forgotten the pain the dumper feels. I still loved Trip; it wasn't enough to save our relationship. I grabbed another tissue from the table and blew my nose. My lip trembled for the millionth time today, and fresh tears streamed down my face.

The front door opened and Dad walked in, stamping snow from his boots. There had been a constant stream of flurries since the breakup. I knew Trip was to blame for it, but I didn't know if he made it snow because he was hurt or just mad at me. I was disappointed in myself for still caring.

"Hey, kid," Dad said, unwinding his scarf. *"Harry Potter?"*

I paused the movie. "Yeah. It's satisfying right now."

He sat on the couch next to me and grabbed a piece of popcorn that had been sitting out since this morning. I'd made a batch earlier in the day but only had a few kernels. In fact, the buttery smell made me a little nauseated. The stress from the breakup was messing with my stomach.

"You know, Bridget, it's going to take some time."

I sniffed. "I know."

"Are you hungry? I was going to make my famous spicy chili for dinner."

I smiled. "I'm not feeling too hungry."

"Well, you should eat something."

"I did." I had a mouthful of cheerios before I threw up and then had a cup of tea to settle my stomach.

"Something substantial. You need your strength."

"For what?" I snuggled into the couch a little more.

"School. You're going tomorrow." Dad stood and patted my knee.

I shot up. "Dad! Please! One more day!"

He shook his head. "Sorry, kiddo. One day of mourning is all you get. Come set the table, and you can finish the movie."

I crossed my arms over my chest. I'd hoped to avoid Trip for the rest of the year. It was bad enough I saw him in school all the time, but we were neighbors, too. I practically saw his house from my front window. I pressed play on the remote and tried not to drown in a new wave of sorrow.

"Bridget, I'm so sorry to hear about—" Bri started, and Annabelle elbowed her in the ribs to cut her off. The next morning, the three of us walked into the front hall of school. I kept my eyes peeled for both public enemies. Thankfully, they weren't in sight.

"It's okay, I'm fine. Just a little tired," I lied. This morning when I'd looked into the mirror, my eyes were still a little swollen from all the crying I'd done. My nose was a faint red, like Rudolph's, and the bags under my eyes reached all the way to my chin.

"If you need anything, let us know," Annabelle offered. She gave me a hug.

"Thanks."

"Are you sure you're okay?" Bri asked. "I mean, I don't mind going over there and kicking him in the shins."

I smiled. In middle school, Bri had always been our bodyguard. No one messed with us because they didn't want Bri punching or kicking them in any sensitive spot.

Annabelle shook her head. "There's something wrong with you, my dear."

"He broke up with our Bridget! He deserves some shin kicking!" argued Bri.

"Guys! I really don't want to deal with this right now. I just want to get to class and make it through my day. Please?" I begged.

Annabelle nodded as Bri looked a little shamed and said, "Like Annabelle said, if you need anything, let us know."

Both girls hugged me and headed off to their classes. I grabbed the books I needed and closed the locker. It felt like every pair of eyes I passed darted in my direction. Dad had been so wrong. I should've stayed home today.

I made it through my morning classes without running into any of the Findlays. Lunch would be the hardest battle since we normally ate together. I braced myself for a sudden patch of black ice or an icicle hurtling in the air toward my heart.

"Bridget!" Cay called to me.

"Hey," I said, walking up to him. He stood and hugged me. "If you need anything—"

"I know, I know, let you know."

He jumped back, feigning offense. "Ow! Retract those claws! I'm letting that slide since you're upset."

I sighed and slung my bag over my shoulder. "I'm sorry. I'm just sick of hearing that. What did you tell everyone?"

"That you're a magical being who dated your evil counterpart but finally saw the error of your ways and ended it." I punched him. Hard.

"I was just kidding! God!" He flinched and rubbed his arm. "I told them you and Trip were over. I didn't go into details. I left it at that. Damn, that hurt!"

"Thanks for having my back on this. I don't want to deal with it." Cay wrapped his arm around me. A wave of comfort flooded through me, and the tension in my body unknotted itself for a moment.

"It'll get better." He scanned the filled lunchroom. "You should get back to your table. People are starting to get the wrong idea about us."

I raised an eyebrow. "Like Kyle?"

Cay looked down for a minute and cleared his throat. Crossing his arms, he said, "We broke up."

"I'm sorry," I replied.

"I'm okay." He hugged me again. "Go on. Get some lunch."

I pulled away and looked around. Eyes focused on me again, but now they brimmed with speculation and gossip. I hated high school.

"See you in class," I said.

Before bed, I looked at a picture of Trip and me at the Homecoming dance. My arms rested lightly on his shoulders as I gazed into his eyes. My face held a smile I was sure I wouldn't see for a while. Trip's hands were wrapped around my waist as he held me close. The smile on his face reached his beautiful eyes, and he radiated happiness. A sliver of cool sadness snaked through my heart. I missed being happy with him. I missed being happy. I locked my phone and dumped it on my dresser. Climbing into bed, I pulled the covers close and watched the snow drift gently toward the ground. It seemed Trip felt better. I snuggled deeper under my covers. If I could sleep through the next three days before winter break, I'd be okay.

Cole stood outside of school the next morning. Panting a little, I walked up to him. I knew he wanted space, but maybe we could heal broken wounds.

"Hey there," I said, nervously.

"Hey," he glumly replied. Cole looked around me for a minute and then returned my gaze for the first time in a month.

"How have you been?" I played with the bottom zipper on my coat.

He shrugged. "Okay, I guess." He looked around again, and I bit my lip.

"Looking for someone?" I hoped the answer was no, though I was confident it would be yes.

He sighed and shook his head. "Not anymore, I guess."

"Are you sure you're okay?" We headed up the steps together; I pushed the door open and motioned for him to go through. It had finally stopped snowing, but the temperature was still below freezing.

"Yeah." We filed behind all the other students moseying their way to their lockers.

"I know you don't want to be friends anymore, but I know you, and you don't sound okay." Holding my breath, I prepared for myself for his response.

Cole glanced at me and puffed his cheeks out but said nothing.

"What's wrong? I've had my fair share of misery lately, and you know the saying." We came up on his locker but were caught behind a couple of kids doing the slow, morning shuffle.

Cole remained quiet, avoiding my gaze. The wind howled from the window behind me.

"Misery loves company?" I prompted.

Still nothing. I cut in front of him. "Fine. I get it. I'm sorry I asked." Shaking my head, I moved around him, heading into the fray and toward my locker.

"Dee left."

I ignored the fire jumping in my veins at the sound of her name and turned to face him. "What do you mean, she left?"

Cole looked up at me sadly. "She and her family left for Scotland yesterday. I got a note tucked inside a basket full of candy on my doorstep last night. They'll be gone all winter long." The fire died out, and my blood cooled. Deidra... Trip. All winter. I had a sinking feeling this wasn't a spur-of-the-moment family vacation. I needed to talk to Cay.

"I'll be okay. I'm just going to miss her a lot." He blushed.

I gave him a tight smile and, impulsively, a hug. "If you ever need someone to talk to, I'm here."

Cole smiled. "I'm sorry. For saying we can't be friends. Dee was making me choose."

I swallowed; bile rose to the back of my throat. "Thank you. I wish she hadn't."

Another student bumped into me, breaking the tender moment.

"I'll see you later, okay?" He nodded and waved. I waved back and dashed off to the bathroom. I closed myself inside a stall and took slow, meaningful breaths. Why hadn't Trip told me? A note or a heads-up of some kind would have been nice. I shook a bit as I let out a breath. I'd be alright. My stomach churned, and I felt like vomiting again. I hadn't really been able to eat since we broke up, but dry heaving in a high school bathroom was not my idea of a party. My eyes watered as I sat on the toilet. I pressed my palms into my eyes to try and stop the tears from sliding down. I was shaking so badly; I couldn't calm down, and I nearly made myself dizzy. I needed to find Cay. *Breathe in through the nose and out through the mouth.* I had to tell him they left. Focusing on the fresh pine from the cleaning solution, I stopped the flow of tears. I let the smell wash over me, and it dislodged the memory of Trip and me training in the pine trees when I'd first learned about my abilities. I cried again, and I rested my wrist on the bar next to the toilet. The cool metal shocked me a little, and I was able to divert my attention. I had to warn Cay's parents that the Findlays were in Scotland. I needed ... to keep breathing. A knock on the metal door made me jump.

"Hey, are you okay in there?" some girl asked.

"Yeah, I'll be fine. Just... something I ate for breakfast isn't agreeing with me. I'm feeling better."

"Okay." I waited for her to leave before I even released another breath. After another few minutes, I grabbed my stuff and hightailed it to class.

When I got home, I brimmed with misery and frustration heading to the kitchen. I was so concerned with trying to find Cay I had missed lunch. I whipped open the fridge. Cay wasn't in class, and he wasn't answering my texts. For all I knew, he was in Scotland, too. Nothing good was in the fridge, so I slammed the door shut. I stomped to the snack drawer, and there was nothing but a box of stale wheat crackers. We desperately needed to go shopping. Frustration morphed into anger, and I whacked my hand on the cereal cabinet handle. I winced and doubled over, holding my hand close to my chest. I hated Trip for leading me on, I hated

Cay for pushing his own agenda, and I hated my powers because they left nothing but problems in their wake. I wished I'd never met Trip and found out I'm a Seeker.

My gaze landed on the backyard, covered in white fluff. Normally I enjoyed snow, the crystals dancing in the air as they fluttered to the ground. But today, I wanted nothing but to melt it. Opening the door, I walked outside without a coat. Depression and anger fueled me as I powered through the mounds of snow. Adrenaline pumped through my system, and my heart raced in my chest. My cheeks burned as soft flakes fell upon them.

I screamed into the silence. Snow slogging off a tree branch was the only other noise in my yard.

Tension, mixed with fury and pain, built in my chest. It formed a tight ball that rose in my throat and bubbled into a scream. I shrieked until my chest burned and emotion took over. With closed eyes, I tilted my head back and felt wet flakes land on my face. My body grew hotter and hotter until the sun was a direct rival; I expected green grass under my feet when I opened my eyes. Instead, it was white. I grew angrier still, and my frustration built in my chest. I half expected it to physically explode from my body. Nothing happened.

"Come on!" I yelled at the snow. "If I'm supposed to be all powerful, why can't I do anything right with my stupid powers?" I stamped my foot childishly, feeling stupid. Of course, nothing happened. I'm *stone*, according to Cay. I turned back toward the house, sufficiently wet and cold and discouraged.

A large crack broke the stillness. I spun around and glimpsed a lightning bolt splitting our maple tree in two.

I could use my powers during winter.

Another crack pierced the air as one half fell on our shed, collapsing the roof. I panted, stunned by the surge of power that had come from me. Frozen in place, my mind raced between how much trouble I was in and how freaking cool that was. I walked carefully to the broken pieces, seeing how much damage the tree had caused.

"Are you okay?" Mrs. Stewart, my neighbor, called from her back porch.

"Yeah!" I called back, giving her the thumbs up sign.

"When I heard the crash, I came out, thinking it was our tree that fell into your yard." Bless Mrs. Stewart. She was eighty and had terrible vision. My heart broke at her kindness for checking on us.

"No worries there. Just our tree." I took a step toward the fence, so she could hear and, hopefully, see I was okay.

"Do you want me to call someone?"

"No, my parents will be home, and I already texted my mom," I lied. "But thank you for asking!"

"Okay, but don't stay out too long without a coat."

"I won't," I promised as she headed back inside. I waited a minute before I trudged back up the steps, where Mom's spade caught my eye. It sat under a splintered piece of wood. Weird. Mom had always locked up her gardening tools before winter. I walked over and bent to pick it up. My fingers touched something underneath the tool, and I drew back, not sure what it was.

It looked like a ring but not one made for jewelry. I brushed away what I could with my hand but wasn't able to see much more than the ring and the metal item it was attached to. Crouching, I used the spade to dig into the frozen dirt. I scraped the top until I found the edge of what looked like a metal container. I frowned. I'd never buried a time capsule here. I chipped away at the dirt until my fingers hurt. Knowing I couldn't use my powers to keep warm, I abandoned the project and headed inside to warm up. I made myself some hot chocolate to sip, and I changed into sweatpants. As the milk warmed in the microwave, I looked out the window and stared at the dig site. Who would have buried something in our yard? My pulse picked up. What if I opened it, and it was love letters from a couple separated by war? Or something from the original owners of the house? What if what was inside was worth millions? I grabbed my coat and shoved my feet into my boots before heading back outside, leaving the milk to cool in the microwave.

I picked up the spade and dug with newfound vigor. The further I dug into the ground, the warmer the dirt was, and I was able to pull out the container. It was a box. I left Mom's spade in the dirt and went back inside.

I flexed my fingers a little and blew on them to regain some feeling. Toeing off my shoes, I padded into the kitchen with wet spots on my cold thighs. I grabbed a sheet from the newspaper and set the box on top. There was a lock on the front of it but no other markings. I jiggled to see if it was loose enough for me to pull open. No luck. Pursing my lips, I went to our junk drawer to see if we had any keys to fit.

Instead, I found a screwdriver and a small hammer. Sitting, I tried using the screwdriver to pry off the clasp. The cold metal was hard to hold for a long period of time. I kept switching hands every other minute to stop my fingers from turning numb. My goal was to jimmy the lock loose, but I didn't do anything more than leave a ton of scratches. I sat back in the chair and pushed a stray piece of hair from my face. What else could I do?

The ice maker hummed from the freezer as it dropped more cubes into the tray. The analog clock on the wall ticked softly in the background, as if the ticks hid behind the ice.

Slightly frustrated, I picked up the box and shook it. Something thumped around. Not wanting to damage it, I placed it back on the table and grabbed the screwdriver again. I wedged the tool just behind the lock and picked up the hammer. Tapping the screwdriver softly and then more forcefully, I was barely able to pull the lock up. My tools weren't sturdy enough. I leaped from my seat, snatched the box, and headed into the garage. Dad kept his best tools here. Finding a stronger hammer and screwdriver, I placed the box on his worktable and wedged the screwdriver in the same spot as before. The hammer made a dull *thwack* against the plastic of the screwdriver as they connected with every tap. It took me a few minutes, but the lock popped open. I lifted the lid only to find a small paper bag inside.

Unrolling the top of it, I turned the bag over and let the unknown object fall into my palm.

My heartbeat quickened.

Out fell the Amulet.

Pronunciation

Cuardaitheoir (koor-DA-hoir)	Seeker
Brighde (Breed)	A Scottish goddess who, with the help of an Amulet, was able to control the Summer seasons (Spring and Summer)
Beira (Beer-a):	A Scottish goddess who, with the help of an Amulet, was able to control the Winter seasons (Fall and Winter)
Tuatha Dé Danann (TOO 'ha dA Dah n'n)	people of the goddess Danu
Neit (Neat)	Scottish God of War; the name of Cailean's dog

Cailean (Kay-lin)

Lugh (Loog)   Brighde and Beira's brother,
               God of Sun, Mastery, and
               Harvest. He helps Brighde
               hunt for the Amulet

About the Authors

Leslie holds a B.A. in English with a concentration in Creative Fiction Writing from Montclair State University. Like Bridget, Leslie was born and raised in New Jersey and inherited her love of reading from her mother. Janice holds a B.S. in Education from Seton Hall University. Her passion for books was passed on to the next generation of her family. Both Leslie and Janice currently live in New Jersey with their cat, in a busy little town, and they couldn't think of a more perfect setting for their heroine. *Brighde Reborn* is their first young adult novel.

What will happen to Bridget, Trip, and the rest of the group from OCHS now that Bridget found one-half of the Amulet? Continue this exciting series, The Amulet series. The next book, *Brighde Redefined*, is coming soon!

Book Club Questions

1. Did you feel it was right for Bridget's mom to keep her powers a secret from her?

2. How did keeping her powers a secret affect the relationship between Mom and Bridget?

3. Are Trip and Bridget meant to be, or do you think Cay manipulated them to be together?

4. If Bridget was told about her powers earlier, would her senior year be less chaotic, even with college applications and standardized testing?

5. Is Cay pushing Bridget too hard, hard enough, or not too hard at all to find out about the family history and the Amulet?

6. Was Deidra's reaction to seeing the Amulet the best way to respond? How should she have acted?

7. Knowing what you know now about Trip, do you feel he really cared about Bridget, or did he date her for the Amulet?

8. Why do you think Bridget's dad kept her powers and the Amulet a secret from her?

9. Deidra spots the Amulet around Bridget's neck at the Halloween dance. Would a different costume have hidden it better?

10. If you were Bridget, how would you have handled the information given to you in Chapter 10?

More books from 4 Horsemen Publications

Young Adult Fantasy

Blaise Ramsay
Through The Black Mirror
The City of Nightmares
The Astral Tower
The Lost Book of the Old Blood
Shadow of the Dark Witch
Chamber of the Dead God

C.R. Rice
Denial
Anger
Bargaining
Depression
Acceptance
Broken Beginnings:
Story of Thane
Shattered Start: Story of Sera

Sins of The Father: Story of Silas
Honorable Darkness: Story of
Hex and Snip
A Love Lost: Story of Radnar

**Leslie &
Janice Sommers**
Brighde Reborn

M.E. Batt
The Syphon's Daughter

Valerie Willis
Rebirth
Judgment
Death

Fantasy

D. Lambert
To Walk into the Sands
Rydan
Celebrant
Northlander
Esparan
King
Traitor
His Last Name

Danielle Orsino
Locked Out of Heaven
Thine Eyes of Mercy
From the Ashes
Kingdom Come
Fire, Ice, Acid, & Heart
A Fae is Done